The Lost Wagon Train

WESTERN NOVELS BY ZANE GREY

Arizona Ames
Black Mesa
Betty Zane
The Border Legion
The Call of the Canyon
Captives of the Desert
Code of the West
The Deer Stalker
Desert Gold
The Desert of Wheat
The Drift Fence
The Dude Ranger
Fighting Caravans
Forlorn River
The Hash Knife Outfit
The Heritage of the Desert
Knights of the Range
The Last Trail
The Light of Western Stars
The Lone Star Ranger
Lost Pueblo
The Lost Wagon Train
Majesty's Rancho
The Man of the Forest
The Maverick Queen
The Mysterious Rider
"Nevada"

Raiders of Spanish Peaks
The Rainbow Trail
Riders of the Purple Sage
Robbers' Roost
Rogue River Feud
Shadow on the Trail
The Shepherd of Guadaloupe
The Spirit of the Border
Stairs of Sand
Sunset Pass
30,000 on the Hoof
Thunder Mountain
The Thundering Herd
To the Last Man
The Trail Driver
Twin Sombreros
Under the Tonto Rim
The U. P. Trail
Valley of Wild Horses
The Vanishing American
Wanderer of the Wasteland
West of the Pecos
Western Union
Wild Horse Mesa
Wilderness Trek
Wildfire
Wyoming

ZANE GREY BOOKS FOR BOYS

Ken Ward in the Jungle
The Last of the Plainsmen
The Redheaded Outfield
Roping Lions in the
Grand Canyon

The Shortstop
Tappan's Burro
The Young Forester
The Young Lion Hunter
The Young Pitcher

ZANE GREY

The Lost Wagon Train

PUBLISHERS Grosset & Dunlap NEW YORK

THE LOST WAGON TRAIN

The Lost Wagon Train

Chapter I

LATCH'S BAND of outlaws and savages hid in Spider Web Canyon awaiting the Kiowa scouts who were to fetch news of any caravans that were approaching.

It was a summer night in 1861. Spider Web Canyon lay up in the first range of mountains rising off the Great Plains. The rendezvous had been a secret hiding-place of Satana, a fierce and bloody chief of the Kiowas. He and Latch had formed a partnership—a strange relation growing out of an accidental joint attack upon a wagon train.

The altitude gave a cool touch to the misty rain which was falling. Camp fires burned under the great cottonwoods shining upon the bronze visages of the savages. A colossal wall of rock rose back of the camp, towering so high and bold that the rim could not be seen in the blackness of night. Across the canyon the opposite wall loomed dimly with a ragged spear-pointed fringe. Night hawks were swooping in the gloom, uttering their dismal nocturnal cries. Voices of men, thud of hoofs, fall of water, mingled with the incessant hum of insects. The fires burned or smoldered, according to the fuel of the moment. Circles and groups of Kiowas sat silently, stoically, their dark faces and inscrutable eyes significant of an impassive destiny.

Satana, the chief, sat with the white men, next to Latch. He appeared to be of small stature, his stooped shoulders covered by a blanket. His raven-black hair was parted in the middle and one braid showed over a fold of the blanket. His visage expressed a tremendous power. It was a pointed face, wedge-shaped, the forehead broad, the chin sharp. In the shadow no lines were discernible, yet that face belonged to a mature Indian with a record of blood and evil. The firelight showed the basilisk eyes, black, cold, with a glitter in their depths.

By reason of his color and costume Satana made the most impressive figure in that group. But Latch's band numbered men as striking of aspect as could have been found round any camp fire west of the Mississippi at the beginning of the Civil War.

Stephen Latch's fine dark face betrayed the havoc of a wild period. He looked to be about thirty years old and was the son of a Louisiana planter, ruined at the inception of the war. Latch had not been accorded a commission in the Confederate army and, bitterly alienated, he had fought a duel with the officer who had forestalled him. With blood on his hands and with all of the Rebel hatred for the North in his heart, he had set out to wage his own battle against the Northerners. From a guerrilla warfare it had speedily degenerated into border outlawry.

North from Texas had spread the deserters, the slackers, the criminals, the parasites that were to live off the vast traffic of the plains—pioneers traveling west, freighters hauling supplies to the forts and posts in New Mexico and Colorado, and gold-seekers bound for California. From the north and east had spread the adventurers and outlaws, the riffraff of the cities, the men who fled to escape the army, and a horde of rudderless individuals without names or hopes or purpose.

From these Latch had picked his band. His gift of command, which would have served the Confederacy well, here found its voice and action. He could read and rule men, and he set himself to develop a following upon which he could depend for the ruthless nature of the strife upon which he had decided.

Nevertheless, despite Latch's cunning, his insight and iron will, his band augmented without his consent, and had left a bloody trail from the big river to the mountains. Liquor and gold were hard masters to contend with, and gambling inevitably led to bloodshed. It was a hard time. Three men, two of whom he had never heard named, had fallen to his own gun, and fights were daily occurrences. Intelligent discipline had been his aim, and sagacity as to deals a paramount issue. There were men in his gang as strong as he, and far more reckless and fierce. With them he had played a far-sighted game, always knowing that those he could not win to loyalty he could kill.

Then had come the fortunate union with Satana. The Kiowas under this chief were implacable toward the buffalo-hunters, the caravans, and the soldiers. Satana had been difficult to deal with, but gifts, and especially firewater, had brought him around, the last of his band to align himself with white men. It galled the scion of a once rich and proud Southern family to see himself despised by a savage for the betrayal of his own people. But Satana was necessary to a terrific purpose and plan. Latch would use the Kiowas and sacrifice them in the end. His great weapon was rum, whole wagon loads of which he had stolen from a wagon train, and had hidden in Spider Web Canyon. Only Leighton, his lieutenant, a Southerner of distant kin, and two others knew where these kegs of liquor had been secreted. Latch realized it would cost him much to keep the secret, and he entertained strong motive to hide the rum in some other place, helped by one or two men he could trust.

"Steve, we want some whisky," Leighton had just repeated.

Latch concluded it was time to declare himself, come what might of it. Whereupon he turned to Leighton the better to see him in the firelight. He need not have done that, for well he had known for years on end how that handsome face looked. But he experienced a slight shock this time.

"Lee, I'm chief of this band," returned Latch, deliberately. "It would not be wise to inflame the Indians now. If any of you drank they would discover it."

"They wouldn't need to know," said Leighton, sullenly.

"These Kiowas can smell rum as far as you can a polecat."

"We'll put it to a vote."

"Who will?" demanded Latch, sharply.

"Some of us."

"You can name your supporters right heah," went on Latch. "We'll have this out."

"Sprall, Waldron, Mandrove, Creik, and Texas, to mention a few," snapped the younger man. He was ready of tongue, yet sullen and unsure, either of his followers or of Latch. Several of their group stirred uneasily and one appeared about to speak. Satana's sudden intensity of gaze betrayed his knowledge of the white man's language.

"All right, I'll answer them as well as you, Lee," declared Latch, forcibly. "I'm running this band and I'll not have any more disobedience. You will abide by my rules and my orders or get out."

"We might start a band of our own," said Latch's kinsman, crisply.

"That's your privilege if you split heah and now. Otherwise you do as I say," replied the leader, ringingly. "And I'll thank you all to declare yourselves quickly."

Latch had by no means felt so secure of his position as his speech implied, but this was the moment to test his strength and he meant to see it through. These men were exceedingly difficult to control when sober. They were foot-loose, restless, careless, and hard. Once under the influence of the bottle, they would be impossible to manage. Latch made his stand, realizing fully that if Leighton and his cronies took the liquor they could take Satana and his savages along with them. The situation was critical, still hardly worse than it had been before.

"What do you say, fellows?" queried Leighton.

Sprall, a wiry little desperado, as poison as a desert viper, leered upon Leighton and Latch.

"Wal, what I want is rum, an' I ain't carin' a hell of a lot how I git it."

Waldron, a self-confessed bank defaulter and fugitive from New York, ran true to the character his weak face expressed. "It's between you and Latch."

Mandrove was a Rebel deserter, a sallow sandy-mustached young man with shifty gaze.

"I'm on Leighton's side," he said.

Latch expected a reluctant admission from Creik, who had been in his father's employ on the plantations. He was a slave-driver, and in other ways than his huge bulk looked the man who could fulfill such position.

"Whisky," was his trenchant reply.

This left one of the supporters Leighton had named, and surely the most important. A gunman from the Rio Grande country, he answered to the name "Texas" and looked as hard as that wild and notorious southern border.

"Wal, I'd take a shot at my own grandad if he kept me thirsty any longer than this," was his reply.

"Thanks for your prompt declarations, men," rejoined Latch, constrainedly. "You can saddle up and get out of heah."

"Stephen, I know where you hid that liquor," spoke up Leighton, a dark flush crossing his face.

"Yes, and by God you'll keep your mouth shut aboot it," flashed Latch, tensely.

The glances of these kinsmen clinched then and that seemed the crucial moment. Latch knew himself, which evidently was more than Leighton knew, for he wavered under a stronger force.

"I didn't say that I'd give it away," went on Leighton, "but I'm good and sore."

"Young fellar, let me have a word," spoke up Old Man Keetch, in deep persuasive voice. "I've been on this hyar border for twenty years. I've seen a heap of men come an' go. I've been in all the tough ootfits from the Brazos to the Platte. An' them thet fought among themselves never lasted long. Shore it's no man's bizness what you want to do with yore own life. But I say there ain't no sense throwin' it away. An' if you-all git drunk an' git the redskins drunk, why, hell itself would be a church meetin' to what this hyar ootfit would become. . . . The boss has a cool haid an' I say we-all ought to listen to him."

"Hell! We're listening. What else is there to do, cooped up heah in this hole? No drink, no money to gamble! I'm sick of it," replied Leighton, disgustedly. "I want action and I don't care a damn what kind."

"Leighton, you can get any kind of action you want," spoke up the latest acquisition to the band.

This individual, a stripling of a boy still in his teens, had followed Latch out of Fort Dodge a few weeks previously and without question or explanation, except to say that his name was Lester Cornwall, he had attached himself to the chief. Later Latch recalled that he had seen the boy in one of the gambling-hells. His face was as fair as a girl's, his eyes were blue as blue ice, his hair shining between gold and silver. And beautiful as a beautiful girl he would have been but for his expression of supreme cruelty. He might have been a son of the god of evil.

"What?" bellowed Leighton, like a bull about to charge.

Cornwall rose with a single action, his right hand sliding significantly inside his vest. The firelight glinted from his pale eyes.

"Guns or fists," he drawled, with the accent of a Carolinian.

Leighton leaped up with a curse, tearing at his weapon. Latch sat closest, but it was Keetch who grasped Leighton's arm and held on until another of the men pushed him down.

"What'd I jest tell you, man?" queried Keetch, testily. "Hyar you air provin' the very thing I said."

"I won't have that white-face boy ——"

"Wal, some one had to call you," interrupted Keetch, coldly. "An' it's shore plain to us if not to you."

Latch for a moment, in the leap of passion, had hoped Leighton would draw on the boy and get shot for his temper. Then he sharply called both the belligerents to order. Leighton vouchsafed no reply, but relaxed and sat back against the log.

"Colonel, I reckon I'm not the only one who's tired of Leighton's gab," coolly responded the youth, and turned his back to step toward the fire.

Latch suffered a twinge at the use of the title given him in private life, but which had been denied him at the advent of war. This young fellow had known him or heard of him. Latch sensed a strange loyalty here,

as well as a remarkable indifference to life. It moved
Latch as nothing else had.

"Listen, men," he began, with eloquent passion,
"Keetch put it right. If we fight any more among ourselves we are doomed. Let us fight for each other and
not with each other. I guarantee the fortune of any
and all of you who stick by me. But my word must
be law. We have had no discipline, no purpose, no
plan, no execution. We've been a gang of border ruffians. My aim is to organize the greatest band ever
known on the frontier. And we'll all be rich."

"Stephen, you talk well," spoke up Leighton, in curious scorn. "But you never get anywhere. What's this
wonderful plan that will gain us a fortune?"

"We will wage an organized war on the caravans
crossing the plains," declared the leader, grimly. "Both
the wagon trains headed west with government supplies, gold, munitions, merchandise, and the wagon
trains returning with the rich furs of the trappers. I
have won over Satana to this deal. He is a crafty
Indian. He sees the bigness of the idea. He controls
five hundred Kiowas, half of whom are with us heah."

"Wal, it's a great idea," interposed Old Man Keetch.
"An' don't you Southerners overlook thet nine oot of
ten caravans air Yankees."

"Yes, we will aid the Confederacy that has outlawed us while reaping our harvest," went on Latch,
bitterly.

"What's your plan?" queried Leighton, stirred
deeply.

"Listen. Few caravans from now on will have an

escort of soldiers. The forts have sent all the soldiers they could spare into the war. Those caravans who do not band together in numbers for protection will be easy picking. We shall choose only small caravans, never over fifty wagons. We shall use our rum to inflame the Kiowas and send them against the damned Yankee freighters. We shall set Satana to kill every last man—and woman, too—of every caravan we attack. It will not be our way to stampede oxen and horses, or to burn wagons. We will make off with every single vestige of a caravan, so that it will simply vanish from the plains. Lost wagon trains! . . . That's all. We can never be found heah, at least not by white men. Satana says we can drive the wagons right out on the high wall below heah and dump them over, where they will never be found. The Indians will take the stock. That will be their pay. Which leaves us the contents of the wagons. Last month one train left Independence with a hundred thousand dollars in gold alone. We could afford to work slowly and carefully for such treasure as that. But any wagon train will yield much in supplies and money. . . . That's my plan, Lee, in the rough. The details can be worked out later. But I must have an united band and keep strict control. . . . Now you and all can speak up."

"I'm for it, Steve," replied Leighton, warmly.

"Daid men tell no tales, huh?" mused Keetch. "So thet's your idee. It's big. But I don't like the complete massacre."

"Nor I. We might attack a wagon train that had women and children. . . . No matter! The Kiowas will do the dirty work. We needn't see it. But for us to make out strong while the South and North are at war we must follow that plan and stick to it. . . . I'll call the roll. Answer yes or no!"

Among the group that Leighton had designated as being of a mind with him the only one to answer Latch in the negative was Waldron, the fugitive from the north.

"What is against your principles as a man doesn't concern me," added Latch, curtly. "Either you go in with us or quit the band. Choose."

"I have no choice," rejoined Waldron, gloomily, as if he indeed saw death near at hand. "I'll abide by your rule."

Black Hand and Nigger Jack, outlaws who had found in Latch's band a haven of refuge, were loud and brief in their acceptance. Lone Wolf, a Texas cowboy of unknown past, dropped his lean tanned face and let silence be his answer. Augustine, the Mexican *vaquero*, spoke softly in his own tongue, "Si, senor." Old Man Keetch parleyed with the chief on the issue of possible murder of women and children. "Cain't we git around thet? It shore goes ag'in the grain. Lots of them caravans have only men." Latch had thought that out, to realize the impossibility of learning whether or not a wagon train had women. Even the freighters always took some pioneers along with them.

"Keetch, we've got to shut our eyes to that," concluded Latch.

"All right, I weaken. But I'll say one word. In the end *thet* will destroy us."

"How aboot you, Cornwall?" queried Latch of the latest and youngest acquisition to his band.

"Whatever you say, Colonel," returned the youth, nonchalantly, his clean pure profile in dark relief against the firelight. Again Latch was struck by the boy's lack of feeling. Fight, robbery, blood, murder, death—these meant nothing to him. Yet he had appeared to be a quiet, intelligent, dreamy young man. Latch awoke with a start from a train of thought he must banish forever.

"It's settled. Latch's band," he said, forcefully, expelling a deep breath. No mind could conceive just what havoc had its inception at that moment.

"Thirteen!" ejaculated Keetch. "How aboot new members? Some of us will git killed. An' in the very nature of our work on this frontier other men will gravitate to us."

"Sufficient to the day. The smaller our band the more profits to each. I don't look favorably on drifters throwing in with us. We will keep this den secret."

"Wal, thet's sense. But it'll not be easy," went on Keetch, thoughtfully. "I've an idee, Latch. You remember, down below, a day's ride, where this canyon opens out on the prairie. There's the wonderfulest valley I ever seen. It'll be settled by pioneers some day. We might locate there, range stock an' cattle, make a blind of ranchin'."

"That *is* a good idea," agreed Latch. "But isn't it too close to this hiding-place?"

"Close! . . . Ain't it the hardest day's ride you ever took in yore life? I heerd you say so. It might as wal be a hundred miles as forty. An' rough! I never seen the beat of thet trail. Sand washes thet leave no tracks, water over hard rock bottom for miles, an' then a jumble of stones not even an Apache couldn't trail us over. No, Latch, we needn't fear bein' tracked in hyar, or even as far as thet Paso Diablo, as Augustine called it."

"Pass of the devil! Very well, it is named," replied Latch. "We'll think all around your idea of ranching the valley below. Later that land will be valuable."

"Wal, it's the finest grazin' an' plantin' field on the west slope of the plains."

"Field? You call it a field?"

"Shore. There's a hundred thousand acres level as a floor. An' a million more in pasture an' timber. Buffalo land in there on the way north an' south. It was a favorite huntin'-ground for Cheyennes an' Arapahoes until Satana drove them out."

"Latch's Field," rejoined the chief, dreamily. "I thought I had done with land—except six feet to sleep in some day, sooner or later."

"Wal, let's mill over thet idee," said Keetch. "Reckon I've always had a hankerin' to locate somewhere an' settle down to farmin'. After the war, if it ever ends, there'll be a spillin' of people all over the west. Shore the South will be ruined, win or lose."

"Aye," echoed Latch, with a haunting bitterness.

"Uggh!" interrupted the Kiowa chief, lifting his head. Three savages had stepped silently up to the edge of the circle. One spoke in guttural tones. Light thud of hoofs came from under the trees. Then lean wild riders entered the light of the camp fires. Wet bronze bodies glistened in the light.

Satana only, of the Kiowas, presented a stoical and unimpressed manner. All the savages round that fire, and those from other circles, came crowding forward as the three scouts faced their chief. Latch had seen a good deal of Indians during his short sojourn on the frontier, but the stride, the mien, the posture of these scouts scarcely required words to express information of most significant and tremendous import for all present.

The spokesman of the trio was known to Latch—a young brave named Hawk Eye, a matchless tracker and rider. He it was who had sighted the Arapahoes in their effort to ambush the Kiowas. His wet braids of raven hair hung over his brown shoulders; he rested his carbine in the hollow of his left elbow; his eyes shone with piercing intensity.

"Keetch, have a care to get all he says," spoke up Latch.

"Wal, he's shore bustin' with news. An' I reckon I wasn't captive among the Kiowas for nothin'," returned Keetch.

The lean warrior spoke as if rendering an oration, making slow and elaborate gestures which had to do with places and distances. Latch thrilled to their meaning. He recalled his boyhood, when he had developed a lust for wild tales of savage warfare on the Texas frontiers. He was now about to inaugurate a newer and bloodier warfare, that united the crafty intelligence of the white man and the ferocity of the savage. Would youngsters of the future ever read his name—Stephen Latch—in the history of the strange disappearance of wagon trains from the plains? The idea appalled him. Here face to face with concrete results of his deliberate plans he suffered his first remorse. Bitter, ruined, vengeful Rebel that he was, he had a glimpse of the horror of his machinations.

At the end of Hawk Eye's speech Satana let out a loud "Uggh!" which needed no translation.

"Latch," interposed Keetch, sonorously, "thar's a heap of that redskin's harangue I couldn't savvy. But the gist of it is thet a train of fifty-three wagons without soldiers left Fort Dodge three days ago, headed for the Cimarron Crossin' an' the Dry Trail to Fort Union."

"Ah! . . . What's the Dry Trail?" panted Latch.

"It's a cut-off of two hundred an' fifty miles. I've been over it a few times. Seldom traveled. Only old freighters an' plainsmen ever tackle the Dry Trail. Water off the trail an' hard to find. Feed scarce. Buffalo chips for camp fires. Been some bad fights along thet road. Point of Rocks a favorite place for redskins to ambush freighters."

"How far?" went on Latch, moistening his lips.

"Two days' hard ridin'."

"Would that place us near this Point of Rocks?" queried Latch, his voice gathering strength. Of what avail fear, vacillation? The die was cast.

"No. We'd strike the trail this side of old Camp Nichols, an abandoned army post. The Cimarron runs along between Colorado an' New Mexico. Wildest kind of country. . . . Looks like this deal was made to order."

Latch turned to address Satana: "Chief, we go daylight."

"Good!" replied the Kiowa, his dark face flashing as he got up.

"We have heap big powwow tomorrow," concluded Latch. "Talk how do fight."

"Uggh. White chief give rum?"

"Yes. Plenty drink."

Whereupon Satana jabbered to his Indians, and they all trooped away from Latch's band toward their own camp fires.

"My God! I believe they're goin' to dance," ejaculated Keetch.

"Wal, good-by to sleep," growled some one.

"Would you sleep, anyhow?" queried Latch, as if addressing himself.

"Reckon I'll have some nightmares after the bloody deal is over—if—" replied Keetch, with a gruff laugh. "Hell! We can git used to anythin'. . . . Latch, how're we goin' to run this fight?"

"I want time to think."

"Thet ain't a bad idee for all of us—an' mebbe Mandrove hyar can offer up a little prayer, like the redskins do. Haw! Haw!"

"Keetch, are you crazy?" demanded Latch, sharply.

"Me? Nope. Reckon I'm the level-haidest of this gang. Mebbe you didn't know Mandrove was a preacher before he turned outlaw?"

"I did not. Is that a fact, Mandrove?"

The Rebel deserter nodded gloomily. Then he spoke:
"I was forced into the army."

"Didn't you want to fight?"

"Killing was against my religion."

"So that's it. You told me you had deserted . . . to join Latch's band! My God, man, but you made a bad choice! You'll have to fight now. But I would not hold you to your word."

"I am in the same boat with you, Latch," he retorted, significantly. "And already a—a murderer."

"Misery loves company! If you failed as a preacher and a soldier, let us hope you succeed as a desperado."

Coarse mirth followed this crisp cold speech of the leader.

"Men, this is where we wipe out the past, those of us who have any to remember," declared Latch. "Honest lives have been denied us. And we *have* to live out our lives whatever they must be. But let's not be a common, thieving, treacherous gang. United we stand! And when the war is over ——"

"Be rich an' can settle down," interrupted Keetch, derisively, as the leader hesitated. "Latch, you're shore a new kind of border outlaw to me. But I'll be damned if I don't like you. An' I ain't sayin' what you plan is impossible. It's worth tryin'! . . . But let's figger on things close to hand."

"You're right—but I want time to think. I've worked it out only this far. We'll ride down to this Dry Trail. Keetch, you can choose the place where we will attack the wagon train. We'll send out scouts to locate it. Then when all is aboot ready we'll deal out rum to the Kiowas. Just enough to inflame them!"

"Don't forget a few drinks to ourselves," said Leighton, dryly.

"I second thet motion," declared Keetch.

"Carried," rejoined Latch, in a hard tone. "We'll be up at dawn. Lee, as soon as it's light enough to see we'll take two men with a pack-horse and get the rum. Remember, all, that the success of our venture depends on our keeping those kegs of rum intact until the hour."

"We'll shore stand by that, Colonel," rang out young Cornwall as Latch turned away toward the dark wall.

He found the shelf where he had left his saddle, pack, and bed, and soon made ready to rest if not to sleep.

Through the misty rain the camp fire shone dimly, crossed and barred by moving spectral forms. His own band stood in a group, talking low. Both factions seemed to have sunk their differences in the common cause of the moment. Latch watched them. How black and sinister! The hatred that had led to this pass for him could not wholly blind him to the truth. His intelligence kept pace with his imagination.

In that hour, if never before or never again, he saw the naked truth. As sure as his ruin, so sure would be his death. Vain mad ravings of a defeated, frustrated man—these plans and hopes for riches, for revenge, to be of some use to the country which had cast him out! He saw all now when it was too late. Death, however, was nothing. He could welcome that. But death was insignificant compared with what he had invited. His soul sickened within him. Yet he had the appalling strength to accept his lot, to fight his better self and kill conscience, good, memory of home, even the thought of the brief, hopeless love which had helped to bring him to this degradation.

How strange that in this devastating hour he should recall Cynthia Bowden! Yet not strange. Was this not the hour when all must pass in review before his tortured sight—for the last time? And Cynthia did come back, not soon to pass! That small regal head, with its crown of auburn hair, the proud dark eyes, the red lips that had been surrendered to his—they came back to make him shudder and sweat there in his cave. All of his misfortune dated from the blunder of that one year of college in the North. Why had he gone the way of wild college youths, sowing a whirlwind that gave his jealous rivals and Cynthia's angered brother a weapon with which to disgrace and ruin him in her eyes? But for that would he be lying here in this Kiowa retreat, a consort of the bloodiest and cruelest of chieftains, self-placed at the head of a border band of cutthroat outlaws? No! The downward steps from that fatal hour were easy to retrace. And his bitter, passionate soul revolted.

Gradually the camp fires flickered and died out, leaving the canyon black as a cave. The trees were barely discernible. A mournful sighing wind breathed through them, with a steady accompaniment of low murmur of tumbling stream, in itself a lonely sound.

Then a sharp cry of wild beast, high on the opposite rim, pierced the silence.

It defined the status of Spider Web Canyon, wildest and most inaccessible hole known to the Kiowas. This place had been worn and weathered out of solid rock by the devil to fulfill a robber's dream. But Latch thrilled no more in the blackness of night. Perhaps when the sun shone again, and the morbid cowardice had faded from his mind, he might feel the same as when he had first ridden into the strange, beautiful, purple rent in the rocks.

The hours wore on, at last merciful to a spent spirit. And he slept. He awoke in the dim gray dawn, aware of a stir out under the trees. Where was he?

A bulge of rock shelved out over his head. A cave had been his roof! Opaque gray gloom enfolded the space out there. Suddenly he remembered the place, the time, the meaning, and a terrible sick hatred of the dawn, of another day, pervaded his soul.

Chapter II

HARD on that sensation fell the bell-like voice of Lester Cornwall: "Mawnin', Colonel."

"It's hardly good morning, Lester," replied Latch, as he flung his blankets back and sat up. "Gray dawn of an evil day, I'd say."

"Evil if Leighton has his way, Colonel," rejoined the youth, in lower tone. "I don't trust that man."

"Did you hear anything?" demanded Latch, hurriedly pulling on his boots. Opposition, some one or something to distrust, stimulated and hardened him to realities.

"It's enough to say now that I'm on your side," returned Cornwall, deliberately.

"Thank you, Lester. I hope you will be justified. . . . Did Leighton send you?"

"No. Nor did he like my snooping into this. I made up my mind last night I was going, and I was the first up. Leighton has Sprall and that Texas gunner with him. They're saddling a pack-horse."

"Humph! And where did you come in?"

"That's what he asked. I told him I'd call you. He thinks you included me in this rum-getting. . . . I'm not apologizing, Colonel. Take me or leave me. It's all one to me."

"Cornwall, I've an idea that whether we fight Indians or make friends with them, massacre caravans **to** turn honest, go to hell or not—it's all one to you."

"I'd stick to you, Colonel."

It dawned on Latch then that this young outcast had answered to some strange attachment born of the inevitable dissension in the band. There was something nonchalant and dare-devil about him which appealed to Latch.

"Heah's my hand, Cornwall," said Latch. "You might have noticed that I have not offered it to Leighton, or any other of our crew."

In the gray cold dawn the younger man's grip closed like steel on the other's hand. Latch imagined himself past any such thing as friendship or trust. Yet here he wondered. What would wild life at a wild period do to him? He realized that there were unplumbed depths in him. Then the gruff voice of Leighton broke that handclasp. Latch buckled on his gun-belt, and examining his six barreled pistol he returned it to the sheath.

Dark figures moved away in the gloom. Latch, with Cornwall beside him, followed them with a stride which soon swallowed up the intervening distance. They kept close to the wall, moving to one side and then the other to avoid obstructing rocks and trees. Sounds of the encampment died away. The gray dawn had imperceptibly lightened.

"Never was any good at location," growled Leighton.

"Wal, if I'd knowed where that gin was cached **you**

can bet your life I'd never forget," replied Sprall, with a hoarse laugh.

"Keep quiet," ordered Latch, in a low peremptory voice. "I don't want the Indians to know where we hid this stuff."

"Hell! They could sure find out quick enough," retorted Leighton.

"Perhaps, if they had time. But there are ten thousand cracks and holes in Spider Web Canyon. It's the damndest place I ever saw."

They crossed a brawling brook and went on at a snail's pace. Latch had his especial signs by which he had marked the cache. And these were peculiarly formed crags on the rim, which at length he barely discerned. Straight into the tangle of trees and rocks he led, over thick grass that left no imprint of foot, and found a crack in the wall.

"Sprall, you stay here with the horse," ordered Latch.

The outlaw demurred under his breath. Latch led into the crack, which was narrow and dark. But by measuring off a number of strides he arrived finally at the point he sought. Feeling with his hands, he located little holes in the wall on the right side, and knew then that he was right. Day had broken and there was light enough to see the caverned walls, pock-marked with holes of every size.

"We should have brought Keetch," said Latch. "Here, two of you help me on your shoulders. One foot on each. . . . There!" Latch reached for a shelf above his head, and laboriously clambered upon it. The wide portal of a cave, unseen from under the shelf, opened in the wall. Back a few feet from the entrance the cavern was full of kegs of rum—three wagon-loads. Latch remembered well, because it had taken days of excessive toil to get those kegs into that hiding-place.

"Throw up the rope," he called. Then he lifted one of the casks and carried it to the edge of the shelf. When receiving the rope he lowered the rum on that, and pulled up to perform the same task for the second keg. The men below quite forgot that he required their aid to descend and packed their precious burden out to the horse. Latch had to get down the best way available, which was not without receiving sundry scratches and a solid thumping fall. Whereupon he hurried out of the crack to the exit.

Already one keg had been looped securely upon the pack-animal, and two of the men were holding up the other keg, while the third made it fast.

"Thar!" ejaculated the Texan, who had been responsible for the securely tied hitches. "Firewater an' delirium tremens for them damned redskins."

"One keg is for us," declared Leighton, with satisfaction.

Latch concluded it wise to hold his tongue. Sooner or later he would conflict harshly with his lieutenant, and a dark certainty suddenly formed in his mind. He followed at the heels of his men, aware that Cornwall, ever vigilant, kept track of him. The rain had ceased, but grass and trees were wet, and water trickled off the cliff. The clouds were breaking away to the eastward. Evidently the day would be favorable for traveling. Latch thought of the strenuous ride ahead and felt grateful for anything that would make it less onerous.

During his absence the horses had been rounded up and fetched in, the score or more belonging to his band contrasting markedly with the several hundred lean and ragged mustangs of the Kiowas. Keetch, a capital camp cook, was dealing out breakfast to the men who had not accompanied Latch. At sight of the rum-laden pack-horse they roared merry welcome. It jarred on Latch. Rum had obsessed these outlaws. Perhaps it contained the oblivion Latch craved, as well as the spirit for evil deeds.

The Kiowas' camp hummed like a beehive, two hundred and fifty half-naked savages, gorging meat before a raid, made a picture Latch had never seen equaled. What would Satana's entire band look like when about to charge a wagon train, or especially in the moment of triumph over the whites? Latch stumbled, having unconsciously closed his eyes. Amid the rough acclaim of his men he sat to his meal.

"Latch, our red pards are aboot to move," called out Keetch. "It'll shore be hell keepin' up with them today."

"Pack light and rustle," was Latch's reply.

In half an hour Latch rode out with his men at the tail end of Satana's band. Just then the sun burst over the eastern rim, transforming the canyon from a dark, gray-fogged, stone-faced crack in the wilderness to a magnificent valley of silver and gold iridescence. The wisps of clouds lifted as on wings of pearly fire, the white cascade tumbled out of a ragged notch in the black rim, to fall and pause and fall again, like fans of lace; the great oaks, walnuts, and cottonwoods, full foliaged, dripped strings of diamonds and rubies and appeared festooned with rainbows; the long grass, emerald velvet, spread away into every lane and patch and corner and niche, and green moss climbed the walls; deer with long ears erect trooped away into the timber; and above the murmur of the stream rose the songs of innumerable birds, over which the mockers held a golden-voiced dominance.

Latch thought it a hideous dream that through this beauty and glory of nature he was riding down to heap blood and death upon innocent people of his own color. Must he steep his brain in rum to carry through this dark project? He divined that he must continually fortify himself against a background of childhood and youth and young manhood. He had not been intended for this devastating business. Strength must come from the past, from betrayed love and frustrated hope, from the poison that ran in his veins. To these he called with despairing passion.

Spider Web Canyon stepped down between narrowing rugged walls, silver reaches and green patches vying with the groves as they all loped down toward a high irregular gap, black and mysterious, where the walls converged. On either side, myriads of rents split the walls, giving them the appearance of colossal fences, with pickets and spaces alternating. Far down, the larger of these were choked with foliage. What singular contrast between this lower end of the canyon and that at the upper where the walls were sheer and in many places for rods without a crack. The eastern wall was lower and perpendicular for all of its full four hundred feet. Keetch had claimed there were places where a wagon could be driven right to the rim. This had given Latch the nucleus of an idea. Why not haul all their stolen wagons to this rim, if that were possible, lower the supplies on ropes, and topple the wagons over, never to be seen again by freighters or scouts of the plains? It was an absorbing thought.

The last red-skinned rider and his ragged wild pony vanished in the green-choked apex that led out of the gap. Keetch, with the pack-horses behind him, slowly approached the entrance to the pass.

Latch, behind the rest of his band, brought up the rear. He took a last look around, the conscious act of a man who hated to leave the peace and solitude of this extraordinary canyon. It was no sure thing that he would come back. The upper and wider part of the canyon could not be seen from his position—only the wild ramparts that seemed to defy invasion of their secrets. But on his right opened the deepest and dark-est cleft so far discovered in the wall, and here a slen-der ribbon of water fell from ledge to ledge. An eagle soared above the notch. Huge boulders fallen from the cliff lay surrounded by magnificent trees, some of which barely reached to the tops of these broken sections of cliff. The sweet, fresh, cool wetness of the morning, the glorious bright radiance on every tree, rock, bush, and plot of grass, the melody of innumerable birds, the presence of wild turkeys, deer, rabbits on all sides, the swallows flitting like a shower of steely sparks, the ripples on dark still pools of the meandering brook, and in the distance the faint roar of the waterfall—all these entered into Latch, and he felt that they were the last of good he would absorb in this life.

What folly to love this canyon—to want to own it all himself—to have it to come to as a refuge! Still he loved and wanted. The perversity of his nature dominated here.

Then he rode on down the winding green lane, into the willows and at last into the brook. Here all signs of tracks and trails vanished. And that brook would be the road of travel for many hard miles. A corner of bronze cliff bulged out over him, and when he turned it he was in the pass where the walls were scarcely forty paces apart, and had begun to sheer up frowningly.

The brook flowed over smooth hard rock that left no imprint of the hoof of a horse. There was a decided current, and in places little steps down where miniature waterfalls babbled and gurgled. Sand and gravel and small rocks had evidently been washed down the floor of this tortuous pass. Willows and cottonwoods fringed the shore lines, except where the wall came down abruptly. At times Latch could see a hundred yards ahead and catch sight of the line of riders lounging in their saddles. The only sounds were watery ones. Latch had as a boy been an ardent angler, and he absorbed himself in watching for trout and other little fish in the deeper places. He was rewarded sometimes by the flash of a silver side spotted with red, and occasionally a fuller view of a lusty trout. And he thought of what wonderful hunting and fishing he would enjoy during the long period when it would be imperative to hide in this fortress.

Some slants in the brook had made it necessary to dismount and wade carefully down where a horse could easily break a leg. And while he amused or interested himself in the course of the stream—anything to keep his mind off the deed for which this travel was necessary—the miles of canyon pass fell behind, and the volume of water mysteriously began to lessen and the walls to grow closer, steeper, and higher until at last only a narrow belt of blue sky showed something over three hundred feet above.

Thereafter the light failed perceptibly and the hour arrived when the walls were so close that only dusk, strange and wan, prevailed under them. Then the green verdure disappeared and nothing but stark, somber rock overhung the subdued and drab brook. Slides of earth and stone from above had choked the space many times, to be washed away. Huge blocks of granite obstructed places, so that it was difficult for a horse to get by. In many cases the packs had to be slipped.

All these details of escape from Spider Web Canyon augmented and at length terminated in a split so narrow that Latch could touch the wall on either side with half extended hand. Last came the deep water, where for long stretches the horses had to swim, and in several instances the men also. Latch's horse was a good swimmer, otherwise Latch would have been hard put to an almost insurmountable task, for he was but a poor hand in the water. The current carried him through narrows where he knocked his knees against the walls. It was these swift places, fortunately short, that had played havoc with the band of outlaws on their way up the pass into the canyon. If the water had not been low the ascent would have been impossible. Also to be trapped there when a freshet came down would have been extremely dangerous.

This constricted part seemed endless in length. Each man had to keep his ammunition dry, and as some of Latch's band used powder-and-ball pistols, this cardinally important task grew almost insupportable if not impossible. But at last, far beyond midday, they got through the Paso Diablo and entered the widening and rapidly descending canyon below. Here again the sun found them and Latch warmed to the golden rays and the ever-broadening stream of blue above.

At sunset the outlaws rode abruptly out of the rock rent into a vast level valley the like of which Latch had never imagined. The Indians had pitched camp in groups under wide-spreading trees; fires were sending up columns of smoke; the mustangs in droves grazed on the green grass. Far down this magnificent stretch, ragged black patches showed against the sunset gold.

"Wal, boss, hyar's your field," called out Keetch, sonorously. "Look down the range."

"Buffalo!" exclaimed Latch, suddenly sighting Indian riders in a chase.

"Shore. An' we'll have rump steak for supper," replied the outlaw scout, cheerfully.

Latch sat his horse and gazed long. He could not

see the extent of this field, but it certainly contained thousands of acres. From where the pass opened, the bluffs extended in wavering lines in an oval curve, growing lower until at length they smoothed out upon the open prairie. Groves of cottonwoods dotted the great field, and a long irregular green line, thick and dark, marked the course of the stream through the range. There were isolated knolls, some circled by big walnut trees, and others with a single tree to distinguish them from their fellows. The golden sun rays paved the meadows and aisles.

"No wonder the red man hated the white man!" soliloquized Latch. "To seek to rob him of this!"

"Colonel, heah's your ranch," spoke up young Cornwall. "And right heah I'm applying for the job of foreman."

"Right heah you get it, Lester," declared Latch, in a glow and flush of feeling which obliterated for the moment how vain his dream was. He knew the Kiowa would trade him this land for guns, trinkets, rum, and then fight to help him keep it.

"Keetch, you called the trick," the leader rang out. "Latch's Field!"

Before dark the Indian hunters returned to camp with buffalo meat, and soon the air was full of the appetizing odor of rump steak, that much-desired delicacy of the plains. Latch ate heartily, and after the meal he walked apart from the members of his band. The long strenuous ride and the conflict of feelings had exhausted him. Soon he sought rest under the cottonwood where he had taken the precaution to put his saddle, bed, and pack with the kegs of rum.

His own men appeared to be a mixed group of merry and somber members. And Latch's keen ears registered the fact that Leighton's coterie of outlaws belonged to the latter. Satana's warriors feasted long and noisily on the choice viands of buffalo meat. He heard Keetch say the "damned red-skinned hawgs ate up five whole buffalo."

Down here in the open, where it was almost prairie, Latch lost the sense of security and insulation furnished by Spider Web Canyon. This field lay at the edge of the plains, high ground without apparent slope, and subject to all the characteristics of prairieland. In the distance bands of wolves chased their quarry, with wild deep bays as of hounds gone mad. Close at hand, bands of coyotes made the night hideous with their sharp yelps. Nevertheless, Latch slept soundly and awoke under the white stars of dawn, rested and himself again.

It was just break of day when Keetch called the men to their meal. "Fill up, you sons-of-guns, an' what you can't eat pack in your pockets. It'll be a long drill to-day an' no cookin' at the end of it, if I don't miss my guess."

Latch hoped the Kiowas would lead off down through the wonderful field, so that he could estimate its size and characteristics. But they took a course straight north, climbed out over the bluff to the up-lands, and strung out, a marvelous cavalcade of color, wildness, and movement. From the last high point

Latch gazed back and down upon the place which had obsessed him. It appeared to be triangular in shape, with the apex at the gateway of the pass, and the broad end some forty or fifty miles across a still greater distance from where he made his estimates. Toward the open range the timber failed, and there strings and patches of buffalo led off from the main black herd. He chose this upper end as his own field, realizing that some day shrewd pioneers would stop to locate on that fertile soil. From this height the scene was beautiful in the extreme, a vast silvery park dotted by trees, basking in the sunrise. Only the dark and ragged break in the western bluff gave any inkling of the rough country in that direction.

Latch made it a point presently to join Satana.

"Chief, I want trade for land," he said, turning to sweep a hand toward the field.

"Uggh. What give?" replied the cunning Kiowa.

"Much. You be friend and keep off Cheyennes, Arapahoes, Apaches, Comanches."

"Good. Satana kill heap red man. How much trade?"

"What you want?" Latch's deal with the savage called for a surrender of all oxen and horses captured in a raid on a caravan. This had appeared to be eminently satisfactory to the Kiowa.

"Heap flour, beans, coffee, tobac," began Satana.

"Yes."

"Wagons."

"No. All wagons are to be run over the cliffs and destroyed."

"Guns, powder, ball."

"Yes. Equal share . . . same you . . . same me."

"Uggh! Good! . . . Firewater?"

"Plenty for Satana. Little for Indian braves. Bad medicine. Make Kiowas crazy."

"Satana trade. Him promise keep."

Latch gripped the lean sinewy hand extended him, and felt that Satana, treacherous savage and deadly foe of white men, would deal with him as he was dealt by. A sense of final committal fell upon Latch. He had chosen his hiding-place, his burrow in the mountains, there to lie concealed until this or that raid had passed into the history of the frontier, forgotten in a few weeks as the unending accidents and disasters befell the travelers to the West. He had traded for his ranch land, where slowly he would develop the resources, build and fence and irrigate, so that when the war ended he could make a home. Home! He railed at his unreasonable dreams. Long before this war was over he would stop a freighter's bullet or be hanged to a cottonwood tree. His trading, his planning, his labor, whatever these might be, would be but vain dreams. Still he persisted in them. There seemed to be an unknown self inside him, a defiant unquenchable self, some man who had a secret and terrific passion. He felt it stirring, boiling, swelling, like the change of a volcano from inertia to awakening for the eruption.

The Kiowas knew the country. They kept on straight as a crow flew, over ridge and across hollows, up and down the barrens, higher and higher across the uplands, ringed by a close horizon. An occasional wolf, lean and old, follower of the pack, watched them from some eminence. Hawks sailed over the swales where scant brush might harbor gophers and rabbits. Latch never tired of the gray reaches, the lonely monotonous eternal gray of the high range. He recognized here something similar to what he had in his mind. And again he was confronted with the thought that unless he became an ordinary ruffian, bent on robbery, gambling, and carousal, he must expect all these strange and illusive things to magnify. Why should he concern himself with what he was then, what he would become tomorrow? The fact was that despite his bitter mocking resignation his dreams prevailed. And he concluded that this was better than dwelling only upon lust for blood and gold. At least he would prolong the period before his inevitable degradation.

The long line of Indian horsemen lengthened out until it covered miles. What travelers they were! Their wild ponies kept on tirelessly. Latch's outfit slowly fell behind. The heavier-weighted horses slowed up toward midday. Leighton had succeeded Keetch as leader of the white contingent. He rode at some distance ahead, shifting in his saddle from time to time, absorbed in his thoughts. In fact, all the men rode apart from one another. Cornwall, however, did not get far in advance of Latch.

Thus they rode on during the afternoon, hour by hour, across the ridges and hollows of the uplands, where the miles ahead appeared like those left behind. Not a track or a trail did Latch's active eye espy. Buffalo did not frequent these barren foothills. Latch had a view now and then of the distant Rockies, rising purple-peaked above the gray land. At sunset the file of Indians appeared to deviate from their straight course north, and turn somewhat to the west. Latch then made note that they had come out on the verge of a promontory.

Leighton and Keetch waited for their followers to come up. Latch was the last to join the group, all of whom were facing intently what lay before and below them. He gathered from their rigidity and absorption that he was to expect some unusually striking scene. Keetch was pointing and speaking.

Presently Latch rode out on the brim of the plateau. His anticipation was vastly overwhelmed. The Great Plains lay beneath him, far below, gray and green, dotted and barren, merging in a dim haze.

"Wal, boss, hyar you are," said Keetch, coming to Latch's side. "Sort of staggerin', huh? . . . You see thet meanderin' line? Thet's the Dry Trail. I wouldn't say it was a line of skulls an' bleached bones. But you'd see some if you rode it. . . . I'm not shore, but I think thet ribbon far out there is the Cimarron. Our wagon train ought to be past the river. The Cimarron Crossin' is where the Dry Trail begins. As I told you, it cuts off near three hundred miles. But it's bad goin'. Some grass. Little water, an' you gotta know how to find thet. I remember some of the camps. Sand Creek's the first. Willow Bar, Round Mount, Point of Rocks, an' so on, only thet's not their

order. We ought to be able to see Point of Rocks from
hyar. But I can't locate it."

"I have a field-glass in my pack."

"Wal, we can use thet tomorrer."

"Are the Kiowas going down to the trail?"

"Reckon only to a waterhole. We'll camp there
an' wait until the scouts locate the train. From what
I gathered, Hawk Eye reckons he'll smoke signal us
day after tomorrer sometime. Thet'll mean the wagon
train will be comin' along the trail, an' be within
strikin' distance in their camp thet night."

"Well, let's follow on down. I'm tired," rejoined
Latch.

Camp that night was something to nauseate Latch.
But for his canteen with water from Spider Web
Creek he would have gone thirsty to bed. His men
grumbled for rum. The Kiowas burned dim fires of
buffalo chips and danced around them, working themselves into a warlike mood. It seemed that their strange
low staccato yells pierced Latch's slumber.

All next day he lounged in camp, in what scant
shade he could find here and there. The Kiowas rode
out to a man, a few of them up the slope of the hills,
and most of them out on the plains to hunt. Leighton's crowd gambled with their share of the expected
raid, using pebbles as counters, and most of the day
they cursed, laughed, brooded the hours away. Some
of Latch's men slept. Cornwall haunted the gamblers,
a watching, indifferent, incomprehensible youth. Latch
marked him for something singular. Often he approached Latch, but seldom spoke.

"Colonel, that outfit is gambling away the contents of your wagon train," he said once.

"They're ambitious—and trusting. Some of them may be dead."

"Queer bunch. I imagine we're all queer, though. I know I am, because I like this life. But not for that sort of thing."

"What for, Lester?" queried Latch, curiously.

"I don't know, unless it's the spell."

"Of blood and death just round the corner. I think I understand. It's got me, too. But it's not a wild joy, a wild freedom from all restraint. It's bitter defiance. . . . What do you make of Leighton's cronies?"

"That Texas gunman fascinated me," replied Cornwall. "He's the only one of the bunch I'd trust. He doesn't talk much. When Leighton taunted him about Lone Wolf, this other gun-thrower from Texas, why he didn't like it a bit. I guessed Leighton wanted Texas to pick a fight with Lone Wolf, just to see which would kill the other quickest. . . . Waldron is a gloomy man, haunted by a bad conscience, but excited about the prospects of gold. Mandrove may have been a preacher, but he's pretty low down now. He too wants the raid on the wagon train to gain him money. I suspect not to gamble with, but to escape with. Creik, the damned nigger, wants some slaves to beat. Sprall itches for fight. He gives me the creeps. I'll probably shoot him presently. And Leighton— what do you think he wants most?"

"God only knows. Perhaps to be chief of this band."

"No. He's just antagonistic to you. He wouldn't have the responsibility. I'm sure he has no great desire for power. Leighton is the kind who live for women."

"What?" demanded Latch, surprised out of his somberness.

"I've studied Leighton, watched him, listened to him. . . . If he's a relative of yours you ought to know something about him."

"Very little. We're only distantly related—third cousins, I think. . . . I believe I did hear something about love affairs—years ago. I forget. . . . Well, it's nothing to me what he was or is."

The day passed and the night. Latch suffered under the strain. He arose feeling like a chained tiger. Cornwall, always active, eager, curious, was the first to report that Satana's scouts were smoke-signaling from far-separated points. They had sighted the caravan. It was a moment of tremendous import. Latch did not realize until then that he had still to make a choice, a decision. Should he go on with the deal with Satana or abandon it to flee across the plains, anywhere to escape? In cold fury he again met the issue.

That encampment became possessed of devils. Satana sent out riders, evidently to get reports from the scouts. He would not allow the white men, even Latch, to climb the hill. He permitted no cooking fires. Dozens of circles of savages were dancing their war-dance. Latch's men eagerly approached him for liquor, and being refused kept up the importunity.

growing sullen and insistent. They had eyes like wolves, except Cornwall's, which resembled blue ice. Latch himself had to fight a need of stimulant. With Keetch he planned an attack on the caravan, drawing maps on the ground, figuring every detail. Satana was a sharp observer of this practice, sometimes approving with an "Uggh!" and more often shaking his head.

"Boss, thet old bird has got a haid on him, an' don't you overlook it. What he's drivin' at is thet we can't plan the attack till we see where the wagon train camps. Unless it's out in the open. Which, of course, any old freighter or experienced scout would insist on."

"Which would be most favorable to us?" demanded Latch.

"I'd prefer a brushy place or willow swale for them to camp," replied the old frontiersman, thoughtfully. "The redskins, you know, can't be held back, specially if they have a little rum—an' it takes damn little to infuriate an Injun. Let's put the brunt of the attack up to the Kiowas an' leave us men to keep back an' do the sharpshootin' from cover. In case the attack is out in the open, some of us are goin' to git plugged. We've got tc put in our lick, too."

"I appreciate that. . . . Well, tell Satana as soon as we locate the wagon-train camp we'll plan the attack. And he must plan the hour."

"Uhuh," replied Keetch, and conversed with the chief. Presently he turned again to Latch. "Satana wants to know when they drink the fire water."

The Lost Wagon Train

"What's your advice, Keetch?"

"Hell! Parcel the rum out tonight. There's twenty gallons, an' a thimbleful of thet stuff will make a devil of any savage unused to likker."

The Kiowa scouts from the south rode in before sunset, reporting that the caravan was on the Dry Trail abreast of Satana's camp, and not far away. Just after dark the riders from the north rode in to report that fifty-three wagons had gone into camp.

"Tanner's Swale," asserted Keetch, after listening to the reports. "Thet's a waterhole off the trail. Brushy with willow an' hackberry. Pretty high banks on each side of the swale, an' not far apart. . . . The damn tenderfeet! Wonder who'n hell is boss of thet wagon train. Reckon they think they can hide. My Gawd! . . . Wal, boss, it's set to order."

Latch stood erect, taut as a wire, with a strange ringing in his ears. Cold sweat broke out all over him.

"Keetch, ask Satana what his hour is for the attack," said Latch, his voice sounding far away to him.

Satana well understood. He made an imperious gesture.

"Dark—before day come."

"It is settled. . . . Keetch, tell him we will follow his braves and fight with them. . . . Spare no man—woman—or—or—child! . . . They are not to set fire to wagons or shoot the stock."

The interpreter made that clear to the chief. "Good!" he grunted.

"Now, men, we can't be cowards and let the Indians do it all. But my orders are to keep back, under cover, and withhold your fire until you see a *man* to shoot at. . . . That's all. Fetch the kegs of rum. Cornwall, get the small cups out of my saddle-bag."

"Aggh!"

"Rush 'em out, Keetch!"

"Boss, how much do *we* git out of thet twenty gallon?"

Presently in the dim light of a buffalo-chip fire Latch was witness to a scene he would never forget. To each of his men, after portioning out the first to Satana, he allotted a full coffee-cup of rum. Then the liquor of one keg was poured out into buckets from which the small cupfuls were swiftly dispensed to the Indians. Silent, with eyes of dusky fire, the savages presented themselves for their portion. Many of the young braves choked as if indeed they had swallowed fire. Their very bodies leaped. From the drinking they went to the war-dance. But this night they made no sound, and the weird crouching steps appeared all the more sinister.

The second ten-gallon keg was tapped and again Latch allowed his men a drink. What heady stuff it was—how it burned his vitals—killed some struggle within—gave rein to the evil in him! It seemed a kind of ceremony, this drinking-bout, for it entailed silence and stilled mirth. His greedy men glared with fiery eyes at these slim savage striplings, erect, proud, fierce, ignorant that their courageous souls had been damned by the white traitors.

Chapter III

BOWDEN'S prairie-schooner had come in for end-less attention all along the trail from Inde-pendence.

Tullt and Co. had built it especially for John Bow-den, and as the plainsman Pike Anderson averred, "shore was a kind of cross between a boat an' a wagon." It did not have square ends and straight sides. The former came almost to a point, like the blunt bow and stern of a boat, and the latter sheered up in a perceptible curve. It was large, heavy, strong, set up on wide wheels, and amazed the freighters by the ease with which it could be pulled.

On the front end was painted against the green background in large red letters: TULLT and CO. NO. 1 A.

At Council Grove this wagon came in for its first more than ordinary attention. Bowden appeared rather pleased, for the prairie-schooner had been constructed after his own plans. From one post to another the caravan traveled, always with Bowden's big wagon to the fore, standing up above the grass like a ship at sea.

Fort Dodge was an important stop on the long trail. Here Bowden expected the soldier escort he had been promised from Fort Leavenworth. But calls for more

43

soldiers to the front in the Civil War made it impossible for Colonel Bradley to oblige him.

"Better wait here until I can give you an escort," said the officer, curtly. "Indians getting bolder since the war started. There have been some serious fights lately."

"How long would we have to lay over?" queried Bowden.

"From three to six weeks."

"Impossible!" ejaculated Bowden, and turned away.

To his niece Cynthia he confided: "I really feel safer out on the prairie than here in these camps. Such a motley crew of men! And they all spot my wagon, just as if their gimlet eyes could pierce that false bottom where I have secreted the gold. Your gold, Cynthia."

"Uncle, it was terribly risky," replied the young woman, seriously. "Hauling gold all the way out to California, where gold is supposed to grow on trees! Dad would turn over in his grave if he knew."

"These are war times, my dear, and if I know Yankees, it's going to last. We could not trust all this money to paper. It might depreciate. Gold is safe and I'm going to get this ——"

"Careful, Uncle," interrupted Cynthia.

Pike Anderson, the scout whom Bowden had engaged at Independence, came up with a companion.

"Boss, this is Jeff Stover, an' he wants to throw in with us far as Fort Union."

"All right with me. Glad to have another man,"

returned Bowden, shaking hands with the newcomer, whose open, resolute visage he liked.

"Got my family an' two drivers," replied Stover. "From Missouri, an' due to meet a Texas wagon train at Cimarron Crossin'."

"That's interesting," spoke up Bowden. "What size train?"

"Sixty wagons. Some old plainsmen an' Injun-fighters with them. You'd be wise to join us. Reckon Blaisdal an' Cy Hunt will take the Dry Trail."

"What's that?"

"It's a cut-off, savin' near three hundred miles between the Cimarron an' the Canadian River. Bad trail. Poor camps. Water scant an' hard to find. Particular pet stampin'-ground for Comanches an' Kiowas. But with Blaisdal an' Cy in charge I reckon we'll go through."

"Anderson, what do you think of this Dry Trail cut-off?" inquired Bowden, eagerly.

"Damn little good," blurted out Anderson, his blue eyes narrowing and his scrubby chin bulging. "Shore it's a cut-off all right. An' if we met Blaisdal's outfit an' if he had sixty wagons, why, I'd say we might risk it."

"Stover, are you sure of your facts?"

"Betcha. The Texas outfit is due at the Cimarron about the ninth of this month. If you pull out tomorrer we could get to the Cimarron by the eighth shore."

"Then, if Blaisdal's train didn't show up in a day or two we could tackle this Dry Trail ourselves or turn back?"

"Shore. But you needn't reckon on turnin' back, Mr. Bowden."

"We'll go!" declared Bowden, forcibly. "I can't 'bide these crowded camps, with their lousy Indians, beady-eyed Mexicans, hard-lipped outlaws, and so on."

"Wal, I'm givin' you a hunch thet you might run into *more* lousy redskins an' tough nuts out there than you do hyar," replied Anderson, sarcastically.

"But can't you take a reasonable chance?" queried Bowden, impatiently.

"Shore, if you give it to me. But this ain't reasonable. It's foolhardy."

"Have you been over this Dry Trail?"

"Onct, an' thet in early spring—which's the best time. I'd rather go around the old trail."

"Are you afraid of Indians and robbers?"

Anderson fastened pale-blue eyes upon his employer and might have intended to make a sharp retort. But he thought better of that, perhaps owing to the presence of Bowden's niece, standing close, her eyes wide, her lips parted.

"Not for myself," returned Anderson. "I've no kin an' I'm gettin' along. One time or another is all the same to me. But, Mr. Bowden, you've got wimmen an' kids in this wagon train. An' this hyar pretty niece of yourn. I'd shore hate to see thet golden haid all gory where thet crown of hair shines now."

"My God, man! Stop such talk! All I've heard since I got to Independence was Indians, raids, burned wagon trains, scalped men, and girls carried off into captivity. And we haven't seen a hostile Indian."

"Wal, if you look around hyar you'll see two, right in Dodge," returned Anderson, crisply.

Bowden turned. Two lean Indian riders stood at ease near at hand. They had long black hair, youthful dark faces of which nearly all points were sharp. Their scant garments were buckskin soiled by long service. One was naked to the waist. Neither, apparently, had any weapons. Their ponies, ragged, wild, fleet-looking mustangs, stood tethered to a hitching-rail.

"Ha! Those Indian boys hostile," scoffed Bowden.

"Kiowas. An' every Kiowa on the plains is hostile," certified the frontiersman.

"Anderson, will you continue in charge of my train?"

"Yes, sir. I had no idee of quitten'. Jest reckoned it my duty to tell you. An' last I'm shore advisin' you to leave Miss Bowden hyar till a train with a guard of soldiers comes along."

"Oh, why, Mr. Anderson?" cried the girl, in dismay.

"Wall, somewhere out hyar thar's a fine strappin' young Westerner thet I don't want you to miss meetin'," drawled the scout.

"Indeed there's no such thing," retorted the girl, with a vivid blush, which enhanced her singular beauty.

"Wal, there ought to be. An' like as not you'll never meet him if you take such chances."

"Uncle John, let us wait for a safer caravan," she said, convinced by the scout's earnestness.

"Nonsense! Just think. We can be in California three weeks sooner."

"Mebbe you can. I shore hope so. I'll do my best," concluded Anderson, soberly, and he led Stover away. As he passed the two Kiowas he gave them a scrutiny which apparently was unnoticed. Nevertheless, Bowden observed that as soon as the freighter disappeared the Indians lounged in the direction they had taken.

Bowden's wagon train arrived at the Crossing of the Cimarron at dusk on the evening of the 9th of the month. No lights on either side of the wide pale belt of sand and water!

The night was sultry and warm. Sheet lightning flashed along the dark battlements of bluffs to the south. An oppressive silence and melancholy pervaded the vast plain. For the first time Bowden experienced a strange sensation such as he imagined was like the uncanny chill old folk were wont to say they felt when some one stepped across their grave.

They went into camp, and as usual drove the fifty-three wagons, two abreast, in a close circle, leaving an opening for the stock. All oxen and horses were put to grazing under guard. Bundles of firewood had been hauled from the last camp. Cheery fire, deep voices of men, prattle of children, color and movement and life disrupted the solitude and loneliness of the Cimarron.

"Blaisdal an' Hunt shore ought to be hyar 'bout

tomorrer or next day, I reckon," Stover went around saying in a loud voice, as if to reassure himself.

Bowden observed that Pike Anderson kept out of his way, a silent, grim man who attended to innumerable tasks. The freighters and pioneers who were crossing the Great Plains for the first time appeared jovial and merry. The experienced had little to say. After supper the former produced their pipes and prepared for a comfortable smoke and talk around the camp fires.

"All fires out!" ordered Anderson, tersely. "I want twenty men—volunteers to go on guard. Our stock will be driven inside."

"What the hell!" declared a farmer from Illinois. The other remained silent.

"Wal, if you won't volunteer, I'll have to pick you out," went on the trail boss. "Smith an' Hall. Dietrich an' Stover. Wallin' an' Bowden." Anderson went on until he had named ten couples. "Keep two together. Spread around the wagons. No smokin'. Watch an' listen. . . . You'll be relieved at twelve o'clock."

Bowden wheeled from his camp fire to stride up to his wagon. Cynthia sat on the high seat and appeared to be fascinated by the dark empty space beyond the river.

"What do you think, Cynthia?" he said, in querulous surprise. "That gloomy Anderson ordered me to do guard duty till midnight."

"Uncle John, you must not shirk your share," replied the young woman, gravely.

"Shirk! . . . That hadn't occurred to me," returned Bowden, irritably. "But that Anderson thinks it necessary riles me."

"How little we know of Western ways! Uncle, all along I have felt something strange creeping upon me. And tonight it possesses me."

"What?"

"I don't know. But there's something out there. . . . When I was little I was afraid of the shadows—of the things that lived in the dark. Tonight it has come back. . . . How terribly lonely and still it is—away from the camp!"

"Child, you've grown nervous from the talk of this crabby old plainsman."

"I dare say. But Uncle dear, I'm no longer a child, except in these nameless fears. I'm twenty-four."

"No one would guess it," replied Bowden, climbing up on the wagon to reach in for his rifle. It was a clumsy heavy gun, a Colt revolving seven-shot arm in prevailing use on the frontier. But he would have preferred a musket.

"Go to bed, Cynthia," he advised.

"Not yet. Oh, I have been so excited and thrilled by this wonderful adventure!" she exclaimed. "Tonight for the first time I can't enjoy it."

Bowden gazed up at the fair face, at the wide violet eyes shining so beautifully in the camp-fire light, at the wave of golden hair above the broad high forehead and level brows; and all at once he seemed stricken with a realization that he was mostly responsible for his niece's presence here in this wild, uncertain country. He strode away with worry beginning to gnaw at his old assurance.

Blaisdal's caravan did not show up the next day, which was the 10th. On the following morning Anderson sent two men with a field-glass to scout from the hilltops ten miles south. That was a hot, tedious, wearing day on those left behind to wait. Toward sunset the riders returned. Smith, the older of the two scouts, had been some years on the frontier.

"Nothin' comin' on thet trail to the south. I could see forty miles of it," he reported.

Anderson ground out a curse that, to judge from the hard glance he flashed on Stover, must have been meant for that worthy.

"Ahuh. What I expected," he muttered.

"Then you saw nothing?" demanded Bowden, incredulously. He seemed to resent this unexpected report.

"Wal, I didn't say thet," replied the scout.

Anderson took a stride which placed him in front of Bowden, and he laid a heavy hand on Smith's knees.

"What'd you see?"

"Wal, for one think I made out two Injun riders way to the south of hyar."

"Riders!"

"Shore. Injuns ridin' 'cross country, haidin' south. I watched them till they went out of sight. Pike, you know how a redskin rides when he's goin' somewhere. Long, even, swingin' lope!"

"An' was thet all?"

"Nope. I seen what I reckoned was smoke risin" above a hill."

"Smoke!"

"Shore. Way off, forty, mebbe fifty miles beyond where I last seen the Injun riders."

"Smoke!" ejaculated Bowden, blusteringly. "What of that?"

Neither Westerner paid any attention to him.

"What kind of smoke?" queried Anderson, gruffly.

"Wal, it come from a fire, thet's shore," rejoined Smith, with a short laugh.

"Was it a steady column of smoke—like from a camp fire?" went on Anderson.

"Nope. Jest yellow puffs, few an' far between. . . . But, Pike, they wasn't plain at all, even through the glass. An' I couldn't see them with my naked eye."

"You mean they might have been dust?"

"I ain't shore. But if you ask me I'd say I wouldn't take any chances."

Anderson whirled abruptly to the leader of the caravan. "Bowden, I advise you not to take the Dry Trail."

"Thet's not new from you, Anderson. You've been against it since we arrived at Dodge."

"Thet was only caution. I'm advisin' you now," rejoined the plainsman, significantly.

"You want to turn back?" demanded Bowden, hotly.

"Yes."

"Why? Because Smith here saw a couple of Indians and imagines he saw smoke?" queried Bowden, scornfully.

"Thet's why," shot back Anderson, in a different tone.

"That does not please me," went on Bowden. "We are taking the Dry Trail."

Two days' travel across the dry undulating prairie, with the gray bluffs to the west imperceptibly rising clearer, convinced even the redoubtable Bowden that the rigors of this cut-off had not been exaggerated.

Anderson failed altogether to find water at the second camp. Next day the caravan went on with horses and cattle wearing to bad shape. The sun shone hot. There was no breeze, except down in the bare swales where whirls of dust rose as if by magic. No living creature, not even a raven or a lizard, appeared to Bowden's searching gaze. The heat lifted in shining veils from the gray grass, the pale mirages wavered in the distant flat reaches. Hazy bluffs, sometimes blue, and again dimly outlined, lifted their ramparts, and seemed to raise a menacing obstacle to the progress of the wagon train. Bleached skulls of cattle and buffalo marked the uncertain trail, which appeared to spread wide over the plain.

Before the sun set, Anderson, riding ahead to reconnoiter, found a waterhole in a shallow rocky gully. At the head of it a bowl protected by rocks caught the trickle from the ledge. Here was drink for beast and man. Bowden was heard to state that he had never appreciated water.

The weary freighters camped, slept, and guarded

by turns, awoke and hitched up for the trail. Camp succeeded camp, meager in water and grass, though having enough to enable the animals to pull on. Skull Rock, named from a ghastly buffalo head stuck upon a rock, proved to be dry. If, on the morrow, after the longest and hardest pull, they did not find water at Tanner's Swale, they faced a catastrophe.

Nevertheless, after a cool night the stock started without distress. Anderson made the most of the early-morning hours, then slowed up and at midday halted to rest. He had been a silent taciturn man for two days, never speaking except to give an order. While he drove Bowden's No. 1 A wagon at the front of the caravan he was observed constantly to watch the gray mounting escarpment rising like a wall. Probably the trail ran along its base as it would to the west.

Noon found them resting. As Anderson gave the word to start again, Smith approached him in haste.

"Pike, I seen smoke signals shore," he said in a low voice.

"What of it? I been seein' 'em all mawnin'—tell that —— Stover!"

Bowden heard this exchange of words, which he let pass without comment. But his stubborn obtuseness had given way to apprehension. Later when he addressed his guide he received no response whatever.

Wearily the oxen and horses hauled off the miles. At midafternoon the caravan was still five miles from Tanner's Swale and perhaps half as far from the foothill which ran parallel to the trail. The bluff at nearer view was a steep yellow hill with a ragged rim extending along the summit, broken in places.

The wagons creaked, the wheels rolled, the horses plodded, the drivers flicked listless whips.

"Ha! There they are!" suddenly shouted Anderson, in a voice that had a sardonic ring.

"Who? Where?" called out Bowden, climbing out to the front seat.

Anderson halted his yoke of oxen. Whip in hand, he pointed toward the top of the hill.

"Oh, Uncle! What is it?" cried Cynthia, emerging from the canvas portal of the wagon.

"I can't see anything," rasped Bowden.

Anderson kept pointing until the foremost wagons behind rolled up to halt abreast, then he leaped to the ground.

Smith, Hall, Dietrich, Walling, Hones, and other drivers viewed him with certainty and concern. Anderson's dark face had lost a shade of its bronze.

"Where's thet —— Stover?" he called.

"Laggin' behind. Not so damn keen as he was fust off," replied some one.

"What you see, Anderson?"

"Why're you holdin' us up?"

Smith answered all such queries by a violent start and a piercing voice: "By Gawd! Look at thet line of Injuns! . . . I felt it in my bones!"

Everyone's gaze followed the direction indicated by Smith's rigid arm. Cynthia Bowden uttered a low cry of terror. Her uncle stared with dropping jaw and popping eyes. The other drivers uttered various ejaculations of alarm, dismay, anger, amazement, according to their temperaments.

Sharp eyes could discern a long dotted line of moving objects darkly silhouetted against the pale-blue sky. Mustangs! Riders! How tiny they appeared— how snail-like they moved! They were Indians. By straining his eyes Bowden could make out the wild lean riders, the wild long-maned ponies. He was struck dumb. Indian riders. He was so astonished that the significance did not dawn upon him. What a line! It extended along the horizon of the plateau as far as he could see, and still that was not the end. They were moving in the same general direction as his wagon train.

"*Turn back!*" shouted Bowden, involuntarily.

"Too late, boss," replied Anderson, with an almost grim satisfaction. "If thet bunch surrounds us out on the open prairie, we're gone goslin's."

"Are they—hostile?" faltered Bowden.

"Haw! Haw! Haw!" roared the scout, harshly.

"Mr. Bowden, all these plains Indians are hostile— when they outnumber the whites," spoke up Smith.

"Outnumber?" echoed Bowden.

The last wagons came lumbering up to be halted by the wide barricade. Stover, with other teamsters, including his two men, came thumping forward.

"Ha!" ejaculated Anderson, giving Stover a hard slap on the breast. "Do you see them Injuns?"

"Hell yes!" shouted Stover. "We got to be makin' tracks."

"Where?"

"Back along the trail."

"Say, I reckoned you knew Injuns."

"You bet I do."

"Wal, you ought to know thet if thet bunch sur-rounds us on the prairie they'll kill every damn soul of us."

"If we can rustle back across the Cimarron we ——"

"You're drunk or crazy," retorted Anderson, an-grily.

"Men, stop arguing," ordered Bowden. "What can we do?"

"Only one thing. Make Tanner's Swale," returned Anderson, tersely. "It's about five miles. Water there, an' good cover. We can make a stand. I reckon we've time."

"Anderson, I'm goin' back with my men," spoke up Stover, dry-lipped. "Any of you fellars want ——"

"You're what?" shouted Anderson, jumping as if stung.

"I'm goin' back. Come on, Bill—Zeke," Stover re-joined, making a stride.

Anderson spun him round like a top. "—— —— —— ——! You got us into this mess. An' you reckon you'll leave us, huh?"

"Thet's what I said."

"Stover, I'm curious aboot you," replied Anderson, slowly. "I ain't so damn shore thet you're what you say you are."

"No matter now, we're turning back. Go on an' git scalped!"

"Man, you ain't goin' back!"

"By Gawd, I am!"

"Not a step. . . . An' if you knowed the West you wouldn't say thet. Else you're a renegade pardner of them Injuns!"

"Aw hell!" snorted Stover, ashen of face. "Lemme by!"

"You ain't gettin' by," returned the scout, low and hard.

"Out of my way, man!"

"Fellars, give us room," ordered Anderson.

The circle split on each side, leaving a wide space for the two men. Bowden uttered a feeble protest. Some other freighter called out: "It ain't no time for us to fight amongst ——"

"Anderson, I'll bore you," roared Stover, suddenly crooking his right arm. That move spurred the scout into action too swift for the eye. Spurt of red and bellow of gun accompanied it. Stover's wrench for his gun ceased as quickly and he fell forward suddenly.

"Thar!" rasped out Anderson, fire-eyed and violent, as he wheeled to leap at Stover's two teamsters. "Drive your wagons out hyar ahaid. Rustle. Or so help me ——"

The two men rushed back without a word and leaped upon their wagons.

"Search him, Smith," ordered Anderson. "Rest of you file out of hyar. We got time to make the Swale."

Bowden staggered to his own wagon to find Cynthia with her white face covered by her hands.

"Oh, Uncle! How—awful!" she cried.

"Cynthia!—you—saw?" rejoined Bowden, huskily.
"I couldn't—help it."

"Damn these crude Westerners! . . . Girl, I suspect we'll see worse. Brace up. . . . We've got to
fight!"

He climbed aboard and drew his niece within the
canvas shelter. Cynthia dropped her hands from a
pale but composed face.

"We should have listened to Anderson," she said,
gravely, dark troubled eyes upon her uncle.

The wagon lurched and rolled on. Anderson had
resumed his seat and whip. There were wagons ahead
and alongside. Gruff shouts and curses attested to
the hurry of the teamsters. It was a slight downgrade
over hard road. Soon the wagons were rolling and
careening. Bowden peered out. The gray bluff rose
against the blue sky. He could see the long line of
Indian riders. What was this that he had so fool-
hardily rushed into? Stories of Indian atrocities returned to fill him with dread and remorse. He had
actually needed a sight of hostile savages to bring
reality home to him. The wagon jolted over rough
places. Dust rose in yellow clouds. Far ahead over the
barren prairie a black patch of timber marked the end
of the open country. A gap showed between two sharp-
banked ridges. The gray promontory loomed higher.

The sun set a strange sinister red. Bowden's wagon
train had reached the coveted swale and had drawn
the fifty-three wagons, two abreast, into a circle in
the thick timber. High banks surrounded the swale,
reaching above the tops of the trees. A stream ran

through the middle of this oval hollow. Oxen and horses had been turned loose down the swale. Grass and willows grew abundantly. Owing to a boxing of the gulch below, the stock could not be driven out at that end. A stampede was here most difficult to effect. A well-armed determined group of men could withstand any ordinary Indian attack. Time and again this swale had resounded to the boom of freighters' guns and the war-cries of infuriated Indians.

Dusk that followed the sunset had likewise a deep red glow.

"Cook an' eat an' drink," had been Anderson's order. "For tomorrow ye die! Haw! Haw! . . . But we might be too busy when mawnin' comes—if we ever see daylight again."

Several fires burned brightly and men and women moved noiselessly around them. Children huddled in a group, wide-eyed and silent, watching every move of the men. Bowden sat on a log, his head in his hands. Cynthia helped around the camp fire nearest to her wagon. Before dark the three scouts returned.

"Nary sign or sound of them Injuns," reported one.

"Vamoosed. I reckon they didn't see us," said the second.

Smith, the last in, had been absent from camp since the caravan had arrived at the swale. His face was gray behind his uncut beard. His eyes had a glint.

"Step aside hyar, you fellars," he whispered, huskily.

Those who heard him moved as one man to a point where Bowden sat upon the log.

"No sense lettin' the wimmin an' kids hear," he said, clearing his throat and surveying the still faces in a half-circle before him. "I've been hyar before . . . know the lay of land. Climbed thet hill. There's another swale down the other side. Old stampin'-ground for redskins. But no wagons can git down there. . . . I heerd the devils before I seen them. Had to crawl a ways over the top—under the brush. . . . Hyar's your field-glass, Mr. Bowden. I shore wish I hadn't had it. . . . Wal, I'll bet I seen three hundred ponies. Then, down in the swale, what 'peared like a thousand Injuns. Some of them was war-dancin'. But farther down, where I seen most of the Injuns—they was Kiowas—it struck me kinda strange. What'n'hell was they doin', I says to myself? Then I remembered the glass. Fust off I spotted white men, ——! An', fellars, what do you reckon they was doin'?"

No one ventured an opinion. Anderson ordered Smith to end their suspense.

"Wal, them white men was dealin' out likker to the Injuns!" concluded Smith, impressively.

"How'd you know it was drink?" demanded Anderson, hoarsely. "It might have been soup."

"Shore. I thought of thet. But soup doesn't make Injuns leapin', boundin', dancin' demons."

"Some white renegades gittin' the redskins drunk!" ejaculated Anderson, wiping the sweat off his brow. "It's been done before."

"Pike, wouldn't you reckon thet means they'll attack us soon?" queried Smith. "Injuns usually wait till just before daybreak."

"There's a white man's hand in this deal," replied Anderson, ponderingly. "The moon's about full an' comin' up now. Soon as it clears thet bluff it'll be most as light as day. I reckon then we can expect hell to pop."

"Anderson, we can pop some hell ourselves," spoke up a brave man. "We got three wagon-loads of rifles an' ammunition an ——"

"Who's got thet?" demanded the scout.

"We have—Kelly, Washburn, an' myself. We didn't tell Bowden what we was haulin' when we fell in with his outfit at Council Grove."

"Wal, fust off thet sounded awful good. But it ain't so good. We might stand off a big force of Injuns, an' white outlaws, too, if they fought in the way frontiersmen are used to. But any redskins even half drunk will rush us. They'll crawl like snakes in the grass. You'll have to kill them to stop them."

"These rifles we're haulin' are the new Colt's revolvin' chamber. Seven shots in two minutes."

"Ahuh. Let's deal out aboot three of these guns an' plenty of ammunition to each man. Put the wimmin an' kids in the inside wagons. Then all of us, two men together, spread out all around under the wagons an' lay down to wait. It's a fight for your lives, men. Our only hope is to keep 'em outside the circle. Think of the little ones an' their mothers. You never can tell. We've got one chance in a thousand."

Chapter IV

SOON after Anderson's last word the moon rose above the dark escarpment, changing the scene magically.

It was a large white full moon, somehow pitiless in its cold brilliance. From the banks above the swale the circle of canvas-covered wagons stood out like silver arcs, and the tents shone as brightly. Shadows of trees fell across them and the few patches of open grassy ground and the open pools of the brook.

Gradually all sounds ceased inside the circle. The freighters, wide awake on guard, lay behind the outside wheels of the first circle of wagons. The night was close and warm. To the east, down across the plains, dark clouds lined the horizon and pale flares of lightning shone fitfully. The horses and oxen that had grazed earlier in the evening, now no longer broke the silence. Not a leaf rustled on the trees. The song of insects died altogether. Nature herself seemed locked in suspense, prophetic of a tragedy.

Before Anderson had placed his men in pairs all around the circle Bowden had approached him, haggard and drawn.

"Scout, if you get my niece and me safely through this night, I'll reward you handsomely."

"Bowden, rewards ain't appealin' to me none jest

now—onless it's one in heaven," replied the plains‹ man, wearily.

"There's a false bottom under my wagon—full of gold," whispered Bowden.

"Gold!" ejaculated Anderson, in amazement, either at the fact or the incredible obtuseness of this East‹ erner.

"Yes, a fortune. I'll pay ——"

"To hell with you an' your gold, Bowden," inter‹ rupted Anderson, ruthlessly. "Gold can't buy nothin' hyar."

Later, when the men were all in position, Anderson and Smith lay under the wagon outside of Bowden's big Tullt and Co., No. 1 A. Its owner had chosen to take his stand in the second line under his own wagon, no doubt under the gold so precious to him and so useless here. In the fifty-three men there neces‹ sarily had to be one without a partner. Bowden was that man, whether by accident or design.

"Funny aboot some men," whispered Smith in An‹ derson's ear.

"Ha! Aboot as funny as death," returned the scout. "The sooner his hair is lifted the better I'll like it. He got us into this deal. . . . But, my Gawd! I feel sick aboot thet lovely niece of his'n."

"Too bad. She's a fine girl. But mebbe ——"

"Sssch! Listen."

A long silence ensued.

"Scout, what'd you think you heerd?" finally whis‹ pered Smith.

"Stone rattlin' down."

"Wal, it's aboot time. Moon must be up a half-hour by now."

"More'n thet. An' I'm up a stump aboot this ambush. It ain't runnin' true to form."

"Pike, hadn't I better crawl back there an' tell Bowden to lie still. He's movin' aboot."

"I see him. An' you can bet some sharp-eyed Kiowa will see him. Let him alone, Smith."

"My turn to hear somethin'," whispered Smith, tensely. "Listen. . . . Is thet an owl?"

From the opposite bank of the swale came the hoot of an owl.

"Uhuh. Damn nice done if it's a Kiowa. Some of these plains Injuns can imitate any critter in natoor. . . . Aha! Get that. Over on this hyar side. . . . Smithy, you can gamble on two red owls around, anyhow."

"Injun owls?"

"Shore."

"Hadn't I better crawl along the line an' tell the men? Most of these men wouldn't know an owl from a canary."

"Wal, I don't know as it'd do any good. I reckon all of them will fight, onless Bowden. He might, too, if he got mad."

Another silence between the two frontiersmen intervened. When a faint rustle of dry grass or leaves came to strained ears, or a far-away rattling of a pebble, or indistinct nameless sounds that might have been imagination only, Smith would nudge Anderson, or that worthy would nudge his partner.

Meanwhile the moon climbed and the silver radiance intensified. Nowhere could the solitude and loneliness of the Great Plains have been more pronounced than at this seldom-visited Tanner's Swale on the Dry Trail. The vast black shadow under the bluff seemed to harbor the devils that lay in wait upon the gold-seeker, the trapper, the pioneer, the freighter, all of the adventurous souls who braved the West.

"Wal, I wish somethin' would start," whispered Smith, restlessly. He could not lie still or keep silent.

Anderson, however, kept his true state to himself. He had faced hazards often, to come out unscathed in most instances. But the oppression of his heart, the cold ache in the marrow of his bones, the settled, somber, nameless proximity of a strange thing about to be—these were different from all sensation and consciousness that had ever before been his experience. He knew. He was ready. He felt grim, bitter, fierce. Better and braver men than he had bitten the dust of these plains' trails.

"Anderson, wouldn't you like to cut the guts out of thet renegade who must be boss of this ambush?" went on Smith, as if the longing had burst from him.

"I shore would. . . . Must be a Rebel. These are war times, Smith. An' ninety out of a hundred caravans are Northerners."

Smith gave his companion a sharp tug. "*Look!*" he pointed up through an opening in the tree tops. Above the black rim of the bluff and sharp against the sky showed a lean wild form.

"Injun! . . . But don't waste your powder. Thet's farther than it looks."

"I see another . . . Movin' along . . . There! Comin' down. . . . Out of sight!"

"Shore. . . . Wal, it won't be long now."

"Reckon we'd better be peerin' —— —— sharp on the ground."

"Ahuh. I'd say. An' up in the trees, too. But thet bright moon makes black shadows."

An instant later Anderson heard a slight sound outside and to the right. That was the belt of cover which not only protected the freighters but also the besiegers. It was grass, brush, logs, and moonlit patches alternating with dense shade. Under the wagons, too, were both bright and dark spots, one of the latter of which the two freighters occupied. Bowden like a hyena in a cage, prowled on hands and knees under his wagon.

Anderson heard a slightly sliddery sound. He lay flat on his stomach, rifle extended. Suddenly a red flash belched out of the shade. CRASH! A heavy report of a buffalo gun almost cracked his ear-drum. But swift as thought he aimed a rifle length back of where that red flash had emerged and shot. Then Anderson flattened himself in the slight depression where he lay. Simultaneously with this action pealed out a mortal cry. Bowden began to flop and thump around under his wagon like a beheaded turkey. A low scream of terror and anguish broke from Bowden's wagon. Bowden ceased his violent commotion. Then followed a singular rattle of boot heels against the wagon wheel. It mounted high, then stopped.

Terrible moments ensued. The scout expected a roar of rifles, a hideous bursting of war-cries. But absolute silence prevailed. Smith, on his left side, squirmed closer till he touched him.

"Gawd Almighty! . . . Thet Bowden should be first! . . ."

"Keep your head down," whispered Anderson, fiercely. "Listen!"

Some kind of sound caught the scout's sensitive ear. He located it near the spot at which he had fired. It resembled a convulsive shuddering contact of something with the earth. He had almost recognized its nature when a hollow gulp, followed by a sound he knew—the death rattle in the throat—made certain the fact that his bullet had found the life of one of the ambushers.

Anderson felt a deadly certainty that this insupportable silence could not last. Bowden's train was surrounded, no doubt, by circle on circle of savages, backed up by crafty sharp-shooting white men on the banks. Still that silence did last. What was holding the horde of Indians from their onslaught?

"Bang! Bang! Bang!" Shots from ambush opened the engagement Anderson had expected. He heard the whistle and thud of heavy lead bullets. One passed closely over his head, the others struck under the wagon. Then the whizz of arrows and the peculiar quivering thud of their impact on wood. Bang! Bang! Bang! These shots from back in the timber indicated that whoever fired them was behind cover. Flares of light showed, but no red spurts of flame. Anderson withheld his fire. "——— ——— shootin' low!" hissed Smith. "Thet arrer skinned my ear. . . . Aha! There go the Colts."

A volley burst from the other side of the circle, and intermingled with it were slighter reports. The battle had begun. Anderson both saw and smelled burnt powder. Down the line ahead of him a freighter opened up. Red flares showed against the black shadow. From high on the bluff pealed down a prolonged yell, unmistakably an Indian war-cry, hideous, piercing, wonderful in its potency. It inflamed Anderson to the point of rushing out to kill, kill, kill and hasten the ghastly end he realized. But he gritted his teeth and shot low, back of a red flash. From his left then, beyond his partner, came the crack of pistols, the boom of rifles, a hollow yell that did not issue from the throat of a white man, and answering musket-shots. This flurry quieted down.

The next quarter for Anderson to hear from was the corner of circle that Dietrich and Walling had charge of. Beginning with a single report, followed by another, then several, this engagement welled to a solid roar of gun-shots. Anderson's fears were thus confirmed. The train was surrounded and had been attacked on four sides.

"Pull thet arrer out of my shoulder," whispered Smith. "Right side—stickin' in my collar-bone. ——— ——— thet redskin!"

The scout laid down his rifle and, careful to keep flat, he felt around to get hold of his comrade. Indeed there was an arrow in him, and deep at that. When Anderson wrenched it out Smith groaned.

"I'd better bind thet up," whispered Anderson, feeling for his scarf.

"Hell! Sooner the better!"

"You're shore bleedin' like a stuck pig, man." Anderson got the scarf inside Smith's coat and under his arm. He then pulled it tight and knotted it above the shoulder.

"Zip . . . Reckon thet one took a lock of my har. Wal, the less in my scalp for some murderin' Kiowa."

"Kill thet ——!" whispered Smith. He's crawlin' up. . . . There!"

Anderson drew a pistol on that bold savage and at the crack he appeared to step, to sag, then melt into the ground. Again Anderson flattened his body in the depression and stretched eager bloody hands to his rifle. At the same moment he became aware that the engagement had become general around the circle.

If cool judgment had not been Anderson's before this moment, he became conscious that he possessed it now. His position was favorable for the time being, and owing to the depression in the ground, the broad-wheel-tire and the ten-inch log that he had taken the precaution to lay against it, he did not run so great a risk of being hit. And before he was through he would account for a good many dead devils. Smith, too, was partially protected in the same way. Smith, however, was a younger man, and not well versed in savage warfare. He let terror and fury dominate him in turn. Whereupon Anderson, as a last admonition, reached a brawny hand to Smith's back and pressed him hard, face and all, to the ground. That done, he grimly addressed himself to the fray.

Flares of light, red spurts, gliding black forms across the silver aisles of moonlight, and a now incessant thudding of lead against the wheels, hubs and bodies of the wagon attested to the swelling of the attack to a point where the inevitable rush was imminent. How wisely and evilly some chief or renegade had coached these Kiowa braves! Surely burning within them was the wild lust to rush to close quarters, to shoot and tomahawk and scalp, to revel in blood. It seemed long in coming, yet perhaps all the fighting had taken only a few minutes.

Anderson wasted no shots. As the savages grew bolder and more numerous he waited until one came into the moonlight, or slid crouching behind a tree trunk, or crawled closer to shoot within a few yards of the wagons. Then the frontiersman sent a hot slug through this Kiowa's vitals. He alternated the buffalo gun with the seven-shot revolving Colt. And he kept the second Colt fully loaded, and his two pistols, ready for the onslaught when it came. If these Kiowas held off much longer, and if his comrades all around were doing stern execution, there might be a chance of driving them back. No Indians had ever long been proof against a steady withering fire. But there appeared to be a thousand of the red devils. Anderson piled dead Indians in a row along the front of his wagon. Smith, too, accounted for one out of every two shots. Anderson's rifles grew hot. He sank back to load them and then pick up the second Colt.

Suddenly Smith let out so deep and horrible an utterance that Anderson heard it despite the roar of gun-fire. He sank back and down. Releasing his rifle, he groped a hand to feel for his comrade. But Anderson did not lift his face from the grass. When he touched Smith he felt a slight tremor pass out of the burly form. Anderson moved his hand, feeling for his comrade's face. It came in contact, however, with his head, and then thick hair wet with something hot and slippery. Hastily Anderson snatched away his hand and wiped it on the grass. For a moment, stern, hard border man that he was, he quailed before the unknown which Smith had met and which soon must be his doom. Yet only for an instant. The unquenchable hatred of a Westerner rolled like a wave through his being and the deadly, cold sickness passed. He gripped his rifle again, raging and reckless now, and peered out into the smoky fire-spotted moonlit night.

He saw a dark round head protrude from behind a tree. It must have belonged to the Kiowa who had killed Smith. Swift as a flash Anderson aligned his buffalo gun with it and fired. Smoke blinded him but he heard a crack as of a melon being split open against the tree. A moment later, as the smoke drifted away, he espied a dark form huddled against the tree trunk, and the slant of a gun in the moonlight.

Then once more Anderson addressed all his faculties to what confronted him. Tongues of flame leaped out of the shade, out of the brush, out of the moon-blanched space. But he did not see any red gun-belch-ings from under either wagon to his left and right. Dead or driven back were those comrades who had helped him withstand the brunt of the attack on that side.

An almost unbroken, rattling, banging roar hung over the swale. It must have come from four times fifty rifles. Certainly it ringed the circle of wagons. The scout had expected to see a wagon with its in-flammable canvas and bedding burst into flames. But this had not occurred. He kept taking snap shots at the flashes out there. Less deliberate, wearing under the strain but not breaking, Anderson fought on.

The time came when he could no longer hear. Then he remembered a slight sensation, as if he had knocked his head against the wagon-bed. He felt light and queer. Meanwhile he could see as well as ever, and knew that another stage of the attack was under way. Dark forms flashed across the moonlit aisles, too fleetly for him to get a bead on. The Kiowas were running, darting, gliding along the side of the circle. He saw them flash by with incredible fleetness, firing under the wagons as they ran. He knew they were yelling now, though he could not hear a sound. What strange silence locked him within its walls! His hearing had gone. Then he felt warm blood creeping down his neck.

The devils raced to and fro, from black shadow to silver lane. Anderson cursed his clumsy aim. His hands felt thick and slow. But he fired as fast as he could aim and work the infernally awkward gun. Presently he would leap out there in the open and club some of those gliding demons to death. Closer to the wagons they ran. They would burst out of the shade into the moonlight and be gone as swiftly. Most of these fleeting Indians were armed with bows and arrows. Anderson felt the wrench of an arrow as it tore through his coat. He became aware then that the increasing flashes of red came from the grass and brush, low down, and that the running lines of savages were back of the line of fire. If he had only guessed that sooner! The dizziness persisted. Closer crept the red-spurting line, and puffs of powder smoke almost reached the wheels. The Indians were crawling up on the wagons. There were enough of them to form a compact line of attack and still leave numbers to run and race and shout from behind. The end seemed near. Anderson rallied his clouding faculties to meet it. He thought only to kill more of these ruthless foes. They were closing in. The red flashes crept out of the shadow into the moonlit space between wagons and timber. Anderson emptied his Colt, and dropping it he drew his six-barreled pistols and emptied them. That left him a seven-shot Colt rifle fully loaded. While he fired this he felt the rend of hot lead in his flesh somewhere. But neither strength nor will was impaired.

Turning the heavy weapon, he seized the hot barrel with hands that made of it a willow wand and crawled out from under the wagon. Leaping erect he made at the dark rising figures and swung upon their shining skulls. But he seemed to have leaped violently against a wall. The brilliant moonlight strangely changed. Where was the clubbed rifle? His nerveless hands! A staggering shock! What?—The moonlight failed—all black—night! ——

Cynthia Bowden crawled under her cot inside Bowden's big canvas-covered wagon. She had just had sharp words with her uncle. Anderson and the men expected an attack from the Indians. Cynthia had been affronted and disgusted at Bowden's offer of gold to Anderson. All day Bowden had been drinking heavily from a jug he had in the wagon. But liquor had not given him false courage. He was a coward and these Westerners had recognized it.

"To hell with you an' your gold!" the scout had said in scorn. And now Bowden was crawling about under the wagon, drinking and cursing, raving that he would hitch up and drive back. At last some stern call reduced him to silence.

Cynthia lay there with her head near the foot of the wagon and she listened with palpitating heart. Silence appeared to be settling down. Black shadows of branches of trees barred the moonlit canvas cover. From under the cot she could see out of the rear opening of the shelter. Bowden had forgotten to close it. Stars were shining. Tips of foliage looked silvered; the top of the next wagon loomed close over her head. What would become of her if the men were all killed? It could happen. Anderson had felt it might. Cynthia had liked and respected this rugged, uncouth plainsman. She could read his mind. She knew what would happen to her if she were carried into captivity. Horrible! She would take her own life. There was a pistol somewhere in the wagon. But could she commit what her religion held a sin? Cynthia wavered and resorted to prayer and hope.

All silent outside! How boding, formidable, hateful! She could not bear to lie there waiting, waiting for she knew not what. Bowden bumped around under the wagon. Perhaps he was feeling for the false bottom that contained the gold. Fool! Could he not feel the imminence of some terrible thing?

Cynthia's delicate sensitiveness registered many sensations—the smell of smoke from afar, the faint whisper of men on guard, the rattle of a little stone falling, the splash of a fish in the brook, and vague undefined sounds and feelings she could not name. Like a heavy blanket these sensations weighted down her breast. They gave a tangible substance to the brooding, charged atmosphere. Something awful was about to come. What Anderson realized from his knowledge of the West she felt with all a woman's inscrutable power of divination.

So her waiting, surcharged faculties were prepared for a sudden bursting gun-shot, almost under the wagon, then a second bang, and a racking strangled scream from Bowden. Involuntarily she let slip a piercing shriek. Then she lay stiff with horror listening to her uncle's boots playing a tattoo on the wagon wheel, in his death agony.

A hoarse whisper, not too faint for Cynthia to detect its grim portent, came from under the next wagon. She wrung her hands in despair. She gasped. Her heart seemed to swell and labor over its function. Her blood flowed sluggishly and cold. What could she do? Why in God's name had she ever come on this mad journey? And into her consciousness flashed a thought of what might have been, a futile remorse which only her present misery could ever have wrenched from her. But if she had only listened to Stephen when he had come to her, shamed with his guilt but manful enough to confess it, and importuned her to elope, to trust him. In this menacing moment Cynthia saw her brother in as evil a light as he had forced her to see Stephen Latch. If she had only listened to the voice of love instead of pride and jealousy! Had it only been two brief years since she had flayed Latch and driven him away? And here she, Cynthia Bowden, heiress and beauty, a runaway from home and courtiers, lay wretched and terror-stricken in a wagon out on the wild plains, surrounded by blood-thirsty savages! It was inconceivable and insupportable. But the hands that dug into her breasts proclaimed the truth.

She thought that she must scream out to rend the unbearable silence. But as she bit her lips to hold back another shriek there rose out of the night stillness a cry so wild and weird, so ringing and sharp, swelling and sustaining its tremendous note of doom that it curdled her blood and froze the marrow in her bones. It shocked Cynthia into a dazed state if not an actual faint.

Reports of guns sounded far away. They came closer and clearer, until she localized them all around her. The attack had begun. Anderson's judgment was vindicated, as had retribution overtaken Stover and Bowden, upon whom rested the responsibility of this massacre. For how could a handful of white men hold out indefinitely against hundreds of savages? Cynthia heard the fire of guns increase, the ping of bullets, and the quivering thud of something into the sides of the wagon. She heard the canvas rip and rip. Some kind of missiles went tearing through the cloth. Forcing herself to face the dreadful issue, she decided that she must find her uncle's pistol and hold it in readiness to destroy herself when all hope failed. Whereupon she crawled out from under the cot to get to her hands and knees. It was almost as light as day under the canvas. Rents let in glimpses of the moon. She saw an Indian arrow sticking under one of the wooden hoops. This spurred her on to a frantic search for the gun. She could not find it and soon the increasing reports of firearms and the tearing of missiles through canvas drove her back under the cot. Here she was reasonably protected, for the sides of the wagon were heavily boarded. And with eyes tight shut and hands clamped over her ears she lay flat.

Then followed a hideous period of increasing terror. With no means of suicide she had no hope except that a merciful arrow or bullet would find her. Then suddenly a calmness of despair settled over her. What avail all this torture of spirit? She crawled from her covert and sat upon the cot, expecting surely a death-dealing missile would find her there. But not one of the hissing things touched her.

All at once the shots of guns were drowned in a

sound so sudden, unexpected, and terrible that she fell
flat, as if actually struck a blow. It was not like any
sound she had ever conceived. But it issued from
throats—from the throats of men, of human beings, of
these wild savages. It was the concatenated, staccato
mingling of hundreds of shrieks, all different, all
pitched high to the limit of vocal power, all pealing
forth the same note, a monstrous and appalling revenge. This must be the notorious war-cry of Indians.
Cynthia recognized in it the great vengeful cry of a
tribe that had been deceived, wronged, robbed, murdered. So Bowden's caravan and many others as weak,
must die for the deeds of white men who had crossed
the plains and left havoc in their trails.

Cynthia had the strength to peer out through the
slit in the canvas door at the rear. The circle inclosed
by the white-tented wagons appeared as light as day.
Slim, nimble dark forms were darting here, there,
everywhere. Savages! She clutched the flaps to keep
from sliding out of the door. And for the time being
she was so paralyzed with a new and mortal fright
that she could only gaze with magnifying eyes.

Red bursts of flames and puffs of smoke blotted out
a part of the silvered circle, and then, as they vanished
there, they appeared at another part, at the far end,
along the opposite line of wagons, and again in the
center. Boom and crack of guns, no longer incessant,
were emphasized by being segregated from a whole.
She could see along the curve of the inner line of
wagons where here and there the wild dark forms came
into sight. Some ran out, others to and fro. Four or

five dragged something heavy and struggling from under the second wagon next to Bowden's. Horrid cries pierced her ears. She saw a white man's face in the moonlight. The fiends dragged him, threw him, to stand over his prostrate body and hack with hatchets. Then they closed into a compact bunch, hiding the wretched victim, tore and fought over him, suddenly to leap up and run, waving arms aloft.

Cynthia saw everything at once, like a boy at a circus, only under a vastly different kind of emotion. She was witness to a massacre. She could not move, nor even close her eyes. Every instant the number of moving figures increased within the circle. Other white men were dragged out before her horror-stricken gaze, butchered and stripped and left stark in the moonlight. Fewer and fewer grew the red spurts of guns. The battle now had changed again. Bowden's men, those that were alive, were driven from their posts into the open, there to contend in a hand-to-hand struggle, a few against many.

From under the wagon next to hers, on the outside, had burst a continuous fire. Streaks of smoke kept shooting out from the wheels. Then through the narrow gap between the wagons, she saw out on the other side, where a giant leaped into sight, swinging a gleaming object upon savages that rose right out of the ground. Yells and shots did not drown sodden hollow cracks. Her distended sight and stunned faculties still retained power of recognition. That giant was Anderson beating at a pack of savages, like a stag bayed by wolves. Then he ceased his gigantic swings, swayed and fell, to disappear under a swarm of wriggling Indians.

Suddenly Cynthia's hands were rudely wrenched from the flaps of canvas. They were spread wide. In the aperture appeared lean dark arms, dark nude shoulders, dark small head. The moonlight fell upon them and upon a barbaric visage—bronze, cruel, sharp features of a savage. His eyes roved from upward glance to downward, then fixed upon her—eyes black as coal, yet burning with a terrific light.

Those hellish orbs and the dark face blurred and faded. Cynthia lost her senses.

When she recovered consciousness she heard and felt the familiar action of the wagon in motion. She opened her eyes, awakening to thoughts: Where was she? What had happened? Why did she lie prone as under a weight on her breast? The canvas let in the sunlight; day had come! Rents and slits in that white canopy showed glimpses of blue sky. She saw an Indian arrow sticking in one of the hoop supports. Ah! All flashed into memory with almost stultifying vividness. Her eyes fell shut as if leaded. The wagon train! The still brooding moonlit night! The awesome suspense! The murder of her uncle that initiated the attack of the savages! The stillness changed to infernal din—and the massacre; then all returned with a violent and unquestionable distinctness. But she had escaped massacre! She felt herself alive. And she opened her eyes to verify that strange idea. She lay on her cot, with feet and hands securely tied, and a scarf bound round her mouth. Captive! Worse than dead! But voices outside, from the driver's seat, suddenly dispelled memory and its consequent despair. Surely these voices were not the jargon of Indians. She listened, to feel her sore slow heart leap with a wild hope.

"Sprall, I hate to admit it, but the chief, once he had his way, planned and executed a great raid."

These words were undoubtedly spoken by a well-educated American, and the leisurely drawl and accent proclaimed him a Southerner.

"Wal, he's got brains, shore, pard Leighton," replied the man called Sprall. "But I give most of the credit to old Satana—bloody devil that he is. We shore didn't git off without a scratch, as my own hurt testifies. I'll be laid up for weeks, —— —— the luck!"

"Man, we got off easy," scoffed Leighton.

"Say, what you call easy? Waldron daid—an' I shore wondered how thet chicken-hearted Yankee bank thief got in front of a bullet. . . . Nigger Jack killed. Keetch crippled, Creik shot through the hand, Augustine packin' an arrow haid in his thigh, Cornwall hurt—and' gloryin' in it—he's shore a strange boy; an' Mandrove bad hurt, but he'll live; an' Black Hand nursin' an' cussin' a bullet hole. . . . Let's see. Thet leaves only the boss an' you, an' our rival gunfighters, Texas an' Lone Wolf, without a scratch. . . . Altogether, as a band I'd say we got a pretty hard knock."

"Little enough for what we earned," returned the other. "It's a rich haul. Three wagon-loads of guns and ammunition. That was lucky. No end of flour, bacon, beans, sugar, coffee, tobacco! Hardware, house-furnishings, bedding. And all that in less than a third of the wagons."

"Any rum?"

"Not so far, which also is lucky."

"How aboot money?"

"We got a pack of greenbacks, gold in money-belts, and silver off freighters. But no search of bags yet."

"Will thet money be divided?"

"Yes. Share and share alike."

"Ahuh. Wal, anyway, the boss is a man you can depend on. We'll go into hidin' at Spider Web an' rest up an' live fat, an' gamble an' fight with one another till this blows over."

"Blows over! It will never be heard of. Just a lost wagon train!"

"Things have a queer way of comin' out, even murder. But it shore was a good job. Not a rag or a tin can left at Tanner's Swale! . . . The boss's idea of haulin' everything away, daid men an' all, shows what a long haid he has. Course the Injuns always pack away their daid an' wounded. We've shore got a load of stiffs on these wagons. Sixty-some daid Kiowas, an' all the wagon-train outfit."

"Not all daid, Sprall," replied Leighton, with a ring in his soft voice. "I've a live girl inside this wagon."

"Yes, an' by Gawd, thet's the only bad move in this deal!" spoke up Sprall, forcibly. "If the boss finds it out he'll kill you. An' me, too, though I had nothin' to do with it, 'cept I happened to find oot."

"He won't find it out now," returned Leighton, thickly. "I was afraid he would, back down there at Tanner's Swale, when I objected to hauling daid Kiowas."

"But man alive, air you oot of your haid?" protested Sprall, in a tone of amazement. "If I got the boss's idee we're to drive these wagons with all they contain across a short cut to the rim of Spider Web. Keetch says no Injuns but Kiowas know how to drive there, same as how to ride into the canyon. Wal, all the stuff is to be lowered down on ropes. The hosses an' oxen go to Satana, as his share of the deal. An' the wagons air to be slid off the cliff where no tracks will ever show. . . . So how'n hell can you hide this girl? She'll have to eat an' drink. An' soon as her mouth's untied she'll squall. Thet'll give us away to the Injuns. I'll tell you, Leighton, it's a crazy idea. I heerd you was keen aboot wimmen. Wal, so'm I. But not in a case like this, or ever on any of our raids. The boss's rule is to kill every last one of any wagon train. So no one livin' can tell it!"

"I don't care a —— —— for him," returned Leighton, passionately. "If he finds out I have this girl I'll swear we didn't know she was alive in the wagon."

"Pooh! You killed thet Kiowa buck in the very act of scalpin' the girl alive. There's blood all over the canvas an' step. Suppose some other Kiowa seen you?"

"I saved her life!" replied Leighton, as if the portent of Sprall's speech had been lost on him.

"Only to outrage her yourself an' murder her presently," rejoined the other in a tone not devoid of contempt. "Leighton, I've cottoned to you 'cause I've no use for our boss. But this woman hunger of yours won't never make a leader of men. Not oot heah on this frontier! . . . I'm givin' you a hunch Take care An' I'm not meanin' the boss. He'll kill you. I'm meanin' my particular ootfit thet has cottoned to you along with me. They won't stand for this break of yours."

"Suppose I let them in the secret—and share the girl—after ——"

"No. It'd split our ootfit wide open. Like as not Texas would take a shot at you for hintin' it. My Gawd! man, this Texas gun-slinger may be the strongest caird you have in a fight, but he's a preacher. He'd shy at thet. Waldron is daid. Creik, the —— nigger slave-driver, he'd shore fall in with your idee. But thet leaves me, an' I won't. So put thet in your pipe."

"All the same I'll go through with it . . . alone!" declared Leighton, in a passion of elation which proved him beyond reason.

"Wal, thet's good," said Sprall, with a hard laugh. "For then you'll shore die alone!"

Chapter V

THE dawn broke slowly and strangely over Tanner's Swale, as if nature were loth to let the light brighten again over the scene of the lost wagon train.

No rosy glow suffused the east. Mist and smoke hung low like a curtain and the shadows persisted. The gray old bluff frowned forbiddingly down upon the monotonous melancholy prairie and the dim meandering trail across the dry sandy reaches.

But the scene that morning was one of extraordinary activity and life. Latch's band and Satana's Kiowas were making away with their prize. Latch sat his horse on the ridge above the swale and watched, occasionally sending down an order by his aide, Cornwall. He never rode down into the swale. Satana was there, astride his white mustang, in the thick and press of the labors. Long since the wild yells of the savages had ceased. In that hour their many dead and wounded warriors counterbalanced any exultation over their triumph.

Rum had failed Latch. It had thickened the tongues and deadened the sensibilities of his men; it had worked its deadly power with the Kiowas. But it had failed Latch. With shaking hand he cast the huge empty canteen down the embankment. Since sunset of yesterday he had recourse to his rum, in a vain endeavor to drown something in him that had the lives of a hydra-headed dragon. It had seemed, however, that the fiery liquor had only heightened his perceptions, augmented his sensations, magnified his thoughts. He had been forced to see in the dark with the eyes of a cat; his ears had gathered an extraordinarily acute sense of hearing. Screams of anguish! They would peal in his ears forever. From that first woman's shriek of terror last night after the first shot, to the wail of a child in the gray dawn, Latch had seemed to hear every sound. And he himself had cried out to the night, to the pitiless stars, to his red devils that he was neither great enough nor evil enough for the work his own brain had conceived. Yet he had to carry it through. This torment was what had caused him to drive his men with the Kiowas—to take their share in the battle. This torture was what had chained him to hot rifles during the thick of that fight. But it was over now. Death had stalked by moonlight. Always to the end of time, specters would haunt that swale when the deceiving moon arose. Dawn had broken. Life had to go on for him until ——

Latch watched the strenuous labors of the Indians and his men. The oxen and horses had been driven up from the lower swale. One by one the white-covered wagons had been hitched to teams and drawn out of the circle into the open. Kiowa braves were filing over the ridge with their ponies. Latch watched the dead and crippled put upon the wagons. Satana had paid a bloody price for this raid.

Young Cornwall rode up with his last report and

for a last order. He was whistling. His beautiful face showed no weariness or pain or remorse. Latch marveled at him. What did this young man lack? Had he ever had a mother, a sister, or a brother? What had killed his soul? He wore his left arm in a bloody sling.

"Colonel, we're aboot ready to leave," he announced, coolly. "The whole swale has been searched. No more found!"

"How many braves did Satana lose?" queried Latch.

"Sixty-nine according to our count. Some of the cripples will die. It's a bloody mess."

"How many—whites" asked Latch, huskily.

"We made no count."

"Any—wounded—left?"

"There was."

Latch gazed away over the gray, barren, lifeless prairie. The Dry Trail meandered up and down to disappear in the haze. Would another wagon train ever venture that short-cut again? There would be nameless sentinels to warn it.

"Tell Keetch to start when there's not a vestige left of the massacre," ordered Latch, presently. "Not a rag—not a shell—not a stain of blood—or a track of wheel or boot or mocassin."

"Yes, sir. They've cleaned up pretty well already."

"Look the ground over yourself," concluded Latch.

"All right, Colonel. We'll not leave a sign."

The oxen toiled up the long gray slope with the heavy wagons. Lines of Indian riders rode beside them, as warriors attendant upon a funeral procession. Far ahead a cortège of wagons drawn by horses led the way up the hill. The white-covered prairie-schooners likewise hauled dead and wounded, but there were no mourners. Latch kept far back in the rear with the cripples who were able to straddle a horse.

There was no road, or even a trail. The wagons zigzagged up a gradual slope, bare patches of hard clay alternating with plots of thick grass. Antelope and deer watched the strange cavalcade drag by. The green spot and the green meandering line that had marked Tanner's Swale soon disappeared under the brow of the bluff. A vague gray waste yawned far out and down—the prairie being left behind for the uplands. Purple domes of mountains stood up above the rolling horizon, and a scant fringe of trees began to top the ridges.

Keetch, with the Kiowa scout, Hawk Eye, led the procession, and two miles back Latch brought up the rear. Lester Cornwall had dropped back to ride with his chief. Their companions were a dozen or more wounded Kiowas, sagging on their mustangs or with bowed heads, or lying prone. They were a silent stoical group, naked, dirty, bloody. Here and there one rider helped another sit his pony. They moved slowly, owing to the tedious progress of the oxen ahead. The sun rose hot; the prairie vanished in haze; the wandering roll of ridges to the fore slowly dropped to show dark hills and purple peaks, ragged clefts and belts of timber.

By midday Latch's band had surmounted the escarpment and were winding over level range or rolling downgrade. To Latch, as perhaps to all the raiders, even the Kiowas, that beckoning broken purple wilderness was an alluring haven of rest, where cool shade and running water meant assuagement of dry choking thirst and labored pangs, where red and white murderers alike could hide in solitude.

At intervals Lester Cornwall addressed his chief, who rode with silent haggard visage bent.

"Colonel, I have to report that I suspect Leighton," spoke up the bright-faced youth, repeating himself deliberately.

The third time this statement fell upon Latch's dull ears the significance of it registered. Latch lifted his head.

"Leighton. . . . What do you suspect, Lester?"

"He's driving a big prairie-schooner, a grand sort of vehicle like a boat. It's new. There are big letters in red on the front. Tullt and Co. No. 1 A."

"Tullt and Co.? I know them. They have the largest establishment in Independence. Rich concern. Outfitters, freighters, fur-buyers."

"I think Leighton has got something in that wagon he's trying to hide," went on Cornwall.

"Why do you think that?" queried Latch, with dawning interest. This boy had the right idea. He was getting at details, facing facts, looking ahead. He had forgotten the past.

"It just struck me. Sprall, that little rattlesnake of a desperado, is on the driver's seat with Leighton. I watched them several times early this morning. They had their heads too close. They talk too much."

"What's in this wagon?"

"I've no idea. It's a big one, fully loaded and has a round canvas top. Look. . . . Leighton is driving halfway between our men and the Kiowas. He has kept that position practically all the way."

"Maybe he and Sprall smelled rum," suggested the chief.

"I'll find out and report to you before night, Colonel," replied Cornwall, and he spurred his horse to a trot.

Latch was left alone with his silent cripples. The momentary curiosity Cornwall had stirred did not abide long in a consciousness that held vast questions to ponder. Latch found himself often gazing back over his shoulder. What did he expect to see on this lonely gray range? He did not know, but certain it was that he looked back. Beyond the sweeping bold horizon line, over the long flat foothill, down off the escarpment there seemed to be something tremendous, intangible, terrible, which could not be named or changed or forgotten or erased. Tanner's Swale! It was a black spot—the period that marked the end of his past and the beginning of his future. Latch realized that he was unfitted for the leadership he had enforced. His intelligence, his executive ability, his power to sway and will to command were enormously handicapped by his imagination, his tendency to deep and poignant emotion. Between these forces he would be fettered to an eternal fear of failure, of betrayal, of death, to a sleepless and horrible remorse.

Far ahead the foremost white wagons wound over the gray waste, sometimes lost to sight under the increasing ruggedness of the rolling land. Then the longer line with its colorful escort moved at slower gait in and out between the knolls. The hours and miles grew apace. A westering sun lost its heat. Green patches of willow and cottonwood showed here and there in recesses, and clumps of trees appeared in the distance. Always the bold domes of the mountains held aloof, far away, apparently unattainable.

Latch's habit of looking back wore away. His band was not leaving many tracks over this gray rolling upland. The summer rains were due, and one storm would obliterate forever the wheel and hoof tracks that led westward from Tanner's Swale.

Before the magenta sun had sunk behind the black ramparts in the west, Latch, who had lagged far behind, rode over a cedared ridge to find the cavalcade had halted to camp.

Latch felt that if he had seen this place before he had suffered the blight to his sense of beauty, it would, in his estimation, have rivaled Latch's Field. A wide low-walled amphitheater nestled between sparsely wooded hills. A brook bisected the level valley floor and shone ruddily under the sinking sun. Cottonwood trees, like stragglers from a herd, led down from the main grove. Outcropping of rock ledges added a gray hue to the green. Antelope and deer moved away in droves. This was evidently another of the verdant spots known only to the Indians.

Keetch had drawn up the smaller number of canvas-covered wagons across the brook just outside the thick grove. Cottonwoods and walnuts, however, gave a park-like aspect to his camp site. Satana and his many followers selected the larger and more open plot for their encampment. With dead and wounded to care for, they sought privacy. Probably they would bury their dead here. Latch had not ordered Keetch to perform a like service for the white people. He had dodged the question. The corpses had been wrapped in blankets and hauled in two of the wagons. But packing such freight across the hot hills was a ghastly business.

Latch gave the Kiowas a wide berth and rode up the amphitheater to cross the brook above. After the long exhausting day how restful the shade and the green, the sense of isolation from the wide pitiless waste of prairie-land! Halting a moment, he took off his sombrero to let the cool breeze fan his heated forehead. He could see Keetch's camp through the trees. The Indians had unhitched the horses, and they were rolling in dusty places. Already a column of blue smoke rose from among the cottonwoods. It seemed like any other camp scene. Only it could not be!

Finally Latch rode on slowly. He hated to face the men, his responsibility, and the irrevocable. But orders had to be given. Leighton would seize upon any show of weakness and work upon it. Leighton! That Southerner wore on Latch's nerves. He rode on under the trees, and presently sighted a large boat-shaped wagon apart from the others. It had drawn up under a huge spreading walnut tree some distance from the camp. Under the adjoining walnut stood an old log cabin with adobe roof partly washed away.

As Latch passed he heard voices on the other side of the big wagon. Leighton's high-pitched voice was always unmistakable.

"Say, what the hell are you sneaking around heah again for?" demanded Leighton of some one.

The reply was indistinguishable to Latch, but the tone was youthful, cool, provocative. That belonged to Cornwall. Then Latch remembered. He resisted an impulse to ride by, noting, however, that the rear door of the big canvas-covered wagon pointed toward the cabin Latch's sharp gaze next took in the red letters on the front—Tullt and Co. No. 1 A. What an odd sensation passed over him! Illusive and unpleasant! Perhaps it was the red color of the lettering. Riding into camp, he dismounted, and throwing saddle and bridle he let his horse go.

The camp scene presented no bustle and cheer common to plains travelers at the end of a wearisome day. Men were moving about, but painfully, silently. Latch approached Keetch.

"How'd you make out?"

"Hard day, chief," responded Keetch. "An' makin' camp ain't no picnic for cripples. Damn me if I can stand up long! . . . Cain't you see that Leighton an' Cornwall lend us a hand? They ain't hurt."

"Yes, and I'll help myself."

"Our redskin pards will be better tomorrer, I reckon," went on Keetch.

"I gather they'll bury their dead here."

"Shore. An' we oughter do the same. But we jest ain't up to that—if you want a safe job done."

"Wait?" ejaculated Latch, harshly.

"Shore, but how'd you like to drive one of them wagons full of white stiffs . . . men and wimmen an' children—all scalped!"

"I can do it, if necessary."

"Wal, I'm glad you could. I'll tell thet to the band. . . . How aboot makin' Leighton drive one? He's took a shine to that big new Tullt an' thinks he owns it."

"I'll see that he ———"

"Colonel," interrupted a cold ringing voice, surely intentionally loud and clear enough for all present to hear.

"Cornwall!" ejaculated Latch, wheeling.

"Leighton has a girl in his wagon."

The leader gaped mutely at his youthful lieutenant. Cornwall was unexcited as usual, except that his eyes emitted blue flame.

Keetch took a heavy stride forward.

"A girl!" he boomed.

"Lester—what is this?" demanded Latch, through dry lips.

"Leighton has had a girl hid in his wagon. I saw him carry her out into that log cabin."

"*Girl!* . . . Alive?"

"Yes, and unhurt, to judge by the way she kicked."

"Wal, by Gawd!" burst out Keetch. "I reckoned Leighton acted kinda queer."

"Where'd he get—her?" queried Latch, conscious of a coalescing fury within.

"Tanner's Swale, of course. She must have been one the Kiowas missed. . . . I had a good look at her. I had slipped up behind the cabin and I peeped out. That was the first time, before you rode by. Sprall was with Leighton then. He had unhitched the team ——"

"Sprall!"

"Yes. He rode all day with Leighton. Well, I saw Leighton drag the girl out of the wagon. He had a hand over her mouth. Her dress was ripped off her shoulders. She had bright long hair which hung down. Colonel, she is a very beautiful girl."

Like a lion at bay, Latch eyed the seven of his band who could stand on their feet and who had grouped behind Keetch. The man Latch sought was not present. On the moment, however, he emerged from between two wagons and came forward. He had been running. His dark wizened face and beady eyes showed concern. But he meant to brazen it out.

"Sprall!" whipped out Latch.

"Yes, boss. I'm hyar. . . . I been lookin' after Leighton's horses."

"Did you ride with Leighton all day?"

"I did. Shore. I had to ride somewhere on a wagon, since I couldn't set hossback."

"You knew Leighton had a girl hidden in his

wagon," asserted the leader, in a voice like steel striking flint.

Sprall had not prepared himself for such revelation. He was staggered. His quick furtive gaze swerved from Latch to Keetch, to the others behind him, and then found Cornwall. Then he fairly bristled. That sudden rage betrayed him. His control and resourcefulness might have saved him with a lesser man than Latch.

"Boss, all day I been tryin' to show Leighton that he was crazy in the haid," said Sprall, in hoarse haste. "But the man is mad about wimmen. I couldn't get him to knock this gurl on the haid. He raved aboot how purty she is. He ———"

"How'd he come to have her in that wagon?"

"Jest aboot the end of the fight he saved the gurl from bein' scalped by an Injun. Shot him daid! . . . It happened in the door of that big Tullt wagon. I was the onlucky fellar to see it. The gurl had lost her senses. But Leighton held her face up in the moonlight. An' damn me if he didn't yelp wors'n a Kiowa. . . . He pushed her back in the wagon, an' gittin' in he tied her up. An' he swore he'd kill me if I gave him away."

"Sprall, I'll kill you for not giving Leighton away," yelled Latch, and swift as a flash he shot the man through the heart. Sprall fell without a sound, but the toes of his boots dug into the ground for a moment. Latch gazed terribly down upon the body, and then at the members of his band.

"That goes for every man who breaks my rule," he said, in cold deadly passion.

"Boss—I, fer one, stand by you," replied Keetch, in a hard tone. But he was the only member of the band to speak. Latch especially eyed Texas, the gunman, the most dangerous of Leighton's supporters. This individual, however, concealed his feelings, if he had any, and preserved his habitual composure. Whereupon Latch sheathed his gun and stalked out of the circle.

When he got somewhat beyond the wagons he looked back. Some of the men were following, and he recognized Keetch and Cornwall in the lead.

It was some distance to the trees where Leighton had left his wagon, too far, perhaps, if the man were absorbed, for him to hear the report of a gun. At any rate, Leighton did not appear around either the wagon or the cabin.

Latch quickened his pace, but took care to keep trees and shrubs between him and the spot he was rapidly nearing. His passion locked on one issue. Yet thoughts whirled through his mind. Chance had offered a magnificent opportunity for him to demonstrate how he meant to rule this band and at the same time to get rid of Leighton. A girl! Long bright hair! A very beautiful girl! . . . What in God's name would he do with her? Here his consciousness encountered a wall. There was no answer.

Gaining the big cottonwood, he swerved from behind that to place the wagon between him and the cabin. He ascertained then that Keetch and the others were following at a respectful distance. That seemed well. It augured fear of him and curiosity about Leighton and his prisoner rather than any will to interfere.

Latch strode around the wagon to face the dark open door of the dilapidated cabin. Here he drew his gun, to be ready if Leighton stepped out. Then his ears rang at the voice of a woman. Latch leaped to the side of the door.

"Oh, my God, have pity on me!"

Strangely that voice tore at Latch's heart-strings. But he thought only of its low, broken, anguished utterance. Then he took a single step to the front door.

Last rays of the sun shone into the cabin. In its light Leighton stood revealed clasping a woman in his arms. A white arm hung limp. Her clothing hung in torn shreds. Her long golden hair fell in a disheveled mass. And the man had his ugly mouth glued to hers.

Latch leveled the gun.

"Damn you, Leighton! Let go that woman!"

So obsessed appeared the man that, though the command seemed to pierce his consciousness, he answered to the violent interruption but slowly. When he broke away from her lips to see Latch, his expression of heat and passion changed to one of intolerant anger. But he had no time to speak. Latch fired point-blank. The heavy bullet whirled Leighton around so that he fell toward the door. The girl collapsed against the wall.

Latch reached her in time to save her from falling. With the hand that still held the gun he sought to draw up her dress to hide her nudity.

Still his vigilance did not relax. Hearing steps and hoarse whispers, he wheeled to see Keetch and Cornwall peering through the door, with others trying to see over their shoulders. Leighton lay on his back, his face half blown away, a bloody spectacle.

"Keetch, drag him out," ordered Latch, sternly. "Lester, guard the door. Keep them back."

"Wal, boss, I reckon our band is some decimated," spoke up Keetch, cheerfully, as he stepped over the log portal to lay powerful hold of Leighton. As he dragged him out Cornwall backed against the door-post, a gun in each hand.

"About close enough, gentlemen," he drawled, and a child might have detected death in his voice.

Latch sheathed his gun, but even then he could not rearrange the girl's torn clothing to cover her. He thought she had lost consciousness, but to his amazement she stirred—she rose from her knees, weakly swaying against the wall.

"Lady, I thought you'd fainted," spoke up Latch.

"Another—white man!" she whispered, scarcely audibly. "Oh—you shot—that beast—only to take me—yourself!"

"No. I'm not so bad as that," replied Latch, bitterly, as he gently released his hold.

A gasp broke from her and she sagged a little against the wall.

"You—don't mean—to harm me—then murder me —as I heard that man ——"

"I killed Leighton for breaking my rule," said Latch.

"Then you—saved me?" she cried.

The broken query brought Latch violently up against the monstrous situation. By his own decree every member of that wagon train had to die. He had shed blood of his own band for this girl, but if he kept his word he must mete out murder to her, also. All at once Latch found himself really seeing her as she leaned face to the wall. The luxuriant hair had a wave, a sheen that acted as a blade driven into his side. Did he know that hair? She was young. The noble contour of her shoulders and neck, and of her white cheek, appeared to confirm Cornwall's estimate of her beauty. Horror began to edge into his realization.

"Yes, it seems I have—saved you for the present," he returned, ponderingly.

A trembling appeared to run over her, ending in a sudden stiffening. She began to turn as if in a giant grip. And when partly around, she moved in a flash, suddenly to disclose her face. White as chalk it was, with strained dark eyes widening—mouth gaping back of quivering fingers.

"Christ, am I mad? . . . *Who are you?*" cried Latch, in a frenzy.

"*Stephen!* . . . You—you! . . . Oh, that you should be the one to save me!"

She sank to her knees, clasping him with nerveless hands.

"*No!* . . . It can't be! Not you! That would be too—too horrible!"

"Yes, it is I—Cynthia," she whispered.

Latch all but collapsed. He shook like a man palsied. His fingers plucked at her, to lift her, but could not take hold. And such a searing agony of spirit claimed him that he might have been in the throes of conscious aggravated torture.

"I've prayed for merciful death," she whispered. "My faith in God—almost failed. . . . But that you —*you* should drop from heaven—Oh, God, forgive me! . . . Oh, Stephen, forgive me!"

"Hush! . . . Don't kneel—to me! . . . Cynthia, you don't realize how awful ——"

"It *was* awful! . . . But I'm saved. By you! I meet you here in this wilderness of cutthroats. Who else could have saved me? I—I would come on this mad journey. Something lured me."

"Get up, please," he begged, huskily. "Cynthia ——"

"No, I belong here at your feet."

"Good God, woman, you're out of your mind!" He laid hold of her with shaking hands, but she resisted his efforts to draw her up. She held him tight, lifting a supplicating face from which a glow of gratitude and love had erased the havoc.

"Don't try to stop me. I *will* tell you," she went on, in passionate aberration. "I loved you. . . . I loved you even when I deserted you."

Latch forgot where he was, what this cabin signi‐ fied, forgot his lieutenant at the door, and the hounds of his band with the dead Leighton outside.

Her eloquent eyes, her clasping arms, her incredible confession transformed him as if by a miracle. He was back in the hour when he had expected his dream to come true. Lifting her swiftly, he held her to his breast.

"Cynthia, you loved me then? . . . Loved me when you cast me off? . . . Let your brother ——"

"Yes, yes! Oh, if I had only known!" she faltered. "But Howard found out your—your affair with—that woman—they told me. They proved it—and, oh, it hurt so hideously. I could have killed you. . . ."

"Cynthia, did they tell you that I never saw that woman again—after I met you?" he asked, gravely.

"No, they didn't. Is that true?"

"Absolutely!"

"But we heard—it was in the papers—your disgrace—your dismissal from the army—your duel—the death of Thorpe."

"Yes, my ruin was well advertised. And here I am. . . . But, Cynthia, I worshiped you. From the moment I met you I was a changed man. . . . I should have told you of my wildness at college and all about that—that affair. Perhaps I might have done so later. But then I didn't have the courage. You, with your uplifted head, your proud eyes! I couldn't! I gambled on every chance. Always I was a gambler. And I lost."

"Then Howard lied," she burst out.

"Lied? My God, yes! He owed me thousands. Gambling debts. So he hatched that plan to ruin me. He and Thorpe hated me. He wanted Thorpe to marry you. It was all so despicable."

"Yes. Of me, as well as of them! But, oh, Stephen, I was jealous. Jealous of that woman! There is nothing so degrading as jealousy. It warped my judgment.

It made me believe my love had turned to hate. . . . But it hadn't. I was just sick—furious. . . ."

"Ah, to learn all this too late!" cried Latch, remembering.

"Darling, it is never too late. Don't turn from me now. I was weak, yes. I failed you. I had to suffer to find myself. And even after I found out what you did to Howard and that you shot Thorpe, I would have eloped with you, if you had come for me. But you did not."

Latch bowed his head over her, holding her close. "Too late," he said again, in a scarcely audible whisper.

"It is not too late—unless you do not want me, love me. . . ." There was fear in the girl's voice.

Latch released her. He had lived one hour too long. If Leighton had only faced him then, there would have been a reversal of the tragedy.

"*Stand back!*" The raucous command tore Latch from the agony of the moment. He turned to see Cornwall backed against the door-post, his two guns extended, his youthful face as cold and gleaming as if cut in ice.

"Cornwall, you ain't meanin' you'd fire on us jest for insistin' on seein' the boss?"

That was Keetch's voice, querulous and rough, indicating that even he had raw nerves on edge.

"Come one more step and see," taunted the youth.

"But, boy, we'll kill you," he remonstrated. "You'd be daid now but fer me. Black Hand, hyar—he's had a bead on you from behind."

"Bah! you're a pack of lousy curs! Shoot and be damned!"

"Lester, what do they want?" called Latch. Nothing could be gained by Cornwall's precipitating a fight; at least not until the demands of the band were heard.

"Colonel, I don't know, and I care less."

"Well, wait." Then Latch raised his voice. "Keetch, what do you want?"

"Latch, personal, I don't want anythin' but a little peace," boomed the old outlaw. "But your shootin' Sprall an' Leighton has upset the outfit. Who next will you shoot?"

"Any man who opposes me. . . . Is Leighton dead?"

"No. But he's aboot as good as daid. An' Black Hand an' Augustine hev gone over to Leighton's side."

"How about Lone Wolf?"

"Wal, he'll stick. But we don't want to fight. An' they hev demands."

"All right, I'll listen. Give me five more minutes."

When Latch turned again to face Cynthia, he found her back to the wall. The softness of love had left her face, and it was now distorted and ashen. To meet her eyes took all the manhood left in him.

"Cynthia, you've heard. I am the leader of Latch's Band," he said, with suppressed passion.

Chapter VI

SHE echoed his words with dry lips.

"Yes," went on Latch, hurriedly. "After killing Thorpe I fled. Out there on the border I organized a band of desperadoes. At first we were guerrillas, fighting independently against the North. But soon we drifted into robbery. From that to crime . . . and lastly to massacre."

"Oh, my God! . . . My uncle's wagon train!" exclaimed Cynthia, in horror. "But those murderers were Indians . . . I—I saw them run and leap . . . saw them brandish tomahawks and scalps!"

"Yes, Indians. My Indians! *I* was the leader, the instigator of that massacre."

"*You!*"

"Yes, I . . . Stephen Latch, son of an old Southern family—college graduate—ruined planter—once a lover of Cynthia Bowden. . . . Now, an associate of outlaws and criminals. A partner of Satana, bloodiest war chieftain of the Indian tribes. In a word—leader of Latch's Band. . . . To this you have brought me!"

"*I!*"

"Surely. Your faithlessness. Your scorn," he replied, bitterly. "I might never have amounted to much, I would have been only another Southerner of my class. But, brutal as it is to say, *you* brought out the evil in me."

"Better that the savage had killed me!" she whispered.

"Better indeed! . . . The law of my band was to kill every soul. To leave no trace! . . . And the horror of this situation is that I fear I cannot save your life."

"I don't want to live—now," she said, brokenly. "But my—my—. . . You will not let these men take me—to—to ——"

"They will have to kill me first, Cynthia."

"But, Stephen, if death is the edict of your band— *you* kill me. . . . The instant you see—it's hopeless . . . I will welcome death at your hands. I have brought you to this degradation; I ought to die by your hand. . . . Swear you will save me that way— if ——"

"*Kill you?* . . . Cynthia—*how* could I? . . . You don't know what you are asking."

"But if it is the only way," she appealed, again at his breast. "Stephen, you say you love me still. Then you cannot see these men defile me . . ."

"No!" he burst out, lifting his head. "I could not . . . I promise. Cynthia! Oh, God—that we should come to this! . . . I'll kill you instantly—the moment I see it is hopeless to save you."

"Thank you," she whispered. "Oh, Stephen, my heart was broken. I am ready to die, at last. . . . To have met you once more—to find what I have done to you—to confess my faithlessness, my remorse, and the love nothing could change—oh, that makes it easy."

For a moment he held her close, then looking to his guns he sheathed them and faced the door.

"Lester, bring them in," he called.

The youth beckoned carelessly with his guns, then stepped across the log threshold into the cabin. First to enter behind him was the lean sardonic gunman, Lone Wolf. The others followed quickly, a lame, bloody, ferocious band of men, inquisitive and baleful.

Lone Wolf turned significantly to back across the room and stand beside Latch. Cornwall came sidewise, still with his guns in hands.

"Keetch, are you with me or against me?" demanded Latch.

"Boss, I stand between. I wouldn't raise a hand ag'in' you or any of my pards. Thet's me."

"Very well. That satisfies me. So it's Cornwall an' Lone Wolf with me against the five of them. Who's going to do the talking?"

"Wal, I've been elected to that," replied Keetch.

"Get back from the door, so I can see you all," demanded Latch, with a gesture. Keetch lined them up in a slant across the opposite corner so that the light fell fairly upon them. Latch's mind had swiftly evolved a plan and set rigidly upon it. He sensed a chance of mediation. But if it did not succeed he meant to wheel and kill Cynthia before he let loose on the men. He could hide his intent. He could fool them, even the Texas gunman, until his vigilant passion-stormed mind divined the issue.

"Now, Keetch, what do these men want?" demanded the leader.

"Wal, boss, they talked it over an' took a vote."

"On what?"

"They reckoned you're no different from Leighton. You wanted the girl, and so you took your law as excoose to kill your men. None of us doubts but thet you'll put her oot of the way when it suits you. But they—an' I mean this majority hyar—figger thet's as fair for them as for you. They want the gurl—to share her same as the money an' rum an' all thet we got there in them wagons."

"So that's your demand," replied Latch, addressing the five dark-faced hungry-eyed outlaws. "Well, men, under ordinary circumstances, that'd be a fair and square demand. In this case, however, it's absolutely impossible for me to give in to it."

"An' why?" queried Keetch, sonorously. "Latch, you hardly need be told that you're on trial hyar by the majority of your band."

"On trial for what?" countered Latch. His game was to play for time, not to force the issue, to match his wit against their ignorance and lust.

"Wal, fust for killin' Sprall, an' Leighton, who's aboot gone."

"You have no right to try me for that," returned Latch, forcefully. "I was absolutely true to my word. It is the law of our band. I killed Sprall on his own word that he knew Leighton had betrayed us. I shot Leighton in the act of maltreating this girl. But not for that. I shot him *because* he had brought her along with us—alive."

"Latch, you swear to thet?"

"Yes, I swear. I never looked at the girl until after Leighton fell."

"Wal, as fer thet, Cornwall told you she was a very beautiful gurl. We all heerd him. An' we all hev eyes for ourselves. But I'll take your word, Latch. . . . Now, men, speak up, yes if you believe the boss, no if you don't. Texas, how aboot you?"

"Yes," replied the gunman.

"No, señor," replied the Mexican, Augustine, and Latch made the mental reservation that that negative sealed the *vaquero's* doom, here or at some future time.

"Yes," returned Mandrove, the preacher who had seen better days.

Creik and another shouted in unison, "No!"

"Wal, boss, countin' me it's a daidlock. Three of us believe you and three don't. Thet's aboot as good as acquittal, accordin' to court rules . . . An' now we'll heah why you won't give the gurl up or share her with your men."

"I'm your leader, I know," rejoined Latch, deliberately. "Satana and I are solely responsible for that —raid last night. His Indians were drunk and you men were merely tools. My orders were to kill everyone, but I can't stand for violation of this girl—or any girl."

"Ain't you gittin' chicken-hearted, boss?" queried

Creik, with a leer. "She'll have to be killed, anyhow, same as the rest of that wagon train."

"That's different, Creik," replied Latch, with difficulty restraining his sudden fierce desire to kill this slave-driver.

"Fellars, it shore *is* different," interposed Keetch. "You know how we all hated to watch them poor wimmen an' kids scalped. Wal, it'd be even wuss for a gang of rowdy ruffins like us to take the gurl— thet way."

"Pards, I'm ag'in Latch," drawled Texas. "But to kill this woman that way doesn't go with me."

"Put that to a vote," sang out Creik.

Keetch, evidently relieved at what seemed favorable to the leader, did as bidden. The vote went against Latch.

"Wal, Cornwall, we don't need your vote, but we'd like to heah it, anyway."

"I'd never vote to save any woman's honor," flashed the youth, with a terrible blaze in his eyes. His tone and gaze were so unexpected that they enjoined silence. Latch was stunned. He felt betrayed by one he trusted.

"Latch, you lost this time," resumed Keetch.

"Can I buy her freedom?" queried the leader. "I'll turn over all money and goods—and the rum back in Spider Web for you to divide among yourselves."

The hot harangue that followed soon ended in a victory for Latch. His tempting offer overwhelmed even the most vicious.

"All right, boss, you buy her freedom," said Keetch, plainly gratified.

"What's he mean by freedom?" queried one.

"Why, her body—while she's livin'," replied another.

"I mean her life, too," rang out Latch.

Passion broke bonds then, and the portent of angry acclaims, of black looks, of surly whispers, argued a ruthless thumbs-down for the captive.

"Latch, air you oot of your haid?" queried Keetch, plaintively. "You cain't make a law for your band— set them to spill blood—and then break thet law yourself."

"If you'll let me explain," burst out Latch, nerving himself for a last stand.

But Lone Wolf interrupted with cold sarcastic speech directed at his rival gunman.

"You never was born in Texas."

The gunman, who had been kneeling on one knee, after the fashion of riders at times, slowly rose to his feet. His lean face turned a scarlet hue, then paled.

"Hell you say!" he replied, coolly, but his eyes gave forth a wicked light.

"Yes, the hell I say!"

Keetch interfered hurriedly. "Hyar, you gamecocks. This is a court, not a place for you gun-throwers to clash."

"Shet up," said Texas, curtly.

"Keep oot of this heah, you old geezer!" added Lone Wolf.

Keetch got back hurriedly. The other men on that side of the room with Texas spread away from him. But neither Cornwall nor Latch moved. Latch scarcely caught the significance, and Cornwall was indifferent.

"Texas, I'm callin' you," went on Wolf. "You're from some nigger country where women air white trash. Not from Texas!"

"I heahed you," rejoined Texas, malignantly. "An' I'm sayin' you'll swaller that—or you'll swaller lead."

They eyed each other. The thing between them was not of the moment. Each would have welcomed any excuse to meet on common ground. They respected nothing on earth except speed with guns. An abnormal curiosity possessed them, yet likewise a monstrous assurance. Latch had always anticipated this meeting. More than once he had interfered with it. Here his lips were locked because he was certain that Wolf would do away with the most dangerous of his enemies. With Texas dead or out of commission the issue narrowed down into Latch's favor.

Probably both gunmen saw in each other's eyes the lightning-like betrayal of thought—motive—stimulus to action. A convulsive wrestling sound ended in the simultaneous flash and bang of guns. Under the smoke Latch saw Wolf stagger a step forward and fall. When that smoke lifted a little it disclosed Texas on his face, smoking gun in hand, and still as stone.

Keetch uttered a hoarse cough. "Aggh! . . . Wal, they always itched fer this. An' one time's as good as another so far's we're concerned. It changes nothin'."

Latch did not agree with Keetch's ultimatum. Few men were wholly impervious to sudden death. Leighton's followers showed something that roused Latch again.

"Men, listen," he began, in a loud voice. "Circumstances alter cases. I feel justified in breaking my own law. I'm opposing you! And I'll fight till the last beat of my heart. Not one man of us will come out of this alive. Now I ask you, hear my reasons before it's too late."

"Wal, boss, speak up," said Keetch, "Thet's fair enough."

Before Latch could moisten his dry lips to give utterance Cynthia moved out from behind him to confront the opposition. She stood erect, with little head uplifted. The sunlight caught the rippling mass of golden hair and made it glow. Every line of her form portrayed intense emotion, courage, eloquence.

"Men, let me tell the story," she began, in a voice that stilled them. "I am Cynthia Bowden, niece of John Bowden, whose wagon train you massacred last night. I—I am the sole survivor. I am twenty-three years old. I lived in Boston. . . . When I was seventeen I knew Stephen Latch. I met him during his last year in college. He was a friend of my brother Howard Bowden. He visited my home. Stephen and I were thrown together, and when he went back home to Louisiana we were interested in each other. He came North frequently. The time came when we fell in love with each other. My brother was a gambler. Stephen won a large sum from him—more than he could pay. And when Howard found out about the attachment between Stephen and me he saw a way to ruin Stephen. He told my father. He used and exaggerated a connection Stephen had had with a disreputable woman. He inflamed me so with jealousy and hatred that I openly scorned Stephen—insulted him—betrayed him—drove him to his ruin. . . . He horsewhipped Howard in the lobby of the Boston Hotel. . . . The Civil War broke out. Stephen offered his services—asked for an officer's commission in the Confederate army. Meanwhile I had allowed the attentions of another Southerner, a friend of Howard's and rival of Stephen's. His name was Thorpe. He had received a commission as colonel in the army of the South. With Howard's connivance and treachery Thorpe disgraced Stephen, so that the commission was denied him. . . . A duel followed. Stephen—killed Thorpe . . . and he fled—an outlaw."

She paused a moment as if to gather strength. Toward the last her voice had begun to break and fail, but her spirit drove her on.

"Surely all of you know how he organized this band, meaning to wage guerrilla warfare against the Northerners—how he fell into robbery—and then to horrible crime. . . . It must have been a strange dispensation of God—that I escaped that massacre—that I was carried away—to meet Stephen Latch face to face. . . . I had failed him, deserted him. I am the cause of his degradation. . . . Before God I must be responsible for his being an outcast—a murderer—a leader of desperadoes—a partner of bloody savages.

That is my story. That is why he bought my freedom from you—why he seeks to save my life. . . . But I am ready to die."

A long pause—which Keetch, with difficulty, broke. "Wal, by Gawd!" he rolled out, at the gaping mute men. "Fellars, did you ever heah the like? . . . Circumstances do alter cases. An' I'm fer lettin' her live."

"Wha-at! An' go oot to put the soldiers on our track?" ejaculated Creik.

"That gurl would never betray Latch."

"If we knowed she wouldn't, I'd say let her go." These and other like comments showed how Cynthia's beautiful presence and tragic eloquence had swayed the outlaws. Keetch turned to her with something of deference.

"Lady, we might break our law an' let you live."

"I—I don't care to live. . . . God has failed me. . . . I have become alienated from my family. . . . My uncle murdered ——"

"Wal, it's shore tough," interrupted Keetch, kindly. "But you're young. Life is sweet. Latch hyar won't always be a robber. . . . Do you still love him?"

"I do—love him. . . . I always did. . . . It has been my ruin, too," she answered, sadly.

"Wal, you can marry Latch," rejoined Keetch, vigorously slapping his leg. "It's the only way to save your life. Will you?"

"Yes," she replied, as if shocked by an incredible and irresistible possibility.

"You cain't ever go back there," declared Keetch,

his broad hand sweeping the east and north. "You'll be an outlaw's wife. You'll have to hide an' live in the loneliest canyon hole in this hyar West. Will you do that, too?"

"Yes—if Stephen wants me ———"

"Want you? My God!" breathed Latch, passionately coming out of his trance. "That idea never came to me. . . . Cynthia, if you'll marry me. . . . Surely I'll not always be ———"

His lips froze over such a forlorn utterance.

"Yes," she whispered, as if dazed. "I said—I'd follow you—to the end of the world."

Keetch intervened to rub his big hands gleefully. "Boss, you win. An' you're a lucky dog. . . . Fellars, drag oot these Texas roosters thet'd rather shoot than eat turkey. . . . Mandrove, I reckon you can do the trick, huh?"

"Marry them?" queried the ex-preacher.

"Shore. Splice them proper an' bindin'?"

"Indeed I can. I've kept my Bible," replied Mandrove, dreamily.

"Haw! Haw! . . . Damn lucky fer the boss. Go fetch it an' somethin' you can write a marriage certificate on. If we haven't got nothin', we'll shore find it in this Bowden ootfit."

Creik and Augustine had dragged the bodies of the dead men outside and could now be heard speculating upon what valuables might be found on them.

"You keep what you see an' gimme what's hid," suggested the slave-driver.

"No, señor, you mucha sleek," declared the vaquero.

Mandrove limped out on his errand, and Cornwall, cold and strange, went to the door to gaze out. This affair did not have his approval. Keetch and Black Hand sat down to wait. Latch had stepped to Cynthia's side, yearning but not daring to take her hand. She seemed dazed, and looked at the blank log wall with eyes no mind could fathom. Moments passed. The smoke slowly drifted through the rents in the roof. Keetch got up to scrape dust over blood spots on the ground floor. Black Hand asked for a smoke.

"Lester, will you stand with me during the—the ceremony?" asked Latch.

"Colonel, if you don't mind, I'd rather not," replied Cornwall.

It struck Latch then that he had seen the youth look strangely at Cynthia. He recalled that Cornwall had a hatred for women. He stalked outside, and Creik and the vaquero entered.

"Señor," said the Mexican, softly, "our niggah-trailin' hombre get beeg roll greenback ———"

"I'll cut your greaser tongue out," interrupted Creik.

"Creik, divide what you found equally," ordered Latch, sternly. "But wait. . . . Here's Mandrove."

The outcast minister had returned with something beside his Bible—a change of mien, of look. Even his voice, as he began to read the marriage service, seemed different. A bloody bandaged hand held the book. He read well and fluently, with an intonation and inflection that caused Keetch to whisper: "By

Gawd! he's a parson all right! I allus reckoned he was
a liar aboot thet."

In what seemed the longest and most poignant moment of Latch's life, Mandrove ended with, "I pro-
nounce you man and wife."

He closed the Bible and knelt: "Let us pray."

The watching members of Latch's Band stared,
with eyes popped out, with grins setting on their
faces.

"Almighty God, let not your holy words fail of
truth and binding right because they are spoken by
an outcast minister, in the presence of men as lost
and depraved as he himself. Out of evil good may
come. I solemnly unite this parted couple as the last
rite of my religious life, and I beseech you, O Lord,
to work upon them and their future in your inscrutable way. It is the fallen who have always had divine
help. Bless this strange meeting of two lovers who
have sinned and suffered. Bless their marriage. Guide
them away from this wicked life of blood and pillage.
Ordain some dispensation of Christ, some immutable
decree of Heaven that they shall be saved in the end.
That at least their souls shall be saved. Who can
tell but Thyself why this man and this woman found
themselves again, out on the naked shingle of this
wild desert? If love ruined them, O Lord, still love
again can resurrect. I pray mercy for him and for
her. I pray you let fatherhood shock him out of this
sordid career of blood and greed. And so through this
woman who failed him in love he may rise again.
Amen!"

Chapter VII

SPRING came early at Fort Union that year of 1863. There had been an unusually mild winter in the mountains of Colorado and New Mexico. The great fur-trading business had passed its zenith years before; nevertheless, trapping was still done extensively by trappers who worked independently. This had been a favorable season for them, and a hundred or more had come down out of the hills with their pelts. Beaver were still the largest assets, but mink, otter, fox, marten, and other furs brought high prices.

There were ten Indian trappers at the fort for every white one, and as the Indians were easier to deal with than the white men the fur-traders reaped a harvest. Tullt and Co. bought one hundred thousand pelts that spring.

By April 10th Fort Union was busier than it had been at any time since the beginning of the Civil War. Two wagon trains had arrived that day, one of one hundred seventy-four wagons from Santa Fe, bound east, and the other of eighty-six wagons under escort from Fort Dodge by way of the Cimarron Crossing and the Dry Trail. This caravan was under Bill Burton, an old scout, and it had come in with some dead and many wounded to report a scrimmage with Comanches. But for the escort of dragoons they probably would have been wiped out.

Burton looked askance at the nine hundred to a thousand Indians of mixed tribes present at the fort. In Burton's opinion there were no good or peace-loving redskins.

What with the tents and shacks outside the stockade, Fort Union presented quite a settlement. Thousands of horses and cattle grazed out on the bleached grama grass of the range. The mountain tops were still white with snow, but ragged black patches and belts told of the ravages of the spring sun. The wide gate to the fort stood open and unguarded, to permit the exit or entrance of anyone at will. Tullt and Co. had their large store inside the stockade, where they kept on hand an immense stock of merchandise, from a caravan wagon to a bag of candy. The Indians bought many of the latter. And often trappers, rich with their winter's catch, purchased a wagon to haul furs that would fetch a much larger price at Independence, Missouri. The Indians presented a motley assemblage. They all wore tight-fitting deerskins and moccasins. Some of them wore white men's hats, but most of them were bareheaded. A few had blankets, and all of them had buffalo robes. The majority were dirty and shiftless, and hung around the stores and the saloon for no apparent reason. There were twoscore and more of white men garbed like Indians and just as dirty and shiftless. These were the riffraff of the frontier, a bane to all the forts. But nothing could be done about it. They came and went, the same as the Indians, and not many of their faces ever became well known to the soldiers. Gambling and drinking went on day and night. Shooting scrapes were not the order of every hour, as at Fort Dodge; nevertheless guns cracked often, and many were heard only by the night hawks and the soldiers on guard duty.

Major Greer had charge of ten troops of dragoons. Before the war he had had twice that number, which, he was wont to state, was far less than he needed. Fort Union was then a distributing point for all New Mexico; and owing to the increasing hostility of the Indians, the movement of freight and the escort of caravans had grown exceedingly difficult to manage.

It was cold enough to make a wood fire pleasant in the bare log-cabin-like office where Major Greer sat at his table. He looked the bluff red-faced plains soldier of the period. But Fort Union was far removed from Fort Leavenworth, where the major had gotten his frontier experience.

"Captain," he spoke up, addressing the middle-aged officer who bent a rugged wrinkled face over a pile of letters, "where'd I hear of Bowden's wagon train before this?"

"Bowden? Let's see," replied Captain Massey. "Sounds familiar. There was an inquiry from Washington ——"

"Hell! We get nothing but inquiries," interrupted the major, testily. "Call Sergeant Riley."

Massey went out, to return presently with a hard-eyed, square-jawed Irishman who would certainly have looked like a frontiersman but for his uniform.

"Sergeant, do you remember Bowden's wagon train, or anything about it?" queried Major Greer.

"Yes, sor. Bowden's wagon train was a lost wagon train."

"Well, this letter informs me of that. Here's the gist of it," replied the officer, scanning the letter. "Over a year and a half ago John Bowden's wagon train left Independence, bound for California. He was traced to Fort Dodge. He left there with fifty-three wagons in charge of a scout named Anderson. They had no escort. They took the Dry Trail and have never been heard of since."

"Major, all we have a record of, if I rimimber correct, is that Bowden's train is one of the missin'," rejoined the sergeant.

"There have been many lost caravans since the war began," mused Greer, ponderingly. "According to headquarters, this Bowden was a man of means and family. His daughter—no, niece, a Miss Cynthia Bowden, accompanied him. It means that she has been left a fortune. They were from Boston. Well, we are instructed to find out what became of Bowden's wagon train."

"Humph!" ejaculated Massey.

"Yes," agreed the major, dryly. "If only some of these desk-chair, big-cigar officers would come out to this God-forsaken West! . . . But here it is. Strong pressure brought upon us. Bowden has powerful relatives or friends. . . . Suppose we call in the scouts. Kit Carson is still here, isn't he?"

"Yes, sor. An' Dick Curtis, Baker, an' John Smith."

"Sergeant, ask them please to come in," concluded Greer.

In short order the soldier ushered three plainsmen into Major Greer's office.

"Major, I couldn't locate Baker an' Curtis," announced the sergeant.

"Howdy, Major," replied Kit Carson to the officer's greeting. The great guide and scout was clad in buckskin. He was past middle age then, but lithe and erect of form, clean-cut of face, with the eyes of an eagle. "You shore know Jack Smith. . . . An' this is Beaver Adams, who knows a blame sight more about the plains than I do."

Greer shook hands with the scouts, and bidding them find seats he offered cigars and briefly stated the inquiry about Bowden's lost wagon train.

"Never heard of it," said Carson, bluntly. "But I've not been to Dodge for two or three years."

"Wal, I have, an' not so long ago," interposed Jack Smith. He was a lean giant of a plainsman who need not have told that he had been on the border for twenty years. "Last fall—October suthin'—I was just down from the Ute camp, an' dropped in at Old Bent's Fort. I heerd a man from Dodge tell aboot that Bowden train. He was talkin' to some new freighters, an' I took it was jest namin' some caravans that has disappeared like jack-o'-lanterns. I didn't mix in that talk. Jest heerd it, an' I never forget anythin'."

"It appears pretty well established that there was a Bowden's wagon train that disappeared," added Major Greer.

"Wal, that's aboot all there ever will be established," spoke up Carson.

"Onless by accident," rejoined Beaver Adams. He was a trapper by calling, as his first name implied, and his quiet deep voice, his sharp eye, and his splendid stature gave his remark an impressiveness that struck Major Greer.

"How do you mean—by accident?"

"Wal, as I look back over my experience in the West I can recall many strange happenings an' stories. Bowden's outfit hit the Dry Trail the beginnin' of a bad summer for all travelers across the plains. Kiowas, Comanches, Apaches, Pawnees, all on the war-path. Bowden had a small force of men unaccustomed to the frontier. I knowed Pike Anderson. He could be trusted. But what would fifty-odd men an' most tenderfeet do against a big force of Injuns? They jest got massacred. The accident I hint of is jest one chance in a million, thet some day some Injun will let the secret slip. Injuns like to brag. An' when they get a drink or two their tongues wag."

"Shore is only one chance in a million," agreed Carson, pessimistically. "But that's an interestin' letter. Thet aboot the big Tullt and Company Number One A wagon. They traced that wagon to Dodge."

"Injuns seldom keep wagons," put in Jack Smith.

"What good would it do to find that wagon?" queried Kit Carson.

"Gentlemen, the idea I gather from this inquiry is the importance of establishing the death of a Miss Cynthia Bowden," went on Major Greer. "A fortune has been left her. Very probably that will be tied up until her death is proved. Law is worse than army red tape."

"If the wagon train was lost, then the girl was lost," declared Captain Massey.

"Shore, but she might *not* have been," interposed Carson. "I see Major Greer's point. If a fortune is awaitin' some other heir, why, it's just too bad. I'd say the thing to do is gamble on Beaver Adams' hunch."

"All right, Kit, talk fast," replied Greer, gathering interest.

"That Dry Trail mentioned begins at the Crossin' of the Cimarron an' runs near three hundred miles west. Fact is it strikes the main trail again at Wagon Mount. Now we can find out if Bowden's caravan ever got that far. I'll gamble it never did. Fort Union is the stampin'-ground of all the redskins an' outlaws from the Staked Plains to Raton Pass an' from the Panhandle to the Pecos. Right this minute there's a redskin out there or an outlaw who knows what became of Bowden's wagon train."

"Huh! an' a hell of a lot more besides," declared Jack Smith.

"Kit is figgerin', as usual," interposed Adams. "An' I shore can read his mind."

"Go on, Kit. It's a forlorn chance," said the major. "But I've been given a strict order. What do you suggest?"

"Major, don't let this inquiry go beyond all present here," continued Carson. "But I'll let Curtis an' Baker in on it. We've all got friends among the In dians. Baker has a squaw wife. A Kiowa. We'll begin a quiet search for clues. Dick is somethin' of a gambler. He can get to gamblin' with the shifty-eyed contingent out there. An' when any one of us gets a chance we'll ask a casual question of anyone we happen to meet. It will take months, an' mebbe years, to get on the track of somethin'. But we might. An' to do a good turn is shore worth tryin'."

"I agree. I'll write the Department and lay stress on the mystery that shrouds Bowden's lost wagon train. And that it will take time to find out, if that is ever possible."

"Major, it ought not be hard to find out what wagon train followed Bowden's over the Cimarron," said Carson, thoughtfully. "Suppose you send word to Fort Dodge for that information. If we find out I'll hunt up the trail boss who had charge."

"He would have reported any sign of a fight, let alone massacre," returned Greer.

"Suppose that particular scout never got here. He might have turned off. With caravans pullin' out every day in season it's like huntin' for a needle in a haystack."

"Do you know a friendly Indian that you could send among the tribes?" asked Greer.

"Yes. An' unless this Bowden wagon train vanished like mist in the mornin' sun we'll get track of it."

"Kit, I'm suspectin' the Kiowas," said Beaver Adams, broodingly.

"That won't tickle Baker," laughed Carson.

"Tell me why Satana is not heard of as he used to be?" queried Major Greer.

"By thunder!" ejaculated Carson, slapping his knee. "*Why?* He shore was a bloody devil."

"Satock is a bigger Kiowa chief than Satana," declared Smith. "He's been the regular war chief since 'fifty-five. Damn bad Injun! He's raidin' all around Santa Fe an' up along the Vermigo River. Lucky the caravan that gets by there without a clash with Satock."

"Bad, yes. But Satock is not Satana's equal for sagacity an' blood-thirstiness. . . . Strikes me queer that it's Satock we hear of now instead of Satana. I wonder if Satana has had anythin' to do with these lost wagon trains."

Kit Carson was obviously becoming deeply interested in the inquiry propounded by the army officer.

"Another thing before it slips my mind," said Greer. "Doctor McPherson dropped in an hour or so ago. Among his patients just now is one he considers worth meeting. Reminded him of Maxwell."

"What! My friend Maxwell?"

"Yes. Doc mentioned your name. Well, this patient is a Southerner of parts. Educated man, handsome, fine type, evidently ruined by the war. His name is Latch. Stephen Latch. McPherson heard one of his men call him that. It appears that Latch has men here at the fort, or friends at least. Now, Kit, you know everybody on the frontier. How about Latch?"

"Never heard of him."

"Any of you?" queried Greer, addressing the others.

"I've shore heard that name Latch," declared Beaver Adams. "But I can't place where or when."

"What of this Latch?" asked Carson, curiously.

"Nothing particular. I was just interested because Mac told me about him. As I get it Latch came here in a wagon train some weeks—or was it months—-ago. He had been badly wounded and was laid up for a long time before he was brought here."

"What is he *now*?" queried Carson, sharply. "Freighter, trader, settler?"

"I'd say neither, from Doc's talk. He has plenty of money. He paid for his keep at the hospital. Has Indian girl nurse in daytime and one of Doc's staff at night."

"If he's a ruined Southerner, where does he get plenty of money?"

"Don't ask me. I'm interested, though, and think I'll call on him. Suppose you come along," returned Major Greer.

"Shore. I'd go far to meet any man like Maxwell," declared the scout.

Stephen Latch occupied one of the army tents in a corner of the stockade. Its isolation would have been significant to anyone who knew Latch. But except for several of his men, no one at the fort had ever seen him. Cornwall, now his inseparable companion, occupied this tent with Latch. It was furnished with more than the usual comforts of soldiers—stove, bureau, mirror, wash-stand, and other articles Latch had purchased at Tullt's.

Latch and his band, about a year and more before, had found it expedient to throw in with a caravan eastbound for Independence. For the time being their intentions had been honest. When the train was attacked by Comanches near Point of Rocks, a noted ambush on the trail, Latch and his men fought with such courage and zeal that the scout in charge highly commended them to the commanding officer at Fort Larned. Mandrove was killed, Keetch lost a leg, and all the others except Cornwall, who bore a charmed life, were wounded, Latch very badly. For months he lay between life and death, often entirely oblivious of his surroundings. Then convalescence was slow. As soon as he was able to be moved he was taken to Fort Union, which was farther south and less rigorous of climate. Here after several weeks he began to mend surely.

On this sunny April day, with chilly gusts of wind swooping down from the snow-topped mountains, the little stove gave forth a cheerful crackling and warmth. Cornwall had had wood hauled in and he chopped it with the gusto of a man who liked to ply the ax. An Indian girl brought their meals from the army cook's quarters. Some days before Latch had dispensed with the services of a soldier.

"Lester, I'd sit up today if it wasn't so damn cold," said Latch.

"Colonel, you're doing fine," replied Cornwall. "It's a spring day. You can smell the odors. And not cold at all. You've lost so much blood. Be patient. You'll be in the saddle in a month."

"Patient? My God!" breathed Latch, drawing his breath hard. "Have I not clung to life? . . . How long is it, Lester?"

"Is what?" queried Cornwall, as he turned to Latch. The youth had passed from his face. Its beauty had suffered a blight. But nothing save death could ever change those merciless eyes of blue.

"Since we—we left Spider Web," whispered the leader. This was his first outspoken query as to the past. But how that had burned in memory!

"Nearly a year and a half. Time flies, Colonel!"

"When did I send Keetch back?"

"Last October. It was just after you were taken to Bent where we expected you to die. But you didn't. Something kept you alive. You had lucid hours and soon as Keetch recovered from losing a leg you sent him back."

"Yes, I remember. I gave him money to build cabins and corrals at the head of Latch's Field. Buy cattle. Start my ranch. Propitiate the Kiowas," replied Latch, with eager fervor.

"I hope the one-legged geezer didn't gamble an' drink the money up."

"No. Keetch is honest. I trust him as I trust you, Lester."

"And—soon you'll be riding back to our lovely canyon—to your beautiful wife?" rejoined Cornwall, jealously.

"Soon! . . . It has been ages. I shall die waiting. . . . Lester boy, you understand?"

The boy who was no longer young drooped his face

over the stove as he put another billet of wood into the fire. His silence seemed something not to violate. But Latch, stirred by memories, and always curious about this youth, surrendered to the moment.

"Lester, didn't you ever love a girl?"

Cornwall lifted a pale face with glittering, terrible eyes. Latch gazed into a chaos of hell.

"Any man but you—I'd kill—for reminding me!"

"Ah—so *that* is it? . . . Forgive me, comrade! Tell me your story some day. You heard Cynthia tell mine that time, long ago, when she saved me. . . . But, Lester, let me ask—don't be hurt—have you no mother—father, whom you love still? I ask because I think we'll give up this game. I have money. I'll stake you to go home—begin life over. Or you can come back to my ranch and have a share in it."

"Yes, Colonel, I have mother—father—damn their souls!"

"Hush, son!" cried Latch, shocked.

"I hate them."

"Hate them! Why?"

"They hated me when I was born—because I came between them. . . . I was her son—but not his!"

"Christ, how cruel life is! . . . No sister to love, still, then—no brother?"

"Yes, I had a kid brother," replied the young man, dreamily. "Cornie, I called him, not because our name is Cornwall, but because his hair was the color of ripe corn. . . . Cornie would be ten years old now. . . . To think I'll never—see him again!"

After that tragic whisper Cornwall started up, as if

recalling the present, and with a gesture of fierce passion he stalked out of the tent.

Latch gazed after him, a prey to conflicting emotions. "What a fine boy gone to hell!—I wonder if it's too late. . . . Yes, for him. He is a cold-blooded tiger. . . . Ah, it's strange and unbelievable, when I think of reality. Here we are, Cornwall and I—robbers, murderers—comrades to the vilest men and fiercest savages on the frontier! . . . So help me God I'm going to end that for myself!"

He indulged in a dream which had grown to be an absorbing passion. He would buy his freedom from his band, go back to Cynthia, and bury the bloody past in honest ranching and unswerving devotion to his wife. He caught his breath in the twinge of agony that always returned when he thought of Spider Web Canyon, of Cynthia, and the lonely cabin where he had left her in charge of faithful attendants.

Having lost all, Cynthia Bowden had created happiness out of love. But during those blessed, lonely months while he hid in Spider Web Canyon she had never rested, never ceased her passionate importunities to wean him from his union with these white desperadoes and with the red Satana. And she had won. But the very day of her victory Indian riders arrived with urgent messages from Keetch and Satana. They had summoned him for a great raid. He swore on his knees that it would be his last, and tearing himself away from the frantic girl he had ridden away to join his forces. Eighteen months! Was it possible that hours, days, weeks could pass so swiftly? But they had been full of hard, perilous, thrilling life until he had been stricken in the fight at Point of Rocks. After that, oblivion for months—and then the slow dull awakening to poignant life again!

Cornwall returned to jar Latch out of his reveries.

"Leighton wants to fetch in these new pards of his," announced the youth, abruptly.

Latch cursed. "——— ——— ———! I wish I'd croaked him sure that day on the trail. He'll finish us yet."

"I'll walk out and kill him now," replied Cornwall, imperturbably.

"Hold on, you damned gamecock! . . . I can't have you shoot Leighton down like that. It will start a lot of trouble. And if you risked an even break with him—you might ———"

"Faugh! I can beat the scar-faced liar to a gun any day. . . . Colonel, I see through this change in Leighton, since you shot him to save Cynthia. It's a grand bluff. He hates you with hate so great that it has transformed him."

"But, Lester, if that is so he could have shot me in the back long ago," protested Latch. "Leighton has changed, yes, but only for the better."

"To kill you wouldn't satisfy Leighton," returned Cornwall, speaking with the cold passionless wisdom of a sage. "He wants a horrible revenge. To put you on the rack! . . . He'll make 'way with Cynthia or do something worse, if that were possible. I feel all this, Colonel. I know the man is playing a waiting game. His patient persistent way of trying to make a friend of me. It's all so clear. This is aside from the bad impression he has made here at the fort. Major Greer and his officers have no use for the outfit Leighton tracks with. And these fox-nosed scouts! Don't let any of them find out Leighton is one of your men."

"Lester, you exaggerate," expostulated Latch, in concern. "You hate Leighton."

"No. I see through him, that's all. Better let me go kill him. That'll end uncertainty."

Latch wavered under the lashing tongue of this young wolf. An instinct of self-preservation warned him. Yet he would not listen. If Leighton had to be killed, Latch wanted to do it himself. That thought found heat in his veins. Moreover, Latch did not want to incite further the enmity of Leighton's friends. It would not be politic in view of his scheme to buy his freedom from the band. Why not let Leighton take over the leadership? That would have been a capital idea but for the certainty of Leighton's continuing to use Spider Web Canyon and Latch's Field and Satana's braves. Latch did not feel up to coping with the problem as yet.

"Cornwall, I'm against that for a number of reasons," he replied, presently.

"All right. You're my boss. But before I give in, let me tell you this. Leighton knows you have a big sum of money in your belt. I could see it in his eyes when he was here. He's always after money. He owes me and every one of the men. The camp women get what he doesn't gamble and drink away."

"That's just why I have held out so much of his share of that September—deal," replied Latch, warily lowering his voice to a whisper. "I've ten thousand here yet that belongs to Leighton, and the others. The rest I sent back with Keetch to be hidden. He had a pack saddle full—some of it gold."

"Don't tell Leighton, and if you give him more money, do it in dribbles . . . Now what aboot these two men he's taken up?"

"Who and what are they?"

"Sam Blaise and Handy something or other. Blaise is a tow-headed lout that I wouldn't trust an inch. Handy is one of the quiet Westerners better left alone."

"Tell Leighton to wait until I'm able to get out. That'll be soon. Ther I'll look these men over. I ——"

"Sssh!" Cornwall peeped out between the flaps of the tent. Suddenly he jerked back, his eyes glinting like sunlight on ice. "Major Greer coming with a scout in buckskin. I think he's Kit Carson. . . . Colonel, heah's where you think quick!"

Latch, after an instant's start, did think quickly. In fact he wasted no time on conjecture or surprise, but braced his nerve and called on all his faculties to meet an encounter that might be friendly; yet could not fail to be scrutinizing.

"Hello inside!" called an authoritative voice.

Cornwall sprang to spread wide the tent flaps.

"Come right in," he said, cordially.

Latch had seen the doughty little officer, but Kit Carson was a stranger, except in name and fame. Many of the great frontiersmen had passed before Latch's gaze. Carson was typical, but he had the clearest, most piercing eyes Latch had ever met. The major greeted him and shook hands.

"This is Kit Carson. You've probably been on the frontier long enough to hear of him. Ha! Ha! . . . Doc McPherson spoke to me about you. Thought I'd drop in. Carson happened along."

"Mighty kind of you, gentlemen," replied Latch, courteously. "I wish I could offer you each one of the easy-chairs on my veranda in Louisiana—also a mint julep. But I cannot, as you see. Pray take a store-box seat. Lester, pass the cigars."

There was not the least constraint. The visitors took both seats and cigars, and faced Latch with interest.

"You've had a long siege, Mac says?" began Greer.

"Long! It seems years. I've been down since last September," replied Latch. "Lester, light one for me. I'll try a smoke myself."

"Bad shot up, I reckon?" said Carson.

"I've just pulled through and that's all," replied Latch. "Perhaps you heard about Melville's caravan being jumped by Comanches at Point of Rocks last September."

"Was you in that? Wal, tell us about it," returned Carson, leaning forward.

Latch had reason to make a clean, straight-forward, forceful narrative out of that fight, and he did it to the top of his bent.

"Nigger Horse, shore as the Lord made little apples!" declared Carson, vigorously. "Major, that Comanche chief has been on the raid lately. If this

Civil War keeps on much longer the redskins will run us off the plains."

"How's the war going, gentlemen?" queried Latch.

"Southerner, aren't you?" inquired Greer. "War's going against the South."

"Yes, but I did not gain the commission I sought."

"Ahuh. Reckon the war ruined you, like it did so many planters?" asked Carson, casually, with those piercing eagle eyes upon Latch's face.

"Ruined? Oh yes, though not financially," rejoined Latch, with the ease and aloofness natural to a Southern aristocrat. "Carson, I presume you hold with the Yankees."

"Yes. But I deplore this war. Not only has it laid waste the South, but told sorely on the West. An' if it lasts much longer no man can foresee what will happen out here."

"You mean a horde of scarecrows will be let loose upon this frontier?"

"Exactly. An' I predict the bloodiest years of the westward movement. My friend Maxwell, a Southerner by the way, claims the worst will come after the war."

"Maxwell of Maxwell Grant fame, out on the Vermigo?"

"Shore. There's only one Maxwell. Have you seen the Maxwell Ranch?"

"Once. And have been fired ever since to go do likewise," returned Latch, warmly. "He is a wonderful man. Indians of all tribes, freighters, scouts, trappers, outlaws, desperadoes—all welcome at his ranch. To come and stay! The whole West his friend."

"Latch, you've got Maxwell right," replied Kit Carson, favorably impressed. "If you have the means to ranch it on the Maxwell scale an' the will to treat red men an' white men the same you could do much toward peace on this frontier."

"You'd certainly help the soldiers' cause," added Greer, heartily.

"Gentlemen, I have the means and the will," continued Latch, rising to his advantage. "What's more, I have found the place. It lies north of here, east of the mountains and the Canadian River, a wonderful range, a valley beyond compare, grass, water, trees, game in abundance—a paradise."

"East of the Canadian?" mused Carson, as if drawing a map in his mind. "That's Kiowa country, Latch."

"The only drawback," admitted Latch, with just the right inflection of regret.

"Do you happen to know Satana?" asked the scout.

Latch met that penetrating glance and query with all the strength and cunning engendered by the realization that Cynthia's happiness and his life were at stake.

"Wal, then how do you propose to propitiate Satana, not to mention that other devil, Satock?"

"I'm gathering a bunch of hard-riding, hard-shooting men with little regard for their status on the plains."

"A good idea, if you can run an outfit of these hard

nuts. Like as not they'll kill you an' take everything you've got."

"I must take that chance, for some years, at least. Then I'll placate the Kiowas with gifts. I'll keep open house the same as Maxwell does."

"Wal, it might work. You are a man of force. But take it slow. Don't throw in many head of hosses an' cattle at first. Feel your way. . . . Did you ever hear of Jim Blackstone?"

"Blackstone? That name ought to stick in mind. No, I can't say I recall it," replied Latch, lying smoothly.

"Blackstone an' his gang holes somewhere up on the Purgatory River," explained Carson. "He's a man to steer clear of. Lately Blackstone has come under suspicion of holdin' up stages on the trail."

"Indeed? I shall look out for him. Thanks for the hunch. All the same, Carson, with Maxwell's way in mind, I'll keep open house for any and all comers."

"Safe enough if you last," concluded Carson, rising. "Wal, Latch, I'm glad to meet you an' shall keep tab on you."

"Do. And run up for a buffalo-hunt next fall," responded Latch, heartily.

Major Greer also shook hands. "Hope you'll be up and around soon. Drop in on me any time. If I can be of service to you, command me."

Kit Carson halted on the way out. "Latch, here's a hunch. If you are wal-heeled you can double an investment pronto. Furs are pourin' down out of the hills in a regular rain. Never seen the like. More than a thousand trappers here! An' you know I was a trapper once. It's just been a bang-up winter for trappin'."

"Thanks. I could readily buy a wagon-load of pelts. But how dispose of them?"

"Tullt will guarantee delivery by escort train."

"Good. Will you buy a load for me? On commission, of course."

"Shore, I'd be glad to."

"Drop over tomorrow and I'll have the money for you. . . . Speaking of money, I'd be willing to take wagon, team, and supplies from Tullt instead of cash."

"That's easy. But let me buy the pelts first," laughed Carson, as he went out.

After the visitors had gone Latch and Cornwall gazed at each other a long silent moment.

"What do you make of that?" finally broke out Latch.

"Greer's a thick-haided Yank!" replied Cornwall, with scorn. "But that Kit Carson is all the West calls him. Colonel, I liked him plenty. How his eyes bored into me! . . . My angle is Greer came in to look you over. But no man could have done more or better. Colonel, you're a master at dissimulation. The Maxwell idea was a stroke. It hit Carson plumb center. And open house for every class on the frontier—that was another. But from this day you're a—marked man."

"By God—yes!" ejaculated Latch, choking over the utterance. "I liked Carson, too . . . greatest of all these great Westerners! . . . And I—Stephen Latch—at the other end—lowest, meanest, vilest of the West's outlaws!"

Chapter VIII

LATCH walked about the fort leaning on Cornwall's arm. He felt in exuberant spirits. The
warm spring sun, the greening grass and bursting buds
on the hackberry bushes, the odor of wood smoke—
all smote him keenly. Before long now he would be
enjoying them in the seclusion of Spider Web Canyon. A certainty that he was starting soon helped to
stay what had been almost insupportable impatience.
And another thought had occurred to steady him. It
was no sure thing that horses could stem the current
of Spider Web Brook swollen from the melting snow
on the mountains.

Tullt's store was so crowded with Indians and trappers that Cornwall insisted on staying out. A new
run of pelts from the hills had come in. Freight was
piled higher than a man's head all around the store.
Two wagon trains had arrived that morning, one to
unload supplies for the West, the other to pack furs
for the East.

"Lester, if we nailed that train of beaver-skins,
we'd never have to work again," said Latch.

"Send Hawk Eye out with the word," replied the
young dare-devil.

"Boy, you're drunk. There'll be over a hundred
wagons with an escort of dragoons. . . . Besides, I
forgot. No more raids for me!"

The youth let loose his cold, tinkling, mocking laugh.

"Colonel, you will die with your boots on," he declared.

"Kicking them at empty air, eh? . . . No, by Heaven! I wasn't born to be hanged."

Latch wearied and had to sit down to rest. His breathing was labored and great beads of perspiration stood out on his forehead. The one wound that had nearly been mortal, though fully healed, pained as if the lead bullet that had made it, still burned in his flesh. But Latch knew Cynthia's hand or cheek on his sore breast, where the hole palpitated and throbbed, could allay all agony, as her love could give him peace.

He watched the throng. Cornwall left him on an errand. Indians, soldiers, freighters, trappers, and all the parasite types of the army camp passed him in review. He realized that he was watching the Western movement in its incipience. He had the vision to see what the future would bring to this frontier. Raw and hard and bloody it was now—a phase in the development of a great country. Somehow the scene of color, action, life, tugged at his heart and touched again his old desire to help the progress of empire. Also he had a divining or intuitive power to read in the mien, the step, the eye of a red man whether he was friendly or hostile. Some Indians were really brothers, but except in isolated cases, from people like Kit Carson or Maxwell, all the Indians received in return was trickery, intolerance, and blood. Latch had been long enough on the frontier now to know that if the Union won the Civil War, it would still have an Indian war to contend with. No army of soldiers would ever sweep the plains free of these proud fierce savage devils. Latch realized that his association with Satana had given him surprising sympathy and regard for the Indian. An afterthought of bitter realization that he was an outlaw—that Greer had cause to hang him—ended his revery.

Cornwall returned and Latch said he felt up to a walk outside of the fort. There were a few rude clapboard structures along the dusty street, and the one farthest appeared to rival Tullt's in bustle and noise. It was a store and saloon combined.

Among the Indians lounging outside, Latch recognized his scout Hawk Eye and another Kiowa brave. They might never have seen Latch before. Their business at the fort was to guide him back to Spider Web Canyon. Latch went on into the saloon with Cornwall. A huge barn-like structure it was, unfloored and unfinished, with the crudest of tables and benches, and a long stand for a bar. Smoke, noise, and the odor of tobacco and rum filled the place.

"Find me—a seat," panted Latch. "Soon as I've rested—we'll get out of this hell-hole."

But he remained an hour, which was far longer than he would have chosen. Black Hand and Augustine approached him, the former drunk and ugly. He bellowed out: "Howdy boss! Gimme stake!"

When he persisted, Cornwall hit him over the head with the butt-end of a gun, which laid the ruffian out.

No one paid any special attention. But Augustine showed his yellow teeth like a snarling wolf.

Next Leighton got up from a table where evidently he had been gambling, and motioning his comrades to stay back he stalked across the room to greet Latch. The last two times Latch had seen his Southern ally had been in the uncertain light of the army tent. Leighton had changed markedly during the five months that Latch had been ill. Had it been only a year and a half since Latch's shot had marred the once handsome features? The left side of Leighton's face bore a crooked, livid, triangular-shaped scar, giving him a deformed and hideous appearance. He had grown heavy in body, untidy of person, and coarse. Nevertheless, he had a pondering look, as if possessed by a hidden thought.

"Latch, my hunch is to rustle away from Fort Union at once," he said, without any greeting. He had never called Latch "chief" or "boss" again.

"What's your hurry?" asked Latch.

"These scouts are too interested in us."

"What scouts?"

"All of them. Not Carson, particularly, though you can't figure him. But Curtis, and particularly Beaver Adams."

"Well, the company you keep is responsible for that."

"You mean Blaise and Handy," returned Leighton, bluntly.

"I do."

"They are no different from a dozen other doubtful hangers-on here. I've been gambling with them all. . . . Latch, I think you are the man the scouts are interested in."

"What gave you that idea?" queried Latch, quickly, ever alert and suspicious.

"Handy. That fellow is a fox. He's been knocking about these forts for years. I don't know what he had seen or heard. But he just tipped me off."

"Call him over here."

Latch had to admit to himself that the stranger, Handy, gave an impression of sterling qualities. He had a fearless, cool, aloof air, a straight hard glance, and a voice that matched both. After a few casual questions Latch came right out: "What's your business on the border?"

"Aw, I'm a gentleman of leisure," replied Handy, with a grin.

"Can you ride?"

"Shore. On a wagon-seat. I began freightin' out of Independence in 'fifty-five."

"Any good with a rope?"

"Wal, I reckon I'll stretch one some day."

"I mean can you throw a lasso?"

"Hell, no."

"You wouldn't make much of a cowboy?"

"Not for work. But I'm handy with a gun."

"That where you get your handle, eh?"

"Wal, it wasn't no pick of mine."

"All right, Handy. I like your looks and your talk. What do you make of me?"

"I had you figgered before Leighton told me."

The old hot passion, dead or slumbering for months, awoke in Latch's veins again. Straightway he restrained it and became thoughtful—compared with this man Latch knew himself to be a novice on the plains. He wondered if Kit Carson and his associates had gauged him as keenly as had this outlaw. Probably they had not. He knew his power of dissimulation and felt convinced that the famous scout at least had not been hostile toward him. Carson, however, had not approached him in regard to the deal in beaver pelts.

Latch asked to meet Blaise, whom he found to be like many other frontier outcasts, dull, negative, indifferent, living from hand to mouth, day by day.

"Any good around a ranch?" inquired Latch.

"Shore am. Was brought up with hosses an' cows. I'm a farmer. Good at graftin' fruit trees. Fair carpenter, blacksmith, an' a good cook. Ain't so poor a doctor an' ———"

"Say, you're a whole outfit in yourself," interrupted Latch, dryly. "Can you shoot?"

"Fair to middlin' at deer an' buffalo. But I've no nerve for shootin' men."

"How'd you last so long on the frontier?"

"Jest luck. An' I can dodge."

"Latch, he packs a gun with six notches cut on the handle," interposed Leighton.

"Shore. They was on it when I stole the gun," agreed Blaise.

Latch came speedily to a decision. This fellow would be less dangerous for the present if he were taken along with the outfit. Latch had no great worry about getting rid of an undesirable. Blaise had had too much of Leighton's society to be left at Fort Union.

"Suppose you throw in with us and take whatever comes along," suggested Latch, to both men.

They agreed without question. Whereupon Latch told them to get horses and packs in readiness. "We have wagon, team, supplies. I'm as weak as a sick cat. But if I can't sit up I'll ride lying down."

They planned to pack that day and leave in the morning with the wagon train bound east. When they got as far as they cared to have company, Latch could explain that he wanted to travel more slowly on account of his condition.

When he and Cornwall left the saloon Cornwall said: "Leighton has some good reason for wanting to pull out quick."

"I gathered that, Lester. Well, the sooner the better. It is not safe for me to have him hanging around these forts. The great mistake all these border outlaws make is to show their faces."

"Colonel, as far as Leighton is concerned the only safe way to have him is dead."

"God! what a blood-thirsty kid you are!"

"I might say, 'God! what a queer dreamer you are!' I see through this border life, and if I cared a jot about living I'd know how to last a little while, anyway."

"Listen to the young sage," scoffed Latch, though

he never took Cornwall lightly. "Just how ought *I* conduct myself on this frontier to survive?"

"Seven out of ten good men will fail to survive this West. Not one bad man ever will. Colonel, you are really a good man gone bad. If you must—well, make wagon trains vanish from the face of the earth, make them few and far between—and expect to hang."

"No rope for me. Not Steve Latch!" replied Latch, breathing hard.

"Why don't you start *now*?"

"What?"

"Your idea of giving up this life."

"I mean to. Will you come with me, Lester?"

"Yes. You'll need some one to help you live down what you've already done. Just so long as one of these outlaws remains above ground you will never be safe."

Latch was glad indeed to reach his tent and to lie down again. He sent Cornwall to the Tullt and Co. store to complete purchase of supplies and to ascertain if one wagon would haul the lot, and if not, to buy another. Thereafter, while Latch was resting and dreaming, the hours passed until late afternoon, when Kit Carson called.

"Howdy, Latch," was his hearty greeting. "Glad to see you can walk about."

"I'm feeling fine. Weak yet. But restless for the trail. I'll be leaving in a day or two."

"So soon? Sorry to see you go. By the way, I slipped up on the deal for pelts. They are pretty foxy in there at Tullt's. My Ute friends had sold out."

"Thanks just the same, Carson. Maybe it's as well. I'm going to get short of funds sooner or later."

"Latch, it'll be sooner if you hit the trail with that Leighton an' his outfit," declared Carson, bluntly.

"You don't say! Well . . . I told you I was hiring a bunch of hard border men."

"Do you know this Leighton?"

"Not very well. He's a Southerner—foot-loose and ——"

"Shore, I appreciate you'd rather have Rebels," interrupted Carson as Latch paused. "Leighton has been under suspicion here. I don't mind tellin' you. Better profit by this hunch. He is playin' a deep game of some kind, most likely against you. If you do take Leighton, be shore an' sleep with one eye open. What-ever Leighton has been in the past, he's headed now on a downgrade. Foot-loose men who drink an' gamble an' cavort with the camp sluts must have money. They are not the kind to help the West along. They hold it back. An' soon they get caught an' stop lead or stretch hemp."

"Have you talked with Leighton?"

"Twice. Yesterday I bumped into him at Tullt's an' I said: 'Say, Leighton, you must have been a good-lookin' fellar before you got that scar? . . . ' He cussed somethin' fierce an' said that was none of my —— —— business. An' I come back at him, 'Wal, I seen you was the kind of man who never wore a glove on his right hand an' was lookin' sharp to see some one first?' . . . I know men on the border. This Leighton is not a clean, hard-shootin' outlaw like

Handy. That fellar won't do you dirt. But Leighton will. I hope you take my hunch."

Latch, after Kit Carson's departure, experienced both elation and misgiving. Carson's friendliness established the fact that Latch was still above suspicion in the eyes of soldiers and scouts at the fort. But never again could he give Leighton the benefit of a doubt.

Three days out of Fort Union the east-bound caravan under Scout Dave Prescott halted at Stinking Springs for camp. It was a big wagon train, with heavily loaded wagons drawn by oxen, and therefore made but slow progress. Prescott was strong for taking the Dry Trail at Wagon Mount, thereby cutting off from ten days to three weeks on the route to Fort Dodge. The caravan, under escort, had little to fear from Indians.

Latch had found riding in a wagon less of an ordeal than he had anticipated. To be sure, his second wagon, affording plenty of room, had been fitted up with a comfortable bed where he could lie at length or sit up and look about as the caravan rolled along. He had his camp separate from the freighters, where his men, Leighton, Black Hand, Augustine, Cornwall, and the two new members, Blaise and Handy, with the two Kiowas, took their turn at the chores. Blaise's boast about his proficiency as a camp cook had not been a vain one.

Away from Fort Union a few days, and gradually working into trail travel, the men settled down into a sort of comradeship. Drink was always the deterrent, and gambling left no chance for naturally agreeable impulses. Latch passed for a convalescent rancher returning to his ranch on a distant range east and south of the Canadian.

"Wal, I don't know the country hyar aboots," said Prescott, who had taken to Latch, "but it runs in my mind thet's Kiowa country."

"Wal, it shore is, scout," drawled Latch.

"How'n hell do you keep from havin' yore har raised, let alone losin' all yore stock?" queried Prescott.

"By being a real friend to the redskins."

"Humph! Readin' a leaf oot of Maxwell's book, huh?"

"Not on such a grand scale. I'm just starting. My range is as fine as the Vermigo. And my place will beat Maxwell's all hollow. Of course, in time. I'm just feeling my way now."

Other freighters joined Prescott around the camp fire where Latch sat propped in an easy-chair. A cigar and a nip of fine brandy awaited all who visited Latch —a fact that was jealously kept secret by the freighters who had discovered it. Among them was Jim Waters, who was to become, a few years later, one of the most famous of the trail bosses, and to lose his life at the great Comanche raid at Pawnee Rock. He was a young man then, a giant in stature, Western born and already a trained scout.

"Latch, you've got the right idea," he agreed.

"Most redskins remember a kindness an' never forget an injury. Do you know Satana?"

"I've seen him once. Why do you ask?"

"Wal, he's the Kiowa chief that pulls a lot of tricks Satock gets the credit for. I know. Both of these chiefs have rid up to my camp fires. I'd be leary of Satock. But I'd trust Satana. Mean-lookin' runt of a reddy. Fierce as hell!"

"Where are these chiefs now?" asked Latch.

"Lord only knows. Your guide is a Kiowa. I'll see if I can pump him," replied Waters, and addressed the Kiowa. Hawk Eye could talk fairly well in the white man's tongue, a fact he concealed here. He appeared to be a proud, calm, taciturn brave. His replies to Waters were brief but instant, and his gestures as ready and expressive.

"Satock is on the war-path with the Pawnees," said Waters, presently. "An' Satana is far south on the Red River, waitin' for the buffalo herds to come north."

"Speakin' of Kiowas," spoke up Prescott. "It struck me that Kit Carson, Beaver Adams, an' them other scouts at Union are damn particular keen this spring."

"How so?" queried Waters. "They're a lazy lot of trappers an' like nothin' better than a powwow around the camp fire."

"Wal, I don't know," replied Prescott, thoughtfully. "They damn near got me drunk before I knowed they was quizzin' me. . . . Waters, did you ever hyar of Bowden's lost wagon train?"

"Shore. I've heahed aboot 'em all."

"Wal, it so happens that I was in charge of the

wagon train followin' Bowden out of Dodge, year
an' a half ago. Kit Carson 'peared not to have any
particular interest. He asked me plumb straight where
Bowden camped last on the Dry Trail. An' I told him
Tanner's Swale. Thet satisfied Carson, I reckon. But
the other scouts talked me dizzy."

"So you was thet scout!" ejaculated Waters.

"Yes. An' I always was a little testy aboot thet,"
admitted Prescott. "You see, I was in a hurry. You
know how a fellar feels on thet Dry Trail. An' I didn't
take no particular trouble aboot Bowden's campin'
at Tanner's. How'n hell was I to know his wagon train
got lost right there? But it shore did. I found no more
trace of Bowden. Reckoned it strange. Didn't bother
my haid. Didn't want to think aboot it. So later at
Independence, when I got called on the carpet aboot
it, I wasn't any too damn pleased."

"Wal, Dave, you ought to have seen more," returned Waters, gravely.

"Hell, yes. But I didn't."

"Have you been by Tanner's since?"

"Nary time. An' I ain't keen aboot it this time.
Shore, we could lick Satock an' Satana with Nigger
Hoss throwed in. But I ain't hankerin' to fight."

"Tell you what, Dave. If this wagon-train raidin'
don't stop I'm goin' to haul a six-pound brass cannon."

"Cannon! What in hell for?"

"To turn loose on the reddys."

Prescott laughed heartily at the idea of a trail boss
imagining he could intimidate or deplete a bunch of
Kiowas with an army cannon.

"Lot of heavy haulin' all for naught," declared he.

"Wal, you wait an' see," replied Waters, doggedly. "I've been a gunner an' I know what I can do."

Latch had felt a slow fire return to heat out the icy terror in his vitals. The camp-fire blaze had temporarily burned down, so that he sat in comparative shadow. What a strained, fixed attention sat upon Leighton and Black Hand! Or was that in himself?

"What about this—Bowden's lost wagon train?" he asked, casually, after puffing out a cloud of cigar smoke. "Runs in my mind I've heard that name . . . Bowden."

Whereupon he was compelled to hear again the story of the famous lost caravan. This time it had an intense interest because related by the scout who had followed Bowden on the Dry Trail. Prescott had more to say than had any other narrator of that tragic event. Another drink of brandy certainly warmed his tongue. He had met Bowden in Fort Dodge and described him minutely. He remembered the red-headed daughter —or was it niece?—and the children. Latch's ears, however, dinned and closed and dinned again around that thundering and terrible juncture of Prescott's story. Prescott remembered having found a baby's shoe—something he said he forgot to tell the commanding officer at Fort Bent. He had recalled it, however, for the scouts at Union.

The camp-fire scene would live in Latch's memory —Hawk Eye watching the glowing embers with inscrutable eyes—Leighton sitting in shadow like a statue—Cornwall in the light, his beautiful face cold, serene, as inscrutable as the Kiowa's—the vaquero smoking his cigarette, his sloe-black gaze on the story-teller—Black Hand dropping his shaggy head. Latch saw only these men who knew.

Next day Latch's outfit slowly climbed the plateau alone. Prescott's caravan already resembled a long white thread growing hazy far out and down on the Dry Trail. All that day Latch lay sick and clamped on his bed in the wagon. But he crawled out at sunset when camp was made in a clump of cedars, high up, with cold water running from the rocks. He walked about, gradually recovering. The loneliness, the wild-ness of the scene, the smell of burning cedar and the trickle of water, the call of the owls and wail of the coyotes—all these prevailed upon his mind and worked on the ever-returning dread.

Days later, when Hawk Eye led the small train down the stony range to the brink of Spider Web Can-yon, Latch was the old Latch again. Strength and force had returned, at least enough to give him activity.

How well he remembered the place—a singular stony surface all along the rim, worn by wind and rain, a hard gneiss—like rock that left no sign of iron-shod hoof or wheel. Cedars grew thickly in spots where there was earth to take root in. A brook slid down a rut in the rock. And the strange cleft called Spider Web Canyon yawned below, filled with sunset gold and purple. This point was a day's ride from that part of the canyon where Latch had established his cabin—

where Cynthia would be waiting. His troubled hungry heart leaped up in his breast. Only stern control kept him from acting like a madman. He walked away from his comrades so he could not hear any more. Leighton's "By God! right there is where my Tullt and Company Number One A wagon went over the rim!" was all Latch could bear.

How well he remembered that red-lettered wagon go sliding down the gradual grade, to gather momentum, to screetch its iron wheels on the rock, to leap off the rim into space! Latch heard again the faint crash come up from below. The Bowden wagon by some chance had been left to the last. All the others had preceded it down that slope into the abyss. All empty except for stinking, putrid bodies of the members of Bowden's lost wagon train! The fifty-three loads of supplies, bedding, tents, hardware, rifles and ammunition, had been cached for pack transportation down the canyon, to be lowered over the rim on ropes—a gigantic labor that took months. All these details came back to Latch while he fought to contain himself, to keep sane a few days longer. And as he gazed the strange beauty and solitude of this Kiowa retreat flooded over him. It was so far down to the rim from where he stood that he could only make out the smoky void. But the opposite rim stood out, limned in gold, ragged with its cedars, cracked and seamed with all the western wall, in strange variance there to the wall farther down, where the rock sheered stupendously high and unbroken. A lonely rent in the earth! A burrow for a hunted man! Latch's blood ran wild, his pulses throbbed, his eyes dimmed so that the purple abyss and the ragged breaks blurred, his dry lips would not have given utterance to the beloved name, Cynthia, even if she had appeared before him. Would she be well, happy, sure of his return, faithful, with those red lips parted? Incredible as he knew his conviction was, yet he felt it in his overcharged heart, in his surging blood. She was one woman in a million, all love, all passion, unabatable and unquenchable. He yielded to thought of her kisses, her embraces. His remorse at the long separation followed in poignant sweeps, like great waves against a dam. But he had prepared her for a possible long wait. She loved solitude, nature. She would never grow tired of Spider Web Canyon. The days would slip into months while she dreamed, worked, studied, waited. Thus he soothed the still small voice of conscience, thus he stilled the thunder of his rumbling heart, thus he clung rapturously to his fool's dream.

A possible wagon route from this camp on the rim of Spider Web down to Latch's Field drew the Kiowa guide back on the high plateau to the north. The supplies Latch had hauled were for the ranch which Keetch had been instructed to develop. So Latch had to forego the tumultuous rapture of a glimpse of Cynthia's log cabin in the depths of Spider Web Canyon. He bore this patiently. Only a few more days!

On the second day, late in the afternoon, Hawk Eye led out upon the edge of the sloping plateau to a

point where the valley containing Latch's Field un-
rolled in magnificent panorama below. The Indian's
gesture had something grand in its slow-sweeping, all-
possessing motion. It thrilled Latch, as if it signified
that here something great would come to pass.

Dry camp was made on this slope. It would require
another day to wind down the zigzag trail and cross
to the head of the valley. Meanwhile Latch sought
a point where he could see to advantage.

The hour was near sunset. Golden rays swept down
from the hills to burn the green of the range and the
timber. Far down the valley black ragged patches
blotted out the gray of valley floor. Buffalo! The
immense herd was on the way north, and straggling
bunches had wandered into the gateway. Satana, with
his hunters, would be down there.

The head of the valley—the thousands of acres
Latch had bought from the Kiowa chieftain and had
called Latch's Field—lay only twelve or fifteen miles
distant as a crow flew. The soft purple of the groves
contrasted vividly with the open spaces of gold. What
a lovely protected valley! It was going to be a home.
And at its back door opened the secret canyon passage
to Satana's hiding. Already Latch felt safe. If he
never committed another crime, surely this valley
would be a haven. Latch longed with a terrible longing to be left alone there with his lovely wife.

With his naked eye he could make out the dark
ragged cleft in the notch of the bluff where Spider
Web Creek emerged, the wandering line of sunset-
flushed willows, the groves of cottonwood and walnut,

the numberless spaces of grassy meadow between the trees, and lastly the open range, rolling vast and solitary down to the prairie.

With the aid of his glass he saw the corrals and barns and ranchhouse Keetch had been instructed to start. The latter appeared an unfinished structure, yellow in the sunlight, with stretched wings like a fort. When completed, this ranch-house would be second only to Maxwell's.

Across the brook and farther down Latch made out log cabins, widely separated. With the cattle grazing around they had every appearance of being smaller ranches that certainly had not been there when last he had surveyed that scene. These occasioned him concern. Keetch could scarcely have gone beyond his instructions.

"Couldn't be settlers," soliloquized Latch. "But I'll not borrow trouble. I'll wait."

Nevertheless, the unexpected edged the first vague uneasiness into his joy. He gazed no more, and toiled back to camp, to rest and eat, to lie wide-eyed for hours, to await another interminable day.

That other day ended with the sun gone down behind the bluffs when Latch's caravan of two wagons rolled to a halt under a great walnut at the head of the valley.

For the last hour Latch had sat out upon the driver's seat, his whole being vibrating like a strung wire.

Peeled logs and picked stones lay around in piles

near where the long rambling picturesque ranch-house was in course of construction. He smelled smoke. Indians and ponies showed off under the trees below. Latch spied a white man who stared at the wagons and then ran for a cabin. The atmosphere of the place seemed strange.

Keetch hobbled out on his crutch. "Wal, by Gawd! if it ain't the boss!" he boomed, with a depth that left no doubt of welcome.

In the gathering dusk the old outlaw's features were not distinct, but they appeared the same.

"Howdy, Keetch," replied Latch, in a curiously halting voice. "I'm glad—to be home."

"Boss, it took you long to come. An' you shore look peaked."

"Man, I lay five months on my back, out of my head. And after that my recovery was slow. God! I thought I'd die getting well. . . . But I've pulled through, and here I am."

"Boss, it's a —a pity—" began Keetch, hoarsely.

"No. I paid. And I'm glad," replied Latch, misunderstanding the other. "No more now. Tell me—how's Cynthia?"

"Latch, didn't you get my letter?"

"Letter! . . . No."

"Wal, I sent one by an Injun rider."

"Where?"

"To Fort Bent. Aw, boss, don't look skeered. I was shore careful what I wrote. . . . An' you never got it?"

"When did you send it?"

"Last fall. November, I reckon. Jest after . . ." Here Keetch drew Latch away from the listening Cornwall and others of the outfit.

"When were you up the canyon last?" demanded Latch, quickly. His impatience made him stern. And suddenly he felt cold. The one-legged Keetch hobbled along on his crutch, dragging Latch to the great walnut tree closer to the ranch-house.

"Not since then," replied Keetch.

"What! . . . Snowed out? High water?"

"No. Wasn't any need, boss," replied Keetch, hurriedly. You see—I fetched your wife down hyar last fall. . . . She was sick—an' it was best. Settler named Benson located across the crick. Good fellar, an' his woman advised . . ."

"Cynthia sick—you moved her!" demanded Latch, incredulously, and gave Keetch a violent blow on his chest.

"Yes. An' it was damn lucky, too," rejoined Keetch, testily. "If only you'd got my letter!"

"Hell's fire!" shouted Latch. "What are you drivin' at?"

"Boss—it ain't so easy!" panted the old outlaw. "I'm tryin' to tell you—aboot Cynthia—thet we couldn't save her—but did save the ———"

Latch scarcely heard. Savagely he ordered Keetch to take him to Cynthia.

"Boss—by Gawd, I'm sorry! . . . She's gone—an' hyar's—her grave," whispered Keetch, huskily, then hobbled away in the dusk.

Stunned by a horrible fear, Latch gazed down at that to which Keetch had directed his attention. A long mound, grassed over, with a white headstone!—A grave!—Then Cynthia was dead. He grasped the fact in a gathering might of agony. With an awful cry, with death in his vitals, Latch flung himself upon that grave.

The long night hours wore away. Coyotes wailed on the levels. Wolves mourned on the heights. The wind whispered through the walnut leaves. Nothing else broke the solitude of the prairie.

In the gray melancholy dawn Latch got up, a broken, desolate man.

Chapter IX

DURING the last year of the Civil War there was less travel across the Great Plains, and as a consequence fewer disasters to wagon trains. Nevertheless, caravans left Westport (later Kansas City) and Independence for the West. The regular freighters could not have been turned back from the Old Trail. But since before the Mexican War in 1846 these adventurers had been learning and had handed down their method to those who succeeded them. When they had escort of soldiers little or no peril attended their travel. Indians of various tribes had from time to time attacked escorted wagon trains, but had seldom caused any considerable loss of life and property.

However, the wagon trains of another kind of adventurer, the pioneer, often left Independence as had John Bowden, in a spirit of irresistible call to the great West. These pioneers were really the men who built the West. The trappers and freighters opened up the vast area; the buffalo-hunters, who fought the Indians to a standstill, made possible the settling of the West, but it was the pioneer who built it. And they wheeled westward, with their trenchant slogan: "Catch up! Catch up!" in ever-increasing numbers.

The Old Trail had three routes from Fort Dodge, the Mountain Trail, the Middle Trail along the Cim·

arron to Santa Fé, and the *Journada del Muerto* (Journey of Death) across the desert of the Cimarron. Despite the tragic stories that never failed to greet the ears of the traveler passing through Independence, there were always men, like John Bowden, who were reckless or dare-devil or ignorant, and pushed on, risking all for the sake of a few days saved in heart-breaking toil across the plains. Many of these had good fortune along with their indomitable spirit and fighting ability, and got across, a wiser, sadder, and depleted caravan. There were many that suffered loss. And there were a few, like Bowden's lost wagon train, that were never heard of again.

They simply vanished. They were not even mentioned in history, nor did they attract the interest and romance which somehow attended Bowden's caravan. With the war coming to a close and chaos everywhere, with the red man steadily increasing in hostility, what was the vague vanishing of a wagon train now and then?

That year there were plainsmen, however, who talked around their buffalo-chip camp fires, about these known wagon trains that had attempted the *Journado del Muerto* across the Cimarron, never to be heard of again. Jim Waters, grown to be a famous trail scout, was one of these. Buff Belmet, who sat his first wagon-seat when he was ten years old, who lost his mother and father in savage raids, was still another. Kit Carson, the best informed of plainsmen, failing to solve the mystery of Bowden's lost wagon train, threw up his hands at the mention of a new tragedy.

But plains rumor kept on. Satana, the Kiowa chief, remained in his retreat in the mountains beyond the Cimarron, yielding the palm of deviltry to his brother chief, Satock, and to Nigger Horse and Soronto of the Comanches, and to warriors of Cheyennes, Apaches, and Pawnees, known to be in active war against the white invasion.

Old plainsmen talked with one another, when they met at a watering-place along the trail; and they had their doubts about Satana. The old rumor of his association with the Bowden tragedy, and with some mysterious dominating white man, did not down. They questioned one another. Why was Satana not on the war-path? Why was he so seldom seen at the frontier forts? What could this wily old devil tell about the vanishing of the caravans on the *Journado del Muerto* during the close of the Civil War? What, particularly, had become of one eastbound wagon train, small in number of men and wagons, but rich in gold from California and beaver fur from Colorado?

"Dog-gone-it!" said Waters, shaking his grizzled head and favoring the leg that had an Indian bullet in the hip joint. "I jest got a hunch Satana is at the bottom of these Cimarron lost caravans."

"Wal," replied Belmet, "your hunch won't fetch them back. All we can do is to roar at Santa Fé an' Independence ag'in' these small unprotected wagon trains ever startin' out."

The end of the Civil War, however, let loose upon the West a flood of penniless, ruined, broken soldiers, many of whom naturally gravitated to wild and vicious life. They came from the South and from the North; and many who had worn the gray and the blue took to the dusty-booted, gun-hipped, hard-eyed riders of the plains. The frontier band of desperadoes became something to be reckoned with in the settling of the West. In fact, these outlaw organizations flourished increasingly for nearly twenty years after the Civil War. The Lincoln County War, a fight between outlaws and cattlemen, culminating in the death of three hundred men, including the notorious Billy the Kid, was the climax of the desperado régime on the frontier.

At the close of 1865 the gun was might and right. Soon the forts and posts from Toas, New Mexico, to Council Grove, Kansas, were crowded with footloose men. Unprepossessing strangers arrived on each stage, and in small bands on horseback. Robbery of stagecoaches grew to be a common thing. The saloon, the dance-hall, the gambling-hall began their bloody era on the border.

Jim Blackstone's gang sprang from obscurity to prominence about this time. He was a huge black-bearded man, formerly one of Quantrell's guerrillas, who had turned robber, and from operating with a few allies he graduated to leadership of a dozen or more of the most hardened outlaws of the plains. Blackstone and his gang had wintered at the various forts during the early stages of the war. At its close, however, it would not have been safe for him to show his black-bearded face at any of them. No doubt Blackstone was accused of many crimes which he never perpetrated. Kit Carson was authority for this opinion: "Jim is black enough," averred the noted plainsman, "but thar's bigger an' more dangerous outlaws that you don't hear so much about."

But for the mass of travelers across the plains these leaders Carson hinted of were mythical characters. They never showed themselves to a large and escorted wagon train. They were heard of but never seen.

Late in the '60's another era had its inception and tremendous advance—the era of the trail-driver and his herds of long-horn cattle from Texas.

The war left Texas penniless and ruined except for the thousands of cattle that roamed her vast ranges. An intrepid Texas cattleman, John Chisholm by name, conceived an idea which, when put into execution, changed the fortunes of the Lone Star State. And that idea was to drive great herds of cattle north from below the Brazos River and even from as far south as the Rio Grande, to Dodge City and Abilene, Kansas. The Chisholm Trail soon marked its rut north over the rolling prairie once traveled only by the buffalo. A wonderful breed of young fighting riders, learning their trade of horsemanship from the Mexican *vaquero*, and developing their own spirit of fire and dexterity with guns, developed to do their part in the empire-building of the West.

A continuous stream of long-horned cattle poured into Kansas. The driving of herds took from three to five months; and was accompanied by all the hazard that attended the freighters across the plains, in addition to the crossing of flooded rivers, the terrible electric storms, the stampedes by buffalo herds, the raids of the Comanches, and many lesser obstacles to travel. But the herds kept coming in ever-increasing numbers.

Dodge City had a marvelous mushroom growth. Almost overnight this frontier post, for many years just an important stop along the Old Trail, whooped into the busiest, noisiest, bloodiest town that ever burst to fame on the border.

During daylight the long, wide, dusty main street, lined by its motley buildings, presented a scene of incessant activity—streams of dusty-booted men, of lithe fire-eyed trail-drivers, of travelers, pioneers, soldiers, adventurers, negroes, Mexicans, Indians, foreigners—all kinds and conditions of men jostling along the crowded thoroughfare. By night and the yellow lamplights the same scene was singularly heightened by strains of music, by half-naked, hawk-eyed dance-hall girls, by the black-frocked gamblers with their pale faces and intent eyes.

It was an enormous floating population, coming and going, owing the majority of its stress to the hundreds of thousands of cattle in the corrals and pastures outside the town.

It was a night in late October at Dodge. A cold raw wind blew from the north down the level Kansas ranges, whipping up such a dust on the main street that the jostling streams of humanity on both sides of the wide avenue could not distinguish each other through the yellow murk. The many lights shone dim and blurred.

Stephen Latch and Lester Cornwall sat in the lobby of the Trail-Drivers Hotel, watching the throng pass. The years of hard life sat lightly upon the handsome head of the younger man. He still held that glow and glaze of youth and that something so marvelously cold and aloof about him. Cornwall seemed a strange combination of eagle and vulture.

But Latch had vastly changed. Maturity sat upon him, markedly in his graying hair, in the sloping lines of his iron, mask-like face, in his heavier frame.

They sat apart from other men in the lobby, and as ever, from long habit, they talked low.

"Colonel, let's hit for the South," said Cornwall, thoughtfully.

"South!" ejaculated Latch.

"I don't mean Texas or Louisiana," replied the younger man, quickly. "God! I never want to see that South again. . . . But I mean let's go south where the winter won't be cold. For years now we've spent the winters in these hell-hole posts and forts. Santa Fe and Maxwell's were not so bad, even in winter. We can't go back there. 'Most all the Western forts are closed to us. We're pushed east farther every winter. This Kansas prairie is a blizzard-swept country where you can't keep warm even in bed or on top of a stove. . . . It's been in my mind for days. Let's go, Colonel."

Latch shook his heavy head as if the idea would not stay before his consciousness.

"What's the sense in this gambling night after night, all winter long?" demanded Cornwall.

"No sense in it, I reckon."

"Is it to amass more money?"

"No."

"Man alive, you have won thousands! You had a fortune hidden in Spider Web long ago. And if your Kiowa riders can be trusted they have safely hidden another fortune for you in that canyon."

"Hawk Eye can be trusted," replied Latch. "I have sent him back six times with packs of gold and currency and jewels to hide. Always he has returned. Lester, if you befriend Indians, especially these Kiowas, they will be true to you."

"I believe that," returned Cornwall, without his usual serenity. "But I was never sure of Keetch. And Leighton's return to Latch's Field—that has never sat well upon my stomach."

"Keetch is all right. He has grown old. He likes the ranch life. His reports make me eager to see the field— when I dare think of—of—. . . But Leighton is a snake in the grass. If he suspected that I was sending booty to be hidden in Spider Web he would search every nook and cranny of the canyon."

"Well, that's another reason for us to go back."

"Heaven! you don't mean to go back—there?"

"I do. It's high time. That last raid of ours—the only failure we ever had—marked you on the frontier. It established your relation to Satana. Jim Waters *saw* you, Colonel."

"Yes. It was bad. I never wanted to tackle that caravan. The east-bound freighters are stronger. They fight harder. But Satana was ugly. He had waited so long! So I gave in to our misfortune. . . . Still, Waters can't prove we were with the Indians."

"Humph! Don't you believe that. His word would go at any post from Leavenworth to Taos. . . . We've skated on thin ice for so many years. Colonel, this is going to break!"

"Why this right about face of yours?" inquired the older man, with scorn. "You used to laugh in the teeth of death."

"I can still laugh. But lately I've weakened or softened. I want to go back to our lovely canyon— and spend the rest of my life remembering. . . . And besides, Colonel, I don't want to see you dangle at the end of a rope."

"Lester, you've been a true friend—a son to me. True as steel! You have killed men in my defense. You have been the fox of my band. Without you I would have been gone long ago. I appreciate all this. You are all I have left in the world. . . . Still, I'm afraid I can't go back—just yet."

"Why, Colonel? It's high time."

"This gambling life helps me to forget," returned Latch, thickly.

"But, Colonel, after all these years it won't hurt you to remember. I never told you my story. It's sadder than yours. . . . Let's go back to the lonely life. I'd like to raise horses. I'd like to hunt and fish. To live away from these vile rum-holes with their smoke and crazy men and hussies! It's been growing on me."

"Suppose I refuse, Lester?" queried Latch, moved by this transformation in his lieutenant.

Cornwall pondered a long moment, his dark marble-smooth face bent.

"I will never desert you," he replied, finally.

"That decides me. We will go, Lester," flashed Latch, unaccountably inspired by Cornwall's fidelity. "Quien sabe? You have guided me right many a time. . . . And after all, I *am* tired of life. Perhaps Latch's Field. . . . Come, we will buck the tiger a last time!"

The Palace of Chance, a drinking, dancing, gambling den, was not felicitously named except in its intimation of the uncertainty of life. It was one of the worst places in Dodge City, where they were all bad.

At midnight that November night Latch and Cornwall sat in a game of poker with a cattle-buyer from St. Louis, a stranger from the East, a manager of one of Tullt and Co.'s stores, and a lean-faced trail-driver from Texas.

The stakes were low, considering what Latch usually played for, and most of them had gravitated to his side of the table.

"Wal, I'm cleaned," drawled the Texan, coolly, as he sat back. "It was shore fleecin' lambs."

"What is?" spoke up Cornwall.

"The way you two Southern gents grab all the coin."

"What do you mean by grab?" queried Cornwall, dropping his cards. His right hand quivered on the table. Latch saw it and interposed.

"Lester, he means we're just good card-players—and lucky to boot."

"Shore I ain't insinuatin' nothin'," replied the trail-driver. "I was jest beefin'. All my wages gone and not even a drink."

Latch tossed him a greenback. "Stay away from poker, son."

The game went on. Luck fluctuated for Cornwall and the other two players, but, as so strangely usual, it held for Latch. His winning at cards was phenomenal. If his game were crooked, no single proof of it had ever been presented. As a matter of fact, Latch was that anomaly on the frontier, an honest gambler. But he was an exceedingly cold, calculating, and skillful one. Fortune merely heaped more money upon him, probably because he cared not at all whether he won or lost.

"Shall we continue, gentlemen?" he asked, as the game momentarily halted.

"I want a chance to get even," protested the Tullt manager.

"Let's raise the limit," suggested the stranger from the East.

Whereupon the game proceeded with an added zest. And it was waxing hot when one of the dance-hall girls came up behind Cornwall to place her hands on his shoulders.

The habitués of this dive called her Lily. She was young, pretty, brazen, and wild-eyed. Her sleeveless gown, cut extremely décolleté gave her an alluring charm. It had been her habit to accost Cornwall every time he visited the place, attracted, no doubt, in Latch's opinion, as so many other girls of like character had been, by his handsome face, his strange, flashing blue eyes, his coldness and unattainableness, and especially his courtesy so marked in that ribald atmosphere.

"Come, Handsome, you've won or lost enough tonight," she said, coaxingly.

Cornwall laid down his cards to remove her hands from his shoulders.

"Pray don't interrupt my game," he said. "Our Texas friend on my right is out. Please devote your blandishments to him."

"Wal, lady, I'd be shore pleased," said the young trail-driver, with a frank smile on his brown face. "But, you see, they cleaned me oot, except for this heah twenty the Colonel gave back. I can buy you a drink. . . ."

She thanked him and put her white, ringed hands around under Cornwall's chin. "Darling boy!—cold iceberg, blue-eyed baby boy! Mama's 'ittle sweet! . . . For God's sake come out and show me you are a man!"

Cornwall flung her hands away as if they had burned. A wave of scarlet amazingly crossed his pale face, to recede and leave it paler. For just an instant Latch saw a flash of something far from hate or disgust in those wonderful blue eyes. He divined that the touch of her bare arms around his neck had revived some poignant memory.

"Lily, please run away and leave us to our game

in peace," said Latch, kindly. "I'll make you a present."

"Aw, go to hell," replied the girl. Then she came
around beside Cornwall, and sitting down on the arm
of his chair she wound a white arm around his neck.
He arose to rid himself of her and did it gently, though
firmly, without a word or glance. Then he resumed
his seat.

"Come away, Lily," suggested the trail-driver. "You
shore don't want to hang around where you're not
wanted."

"Funny how I love the damned cold brute!" she
exclaimed, with a hard laugh. "But even as a kid I
liked 'em shy."

Cornwall picked up his cards. Latch observed that
his fingers quivered. He also observed the leaping light
in the girl's eyes. The situation might develop nastily
if one of her admirers happened in. The stranger from
the East regarded her with distinct favor.

"I'd like to substitute for our indifferent comrade,"
he said. "No doubt he's a woman-hater."

"Don't get personal, sir," cut in Cornwall, danger-
ously. "You are quite welcome to appease the young
lady, so far as we are concerned!"

"No offense. I was just trying to step into the
breach," rejoined the Easterner, suavely.

"Listen, Handsome," resumed the dance-hall girl.
"I don't care a damn about you. Really. But I made
a bet with that French tart. She says, 'Ees a frozen
—what you call eet?—turnip?'—and I bet her fifty
I could thaw you. Be a sport now and help me win."

"To what extent do you want me to be a sport?" queried Cornwall, evidently arrested.

"Come with me—dance—make love to me," appealed the girl, eagerly. "There's the damn Frenchie now."

A striking, dark-haired, dark-eyed girl entered the gambling-den. She was attended by a heavy man, of bold mien. They walked arm in arm between the tables, stopping here and there to speak to gamester acquaintances. Then they espied Lily. This not only appeared to be a signal for them to approach, but also it prompted Lily to desperate ends. Turning her back to the table she sat down on the arm of his chair and, face to face with him, she attempted a passionate embrace.

"Lay off me—you lousy slut!" flashed Cornwall, and repelled her so violently that she went sprawling upon the dirty floor.

Like a cat she leaped up. Her scream of rage drew all eyes. And she stood beside Cornwall, her clawed hands uplifted, as if about to rend him. Cornwall might not have been aware of her presence. Cold-faced, imperturbable, he bent over his cards. Suddenly, before even the sharp-eyed Latch could move or speak, she snatched the Texan's gun from his belt and shot Cornwall in the head. Without cry or quiver his face drooped to the table. The startled observers, dumb for the instant, saw a dark thick stream obliterate the cards under Cornwall's nerveless fingers.

Gray dawn brightened the casement windows of the

hotel room where Latch had spent the last hours of that night. Oblivious of the cold, he sat there, smoking and thinking.

Always Latch had been prepared for death in any form for himself or his comrades. Yet Cornwall had seemed to bear a charmed life. He had seemed immune. He, at least, would escape the rope and the bullet. No doubt a woman had ruined him; certainly a woman had murdered him. Latch took the blow second to the hardest he had ever endured. Cornwall had been incredibly faithful. He had been Latch's genius. He had understood Latch, served him, surely had loved him. And now he was dead—gone with Augustine, and Black Hand, Nigger Jack and Lone Wolf, Sprall, Creik, Waldron, Texas, all of the old and original outfit except Keetch and Leighton. His place could never be filled.

The sting of this tragedy awakened Latch's steeped mind into something of its old introspective power. Stern probing of his gloom-pervaded brain discovered that he did not want to die at the end of a rope or as poor Lester had. With this fact established, he had to face the alternative. Wherefore, the loss of Cornwall turned him abruptly back upon the enterprise to rival Maxwell's Ranch. But the old ambition, the old thrill in a landed estate, great troops of horses and herds of cattle, a pack of hounds to follow in the chase, and all that had been a dream of youth— these seemed dead as cold ashes. Nevertheless, there was Latch's Field down across the prairie and the *Journado*—the beautiful valley and the lonely canyon, the ranch developed by Keetch, and the stock that had accrued since his trade with Satana. He counted the years—five—six—nearly seven years, and was incredulous.

At least, an intense longing to rest and hide, and a curiosity to see his property, brought him with bitter remorse to go back, as Cornwall had entreated. Too late for that strange, seemingly cold youth whose heart in fact must have been a volcano!

A belated caravan, the last one of the year, left Dodge City the 1st of November, and Latch with two pack-horses and a young *vaquero* rode out with it across the bleak prairie.

At the Cimarron Crossing—fateful deciding-point for so many wagon trains, the trail boss took the middle course along the famous river. Latch imagined for this reason he would be spared painful memories. But he was not. At Wagon Mount, where the Dry Trail again met the Old Trail, Latch left the caravan and headed south.

Jim Waters had been the scout and boss of that big west-bound caravan, a fact Latch had not been aware of until the start was made. Then it was too late. He sensed Waters' curiosity and suspicion. There was nothing for him to do but be frank and friendly with freighters and plainsmen, and around the camp fire. As always, he made a favorable impression. Nevertheless, Jim Waters kept aloof. At Wagon Mount, when Latch got in his saddle to ride after the *vaquero*,

Waters strode up with a sharp glint in his plainsman's eyes.

"Wal, Latch, you're off, eh?"

"Yes. Sorry I have to part company with such a fine caravan," returned Latch, easily.

"Wild country south of hyar. . . . Must be friendly with Satana?"

"I bought Latch's Field from Satana. . . . So far he and his Kiowas have tolerated me."

"Ahuh," rejoined Water, bitingly. "Wal, I'll report at Fort Union thet thar's *one white man* the bloody old devil tolerates."

Before Latch could retort the scout wheeled on his heel to stride away. Other freighters had heard that parting shot. It was what Latch might have expected; nevertheless, a grave and thought-provoking circum- stance. Could he ever live down suspicion? Could he obliterate the shadow upon his past? Could he ever forget the stealthy steps upon his trail?

To Latch's surprise and regret, he found a road of well-defined wheel tracks leading out of Wagon Mount, in a southeasterly direction. Caravans from Texas, instead of taking the old trail up to the Cimar- ron Crossing, evidently had climbed the plateau. He wondered if that road bisected Latch's Field.

Latch's desire for loneliness increased as he rode over the gray landscape. If the Kiowa Valley where he had located his ranch ever became populated, he could retire at will to the solitude of Spider Web Canyon. His fears seemed ungrounded, however, for the well-defined road gradually faded into various wheel tracks, old and dim, covering a wide belt. And he decided that separate wagons traveling at different times had made the tracks. Several times he was at a loss to keep to the old trail he knew. His Mexican rider had never been in that part of the country. Latch had to be his own guide, a fact which slowly began to dawn upon him with interest.

He had packed a number of canteens. There were springs and water-holes on this route, and the season was late fall when they ought to be full, but he did not take any risks. The first day away from Waters' caravan passed so swiftly that Latch was overtaken by sunset before he realized the passing of the hours. Dry camp was made near a brushy plot from which a meager quantity of firewood could be procured. The Mexican was lazy, but a cheerful whistling companion. Latch lent a hand to tasks he had once liked, and now for several years neglected. He found himself presently conscious of a vague pleasure in breaking dry sticks, in kindling a fire, in the smell of smoke, in the necessity of using his hands.

Dusk soon mantled the shallow basin. Coyotes ranged about, yelping and barking, and the mourn of wolves emphasized the loneliness. Unconsciously old associations wedged into the insulated poverty of his thoughts. Away from men and noise, out in the open, under the velvet dome with its white stars he seemed to be worked upon by inscrutable forces. But he did not give much heed to these or any sensations. He made his bed and rolled in his blankets with a feeling

that it did not matter whether a Comanche toma-
hawked him or not. And, tired out, he fell asleep.

The *vaquero* awakened him. Day had come, cold
and raw, yet welcome despite things he did not ana-
lyze. How good the fire felt! and the savory odor of
ham made his mouth water. After all, he could not
help these sensations. He was still alive in flesh. Nature
made her old demands. Before sunrise they were on
their way.

At once Latch's interest was roused. Deer and wild
mustangs covered the bleached plain. After the sun
had been upon him for an hour the raw cold tempered.
He remembered that he was traveling south, away
from the blizzard zone of Kansas. They had good
horses, and the pack-animals, lightly burdened, kept
at a trot over the rolling land. When Latch topped
a rise of ground to see dark blue domes of mountains
to the southward he sustained a singular thrill. He remembered that range. So clear and sharp they looked,
scarcely ten miles distant! But he calculated they were
seventy-five or a hundred. Somewhere along their base
sloped the plateau which Spider Web Canyon cut
through in its dark deep defiles. Straightway Latch
became thoughtful. He was taken out of himself. He
rode on eagerly, watching for other landmarks he
knew. When they rode down into a thicketed swale
Latch regretted the vanishing of the sunset-flushed
patches of snow on the distant peaks.

He had camped in that swale with his band and
three hundred Kiowas. Were the gray and black circles of ashes, the remains of camp fires he had known?

But these had been lately burned. And six years had passed by since he had camped there.

Before the *vaquero* had wholly unpacked Latch had shot a deer and wild turkey. Again he was annoyed and puzzled by odd pleasurable sensations. Still these did not inhibit the camp tasks he set himself. He wondered vaguely. Once he thought with a pang how he missed Cornwall! Henceforth all the rest of his life he must be alone. It struck him as something impossible for a sane man to endure.

The third or fourth day from that camp, when the westering sun had gone down behind the purple range, the trail Latch rode with an ever-increasing impatience that left his *vaquero* far behind let out abruptly upon the rim of a high bluff.

A gray triangular-shaped valley, vast in extent, widening away from him, and wondrously beautiful with its silver and green parks and pastures, its round-foliaged, tree-dotted ridges, spread away from under him in a vast field. It was Latch's Field. Violent pangs assailed his breast. He had come back. The impossible was realized.

Only the upper reaches of that lovely valley had been changed. Long gray-roofed ranch-houses lay hidden in the velvety green. Barns and sheds were more wholly concealed; bright little lakes rimmed by willows shone out of the green; lanes and patches of gold puzzled his searching eye until he recalled his favorite among plants—the sunflower. Fenced pastures of hundreds of acres stretched down to the open prairie.

Across the shining stream, however, still greater

change riveted Latch's eye. Houses, cabins, shacks, tents! He was nonplused. What had Keetch been about? Only a moment, however, did it take for the significance of what he saw to dawn upon him. A village, a settlement on his own field! Rage possessed him. And for the spell of a few moments he cursed Keetch and all who had come unasked into his lonely paradise. Soon it came to him that two miles, perhaps more, separated the ranch-house from this eye-sore of a town. Keetch had preserved his field. All habitations as far as Latch could see lay beyond the stream, at the base of the waning slope on that side.

Latch rode down the zigzag trail, a prey to emotions. His disappointment seemed all the more intense because of his astonishment that he could care at all.

His first impulse to kill Keetch slowly faded. What a marvelous place! Maxwell's ranch-house was more commodious, more like a feudal baron's fortification, but could not compare with this for beauty. Latch rode across the level, nearing the ranch-house and the huge walnut and cottonwood trees which stood in stately isolation. A wide porch, evidently at the front of the house, faced these great trees. All in front there appeared to be as green and smooth as if it were a well-tended park.

No person showed in sight anywhere on this side. Nor was there a horse or cow. Latch saw squirrels and long-eared rabbits and deer that paid no attention to him. Halting before the wide porch, he hallooed. No answer! As he dismounted he saw his *vaquero*, and the pack-animals silhouetted against the skyline on the bluff. Latch called again.

This time a little girl with red-gold curls came running out to fix dark, wide eyes upon Latch.

Chapter X

A MEXICAN woman followed the child out on the porch. Latch was about to hail her when a white woman, pleasant of face and buxom of form, came to the door. She gave Latch a look, then, obviously startled, she disappeared within. Latch heard her call, and presently a deep voice and the thump of a crutch gave him thrilling expectation of his henchman, Keetch.

The man who appeared was indeed Keetch, gray and grizzled now, but no longer stern of face and hard of eye.

"My Gawd! if it ain't Latch!" he boomed, with incredulous delight. And he stumbled in his haste to cross the porch.

Latch dropped his bridle and met Keetch at the steps, where they gripped hands and locked glances. Latch felt and read the loyalty he had always gambled upon in this outlaw.

"Howdy, Keetch," was his greeting.

"Wal!—I be'n lookin' for you every day these last two years. An' I shore am glad to see you, boss," replied Keetch, warmly. "Git down an' come in, chief. We've shore got some surprises fer you."

"Just a moment—Keetch," rejoined Latch, panting a little. "One thing—at a time."

"Air you alone, boss?" queried Keetch, in a lower tone.

"Yes, except for a Mexican. . . . There he comes with my packs."

"Ahuh, I see. . . . Wal, thet's good. We've got enough men hangin' around hyar now."

"That so?" returned Latch, easily. "Come out, Keetch." Then across his saddle while he loosened the cinches Latch bent penetrating gaze upon this trusted ally. "Wonderful house, Keetch. How'd you ever build it?"

Keetch beamed. "Wal, thet's shore a story. Mebbe you didn't know I was once a carpenter. Before I become a gentleman rider of leisure. Haw! Haw! All the same I was. An' it come in handy hyar. Latch, I was nigh on three years on all the buildin'. An thet with plenty of help."

"You don't say! I'm amazed. Where did you get the lumber?"

"Floated it down from Spider Web durin' spring freshets. The walnut we cut hyar in the valley. Ripsawed every board! Damn few nails used, 'cause we didn't have them. An' you gotta give Benson credit—as much as me."

"Who's Benson?"

"Gosh! Didn't I tell you when you was hyar last? I guess not . . . wal, Benson an' his wife rode in hyar—lemme see—seven years ago this last spring. They escaped a Comanche raid down on the Red River, got lost, an' wandered in hyar. I reckon without them I'd never have made a go of it. Mrs. Benson is shore a darn fine little woman. It was she who took care of your wife when ———"

Latch had prepared himself for rending words and facts, but at the first wrench of the old wound he held up a hand.

"Bensons, eh? . . . So I owe them something. . . . They have shared your work and lived with you?"

"Wal, I should smile. Made home out of this ranch. Why, man alive, you'll be knocked off your pins when I tell you all. . . . But Benson, figgerin' on the future, staked out a ranch below an' works thet at odd times."

"Leighton?" queried Latch, sharply.

At this juncture the *vaquero* rode up with Latch's pack-animals. Keetch directed the Mexican to throw the packs on the porch and take the horses around to the corrals. Then Keetch, leaning closer to Latch over the hitching-rail, and with slow cautious look all around—an action that awakened old associations in Latch—continued in a whisper:

"Leighton rode in hyar a couple of years after you left. Wintered up Spider Web. Come back now an' then for a couple of years. An' seein' the drift of Latch's Field, he built himself a big place out hyar across the crick. An' he has been runnin' a saloon, gamblin'-hall, an' hang-out for men who don't like the Kansas plains in winter. Haw! Haw! Do you savvy, boss?"

"I think so," replied Latch, thoughtfully.

"Leighton has his cronies—as bad a lot as we ever

traded with," went on Keetch. "I'm wonderin' if you knowed Bruce Kennedy?"

Latch repeated the name. "It's familiar. But he was never in my outfit."

"Bad hombre! An' there's Smilin' Jacobs an' Wess Manlay. These three are Leighton's bosom pards. Besides thet, some of your old hands are hyar for the winter. Jerry Bain, Seth Cole, Tumbler Johnson, Mizzouri, an' Plug Halstead."

"Good men and true, except Halstead. Mizzouri is the salt of the earth," mused Latch. "I should have expected this. But I never thought—I never thought . . . Who else, Keetch?"

"Aw, there's a score of men whose names I never even heerd. An' across the ridge in the next valley— ride of a few miles—Jim Blackstone is winterin' with his outfit."

"Hell you say! I don't like that," flashed Latch.

"Wal, it's so. You gotta make the best of it. I'm bound to admit they make no trouble for us. They're hidin' out, boss."

"Do these strangers know of Spider Web Canyon?"

"I reckon not. An' they wouldn't go up there if they did. Satana has been winterin' in Spider Web. I'm tellin' you, boss, the old Kiowa has no use for these strangers. But he lets them come an' go."

"Do these strangers associate me in any way with the Kiowa?"

"Not atall. Leighton is close-mouthed where his own hide is concerned. It has jest gone out over the range that any man is welcome at Latch's Field."

"My own words!" ejaculated Latch, throwing up his hands.

"Shore. An' it's gonner be embarrassin'."

"Rather . . . Keetch, how many times has Hawk Eye come to you with packs and letters from me?"

"Six times. I don't need to count. An', boss"—here the outlaw again glanced about warily, as if he could not trust even the air—"every damn bag you sent is safe hid."

"In the secret cave in Spider Web?"

"No, by gosh! I couldn't risk that. Leighton knows there's rum an' treasure hid in Spider Web. He goes up there every spring an' fall. To fish an' hunt, he says! Bah! At thet it may be to hunt. But not for meat! . . . So I couldn't risk Spider Web. . . . Boss, I dug a secret cellar under this hyar house. An' all you sent is hid there. I didn't trust even Hawk Eye."

"Old man, you're a good and faithful fellow," returned Latch, feelingly. "So here I am, Keetch. Back for good! The great ranch and money to buy what I want—live as I choose. Go even Maxwell one better! But for one thing!"

"What's thet, boss?" asked Keetch, hoarsely.

Latch whispered. "The shadow of Bowden's lost wagon train hangs over me. . . . Keetch, the scouts and plainsmen look on me with suspicion. It may be Kit Carson's step I hear on my trail."

"My Gawd! Latch, thet's shore bad news. . . . You gotta quit Satana!"

"I have quit that old deal."

"Latch, you've pulled your last deal of any kind on this border—except honest."

"You speak my mind, old timer. From now on it's another kind of a fight—to live down the past. But let that go for the present. . . . Who else drifted into Latch's Field besides our undesirable comrades?"

"Latch, you'll be glad to know your valley has held a lot of settlers who happened across it, one way or another. I reckoned the other day thet there was fourteen honest settlers in the valley. An' all ranchin' it an' lookin' to the future. Thet doesn't count Jud Smith, who keeps a store hyar an' trades with the Injuns. An' Rankin, the blacksmith, who has two sons. An' Hep Poffer. He's a farmer an' a grafter of fruit trees. He has freighted in a lot of trees. You have a fine orchard, boss."

"Honest men . . . pioneers!" exclaimed Latch, overcome. "Keetch, do these honest men *know* Latch's Field is a rendezvous for outlaws?"

"Wal, if they do, they ain't sayin' so. Benson shore knows, though I never told him. But I reckon it wouldn't make a sight of difference to any of them. Thet is, up to now."

"Keetch, you intimate that Latch's Field has a future."

"Boss, it shore has."

"To what do you attribute this trend?"

"Wal, since the war there's been a boom. It ain't only the broken-down soldiers who're emigratin'. Take this Chisholm Cattle Trail. Have you heerd of thet?"

"Rather. I just came from Dodge City, which is the

western terminus of Chisholm's Trail. From a sleepy freightering post, Dodge has leaped to a roaring metropolis. They burn daylight there. More hell in Dodge in one hour than any night sees in another Western town!"

"I can jest figger thet. Wal, the cattle herds comin' up the trail have had somethin' to do with the turrible growth of Latch's Field. Haw! Haw! . . . You see, boss, it's only around hundred an' fifty miles as a crow flies to where the Cimarron crosses the Chisholm Trail. An' mebbe another fifty miles down the trail to Camp Supply, an army post. The North Fork of the Canadian River crosses the Chisholm Trail there. A wagon road runs now up the North Fork, for the most part, an' comes right up into our valley. Spider Web Creek is one of the heads of the North Fork. Thet accounts for most of the travel up this way. Of course the caravans don't tackle it. But a lot of wagons come along, sometimes single, an' then in twos an' threes. A few of these settlers have stuck. Webbe an' Bartlett air both married Injun fashion, one to a Kiowa squaw an' the other to a Cherokee. Some of the other settlers have families. They're darn good fellars to have around us—*now*."

"It's a bitter pill, Keetch. I don't see just why. But I swallow it. I'll make the best of everything. One more question about them. It's cattle, of course, these settlers expect to realize on?"

"Shore. An' it's good figgerin'. Cattle will dominate the West. Soon as the buffalo air killed off. Thet's goin' to be the hellenest time this old border will ever have. I see it comin'. The Injuns will fight for their buffalo. Poor devils. I shore don't blame them. An' in the end it'll be the buffalo-hunters, not the soldiers, thet'll lick the Injuns an' make possible the openin' of the West."

"Keetch, you've got a long head," replied Latch, admiringly. "I've forgotten my instructions about cattle, if I ever gave any. What stock have I here in the valley?"

"Wal, I cain't say correct. Around ten thousand head of cattle an' mebbe a thousand of horses. I hate sheep an' hope you won't throw them on this range."

"So much! Well, I'm a rancher before I knew it. Who runs all this stock?"

"They don't need much runnin' in this valley. Not yet. Lord knows what'll be needed when the hoss an' cattle thieves come. Which they will! At present all our help except the Bensons is Mexican. They're cheap an' they're good."

"Keetch, all wonderful news! I won't attempt thanks now. And that'll do for the present. . . . I'll be in—presently . . . after I spend a little while—by Cynthia's grave. . . . You've cared for it—of course?"

"Shore have, boss," returned Keetch, hurriedly. "It's right there, under the first big walnut, all fenced in an' kep' green. Flowers, too. But the frost will nip them soon. I seen the walnut leaves fallin' today . . . No, boss, we never forgot. An' Mrs. Benson an'—an' Estie. . . . Boss, wait—I—I got more to tell."

Latch waved him silent, and strode slowly toward

the huge walnut tree. The sun was setting. Rays of gold filtered through the foliage upon the greensward. Through the trim pickets of a little fenced inclosure the golden light shone upon a stone headpiece. A rabbit slipped between the pickets and hopped away. Leaves were falling, like flakes of yellow snow. Latch was conscious of faint sounds at a distance—the bray of a burro—the low of cattle—the languorous music of a guitar.

He leaned against the huge, brown-barked tree and gazed down into the little inclosure. Narrow green mound—crude monument—blossoms smiling pale-gold from the grass! His heart was oppressed. There seemed to be great strain and strife within his breast, as if long-strangled emotions were awakening to a poignant present. This vigil would not be what he had feared. He was going to endure it. Cynthia! All the loveliness, all the sacrifice and atonement, the passion she had given him, lay interred here. Had the wild life he had led killed his grief, his repentance? His breast labored with a dull pang. But he did not feel acute, alive, vibrant. This grave was the end of his journey. His tremendous will to go on found no impetus here. He had only to get back to Latch's Field to realize he had nothing left to live for. So his journey had indeed been a *journado del muerto*. What could a ranch that rivaled Maxwell's be to him now? In that moment Latch would have told Kit Carson who had been responsible for the loss of Bowden's wagon train. What could the gaming-table mean to him henceforth? There was no rest, no hope, no peace, no work, no good, no use for him any longer on the earth. And a long shuddering sigh of resignation escaped his lips.

At this moment something encircled his leg. He looked down to see the little girl who had run out upon the porch. Her head with its red-gold curls reached to his gun-sheath. She was looking up at him with the wide dark eyes that had struck him at first sight.

"Little girl, please go away," he said, kindly. "I wish to be alone."

"Daddy," she replied in a low, flute-like voice.

"My child, I'm not your daddy," returned Latch, vaguely perturbed.

"I'm Estie. Didn't Uncle Keetch ever tell about Estie?"

"No. Uncle Keetch never did. He's a very poor letter-writer. . . . Please run away now, Estie. . . . This is the grave—of one very dear to me."

"Oh, I know," she said, in grave wistfulness.

"Child, what do you know?" queried Latch, strangely impelled out of his dark mood.

"I love her, too. Every day I come here."

"That's good of you, Estie. Thank you. I—I. . . . But, child, why do you come here?"

"It's my mamma's grave."

Latch heard. His reaction was not instant. When that message reached his brain it seemed to be a paralyzing terror.

"I'm Estie. Uncle Keetch sent me to tell you," the child said, earnestly.

Latch's lips barely formed the hoarse whisper.
"Estie—who?"

"Estie Latch. My name's Estelle, but Auntie Benson calls me Estie. She teaches me. I was going to
write you to come home."

"God in heaven!" whispered Latch. He knelt to
take the pretty face between his shaking hands.
"Child, who—are—you?"

"Estie Latch," she replied, softly. "Don't you believe? I was born here. I'm nearly seven years old.
. . . This is my mother's grave. . . . You've been so
long coming home, Daddy."

Then the agony that gripped Latch seemed pierced
by the almost incredible truth. A last slant of sunlight
fell upon those red-gold curls. How like the hue of
hair that had once waved across his breast! Cynthia's
eyes looked into his. The same dark violet eyes that
had been Cynthia's greatest beauty!

"Call me—that—again," he whispered.

"*Daddy!*" She put her arms around his neck.

Suddenly Latch snatched the child to his breast.
Cynthia's child! There had been a baby. His baby!
A little girl with red-gold hair and violet eyes! And
he was struck to his soul by the ecstasy of the truth,
by the horror of it. This was why the fire and fury
of the frontier had failed to make an end of his life.
Murderer of innocent children, he had the awful fact
to face—a child of his own—the image of the woman
who had loved him, ruined him, died for him. His
own little girl—Estelle Latch! She had her arms
around his neck—a wet cheek tenderly against his.

She had been taught to love her father. That crazy old man Keetch—this woman teacher—had taught the child love. Love for Stephen Latch, partner of the red-handed Satana!

But little Estelle must never know. All the great evil of this unfortunate man burst into new fire to burn away anything or anyone that might destroy the happiness of Cynthia's child. Holding her there, all his passions concentrated into the single one of living for Estelle, to save her, to atone to her for all that he had made her mother suffer. Life would never hold another moment of peace for Latch. Not with that shadow on his name—with that step on his trail! But he prayed for nothing except life, courage, cunning to meet all issues.

A thousand thoughts, ideas, plans, whirled through his mind. He could leave the child to this kind woman and go out to be hanged as he deserved. Impossible! She had learned to love her father—had waited for him—had looked at him with Cynthia's eyes. He could never leave her. Nor could he take her and go to a far country. No! Latch's Field held too much to leave. Cynthia's spirit seemed to call upon him to keep Estelle there in the purple land where she had been born of such a tragic and beautiful love. Estelle would be her mother all over again. She would be a flower of the West; she would love the West; she would become a factor in the progress of the West.

Latch sat with the Bensons in his big living-room.

The Lost Wagon Train

A bright fire blazed in the huge stone fireplace. Outside, the November wind moaned under the eaves with a portent of storm.

Alec Benson was about forty years old, a sturdy farmer from Pennsylvania. His wife was younger, a comely strong woman, fit for a pioneer's wife. They had come West to grow up with the country.

Latch had listened silently to Mrs. Benson's story of Estelle's birth and Cynthia's death. If he had not rushed away that night long ago, mad in his grief, he might have saved himself six years of vicious life. He would not have had so much more crime to live down. He would have had Cynthia's child to comfort him.

The part of the woman's story which troubled Latch most was her iteration of the fact that Cynthia had tried desperately to leave a message. But she had died trying. Letters—birthright—fortune! These disturbing words were all Mrs. Benson could distinguish. Latch put the thought-provoking words out of his mind for the present. That they would bear future fruit, far-reaching and important, he had no doubt.

"I owe you much," he said to the couple. "My thanks must show in deeds, as your goodness has shown in service to me. . . . Benson, if you came West to make your fortune, you need go no farther. You can make it here with me. We are on the ground first. Take your place as superintendent of my ranch, and meanwhile develop ranch and cattle of your own. Will you accept?"

"Will I? Why, Mr. Latch, I'll be the happiest and luckiest man alive," returned the farmer. heartily.

"It's settled. You will live here with me. Later we will talk of plans to improve the ranch and develop for the future," replied Latch, and then turned to the man's wife. "Mrs. Benson, your kindness to Cynthia can never be repaid. Nor your mothering of my little girl. But if you will go on with Estelle's education I'll repay you well."

"I would do all I can for nothing," rejoined Mrs. Benson, her blue eyes bright and warm. "I love Estie. She is a strange, adorable, wonderful child. . . . I used to be a school-teacher. I can answer for her up until she's ten or possibly twelve."

"That is splendid. When Estelle is twelve I'll send her to school in the South."

At a later hour Latch sat in his living-room with the men Keetch had summoned. Strong drink went the rounds, and then cigars. Latch sat back and gazed from one to another of these outlaws who had at one time or another been members of his band.

Leighton, barring the deformity of his face, appeared to far better advantage than when Latch had seen him last. He was lighter in weight and cleaner in garb. A soddenness from the bottle and evil courses did not show markedly. But more potent than ever was the man's incrutable force—the dominant passion that radiated from him.

Jerry Bain, the merry little outlaw of whom no stranger would ever think evil; Seth Cole, big, bland, lazy, a man who had drifted into outlawry because it was the easiest way; Tumbler Johnson, the mulatto circus performer, a good friend and dangerous enemy; Mizzouri, the old, drawling, sandy-haired, freckled-faced cowman gone wrong; and lastly Plug Halstead, one of the glinting-eyed fraternity of the border, one to whom trouble had gravitated and only the gun could end—these members of Latch's Band in the past, carefully chosen and fairly treated, had never failed him in the slightest.

"Men, I have a surprise for you," spoke up Latch, after an hour of talk. "You will remember how I always used to come to the point."

"Yes, or come to the draw!" retorted Plug Halstead.

"Wal, chief, shoot," said Mizzouri.

"Latch's Band is no more! It is ended—through. . . . I am asking each and every man of you to turn honest."

The amaze aroused by that request was depicted in the hard faces; the receipt of it in utter silence attested to its shock.

"The rest of my life will be honest," went on Latch. "Devoted to thinking, fighting, living down the past. The odds are against me. It is an open question whether I can succeed. A shadow hangs over me. There is a step on my trail. Kit Carson, Dick Curtis, Beaver Adams, all the scouts suspect me. The plainsmen and trail bosses like Jim Waters *know* I've been leagued with Satana. All of you come under this sinister bar. You've all been under me in Satana's raids. If I am found out you will be found out. So much for the past. We face the future. I can see the day when the

West will not abide the outlaw. Maybe not in our day. But that's not the point. The great drive is on. The empire-building era of the West has started. The freighters will go, the caravans, the plainsmen, the scouts, the soldiers, and with them the Indians, along with every kind of border criminal. What I respectfully call to your attention is the fact, the movement. Not the finished result! None of us will live to see that. . . . Now, speak up, each of you—whatever my statements strike from you."

"Wal, Colonel," began Keetch, sonorously, "I take it you mean this movement on the border will rub out the old outlaws pronto—if they keep on."

"Exactly."

Mizzouri puffed his cigar and eyed the blue cloud of smoke as if it was as new to him as the idea Latch propounded.

"Thar's a lot in what you say, boss. I've always been for you, an' if you're turnin' honest, so am I."

"Sho, Kurnel, I've always done expected to tumble on the end of a rope," spoke up the negro.

"Latch, me an' Jerry Bain was talkin' thet very thing over not so long ago," added Seth Cole, ponderingly. "An' we agreed. . . . The wust about turnin' honest is how'n hell are we goin' to make a livin'?"

"Colonel, you always knew that bein' crooked was forced on me," said Plug Halstead. "It seems to me men of my callin' have to keep on bein' crooked— if it's crooked to throw guns. Suppose I turned over a new leaf. Suppose I became a judge or preacher.

Pretty soon some hombre would come huntin' me—
to see if I could draw a gun quicker'n he."

This sally elicited a laugh. Leighton was now the
only one left to give his opinion, if he had any.

"Latch, your idea is sound," he concluded, with his
baffling smile. "As for me—I always intended to turn
over a new leaf. Probably there couldn't be a better
time for me to try it."

"Settled!" rang out Latch, rising to pace the floor.
"Now for ways and means. . . . This valley will
graze half a million head of cattle—if we keep the
buffalo out. The cattle era has begun. Fortunes are
made in Dodge City. Trail-drivers buy cattle for two
and three dollars a head. Sell them at Dodge for fifteen! That price will go up and up. In a few years
it will be forty dollars. Forty dollars a steer delivered
at Dodge! . . . Men, we'll all get rich. We *are* rich,
right now."

"Boss, s'pose you prove that statement," drawled
Mizzouri.

"We're here first. This valley is mine. As you know,
I bought it from Satana. It is wonderfully rich in
grass, water, climate. Farms will prosper here. Game
abounds. The hills are covered with timber. . . . My
proposition to you all, except Leighton, is this. I'll
start you with a ranch and cattle—say five hundred
head each. A fine start! Also five thousand dollars
each. Bunch together with some Mexicans, and Keetch
here to superintend, and throw up cabins, corrals,
barns. Build homes. Get yourselves wives, even if

they have to be squaws. Work. And live down the past."

Keetch made a great thump with his crutch as he got up to support his master.

"Fellars, it's a grand idee. Any man of you can see the sense of Latch's plan, as wal as his generosity. Come! you can all have many years to live yet. Honest years!"

The negro tumbler rolled his great ox eyes. "Marse Latch, I done knowed you wuz a good man. All the time I knowed it."

"Hell yes!" shouted Mizzouri, roused out of his good-nature.

Bain, Cole, and Halstead in quick succession, moved by the fire of the moment, acquiesced dramatically.

"Leighton, you don't need a start in ranching. You are already doing well, Keetch says, on the way to prosperity. Are you with us?" Latch halted to bend eagerly over his one-time confederate.

"Latch, I prefer to go my way alone," returned Leighton, inscrutably. "But I'm with you so far as the secrecy of our old band is concerned."

"You don't join us in this turn to honest living?" queried Latch.

"I will never join any band again," replied Leigton, harshly. "But I approve of the plan. Only I'll make my own turn."

"Fair enough," interposed Keetch. "Let Leighton go his own way—so long's it's honest."

"I agree to that," added Latch.

"How do you propose to placate Satana?" queried

Leighton. "I just lately came down from Spider Web. Was up on a hunt. . . . The old chief is restless. It was our deals, you know, that kept him off the war-path. He'll be hard to handle."

"That will be my job and my expense," declared Latch.

"Here's a harder job. What to do about the, well, men of our old calling who come heah, more and more of them, every winter."

"They will be welcome. Outlaws, Indians, every kind and class of men will be welcome. We'll keep open house. We'll hide them, if necessary, feed them, be friends with them. . . . *Only, we have turned honest!*"

Chapter XI

CORNY wrenched his gaze from the set eyes and twitching face of the prostrate trail-driver. Suddenly sick and cold, he turned away.

"He forced you to draw, Corny," spoke up Weaver, the trail boss, in hoarse and hurried tones. "We all seen that. But he was Lanthorpe's favorite an' you know Lanthorpe was already sore at you. Fork your horse, boy, before he gits back."

"We air damn sorry, Corny," spoke up a lean-jawed rider. "None of us had any use for Pitch. He was an ornery hombre. An' he got what he always expected. But as Weav says, Lanthorpe was some kin or other to Pitch. You gotta rustle."

"Wal, I've a mind to stay," drawled Corny as he flipped his gun and sheathed it.

"Yes, an' like as not bore him, too," added Weaver, earnestly. "Don't do it, Corny. I bet it'd make you an outlaw. Wouldn't it, Chet?"

"Shore as hell. And we're jest too fond of you, Corny. If you don't care aboot yourself, why, think aboot us."

"If you put it that way——" returned Corny, ponderingly.

"Listen, cowboy," interrupted Weaver, so relieved that he seemed tense. "We'll keep this from Lanthorpe

as long as we can. You ride down along the river,
back to town. There's a wagon train got in last night,
an' it'll be leavin' this mawnin'. Fall in with it,
Corny."

"Wagon train! Weav, I'll hit the next trail-herd
boss for a job—an' see you in Dodge."

"No, you won't, Corny," returned Weaver, emphatically. "You've wore oot this heah trail-drivin'.
Texas ain't big enough for you, no more. . . . Corny,
don't argue an' don't git sore at me. Take my hunch
an' hit for the West."

"Where?" queried Corny, as if intrigued by a new
idea.

"Anywhere West. Even Californy. . . . Corny,
you've spent six years up an' down this Chisholm Trail
—huntin' for thet—thet brother. . . . Forgive me,
Corny, but this is straight talk . . . you'll *never* find
him. So git off the trail where you've earned so bad
a name for throwin' a gun. Go where you've never
been heerd of—an' begin all over."

"Corny, it's more than straight talk," added the
other driver. "It's sound sense. You're no low-down
hombre of a gun-slinger. Corny, you're good old Texas
stock an' ——"

"You-all win," interposed Corny, coldly. "Don't
rub it in. . . . But where in hell will I go?"

"I was aboot to tell you," continued Weaver.

"Rustle, boss, I see Lanthorpe comin'," spoke up a
driver in the background.

"Ride oot with thet caravan," went on Weaver,
hastily. "They're travelin' west on thet Lyons wagon

road. Go with them—as far as the Canadian River, anyhow. Try your hand at buffalo-huntin'. This'll be a great year for buffs, Corny . . . or better, ride on to Latch's Field. Steve Latch is runnin' Chisholm a close second these days. They say Latch has a wonderful range up on the North Fork."

"Latch's Field! But that's an outlaw rendezvous— didn't we heah? Some stranger rider down on the Brazos."

"Range gossip, boy, so far as Latch is concerned. But at thet in Dodge you heah aboot outlaws holin' up in the bad lands west of the Cimarron. As for thet, Corny, where can you go these days an' not run into gangs of bad hombres? Look at this old cattle trail since the buffalo hide-hunters have got so thick! But back off the main roads an' trails! Thet's your deal, boy."

"Wal, I'm thankin' you-all," replied Corny, and made for his horse, just saddled for the day's drive. He led the horse away from camp, to the bank of the river, where a fringe of willows and cottonwoods soon hid him from sight. As he strode along he concerned himself with fighting the bitter nausea that possessed *his* vitals. Coming to a grove of cottonwoods, he halted to sit on a log and roll a cigarette.

"I wonder if Weav was right aboot Lester," he soliloquized. "I reckon. . . . But all I hoped these years was to find out what become of him. . . . Wal, wal! . . . That'll never be."

The long-lost brother was to become only a memory. Corny experienced a relief at the actual abandoning of a search that was hopeless. He felt glad, too, that the Chisholm Trail had seen the last of him. He had been a trail-driver since he was sixteen. It had suited his wild nature, this roaring cattle drive from the Rio Grande to the markets in Abilene and Dodge. The constant action, the ever-present peril of stampedes, floods, storms, Indians, buffalo, rustlers, the conflict with as fiery, ruthless, and devil-may-care young men as himself, the romance and magic of the greatest movement of cattle the West was ever to know—these had filled out Corny's restless, unhappy life, these things alone could have saved him from becoming a gun-packing tramp. He loved Texas. It hurt terribly to give up the long, endless ranges, the sight of the white *L'lano Estacado*, the fording of the Nueces, the Brazos, the Red, the Canadian, all those rivers so dear to him. But on the other hand it was well that Dodge and Abilene and Hays City were to see him no more. "Corny barks too often with his gun!" an old trail boss had averred. Corny confessed it. All the same he knew more than anyone else how he had been barked at.

Corny smoked another cigarette and then mounted his horse to ride up on the bank where he could see. Lanthorpe's big herd was crossing the river above— a long, moving, spotted line breaking the bright serenity of the stream. Soon a moving bridge of long-horns spanned the space from bank to bank. The drivers were having trouble with the rear end of that tri-angle-shaped herd of three thousand cattle.

"Wal, Weav will shore miss me when it comes to

drivin' the drags," said Corny, with pride. He was proud of his reputation as the best rear-end driver on the trail. Corny gazed once more. This was his farewell to the Chisholm Trail.

A dull thud of hoof on soft ground caught his ear. There was a horse moving down in the willow brake under the bank. Presently he espied the sombrero of a rider. One of the drivers was trailing him. Corny rode back to where he had climbed out, and it was not long before the lean-pawed trailer confronted him.

"What you countin' my tracks for, Jeff?" inquired Corny.

"Jest wanted to say good-by an' hand you this," returned the other, and he handed Corny a roll of greenbacks.

Corny stared at the money and then at Jeff. He was trying to roll a cigarette while engaged in watching Corny appealingly.

"Gosh blast it, pard! Thet was Weav's idea. He knowed you hadn't a dollar. An' Weav said we'd all chip in. Didn't want you to start a new trail without some money. Only don't hit the bottle, Corny. . . . An' Weav says for you shore to write him home at Santone. An' he'll let us all know how you air."

This kind thought of Weaver's, the gift from all his trail comrades, the faith and hope expressed in the wish to hear from him—these broke down Corny's reserve and he bowed his head over his saddle.

"My Gawd! . . . an' I never cared for—nobody— but *him*!"

"Shore. We understood, Corny," replied the other, softly. "An' thet is one reason *we-all* cared so much. . . . Good-by, old man. Weav says to go straight. I needn't tell you to shoot straight."

Jeff wheeled his horse, and piled over the bank so quickly that when Corny looked up he was gone.

"Tell Weav I will," called Corny, hoarsely, down into the shaking green foliage. "Good-by, Jeff."

Corny rode away from the river bank across the flat toward the post. The sun was well up now and warm. Birds flew from the brush and rabbits scampered before his horse. Soon he saw blue columns of smoke and then the outlying gray shacks of Findlay. Corny remembered when the little settlement had once been a single trading-store, a landmark on the long trail of the drivers. A stench of buffalo hides assailed his nostrils. Huge bales of the shaggy pelts lay scattered around. Freighters were busy packing. Corny passed them. He rode on to a camp on the outskirts of Findlay and inquired if a wagon train bound west had passed.

"Left before daybreak," replied a red-whiskered hide-hunter, bending a curious glance on Corny. "Didn't I see you with Weaver's trail herd?"

"You might of. Mawnin', friend," drawled Corny, and turned west on the dusty road. He put his horse to a lope until over a rolling ridge out of sight of the camp, and then slowed to a walk. The long road wound to the west, disappearing here and there over ridges, to come into sight farther on. Evidently it followed a stream-bed, a branch of the river, where

fringe of willows and clumps of trees marked its
course. Corny bent experienced scrutiny upon the
wheel tracks in the road. The caravan was hours
ahead of him. Corny decided to travel leisurely so
that he would not catch up with the train before camp
that night. A long day on the lonely road in which to
think! He had bade the old trail and his driver comrades, farewell. He must by some power of mind
place the deed that had forced him to part with them
far back in the past. He had done that before. And
when he looked up from the dusty road again to face
the vast purple rangeland it seemed with strange
relief, certainly with resolve. Something beyond the
dim bold hills called him.

Midday found Corny topping a high ridge from
which he saw dust clouds rising far ahead and also
behind. The wagon train he was tracking no doubt accounted for the former, but who was raising dust in
the rear? Corny made the acquaintance of what Westerners called a step on his trail. Lanthorpe was quite
capable of sending a posse in pursuit of him. But reflection showed the fallacy of this thought. Weaver
and the other drivers had long ago pointed the big
herd of cattle to the north and somehow they would
circumvent any attempts of Lanthorpe to catch him.

He rode on down the long slope, to a pleasant valley
bottomland, where groves and patches of prairie grass
bright with flowers bordered a meandering brook.
Shade invited a rest. Corny let his horse drink and
then led him across the brook into a grove some rods
from the road. Then Corny retraced his steps and

found a shady covert where he proposed to wait until whoever was raising the dust should pass.

The nook was cool and restful. A noonday breeze rustled the leaves and pleasant sounds came from the grove. He had difficulty in keeping awake. When had a trail-driver ever had enough sleep? In less than a half-hour, however, he heard the clip-clop of two horses on the hard road. His position was such that any riders happening along must pass before he could see them. Presently two rough dark-clad men, astride bay horses, came into sight riding off the road. They had a look trail-drivers were wont to regard with suspicion. Dismounting at the brook, they watered their horses, then led them back of the thicket where Corny lay concealed. Too close for comfort! Yet Corny could not distinguish the low deep voices. He sensed, however, that something was afoot; with his unfailing misfortune and fatality he had gravitated to another incident, probably calamitous. Riders did not dismount and hide along the road just to rest in the cool shade.

Corny guessed that other riders and perhaps a belated wagon belonging to the caravan were coming along. These two men in hiding were highwaymen. Robbery along the trails and roads of Texas in that day was a frequent occurrence.

Keen as Corny was, however, he had not prepared himself for the rhythmic trot of four horses and the rolling sound of a stagecoach, coming also, evidently slowing up at this point for water.

At this juncture, scrape of boots and jingle of spurs

made Corny aware that the two ambushers were coming round in front of the thicket. Corny peered through the brush to see them slink by.

"Steve Latch would pay handsome to git thet gal of his back alive," said one, gruffly.

"I'm leary of the idee. We don't know this country. But let's see how they're heeled before riskin' any more'n a hold-up," returned the other.

They passed on out of hearing. Corny was taut with excitement. He whispered under his breath: "Wal, what the hell have I run into now? Steve Latch's gal!" He got up noiselessly, and bending low weaved to and fro through the thicket until he approached the road. This he could not see, but the near approach of horses slowing to a walk acquainted him with his position. What he wanted to find out was where the two robbers had located.

Corny ventured crawling to the edge of the thicket. From here he could see the road a few rods out, but could not detect the whereabouts of the two men. They must be close, and would presently leap out to hold up the stage-coach. Corny pulled one of his guns, the new Colt. There was a grim little laugh behind his set lips. Fine chance he had of avoiding gun-play! But this deal sent sharp thrills over him.

Suddenly a crash of brush in front sent a hot gush of blood after the thrills.

"—*Hands up thar!*" pealed out a stentorian command.

A girl's scream, pound of hoofs, startled voices, and scrape of wheels attested to a halt. Corny put his head out of the brush. Robbers and victims were just out of sight around the corner of thicket. Corny crawled out, ran with light steps, halted for a deep full breath —then leaped.

This action brought him within a rod of the two dark-garbed robbers, standing with backs toward him, their guns slanting up at the driver and his companion on the seat of the stage-coach. Their hands were high above their heads and the driver still held the reins of the restive horses.

"*Heah!*" yelled Corny at the top of his lungs.

The robbers wheeled with wide sweep of guns. Corny's two shots broke that action. One of the high-waymen discharged his weapon as he fell. The other merely sank like an empty sack released.

"Whoa! Whoa!" bawled the stage-driver to the plunging horses. They lunged to drag the coach beyond where the robbers lay.

As Corny ran along side he caught a glimpse of three white-faced girls and a negro woman whose countenance appeared extremely black by comparison. One of the lead horses on the left side still plunged in fright. Corny reached an iron arm to drag him down. In a moment more the horses were tractable.

"Driver, was you goin' to water heah?" queried Corny.

"You—you ain't with them hombres?" blurted out the driver, evidently gripped by both anger and fright. The negro sitting beside him showed only the latter.

"Nope, I'm all alone," replied Corny, and sheathed his gun.

"——— ——— ——— ——— their lousy hides!" cursed the driver. "You bored 'em, cowboy. You shore bored 'em. . . . Yes, I was intendin' to water hyar. . . . S'pose you lead thet haid team for me."

Corny took hold of a bit strap in each hand, and backed into the shade, drawing the horses with him. Here the driver leaped down.

"Put her thar, cowboy," he burst out, heartily, extending an eager hand. "What might yore name be?"

"Wal, it might be Jeff Davis, only it ain't," replied Corny.

"Ahuh. Mine is Bill Simpson, driver for Latch of Latch's Field."

"Howdy. I reckon you're a powerful careless driver to work for Mr. Latch, if all I heah of him is true."

"Careless? My Gawd yes! Wuss than careless. But it's Miss Estie's fault, cowboy, an' you can believe me," declared Simpson, beginning to unhitch. "Pile off, Moze, an' help hyar. . . . You see, stranger, it was this way. I'm drivin' Latch's daughter an' two of her friends from New Orleans to Latch's Field. We'd never been alone a mite of the way till this mawnin'. We was to start out with Bridgemen's wagon train. But the girls couldn't be got up, an' when they did Miss Estie said we'd hurry on an' catch up with Bridgeman. That is what I was doin' when them hombres busted out of the brush. I seen them hangin' around this mornin'. An' if that thick-set, pock-marked fellar hasn't been at Latch's Field I'm no good at rememberin'."

"Wal, lucky I happened to be restin' in the shade," said Corny.

"Lucky for us. An', say, cowboy, lucky for you if you ever drop into Latch's Field. . . . Soon as I water the horses we'll go back an' have a look at them hombres. . . . Yes, Miss Estie, we're all right now, thanks to this cowboy."

"Please wet my scarf. Marce fainted," replied the same musical voice that had called Simpson.

Corny leaped to take the scarf from the gloved hand extending from the window of the coach. He ran into the brook, and saturating the scarf he hurried back with it to the stage-coach. The same small hand received it, only ungloved this time. Its owner bent over a pale still face lying on the lap of the negress. The third girl sat back limp as a rag. The one Corny took for Miss Latch had red-gold hair waving from under a bonnet that appeared awry. He could not see her face.

"Dar, she's sho comin' to, Mis' Estie," spoke up the negress. "I was scared mos' to faintin' myself. . . . Dar, set up, Mis' Marcella."

"Marce, you're all right. You fainted," said Miss Latch.

"I did? How silly! . . . Oh, you've drowned me. . . . What happened to those—dreadful men?"

Simpson approached to take a peep in. "Aw, Miss Marce, I'm shore sorry you had a scare. But all along you've wanted somethin' to happen. It did. An' it could have been wuss . . . Meet our cowboy friend, hyar—who says his name might be Jeff Davis, only it ain't."

The young ladies appeared on the moment too perturbed to be aware of strangers or introductions. Whereupon Simpson drew Corny out of the shade to the road, and thence on to where the robbers lay.

"Excuse me, Simpson. You search them hombres an' identify them, if you can, while I let their horses go," said Corny.

Corny had vastly more consideration for the horses than for the men. Freeing them of bridles and saddles, he left them free to roll. Then he went across the brook to fetch his own horse, and took his time about the task. Upon returning, Corny found Simpson hitching up the teams.

"Wal, I'll ride along behind you 'til we catch up with the wagon train," announced Corny.

"Cowboy, I'll feel in damn good company," rejoined the driver.

"Please come here, sir," called a rather imperious youthful voice.

Corny seemed forewarned of a stupendous event, but not forearmed. Owing to the tragedy of his brother's life—wholly on account of a girl—Corny had never given in to his natural tendency. He feared girls, distrusted them, and his own vague stirrings. Removing his sombrero and with the bridle of the horse over his arm he approached the stage-coach. If he had ever seen a lovely face before, this pale sweet one, with its violet eyes and red lips, eclipsed the memory.

"Sir, you saved us from being robbed, if not worse," she said, gravely. "Robbery would have been bad enough. We are carrying home a considerable sum of money of my father's. Stephen Latch of Latch's Field. I am Estelle Latch. And these are my friends Miss Marcella Lee and Miss Elizabeth Proctor."

Corny bowed low. "I shore am glad to meet you-all," he drawled, and let a smile relax his set face.

"To whom are we indebted for this rescue?" spoke up Miss Lee, weakly. "I want to thank you—first for saving us, and secondly for the lesson I deserve. I've prayed for something wild to happen."

"Aw, lady, don't thank me," replied Corny, in his easy, careless way.

"But we do thank you," interposed Miss Latch, gravely. "And we want to know who you are."

"Wal, Miss Latch, I reckon it doesn't matter much who I am," replied Corny, and his eyes sought the distant range. "I'm only a no-good trail-driver that lost his job this mawnin' an' I happened to be restin' heah."

"Are those—bandits dead?" queried Miss Latch, haltingly. But she appeared composed and as truly Western as Corny might have expected a daughter of Stephen Latch to be.

"Wal, fact is I didn't see," drawled Corny. "Looks like they was takin' a siesta."

"Mr. Trail-driver, you are pleased to be facetious. Which is certainly not what you were when you jumped out of that thicket."

"I reckon I did 'pear sudden," replied Corny. "Wal,

the fact is, lady, I heahed one of them say your dad would pay handsome to get you back alive. So I wasn't actin' with much compunction."

"How awful!" exclaimed Miss Latch. "Girls, did you hear? Those ruffians meant not only robbery. . . . My father must hear of this, sir."

"Wal, I've no objection to your tellin' him, lady. Only don't rub it on thick. 'Cause there isn't much credit due me for just bein' heah."

"You are a very strange young man," declared the girl, sweetly, and again the wonderful violet eyes took him in from head to foot and back again. "Don't you know my dad would reward you—give you a job —make much of you—for this service to me and my friends?"

"I reckon he would, lady. An' that's why I'll not ride Latch's Field way."

"You will not accept anything for what you have done for us?" she queried, in surprise.

"Wal, nothin' much," drawled Corny, finding this interest sweet as nothing had ever been. "Shore not money, lady. But if you an' your friends are daid set on rewardin' me I'll compromise for a kiss."

"Don't be rude, sir," hastily expostulated Miss Latch, blushing scarlet.

"No offense, lady. I was only talkin'."

"Estie, *I* don't think it's rude," interposed Miss Lee, spiritedly. "I will—if you and Elizabeth will."

Miss Latch looked vexed and embarrassed, but young as she undoubtedly was, she had dignity and

restraint which no romantic sentimentality could upset.

"Marce, this young man is not in earnest," she said,
reprovingly. "Can't you tell that he is teasing?"

"Are you?" retorted Marcella, leaning out of the
coach window.

"I reckon I was, lady," replied Corny. "Miss Latch
is shore tellin' you that it isn't becomin' of a stranger
to spill blood an' ask for kisses in almost the same
breath."

"It's most extraordinary, if nothing else," declared
Miss Latch. "But we are silly—excited. . . . Mr.
Trail-driver, we must catch Bridgeman's caravan for
camp tonight. How far are we behind?"

"Ten miles or so. You can catch up before sundown."

"Will you accompany us?"

"Wal, I'll ride along behind if you want me."

"Please do. We shall feel safer. If only you could
ride ahead, too! . . . Please come to me while we are
in camp. I—I would like to speak with you again."

"Wal, it's a turrible risk, Miss Latch, but I'll do it,"
drawled Corny.

"Risk of what?" she queried, swiftly. "Is there a
sheriff after you or—or ———"

"The on'y sheriff I ever met on the Chisholm Trail
is daid. It couldn't very wal be him . . . No, the risk
I meant is more turrible than trailin' sheriffs."

"Indeed!" replied Miss Latch, her color mounting
in a wave. "Pray let us see if you can dare such terrible risk as bravely as you faced these bandits."

Corny turned to mount his horse. And when he got up the stage-coach was in motion. He rolled a cigarette, noting that his fingers were not shaking. Singular! They certainly had shaken that morning. But somehow this was different. Corny never even glanced over his shoulder toward the spot where Simpson had dragged the bodies off the road. Presently Corny fell in behind the stage-coach and kept about the same distance, except on the upgrades, when he dropped back a little.

It was some time before he realized that no other adventure of his life had affected him like this one. When he discovered that for miles he had not had a thought of anything but this violet-eyed Latch girl he was amused, then chagrined, and finally bewildered. "Gosh! I just bored two hombres an' heah I am dreamin' of a girl's violet eyes an' cherry lips! Dog-gone it! I'm out of my haid!"

He rode on and straightway fell under the magic spell again. She could not be a day over sixteen and she was as lovely as the cornflowers he and Lester had loved as children. He remembered that her hair was gold with a glint of red and that her eyes were a changing purple. But he could not recall the rest of her face. How strange that Weaver should suggest that he ride west to Latch's Field! The idea held a nameless and incalculable charm. But he could never yield to it. Even to watch this girl from a distance was out of the question. He was nothing but a *vaquero* and he had blood on his hands. Somehow never before had he regarded this fact of self-preservation as a crime. Her eyes had dilated and she had averted them. Still, he reflected, she was Latch's daughter. She was a Southerner, surely a Texan. The spirit of the Alamo, the blood of fighting martyrs, might run in her veins.

Corny tried to recall all that he had ever heard about Latch's Field and the man who had made it noted on the border. Somewhere down on the Brazo's at Dean's Store, on the trail to Abilene, and in a gambling-hell, vague range gossip had met his ears, not to be retained. Nevertheless it whetted his curiosity. What kind of man was this Steve Latch? Another Maxwell, no doubt, or a Colonel St. Vrain, or Don Esperanza, or a rich cattle baron like the Chisholms. Corny would have been proud to ride for such a man, if that were possible.

Thus Corny dreamed and thought as he rode on, keeping the stage-coach in sight. Progress had been gradually slower owing to an almost imperceptible upgrade. His habit of looking back had made him aware of the rising trend of the prairie. And every time he looked he felt a regret for the old cattle trail. He should not have regretted it. The Chisholm Trail had given him toil, privation, a quick trigger, and a hard name, and at last had turned him away, if not an outlaw, at least an outcast trail-driver.

The sun was westering low over the bold uneven horizon when Corny espied the caravan wheeling off the road to make camp. The white canvas-covered wagons, the horses and oxen, the meaning of their presence and movement, struck Corny to admiration and respect. Pioneers! Builders! The thought had never before intrigued him. Then the setting was so wild and picturesque. A small herd of buffalo was raising the dust off to the right; deer were retreating into the willow brakes; the little valley was dotted all over with trees; and the setting sun flushed the long grass into rose.

Sight of camp in the making reminded Corny that he had to meet Miss Latch again—a perturbing thing to look forward to. His horse, sensing relief and water and grass, repeatedly broke out of a walk. And at last Corny let him go. The stage-coach rolled off the road down a slight grade, to halt at the first wagons. Corny followed, but, once down in the valley, he swerved to the right to dismount near a big prairie-schooner.

"Howdy, rider," greeted a tow-headed emigrant, cheery and hearty. "Was you with that coach?"

"Shore. I was scoutin' behind. But I can eat with you if you ask me," replied Corny, genially.

"Haw! Haw! You're welcome, cowboy. Throw your saddle an' grab the ax."

Straightway Corny found himself an object of interest to a family named Prescott, consisting of father, mother, grown son, a daughter about eighteen years old, and a lad of ten. Corny guessed they were from Georgia even before he heard them talk. They were solid plain folk bound West to win a livelihood out of the soil. The girl was shy, yet treated him to most complimentary glances. Corny made the mental observation that now, having given up the lonely trail of the cattle-driver he might expect to meet a girl anywhere on roads, at the military forts, the trading-posts and ranches. It was a disturbing thought. Girls never left him to himself. That had always been something incomprehensible. Unless it was because he is a cowboy, wore a huge sombrero and spurs, and packed guns, he had no idea why.

"Say, if you left them guns off you could set down to eat," said the lad, practically, as Corny knelt cowboy fashion to partake of his generous supper.

"That'd never do, sonny. When the Comanches come swoopin' down a fellow wants to be ready," replied Corny, not unmindful of the large dark eyes across the tarpaulin.

"Shucks! The Injuns I've seen wouldn't swoop on nothin'," replied the lad, disgustedly.

"Wal, wait awhile till we get farther west along the river. The redskins are with the buffalo."

"Haven't seen no buffalo, nuther."

"If you look sharp you'll see some tomorrow."

The father of the lad had been late with his chores and was washing his hands at the wagon when another member of the caravan strode up.

"Bill, that stage-coach was held up by bandits back a ways on the road," he declared, loud enough for all to hear.

"Hell, you say!" ejaculated the other, straightening up.

"Yes. Two men follered the coach which was tryin' to catch up with us. They was both shot by a cowboy. Accordin' to the driver, thet cowboy come along

with him, ridin' back a ways. He must be heah some-
wheres. Bridgeman wants him."

"Ahuh. I reckon your cowboy is eatin' with us."

Corny heard it all with lowered face. What was the
use? He must always be a target for notice.

"Aw!" burst out the lad, breathlessly.

Slowly Corny arose to meet the messenger. The girl's
big startled eyes appeared to express what had fascinated her in him.

"Are you the rider who came along with the Latch
coach?"

Corny nodded coolly.

"Boss wants to see you."

"What aboot?"

"Didn't say. I reckon he wants a report of that
hold-up."

Corny allowed himself to be led toward a semi-
circle of wagons. Smoking fires and fragrant odors,
with people sitting and bustling around, attested to
the camp meal. Latch's stage-coach stood at one side
under a tree, with the tongue propped on a branch.
Out of the tail of his eye Corny saw a number of the
opposite sex, but he did not look closer. He did not
like this situation. Still, he supposed he should permit
himself to be interrogated out of courtesy to Miss
Latch.

"Heah's your cowboy, Bridgeman," spoke up
Corny's companion as they entered the circle to encounter several men.

Corny's glance never got any farther than the foremost—a tall rugged Texan with gray eyes like gim-

lets. Corny recognized him, but had never known his name was Bridgeman.

"Dad-gast my soul!" whooped out the caravan-leader, a warm bright smile breaking the hardness of his visage. "If it ain't Corny!"

"Wal!" ejaculated Corny, and it was certain he felt a rush of relief and pleasure.

"I shore am glad to see you, cowboy," declared Bridgeman, extending a huge hand. "How come you're so far off the trail an' the drags?"

"So your name's Bridgeman?" drawled Corny. "Dog-gone! I've heahed of you. An' all the time I knew you! Shore glad to see you again, old timer. An' I might ask what're you're doin' so far off the Old Trail?"

"I sold out, Corny. An' I'm goin' West to grow up with the country."

"Dog-gone! 'Pears to me a lot of good folks are doin' that."

"You bet. Why not try it yourself? . . . Corny we all heahed aboot the little service you did for Miss Latch an' her school friends."

"Yeah? Somehow a fellow cain't fork his hawse or doff his sombrero to a lady without it travelin' up an' down the range," replied Corney, cool and nonchalant, sure of himself now that Bridgeman was going to ease the situation for him.

"Folks, if I wasn't afraid to embarrass this cowboy I'd tell you aboot him. It's enough to say thet he happened around for *me* once, or I wouldn't be heah. But don't ask him no questions."

"Wal, if anyone asks me what a liar you are, old timer, I'll shore answer that," retorted Corny.

Bridgeman turned to the girls edging into the circle.

"Miss Latch, it has turned out thet the hero of your little experience down the road is an old friend of mine," he said, evidently desiring to impress and please. "I'm sorry, though, I cain't introduce him by name. All I ever heahed him called was Corny. . . . Cowboy, meet Miss Estelle Latch an' her friends."

"Good even, Mr. Corny Trail-driver," spoke up the girl between the other two girls.

Corny remembered the voice. But could this be the Latch girl of the stage-coach? Divested of the linen coat and veil and bonnet, standing on the ground to disclose a slender rounded form and a beautiful face, this girl was vastly transformed, if she were the one who had dominated his thoughts all afternoon. Then he saw her eyes.

"Evenin' Miss Latch—an' you-all," he said, composedly, and bowed to the three. "I'm right glad you're safe with my friend heah, Mr. Bridgeman. Funny how neither of us knew the other's name."

"Indeed, it is very funny how some men forget their names," returned Miss Latch. "But my dad always said that names don't count for much west of the big river. It's what you *do* and *are* that counts."

"Wal, sometimes what you do an' are make it good you have forgotten your name."

"Will you walk with us a little?" she asked, sweetly. "We are cramped from sitting all day. And

soon it will be so dark we'll be afraid to venture away
from the camp fire."

"Shore be glad to."

They strolled under the trees and along the brook.
Corny had never before been so free from confusion
in the presence of young women. Nothing was said
about the incident of the day. No questions were asked
Corny. The Latch girl talked about the caravan and
the band of Kiowa Indians, friendly with her father,
that was to meet them at Adobe Walls and escort them
to Latch's Field.

"Oh, girls, Adobe Walls is the most interesting
place," she exclaimed, thrillingly. "There was a terrible fight once. A handful of white men held off hundreds of Indians . . . Mr. Corny, did you ever hear
of that battle?"

"Shore have. It was a humdinger."

"The ride from Adobe Walls to Long's Road, where
we branch off, is about like this. But from there on it
grows wilder and rougher. My valley is the most wonderful place in the world."

"It's all so wonderful," murmured Marcella Lee.

"What a pretty spot!" exclaimed Elizabeth.

They had come to a glade perhaps a quarter of a
mile below camp where the brook, bank-full and bordered by high grass and flowers, appeared to rest and
eddy, reluctant to move on. The water glided smoothly
on, flushed rose by the sunset glow. Horses and oxen
were grazing down the glade.

"It is pretty," agreed Miss Latch, demurely.

"Marce, you rest here with Elizabeth a little. Mr. Corny and I will walk to the big log yonder."

"Well, Estie Latch!" ejaculated Marcella, aghast. Elizabeth giggled. "So that's why you took us walking!"

Chapter XII

CORNY walked beside her as one in a dream. Still he divined that this was to be the most extraordinary event of his life. She was not such a little girl, after all. The small head, crowned with wavy red-gold hair, came quite up to his shoulder. She stepped daintily, lifting her skirts clear of the weeds.

A huge cottonwood tree had blown down to make a bridge across the brook. Though half uprooted, it still kept fresh green foliage.

She put her hands on the log. "If there was a stirrup to put my foot in I could make it," she said, and turned. "Lift me up."

Corny put a hand to each side of her slim waist and tossed her aloft. But she appeared more substantial than he would have guessed.

She smoothed down her skirts and then looked straight down upon him, as he leaned against the log. If Corny had known anything about girls, he would have seen this one was quite pale and very earnest.

"Can you imagine this is a most unusual proceeding for Estelle Latch?" she asked.

"Wal, no, I cain't. But it's shore unusual for me!"

"A trail driver is not used to girls—like me?"

"This heah trail driver is not used to any girls," he flashed, in reply to the significance of her query.

"Marcella and Elizabeth think me a flirt," she went on. "I have fun with their brothers, and we had parties occasionally at school. But I'm really not a flirt."

Corny could only be sure of what she looked like and there was no word in a trail driver's vocabulary to do her justice.

"I reckon you needn't have told me that," he said, and looked away from the penetrating eyes.

After a pause she went on: "So you are not really a no-good trail driver who has lost his job?"

"Wal," he laughed, "I've shore lost my job, all right."

"I saw Mr. Bridgeman when he greeted you. I heard him. He must have a very high opinion of you."

"Aw, he overrates a little service I was lucky enough to do for him," replied Corny, impatiently.

"A service like the one you did for me, probably."

"No. It wasn't like that atall."

"Never mind, Mr. Cowboy. Modesty is becoming to some young men. Mr. Bridgeman established your status to all who heard. . . . But he hinted that no one should *dare* ask you questions."

"Wal, it's not exactly safe," replied Corny, with a smile that disarmed his words.

"I was afraid of you at first. . . . But I'm not now. You're like a boy my dad used to tell me about. A wild strange boy who was killed saving Dad's life."

"Lady, I reckon I'm wild an' strange, all right, but hardly worth your interest for that."

"How did you come to lose your job?"

"Wal, there was a driver who had a grudge against me. An'—I couldn't keep out of his way forever."

"You fought?"

He let silence be his answer.

"Mr. Corny, you hint you're a very bad fellow."

"I reckon I am, dog-gone-it!"

"What do you mean by bad?"

"Just no good, Lady."

"Do you gamble and drink?"

"Wal, I used to—some," he confessed, "till I got sick of it. Always got me into trouble."

"I imagine from one thing you said—that you never ran after the dance-hall girls at Dodge and Abilene . . . Oh, I know all about them."

"No. I never run after them—or *any* girls," he replied, a little stiffly.

"Then—are you a rustler and a horse-thief?"

"My Gawd, no! . . . Lady, I'm not that kind of bad," he replied, bending stern eyes upon her.

"I knew you weren't."

"Aw, what can a slip of a girl tell aboot men?"

"It's something she feels," she rejoined, eloquently, and leaned closer. "Listen. You know who I am. My dad is Stephen Latch, whom you've heard of. Everybody knows him. He is a Southerner and has been on the border for nearly twenty years. I am sixteen years old. I was born in Spider Web Canyon, the loneliest and most beautiful place on earth, I think. All I know about my mother is that she came from the East and belonged to a rich and cultured family. There's a secret about her—she died at my birth—

which Dad promises to tell me when I'm eighteen.
. . . Up until I was ten years old I never was away
from Latch's Field. Mrs. Benson brought me up—
taught me. She has been a mother to me and I love
her. When I was eleven Dad sent me to school in New
Orleans. Oh, how I hated being away at first! But
I came home to spend the summers. And I'm going
home now for good. Dad doesn't know that yet. . . .
Now, Mr. Cowboy, will you tell me as much about
yourself?"

"Aw! . . . It's awful nice an' kind of you, Miss,
givin' confidence to a stranger," he burst out. "I shore
appreciate you. But I cain't understand why you did
—or why you want to know aboot me."

"Because I'm going to persuade you to come to
Latch's Field and ride for my dad," she declared.

"You're what?" he demanded, incredulously.

"I think you can help Dad—and make my home a
happier place," she replied.

"Lady, you're payin' me too high a compliment.
But what aboot your dad?"

"Last summer was different," she went on, swiftly.
"Up to then I was the happiest girl in the world. But
troubles for Dad multiplied. Oh, I can't take time now
to think of them. But they distressed me. Dad thought
he kept them from me. I found out that Dad had
enemies. There's a man at Latch's Field—his name is
Leighton. He runs a gambling-den. Of late years he
has grown rich. Land, cattle, horses, merchandise—he
has prospered. I *know* he is my Dad's greatest enemy."

"Shore. On this border any big man will have enemies. Go on."

"Then, just before time for me to go away to school something dreadful happened. Strangers are always coming to Latch's Field. This one wanted money—threatened Dad with something—I know not what. And Dad shot him! . . . I was there on the porch. Saw the guns drawn. . . . Saw that man fall off the porch—to beat and flap in his own blood—like a chicken with its head cut off. . . . Oh, horrible! It made me sick. I'd seen fights before, ever since I was old enough to remember. . . . Dad was shot, too, but not seriously. . . . Well, I had to go to school again. This last has been the longest and hardest winter away from home. Only two letters from Dad in all those months! I'm worried."

"Wal, I reckon you're borrowin' a lot of trouble, Miss Latch," replied Corny, kindly.

"Since last summer I've felt a shadow hanging over me. I can't explain. It's something I feel. I hope, once I get home, that it will be dispelled. . . . Now, Mr. Cowboy, I've told you my story and asked you to come to Latch's Field. Will you?"

"Just why do you want me, Miss?" he queried, curiously.

"I—I don't know, unless it was what Mr. Bridgeman said."

"Like as not your dad wouldn't hire me. I have no recommendation."

"You have mine," she retorted. "*I* will promise you a job."

"Excuse me, Miss, if I laugh," drawled Corny, amused. "The idee of a kid like you rulin' your dad. I'll bet Latch is another Chisholm or Maxwell, an' maybe more."

"He would do anything for me," she declared, proudly. "He's the best dad in all the world."

"Wal, that's not to be wondered at. But to let you run his ranch an' hire strange riders—umf—mmm, Miss Latch, I cain't see it."

"Never mind that. I trust you without knowing even your name."

"Shore. An' you're a dog-gone little fool. Suppose I did turn out no good?"

"Every word you say strengthens whatever it was that prompted me to ask you. But I cannot go any farther than—ask."

"You make me ashamed, Miss Latch. Fact is, I was only thinkin' aboot sparin' you. I'm an unlucky cuss. Things always hunt me up. Still, the truth is that doesn't prove I cain't help your dad an' ease your mind. . . . So, I—reckon I'll come."

"Thank you," she replied, radiantly, extending her hand. "Shake on that."

He squeezed her little hand, finding it strong and not too soft, surely one that had known work and the pull of a bridle. Without boldness or intent he retained it in his own.

"I'll come, provided you don't tell your dad anythin' aboot me atall."

"Oh, it's only fair he should know of the hold-up, at least. Bill will tell. The girls couldn't keep it."

"I'll take care of Bill an' you keep your friends from ravin' aboot me. Then maybe Latch might take me—on my merits as a trail driver."

"Very well. . . . Mr. Cowboy, you are still holding my hand," she said, as if wondering at the fact.

"Wal, so I am," drawled Corny, not in the least abashed. "You forgot aboot that turrible risk."

"You said *you* would run that," she retorted, with almost a touch of roguishness, and pulled her hand free. "I might let you hold it, but for those sharp-eyed girls. What would they think?"

"Gawd only knows!" ejaculated Corny. "What would anyone think? . . . Miss Latch, I'm askin' your pardon. You see this is the first time I ever met a girl who wanted me to ride for her."

"I'm glad no other girl ever did," she replied, laughingly. Then she grew thoughtful again. "It's getting dusk. We must go. But first—who are you? Please tell me something about yourself?"

"Shore. There's not much interestin' aboot me. My name's Cornwall. I'm twenty-two. Born in Santone. My father run a string of stage-coaches before the war. . . . I—I had a brother . . . Lester. He was much older . . . but we were playmates. Went to school together. Then somethin' turrible happened. We were close friends with another family. The boy in that family was Lester's best friend. . . . Lester was in love with the prettiest girl in Santone. She was part Spanish. . . . Wal, she ruined Lester—betrayed him with his best friend. . . . Lester did somethin' awful. An' he ran away. Mother died, an' father went to war. I never heahed from him again. I worked on ranches till I was fifteen. Then I took to trail drivin'. I was six years riding the Chisholm Trail. Have driven herds of cattle clear to Montana an' Wyoming. Always I was huntin' for Lester. But I never got any trace of him. Reckon he's gone—long ago. . . . Wal, trail drivin' suited me. All day in the saddle an' most of the night, sometimes! The long slow drive, grazin' along. Ten miles a day was good travel. Hot sun— aw, I know these scorchers. An' the *del norte* of the Mexicans. North wind out of a clear sky—freeze your marrow! But the turrible storms an' floods, the stampedes, the roarin' herds of buffalo, the maraudin' Injuns an' the thievin' rustlers, the tough hard riders in every camp an' on every trail—they all seemed to ease me—to call to that fierce wild somethin' in me. . . . An' so, Miss Latch, I grew quick with guns an' patient with the drags—an' by drags I mean the slow, lame, worn-out cattle that dragged behind the herd. . . . I reckon not all trail drivers will speak so fair of me as Bridgeman. . . . Wal, it had to be good-by to the Old Trail. An' heah I am, Miss Latch, shore lucky at last, an' swearin' you will never regret your faith in me."

"I shall not. . . . Oh, what a sad and wonderful story! You must tell it all to me some night when the *del norte* blows and we are sitting beside Daddy's great fireplace. . . . It is almost dark. Help me down. Where are those girls? If they ran off, I shall murder them. . . . Mr. Corny Cornwall, I declare if you are not holding my hand again."

"Dog-gone! I'm shore absentminded," drawled Corny, ruefully. "Wal, heah come your friends, I'll bet huntin' you up. Lady, I reckon I want to run."

"Please don't. At least leave me my hand . . . Stay, Corny! They will be merciless. . . . Hello, girls! Here we are. We've been waiting—the longest while."

Corny camped with the family from Georgia and made himself useful during the four days' ride to Long's Road.

He saw but little of Miss Latch and her friends, an omission partly owing to his reluctance to approach Miss Latch again. He thought of her all day long, watched her from a distance, longed to go to her. But the one time he did venture to visit her camp fire there were feminine members of the caravan present, besides her girl friends, so that he had only a greeting from her. This seemed a little cool, he thought, and her dark, doubtful eyes on him further rendered him diffident.

On the fifth day, however, when the wagon train went on, leaving the Latch stage-coach and occupants to the escort of Kiowas, Corny learned a little more about the complex nature of girls.

"Good mawnin'," drawled Miss Latch, imitating him as he led his horse by the coach. "We thought you had gone with the caravan—and the big-eyed girl from Georgia."

Corny was as one thunderstruck. He stared at Miss Latch. Her face appeared a lovely mask. It seemed to deny all that he had built upon. Astounded, bewildered, he could only resort to the nonchalance of a trail driver.

"Mawnin', Miss Latch. . . . Shore I'll catch up with them before they get over the hill."

A little later, while fumbling over his saddle-cinch, utterly at a loss for what to do and cursing his stupidity, he was confronted by an entirely different Miss Latch.

"You don't mean it? . . . You're not going with that caravan?" she demanded, in a low and furious voice. In all his life Corny had never gazed into such blazing, unfathomable, wondrous eyes.

"Wha-what?" he stammered.

"You couldn't be so—so unkind. Such a liar! . . . Oh, I've watched you night after night—talking to that Prescott girl. She's very pretty and nice. I met her. I don't blame you. I can make allowance for you. My camp fire was always surrounded. But to desert me now—after promising to come help me—and Dad— oh! that would be despicable! . . . For a country girl with red hands and big feet! . . . Oh, I wondered about you!"

"Yeah. So you wondered aboot me, Estelle?" drawled Corny, thrown suddenly into a blissful paradise.

"Yes, I did," she cried, nodding her bright head until the red-gold curls danced. She was only a child. Her eyes burned dark reproach. "All that blarney of yours about so little knowledge of girls! Oh, I'll bet you have been a devil with women."

Corny looked across his saddle at the lovely betraying face and he thought that it was well his horse stood between the girl and him. Something like a bursting comet scintillated in his mind.

"Estelle, a fellow can fall so turrible in love with one girl that he runs ravin' to another," he said, deliberately. And then the instant that unwitting and astounding speech was out he stood appalled, actually trembling in his boots.

"*Oh!*" she breathed. "I—you—" she gasped. The purple flame vanished from her eyes that dilated, grew wide and round in wonder, and suddenly fell as a tide of crimson flooded up from her neck to cheek and brow. Then she fled.

Corny rode out in front with the Kiowa guides, one of whom, a magnificent Indian, surprised him by saying:

"How, cowboy. Me see you Dodge. Me Hawk Eye."

"Wal, howdy yourself, Hawk Eye, old scout," replied Corny, who was in a state of mind bordering on delirium. At this moment he felt hilarious; the next he was sure to plunge to the depths of misery. Then he would be cold and again hot. He had a madness to run his horse out on the prairie, only there was something binding him to that stage-coach.

Hawk Eye was not loquacious. Corny soon exhausted the Indian's stock of English, or at least all he chose to divulge. Corny knew Indians pretty well, and he was not one of those Westerners who believed the only good Indian was a dead one. Hawk Eye had been well named, so far as his eyes were concerned. His bronzed lineaments appeared to mask wonderful experience and cunning. Corny decided to cultivate Hawk Eye.

The road wound through one narrow valley after another, following a stream Simpson had called Major Long's Creek. A detachment of soldiers under Long had worked out this route in 1859. It did not appear to have been traveled much and in some places the stage-coach made but slow progress. Corny was not sure of himself when he thought this country the most beautiful he had seen. The rich golden light on the waving grass, the brightness and color, the reflection of white clouds and blue sky in the streams, the glamour that lay on the lonely purple ridges— these might have been an exaggeration of Corny's state of mind. He was sure, however, of the topography of the valleys, the groves and glades, the deer in the swales and buffalo on the ridges, and the tips of blue mountains that stood up in the notches.

These Kiowas were travelers. They kept their ponies on a trot. When the coach got stuck in a mud-hole or a sandy wash, they got off and dragged it out. Corny likened them to trail drivers. They made upwards of forty miles, Corny calculated, and halted for camp early, in a sheltered oval between hills. Some of the Indians rode off to hunt meat.

Corny had nothing to do but unsaddle and hobble his horse, then present himself to Simpson for camp duty.

"Any good as a camp cook?" queried the driver.

"Turrible," replied Corny.

"Never seen a cowboy who wasn't. Rustle wood, build two fires, one hot, an' pack water."

The young ladies appeared to be having the time of their lives. Miss Latch giggled and played about quite as obstreperously as her girl friends. Corny observed, however, that she studiously avoided looking in his direction, which fact first relieved and then annoyed him.

Presently it was Corny's task to spread a canvas on the ground and get ready for supper.

"Say, girls," he drawled, " 'pears to me, if you-all are goin' to marry Westerners, you oughta learn somethin' aboot camp chuck."

Elizabeth and Marcella came running, only too glad to help, but Miss Latch apparently had urgent business in the stage-coach. She had to be called twice. Corny ate his supper standing at the camp fire, while Bill waited upon the young ladies. They had a merry meal.

"Estie, if you find me a young man as handsome as our cowboy, who can cook as well as Bill, I'll marry him," vouchsafed Marcella in anything but a low voice.

That remark destroyed Bill's equilibrium and put a sudden end to Corny's listening. "Dog-gone!" he muttered. "They shore got me buffaloed."

Still, a little later, he had the courage to suggest that they allow him to spread their blankets under a tree, where they would be more comfortable than in the coach.

"Thank you," replied Miss Latch, coldly. "We'll feel safer inside."

Corny turned to his tasks, effectually rebuffed. Nevertheless, there edged into his dismay and bewilderment a sense of gladness, of charm, in thought of the future. This journey would go on, days on end. She would be there. Already he was serving her. That brazen remark of his to her had been a blunder. Moreover, it was not even true. Suppose she took that for truth! Corny squirmed in his fright. And the next instant stole an unobtrusive glance at this young feminine person who had changed the very current of his life.

Darkness came on, with the Indians smoking round the camp fire. Coyotes began their thrilling chorus. The girls were entranced with it all. Bill coaxed them to go to bed, pleading a start at dawn next day. Finally he grew exasperated.

"Say, cowboy, pack these gurls to their boodwa," he called to Corny, who was making way with the scout Hawk Eye.

"Shore, Bill," replied Corny, placidly, as if the order were a routine of camp tasks.

Like naughty children the girls fled to their refuge, but not before Corny had ascertained that it was Miss Latch who led. "Bold thing!" he heard her say to her friends. "I believe he'd have packed us in as if we were sacks."

"I sort of like that boy," Marcella replied.

Corny sought his hard bed, which consisted of a saddle blanket and a coat. He began to evolve in his mind a cowboy trick to play upon the girls, and was deep in machinations when he fell asleep.

Dawn did not stay for dreams. Another day came and passed, and then four more days in succession, all alike in travel and incident, yet strangely, almost imperceptibly, different. They mounted in romance. Still he kept aloof from the girls, scarcely ever addressing them unless necessary or instructed to do so by Simpson. Marcella and Elizabeth manifested signs that even Corny could not fail to see. He pretended to be wooden, however, and certainly felt easier that Miss Latch deigned him only little notice.

The long succession of ridges seemed but waves of the prairie climbing to the foothills. The morning arrived when Hawk Eye led around their base to a vast tableland, green and blue and yellow, far as eye could see. Black patches out there meant herds of buffalo to Corny. That day they heard the boom of guns and saw Indian riders in the distance. They passed a squatter's hut, and ten miles farther on stopped at Hartwell's ranch, where a pioneer lived with his squaw wife.

Next morning as Corny rode out with the Kiowas he saw a strip of purple land rising above the prairie straight north. This was the northern prong of the bluff that ran down from the foothills, and formed one of the boundaries of the triangular valley Latch claimed as his range. The line of ridges Hawk Eye had been traveling along soon turned abruptly west, and this, Corny decided, formed the southern boundary of Latch's valley. It certainly was a magnificent range. Herds of buffalo showed in clusters out on the rich prairie grass.

Late that afternoon Corny made out cattle, and then he realized he was getting somewhere. Camp that night was made near the first ranch in the valley. Corny was so keen to talk to a cowboy that night that he forgot some of his camp chores. Casual interrogation of this range rider acquainted him with much he never could have learned from Miss Latch.

Before sunrise next morning the stage-coach was hitched up and loaded, with Bill at the reins and the girls gayly excited. Latch's Field only thirty miles! Corny leaned with an arm over his saddle as Bill cracked his long whip. The coach groaned and the wheels rolled. Then Corny, waving to Marcella and Elizabeth, suddenly gave a start to discover Estelle giving him her eyes for the first time since the upheaval at Long's Road. What a strange, dark, wondering glance! It held a long moment. Then she waved a gloved hand and averted her face. Corny was flung aloft to the skies in ecstasy. Did not that look, that farewell wave of hand, signify forgiveness? Could they have meant more? It took many a long mile of riding for him to wear out that mad hope.

Late that afternoon Corny rode alone on the last few miles into Latch's Field. The Indians had gone on ahead. Corny was content to walk his tired horse, to have time to form his impressions. He passed a dozen prosperous-looking ranches and thousands of cattle and horses before he came in sight of the head of the valley. A fine willow-bordered stream flowed down the valley, cutting one-third of its width off on the left, where between it and the gray bluff all these ranches were located. Nothing but open range on his right! The brand on the stock on that side appeared to be an L F. This manifestly was Latch's brand and cattle dotted the whole expanse across the miles of valley to the north bluffs.

Like all the valleys in this region, Latch's headed in a notch under the hills. Only this one was by far the most imposing and beautiful of all he had seen. Green squares attracted his speculative eyes, groves of cottonwoods and ridges with a line of walnut trees marched across to the opposite wall, meadows like parks of golden grass shone against the sunset.

"Dog-gone!" soliloquized Corny, in the rapture of a true rider of the open. "Shore Latch knew what he was doin' when he bought this range from the Kiowas. Prettiest place I ever seen. An' shore a gold-mine if the Old Trail keeps pourin' cattle north."

Soon Corny made out Latch's ranch occupying much of the upper end of the triangle, and separated from the town by a mile or more of orchards and high fences of cottonwood trees. Corny had never seen Maxwell's Ranch, but he would have wagered this one of Latch's would run it a close second. For the first time in his life Corny saw a place where he would like to stay indefinitely. But he admitted he could not be sure this feeling was not caused by thought of the violet-eyed girl who would some day own that ranch. Still, it would have been a pretty nice place even without the girl! Orchards on two sides, big trees and grassy parks to the north, lakes and gardens, and everywhere gray roofs showing out of the green—his experienced eye acclaimed all this a glorious ranch.

Near the town of Latch's Field were a number of substantial log ranch-houses perhaps a half-mile or less apart. All these had been built at one time, as had the barns and corrals. The planting of cottonwoods for shade, and the orchards, indicated the foresight of Latch. The farms adjoining were fertile and well tilled, and farther out great herds of cattle roamed.

When Corny entered the town he saw that Latch's Field was no different from any other Western town in an isolated district. One long wide dusty street was spotted with vehicles and lined by a motley assemblage of buildings new and old, large and small, most of which had high board fronts. Corny rode on leisurely, to pass Indian shacks and Mexican huts, tents white and tents dirty, cabins of various kinds, until he reached the zone of larger buildings. Here he passed a row of saloons. "All same Dodge!" he laughed. "Dog-gone! This heah burg's no place for the future Mrs. Cornwall!"

In the center of the more pretentious section he espied a big signboard upon which shone in large letters the single word "Leighton's." Corny rode by with more than interest, with a return of his old, cold thrill. "Shore as hell I'll bore some hombre in there!" he muttered. Leighton's place was huge. A porch ran along the whole front. "Ahuh. Mr. Leighton runs a whole show." And by that Corny meant store, hotel, trading-post, and a saloon with its vile accessories.

The town appeared to be alive. A few loungers, a few riders, teamsters driving along, groups of dusty-booted men, a pedestrian in his shirt sleeves here and there—all these attested to the leisurely activity of Latch's Field at sunset.

Some minutes later Corny rode down a lane into Latch's ranch. He preferred to go in the back way, as more becoming a trail driver. Inquiry of a Mexican directed him to a huge courtyard surrounded by cor-rals and barns. It bore the action and odor of use, though vacant of riders at the moment. Fine horses were drinking from a pond in the center; from some-where came a sound of running water; burros were braying, horses whinnying, a stallion was whistling. A wide opening in the circle led to a barn, the mag-nificence of which was a climax for all this approach. Corny decided that he was going to stay. And then he laughed inwardly at the thought of how impossible it would be to leave.

A long slant up to the wide-open entrance of the barn led Corny's slow gaze to rest upon riders with horses, and several men. He rode toward them, rolling a cigarette on the way. If the tall man in black som-brero and high-top boots was Mr. Latch, as Corny guessed, this moment was most auspicious. But Corny was never sanguine about meeting men. He always had his mind made up before he confronted anyone. A big bearded man leaning on a crutch, and a bow-legged cowboy, directed the attention of the tall man to Corny's approach.

In another moment Corny did not need to be told which one was Stephen Latch.

Reining in, he shifted a leg over the pommel, always a sign of friendly intent, removed his cigarette, and addressed the trio.

"Howdy." And he looked from the cripple to the cowboy, and then to the man in black. He saw a handsome face, a mask of fine lines, a record of havoc, and eyes of piercing fire.

"Howdy, yourself," retorted the rancher, curtly.

Corny felt at ease. His presence with the Kiowa escort, his rescue of Miss Latch and her companions, had not been divulged.

"I'm lookin' for a job," went on Corny, placidly.

"Talk to Keetch, here. He's my foreman."

"Excuse me, sir. Are you Latch?"

"Of course I'm Latch," rejoined the rancher, impatiently.

"Wal, if you don't mind, I'll talk to you," drawled Corny, with his slow smile.

Latch laughed at the rider's impudence.

"Fire away, son. But you can't fool me. You saw the stage-coach come in."

"Ump-umm," declared Corny. In his second glance at Latch he satisfied himself that he had judged the rancher correctly. No ordinary man could achieve the ownership of Latch's Field. And that invitation to declare himself won Corny's liking on the instant. "I shore didn't see no stage-coach come in. But I heahed some hombre in Leighton's say, 'Latch's trouble is heah,' so I reckoned I'd come over to offer you a handy boy."

"Leighton's!" Latch might have been stung. Then with a laugh he bent penetrating eyes upon the rider. "Thanks, cowboy. But we don't need any riders."

"Aw, you'll always need a boy like me on this heah ranch," returned Corny, coolly.

"Suppose you tell us just why you think that."

"Wal, I see you have a lot of redskin hunters to pack meat in, an' greaser farm-hands to dig fence-post holes, an' you shore have some riders judgin' from this heah nice-lookin' low-laiged chap. An' your foreman is lookin' me over pretty pert, which shows he's not to be fooled by lousy no-good strangers rollin' in."

"Well?" demanded the rancher, sharply, as Corny paused.

"So I just thought you ought to take me on."

"Cowboy, you've got nerve. Get down and make yourself at home. Stay to supper with the men. But don't bother me any more."

"Sorry, boss, to bother you," drawled Corny. "But this is serious for me. I heahed down on the trail that you never turned a rider away from Latch's Field."

"Didn't I ask you to stay to supper?"

"Shore. An' thanks. But I want a job with you."

"What kind of a job?" demanded Latch, his keen eyes studying the rider.

"Aw, I can do most anythin' aboot a ranch that isn't

hard work. But my specialty is heah," drawled Corny, and then, in a flash, there he was extending a gun by the barrel.

"Oh, I savvy," declared the rancher, slowly taking the gun. His mobile hand closed over the butt and Corny knew that he felt the notches there. Then he looked up with a peculiar gleam in his falcon eyes and returned the gun to Corny. "Are you drunk, son, that you brag of gun-play?"

"Nope. I'm not the bottle-lovin' kind, Mr. Latch. I just had a hunch you might need a handy hombre like me. An' if you want to know, ridin' heah to Latch's Field hasn't changed my mind."

The bow-legged cowman gave a snort and, throwing up his hands, strode away into the barn.

"I'm sorry, son," returned Latch, apparently in doubt of both his visitor and himself. "But despite your nerve and your estimate of your worth and my needs—I don't want you."

"No offense, I'm shore," replied Corny, shifting his leg back over the pommel, and turned his horse away. When he got a few paces distant he heard the foreman say to Latch:

"Boss, let me call that cowboy back. Thar's somethin' ——"

Corny distinguished no more. He rode out satisfied that he had gauged Latch correctly. If the rancher had not really been in trouble, had not been haunted by enemies, he would have reacted differently to Corny's cryptic proposal. "Good!" soliloquized Corny, falling into his habit of lonely trail driving. "He shore needs me, but wouldn't take me on. That'll give me a chance to size up this heah town. . . . Wal, wal! An' what'll little Estelle say aboot this? Dog-gone! If I don't miss my guess she'll raise hell with Dad."

Chapter XIII

LATCH'S joy at the return of Estelle, the precious treasure for which he labored and fought and lived, minimized the multiplicity of troubles that assailed him. With Cynthia's daughter in the house, puttering and bossing around, singing new songs, screaming in delight with her girl friends, revealing her love for him in a hundred ways, Latch's spirit leaped to its former heights. Cynthia had been eighteen years old when he met her first, a reserved, dignified young woman—still water running deep. Yet this gay teasing little minx reminded him endlessly of her mother. Her mouth and her voice were Cynthia's.

It was impossible for him not to be happy. Nothing could have killed that deep, rich, wonderful joy except for Estelle to discover the truth about his terrible past. She worshiped him, she believed him a hero of the West, a blue-blooded Southerner who had devoted his life to placating the savages, to making friends with them, to keeping open house for all the wanderers of the range. To her he was good and great—a father to be proud of. Yet Latch lived perpetually in a haunting fear—that his sins would overtake him—that Estelle would find him out. And he would die with his back to the wall to keep his secret.

"Dad, I'm home—home to *stay*!" she cried, with her

arms around his neck. "I'm not going back to that dog-gone school."

" 'Dog-gone'! Surely you didn't learn that lingo in Miss Delorme's school?"

"No, I didn't. And I like it better than French. Dad, I should have taken Spanish. Why, most of your help speak Spanish."

"Mexican, my dear. . . . But you must go back to school with your friends."

"Dad, they can stay only a month. Mr. Lee has already arranged for them to go to Fort Union to travel with an escorted caravan. But I wouldn't go if they were to stay until September. . . . Dad, I've had enough school. I want to stay home—to help you —to share your troubles."

"Why, you darling child, I have no troubles!"

"I suspect you are an awful liar."

"Estelle!"

"Let's not argue now."

Always her slightest wish had been law to Latch. Long ago he realized he had spoiled Estelle, but even knowing it did not change him. All of the frustrated love and passion of his maturity centered in her. All that he thought of was to make her happy. To atone in some slight measure for the tragedy he had brought upon her mother!

"Very well. You shall stay home," he said. "I have thought only of your education. For me it will be glorious. But, Estie, what will you do—after the novelty of being home wears off?"

"It never will. Anyway, I'll ride all the horses, boss

your *vaqueros*, keep your books, run the house—and look round for a husband."

Latch was too nonplused and startled to laugh. Estelle had grown up.

"Husband!" The word was a blade piercing his heart. "Where, for Heaven's sake, will you find him?"

"Where do you think, you goose? Shall I go to Boston to look for one, or back to New Orleans? Not much! I want a big sombrero and a pair of high boots with spurs. . . . Don't look so shocked, darling Daddy. It will probably take me some time. Because he must be like *you*!"

Latch burned under the fire of that innocent expression.

"In that case I will try to possess my soul until such dire event comes to pass."

That conversation occurred the very hour of her arrival. And every time thereafter when she sought him or happened to run across him the effect of her presence was the same. She was a vivid, intense personality, beginning to manifest some of the depth that had characterized her mother. She ruled Keetch absolutely. The old outlaw's eyes had the warm loving light of a spaniel for its master. The Bensons had no child of their own, and Estelle's home-coming was an epochal event for them. Mrs. Benson said to Latch, "Now your old rancho will hum!" and did not explain why she seemed vastly concerned. The Mexican servants in the house, the stable-boys and laborers, the *vaqueros*, all trooped to welcome the young señorita. As if by magic the life of the ranch seemed trans-

formed. Latch's heart swelled. Always he had borne
in mind that this hour would come. He accepted it,
rejoiced in it, and received from it a strength which
braced him to confront the last stage of Stephen
Latch's stormy life.

The great living-room, built of walnut cut in the
valley, with its dining-table for fifty guests, its wonderful huge stone fireplace where oak logs blazed on
this cool spring night, the polished walnut walls
adorned with horns and skins and Indian trappings,
the enormous buffalo bull head over the mantel, the
rugs, the easy-chairs, the wide high-backed divan and
the brightly colored lamps—all seemed to have been
waiting for Estelle, to take on the meaning of home
for some one beloved.

After dinner, which on this occasion had been shared
only by the Bensons and Keetch, they sat before the
glowing logs.

"Boss, did you tell the gurls aboot thet young
rooster who wanted a job so bad?" queried Keetch,
as he settled comfortably for a smoke.

"No, Keetch, I forgot it."

"What young—rooster?" inquired Estelle, turning
irresistible eyes upon her father.

"Some cowboy who rode in while I was at the barn
this afternoon late. Impudent rascal. He declared I
needed him whether I wanted him or not," replied
Latch.

"How interesting!" exclaimed Estelle.

The other girls evinced something even more than

interest. Latch, keen to grasp subtleties, wondered if they knew anything about this young man.

"Keetch, you tell them," said Latch.

"Wal, jest before sundown a young fellar rode into the court," began Keetch, genially, as one who liked to talk. "He came up, said howdy an' throwed his leg across his hoss. I've seen a sight of riders in my day, but never only one thet beat him. . . . Boss, do you remember who I'm thinkin' aboot? . . . Wal, he wasn't as skinny as most cowboys. Built like a wedge, all muscle, an' straight as an Injun. Handsome, too, gurls. Lean face, tanned dark, cut sharp an' fine. Sort of cold, 'cept when he smiled. He didn't take off his sombrero, but I reckon he was tow-haided. An' he had the damndest pair of eyes I ever looked into. You-all shore would have liked him."

"I think we would," agreed Elizabeth Proctor, demurely. Marcella giggled, while Estelle sat straight and tense, anticipating Keetch's conclusion to this long preamble.

"He packed two guns. Did you notice thet, boss?" went on Keetch. "An' darn me if he didn't flip oot one as a callin'-caird. Fact is he struck me like one of them trail drivin' *vaqueros*. Salt of the earth! . . . Wal, this boy wanted a job bad. He was kinda testy aboot it, an' I reckon gave yore dad a poor idee of ——"

"Not at all," interposed Latch. "He struck me most favorably. I sent him away because he reminded me of the same boy of whom he reminded you, Keetch."

"Ahuh. I shore pondered aboot thet. Fust rider you

ever refused, boss. . . . Wal, anyway, he gave us a cool stare an' rode back the way he come. Somehow I was sorry to see him go."

"Dad, is *this* boy really the first rider you ever refused to help?" asked Estelle, swiftly, her color coming.

"If Keetch says so it's so," rejoined Latch, regretfully. "I'm sorry."

"He reminded you of some other boy?"

"Yes, dear, indeed he did. One I loved greatly and owed much."

"Oh, Dad, you've *told* me about him. How strange!" Her eyes quickened and dilated with thought. "Father, it is too bad you didn't hire him."

"Why so?" inquired Latch, with his indulgent smile.

"Because you will now have to hunt up this cowboy and give him the job he asked for," declared Latch's daughter, spiritedly.

Keetch enjoyed this hugely, grinning broadly behind his hand.

"Child, I can't do that. I refused him before Keetch and Reynolds. It was easy to see Reynolds didn't like him. I don't say things, then retract them."

"Father darling, if you don't hunt up this cowboy and give him a job—I will," said Estelle. She spoke too sweetly, too coolly, she was too pale and dark of eye not to be taken seriously.

"Estelle, if you think I was unjust I will reconsider," declared Latch, hastily. "Certainly I would not permit you to ask him. That would make him a marked rider in Latch's Field. But why are you so insistent? This isn't one of your whims, dear."

"Dad, if it hadn't been for this cowboy I wouldn't be home tonight. . . . I'd be out on the range somewhere, kidnapped by two ruffians, held for ransom, because one of them said, 'Latch will pay handsome for his girl back alive!'"

Latch got up to face his daughter. With subtleties and uncertainties over, he reacted to stern facts as he had a thousand times.

"Estelle, what have you kept from me?" he demanded.

She turned quite pale. "Father, at Findlay we slept late—missed Bridgeman's caravan. Bill was wild. But I made him drive out to overtake the caravan. . . . Well, we were held up by two bandits. No sooner had Bill stopped the horses when we heard a yell, '*Heah!*' . . . The bandits whirled around with guns aloft. The brush crashed—a man leaped out . . . Oh, Dad!— He shot—bang—bang! One of the bandits' guns went off in the air. They fell. He had killed them. . . . Oh, it was dreadful! . . . Marcella fainted. Presently I saw Bill had driven off the road into the shade. I called for water. The young man took my scarf, wet it, and we brought Marce to. . . . Well, he was a cowboy—had just happened to be resting there. He saved all that money we had for you, Dad, and *me*. . . . He said he was only a no-good trail driver out of a job. I told him we'd feel safer if he rode along with us. He did so—stayed with us all the way to

Latch's Field. And he—I—well, I asked him to ride for us."

"Estelle Latch! You kept this from me?"

"Yes, I—I didn't want to distress you the very first thing," she faltered. "Besides, he said he wouldn't ask you for a job if I told you. That you'd overrate a little service. Wanted you to take him for himself. I had a time persuading Bill not to tell you."

Latch thoughtfully rubbed a slightly quivering hand through his scant beard. Verily this precious daughter was the vulnerable spot in his armor.

"Mrs. Benson said that now my old rancho would hum," declared Latch, with dry humor. . . . "My child, who has grown up—she was right. . . . But you should have told me at once. I understand the boy. But now I dare say he won't work for me."

"*I* can get him to," replied Estelle, shyly.

"Oh, I dare say. Maybe you had him in mind when you made that—er, remarkable statement today."

"Daddy!" she cried, blushing furiously. "It was only in fun."

"Estelle, we shall make amends one way or another. . . . Now you girls run off to bed. You're fagged out."

Estelle kissed him good-night, obviously relieved and mysteriously upset, glad to run off with the girls.

Latch stared into the fire.

"Gimme a cigar, you —— —— —— of an old outlaw!"

"Haw! Haw! Don't care if I have one myself. . . . Boss, ain't she a little wildcat? An', my Gawd! how sweet! . . . Wal, I'm gonna grow young again."

"Keetch, I've had that thought, too, God bless her!"

They smoked and gazed into the fire. Keetch had grown old in Latch's service. And Latch himself had begun to feel the stress of too full and violent years. They were old tried and true comrades now.

"All for the gurl, Kurnel. I seen thet long ago," said Keetch.

"All for her, old-timer," replied Latch, sadly. "But shall we be able to—to ——"

"So help us Gawd! . . . Boss, thar's only one man livin' now who can *prove* ——"

Latch lifted a hand to enjoin silence or discretion.

"I said prove . . . Kit Carson is daid. Jim Waters is daid. Blackstone an' his gang, Charley Bent, the white-livered renegade—Satana an' his red divils, *all* wiped out last year in thet turrible fight with Buff Belmet's caravan at Point of Rocks. . . . All daid but Leighton—all who could *prove* ——"

"How do we know, Keetch?" queried Latch, clasping and unclasping his hands. "It's not possible that Leighton has not told.

"Keetch, I should have shot Leighton long ago. It may turn out just as well that I haven't. For we may find out what late cronies of his he has told."

"Ahuh. We agree. . . . Kurnel, what struck you hardest aboot this trail driver who rode in on us to-day?"

"He looked like—Cornwall. . . . My God, how it hurt! That boy so like a son to me! . . . Keetch, I'll never forget him."

"Nor I. . . . Wal, thet struck me, too. Somethin'

strange aboot this rider—same as aboot Cornwall. I don't know what onless it's the way they both looked at you."

"Keetch, did I ever tell you Cornwall had a younger brother of whom he often spoke? So sadly—bitterly!"

"Wal, you don't say. Thet's news to me, boss. By damn, it's shore interestin'. A brother? . . . This fellar is bigger. You can see he was born on a hoss. He has the range-rider's eye. A lazy, cool, soft-spoken Texan, young in years, old in trail experience. Boss, the iron hasn't stuck in this lad's soul. Thet's the great difference, if he *is* Cornwall's brother. Reckon we'll never find oot. . . . Wal, an' what aboot him struck you second?"

"He roused that old deadly fear in me, Keetch," whispered Latch, hoarsely. "How I have felt it— fought it all these years! *What does this stranger know?*"

"Shore. We've lived under thet shadow. But hyar we air, Kurnel, kickin' yet. An' Estie is sixteen years old. By Gawd! we'll run the race—we'll finish. . . . But listen, boss. This trail driver saved Estie—more than her life, mebbe. He rode days on end with her. An' you can bet your last dollar thet whatever he knows now or ever finds oot hyar, will never hurt *her.* I love that kid, an' I'd kill any livin' thing thet'd threaten her."

"Keetch, you were always keener than I. You may be right."

Next morning Latch strode down to the corrals to

have it out with Bill Simpson. He found the driver on the bunk-house porch with Reynolds, Keetch, Simmons and some of the Mexicans. Bill knew what was coming, but did not flinch. Latch thundered a wrath that was not altogether genuine. But he had to be Latch still. He called Bill every disreputable name known to the range. Then he spun him around and booted him in the rear. Bill sprawled to his hands and knees. Then Latch booted him again, off the porch this time. Bill hopped up, red in the face, mad as a wet hornet, and exploded while he brushed the dirt from his clothes.

"I can stand thet once, Steve Latch," he fumed, after his profanity was exhausted. "But don't you never kick me no second time!"

"Don't you keep things from me—you damned old sentimental jackass," replied Latch, and called for a horse.

He rode to town alone. It was fairly early and he doubted that the trail driver would be up. Hitching his horse, he went down the familiar street, stopping in at the stores, peeping in the saloons, except Leighton's, which he always gave a wide berth, but he did not find whom he was looking for. Whereupon Latch made a long-neglected visit to his rancher allies, old members of his outlaw gang, who with him had turned honest. Each had been true to that vow. And all were living except Plug Halstead, who had been killed in Leighton's gambling-den the preceding year. They were prosperous ranchers now. Tumbler Johnson was the only negro on the border known to be a squaw-man. Mizzouri had a wife and two children and was happy—a most amazing fact. Latch spent the morning with these old friends, invited them to the party he was giving Estelle on her sixteenth birthday, and rode away, as always, somehow warmed deep down by the truth of what he had brought to these men who at one time lived in the shadow of the noose.

Upon riding into town again Latch espied his quarry lounging in front of Rankin's store, talking to Jim Rankin, the older of the two Rankin boys.

"Come here, cowboy," called Latch, as he dismounted at the hitching-rail. "Jim, you go back to work. I've got business with this hombre."

Jim beat a hasty retreat while the cowboy leisurely advanced to meet Latch. They locked glances. Latch, on his part, felt relief. He thrilled. What a magnificent stripling! He suffered a qualm at thought of Estelle.

"Howdy, Mr. Latch. I see you've looked me up," drawled the cowboy.

"Howdy. I'm sorry I can't take credit all myself for looking you up. . . . You should have seen me boot old Bill this morning."

"Dog-gone! I'm shore sorry. That was my fault, Mr. Latch. I just didn't want you to know aboot the hold-up, till after I'd seen you."

"Why didn't you want me to know?"

"Wal, I'm queer, the boys say. I'd shore liked to have rode for you, on my merits. But I reckon I wouldn't take the job now."

"You wouldn't take money or horses or land—anything?" asserted the rancher.

"Nope, I reckon not. I'd have done that for anyone. But it's shore nice to remember it was for Steve Latch's girl."

"But listen, boy. You just can't refuse," protested Latch, earnestly. "Honest, you're the first rider ever turned away in all these years. It wasn't because you were a—a little queer—or swaggered some . . . but because you reminded me of a boy who was true to me once—who was more than a son to me."

"Hell you say!" came in the soft cool voice, accompanied by a flash of eyes that made Latch think of blue lightning. "Why are you askin' me now?"

"Well, as I'm being honest it's because I'm in bad with Estelle. She said if I didn't give you a job she would. And I'll be darned if I don't believe she's up to it."

"Dog-gone!" ejaculated the trail driver, visibly disturbed. "Did she tell you the—the story I told her?"

"Not a word. She told only about the hold-up."

"Latch, you cain't let this girl of yours come offerin' me jobs. Folks will talk. This is a hell of a place for talk. I shore got on to that last night."

"Of course I cain't. That's why I hunted you up."

"Wal, you tell her you did ask me an' that I said no," replied the young man, ponderingly. "An' thet you reckon I'm a no-good trail driver drove off the trail."

"I'll not tell Estelle that, because I don't believe it. What's your game, boy?"

"Wal, Latch, I'm not sayin' much aboot myself."

"Yes, I get that. And I think you're wrong. You be-

friended me. You saved me ten thousand dollars—
the last money I have, to be confidential. You saved
Estelle, which was more than all the money in the
world. Why shouldn't you let me make some return?"

"Pride man, pride. . . . She's the wonderfulest girl
—the loveliest I ever seen. A little lady—sweet and
innocent. Full of fire an' romance. Why, she'd turn
any man's haid. But that wouldn't phase me. Suppose
she took a shine to *me*? My Gawd! I couldn't let her,
Latch! She's a kid. Just out of school. You've kept her
too—too close. She never had a beau. Oh, I heahed
the girls talkin'. . . . Wal, she's your daughter an'
she'll be a rich an' great young lady before long. Not
for a gun-throwin' trail driver!"

"Now you've got me in deeper. I won't take no for
an answer. I'll take a chance on Estelle. And I'll take
one on you. Come out to the ranch."

"Damn it, man! When I talk straight out to you!"
ejaculated the youth, his cool equanimity ruffled.

"Straight talk always goes far with me. Besides,
you haven't said that you were no-good."

"Latch, how'n hell can I say so when I reckon I'm
as good as anybody?" demanded the cowboy, hotly.
"But you know what I mean? I'm a tramp rider.
Haven't a dollar 'cept what the boys chipped in an'
give me. All the boys an' bosses on the Chisholm Trail
—an' all the cattlemen I ever rode for but Lanthorpe
—they are my friends. Yet I got a bad name. It'll
follow me heah. I come from as good Texas blood as
ever flowed in any man's veins. But I'm poor, unedu-

cated, alone. An' I'll never risk makin' any girl
ashamed or unhappy."

"Son, then why did you ask me for the job?" queried
Latch.

"I knew damn wal I could ask so you'd refuse."

"The boot's on the other foot now. I'll gamble on
you. Come."

The cowboy made a gesture of despair, singular in
one who seemed so mature in harder ways. But it had
an air of finality. Latch thrilled again at some nameless quality familiar to him in other days.

"Wal, dog-gone!" drawled the cowboy, tossing his
cigarette and facing Latch with all fire and hostility
and aloofness gone. He seemed very young then and
singularly winning. "You an' your daughter are shore
chips from the same block. You win, Latch. But,
heah's my condition . . . I'll come to you presently,
an' work faithful an' true, an' stick till hell freezes
over. Only there's somethin' I want to do heah first.
Never mind. You gotta trust me. Meanwhile tell your
daughter I am no-good atall. But you're not to believe
that or anythin' you heah aboot me. Savvy? Is that
clear, Latch?"

"No. It's not. But I'll agree and I'll gamble on you,
whatever you do. I've had some dealings with men in
my day. You've got something up your sleeve, son."

"Aw, it's only a gun, Latch."

They shook hands without more words and Latch
mounted his horse to turn thoughtfully homeward.

"Wait, boss. I forgot—I shore forgot," drawled

that soft voice over the hitching-rail. "When I first went trail drivin' they called me Slim Blue."

Latch had been too generous with gifts of money, cattle, land. He had staked more men than he could remember, only a few of whom stayed on the range. This was in the heyday of his prosperity in 1875 when the number of cattle marketed at Dodge City had grown exceedingly large. The rancher who raised his own stock made enormous profit. Latch, driving thousands of head to market every season, believed his business would increase for years, and hence spent and gave prodigally.

But the years following had been increasingly evil ones. Leighton put on the screws in his demands for money. First he had borrowed and then he had extorted. Satana was easy to appease until all the rum stored in Spider Web Canyon was gone. Then Latch had to buy more and freight it in across the *Journado del muerto* at enormous expense.

Every year Blackstone and his gang had wintered at Latch's Field along with other outlaws, some notorious and many unknown. They all came to Latch for money. He was a friend. He had to give to save himself. They knew he had been one of them in earlier years and with the honor of thieves they had never betrayed him. When Blackstone and many other of the leeches who preyed upon him were wiped out in the Point of Rocks ambush, where Buff Belmet turned the tables on the ambushers, Latch was freed of much of the drag upon his resources.

But for him, at least, the advent of the buffalo hide-hunters on the range brought a most disastrous period.

Most of the great cattle barons were located on accessible ranges where cattle-rustling did not become wholesale. Jesse Chissum, of the jingle-bob brand of cattle—a peculiar way of cutting the ear of a calf so that the flap would dance up and down—was located on the Pecos River with other ranchers. He was the only rival of Latch's in that country, but he suffered comparatively little from rustlers, while during the rise of the hide-hunters to excessive numbers, Latch was hard hit. Among the hordes of these hunters there were many rustlers who profited mostly by their opportunity. One band would ride up from the Canadian River or the Red, make a raid and never come back or leave a trace. Then another band would do the same. Latch felt that he would be reduced to grazing small herds on close ranges that could be patrolled by *vaqueros*. This would not do for him, nor half pay his expenses.

His call upon Mizzouri, Seth Cole, Bain, and Johnson, increased his suspicion that some one in Latch's Field was coöperating with the fraudulent hide-hunters or else was rustling on his own hook. Latch employed only Mexicans, in charge of Reynolds and Simmons, and they were not the fighting breed of cowboys. He formulated a plan of combining forces with his old comrades to make a stand against this evil. But he abandoned it when he became convinced that it would bring ruin to them. The amazing fact was that neither Bain, Cole, Johnson, nor Mizzouri was losing any stock. This revelation caught Latch by the head. On any raid of rustlers from the hide-hunting camps below these ranchers would surely lose a few straggling head of cattle. It added to Latch's problem.

A year or more before he had banked ten thousand dollars in New Orleans for the purpose of making a cherished cattle deal and driving a new herd up from Texas. He had abandoned this, sent word and papers for Estelle to fetch the money, which he thought he had better use to pay long-standing debts.

Minor troubles added not a little to Latch's worry. Poisoned water, burned haystacks, broken irrigation ditches, cut fences, stolen horses and saddles, disappearance of faithful *vaqueros*, despoiled orchards, an increasing difficulty in hiring Mexican labor—all these and many more incidents of a rancher's life began to have a look far from accidental.

Lastly, and more disturbing than all else, of late he had observed a coolness in the attitude of Rankin, the blacksmith, and in Jud Smith, trader and storekeeper, both reliable and honest men who had chosen to settle in Latch's Field. Also Hep Poffer, the farmer and fruit-tree grafter to whom Latch had paid much money, had been decidedly uncivil of late. Latch had no false pride. He could not chafe under these real or imagined indignities. If they were true they were justified, and they meant that the old suspicion formed at Fort Bent and Fort Union had taken root in the very town Latch had founded, owned, and given away.

So in reality that old specter had never vanished.

For himself he cared little about ruin, disgrace, or death—though he would never die at the end of a rope! It was for Estelle that he minded. How poignantly he regretted not having sold out long ago and taken his lass to some distant place! But he loved Latch's Field and Spider Web Canyon. He had vacillated and lived on until too late. Some day his range would be worth a fortune—one that he swore to leave to Estelle. He must retrench, gird up his loins again, and beat down these baffling unknown foes for the sake of Cynthia's child.

Chapter XIV

CORNY in his six years of intensive trail driving had met thousands of men who lived one way or another on cattle. His had been a long search and for every stranger he had at least one question. For a long time he had not been conscious of a singularly acute intuitive genius. Knowledge came to him first through the rare gift of the gunman—to read the intent, the stimulus to action, in the eyes of his opponent. Thereafter he developed the power consciously. He was essentially a lone wolf in soul. But continuous contact with thousands of men along the trail—drivers, cattlemen, buffalo-hunters, scouts, soldiers, adventurers, pioneers, and a horde of the outlawed, had trained him in a marvelous school.

A shadow of the range hovered over Stephen Latch. Corny had sensed this in Estelle's vague dread—of something, she knew not what—in her simplicity and earnestness to secure his championship of her father. With it returned gossip of the Old Trail. Rumor of Latch's Field as a rendezvous for outlaws had drifted from camp to camp along the hard-beaten path of cattle empire. Where there was smoke, there must be fire. Corny's aggressive interest leaped on behalf of Estelle Latch. Just one shadow in her violet eyes— the shadow that hovered over her father—was enough to start the flame always smoldering in his breast. But there seemed to be other incentive, what he could not grasp, unless it was a nameless portent of a part he was destined to play in their lives.

Corny wanted a day, a week, a month, or more to probe into the dens of Latch's Field, into the dark minds of those inimical to the happiness of the Latches. He wanted to give substance to some intangible thing he felt.

What stranger thing could have come to pass, what stronger proof of his foreboding, than the moment he entered the Hall of Chance that night to encounter Leighton, to see the disfigured face, the brooding eyes of a passion-driven soul, the furrowed brow of a man possessed by devils, to feel anew the icy sickening freeze of the marrow in his bones at meeting another man he was going to kill. Corny had suffered it often on the trail. But in front of Leighton it was a flashing regurgitation, gone as swiftly as it had come, leaving him cold and sure, secretive and cunning as a snake.

Glancing around the big saloon, at tables and gamblers, through the wide door into the dance-hall, back to Leighton and his several companions at the corner of the bar, Corny felt transported to Dodge or Abilene. Still there was a difference. As he halted he became aware of the familiar searching gaze hard men at a hard period bent upon strangers.

"Howdy, cowboy. Just ride in?" greeted Leighton, sweeping Corny from head to foot. On the return sweep his eyes tarried a shifty instant on Corny's guns, worn low, dark-butted, dark-sheathed, inconspicuous against his dark garb.

"Yeah. Dog-gone tired, too," drawled Corny, lazily.

"Looking for anyone?"

"Nope. Not if nobody's lookin' for me. . . . Any sheriffs aboot this heah Latchfield?"

"That's a good one, Bruce," said Leighton, turning to one of his comrades, whose features would have marked him in any community. "Latchfield! Funny no one ever connected the two names. Cowboy, you've made a good start by naming this town. . . . And you can rest easy. No sheriff nearer than Dodge. And only one ever tackled the *Journado* to get heah. He's daid."

"Dog-gone! I shore am glad," replied Corny, with his careless good-natured grin. He knew his part. It was to represent any of a hundred trail drivers he had known. It came like second nature.

"Where from?" queried Leighton's vulture-beaked companion.

"Hell! Where do I look from?" drawled Corny.

"Hard to say. You got Red River mud on your boots."

"Shore. I forded the old Red—a last time, I reckon. . . . From Findlay I rode with Bridgeman's caravan."

"Ahuh. . . . Cut off at Long's Road with the Kiowas escorting Latch's stage?"

"Nope. I trailed that Indian outfit heah."

"Have a drink."

"Wal, thanks. Don't care if I do. . . . But I shore gotta swear off on the bottle."

"You look broke. But you might be heeled. What say?" returned Leighton, as he poured out drinks.

"Wal, I don't need to be grub-staked. . . . Heah's to Latchfield!"

Leighton leaned over the bar with an expression impossible for Corny to read.

"Stranger, excuse a personal question. We're not inquisitive heah. But I've a reason outside of curiosity. . . . Is your name Cornwall?"

Corny, fortified against any intrusion, hid the leaping pang in his breast and of his amaze. "Nope, my name is Slim Blue."

"Sorry. You look like a boy I knew years ago."

"Where?" queried Corny, with just enough casual curiosity.

"I forget. You just reminded me. . . . Make yourself at home, Blue. We provide entertainment heah for any pocket."

That had been Corny's introduction to Leighton and to the activity of this settlement he dominated. Corny affected a natural easy-going negative character, too indifferent to make advances. He strolled and lounged around, he sat for hours doing nothing, he listened when he appeared asleep, and he waited. His part was that of another outlaw passing time.

More than at any time before in his experience, however, boys, men, girls, everyone with whom he came in contact, gravitated to him in friendliness. Corny had only to be his idle careless self. One of Leighton's dance-hall girls swore she had seen him at Dodge and by her advances subjected him to embarrassment. But by being shy, along with his lazy way, he fooled her, intrigued her, piqued her vanity, and so began to learn the undercurrent of outlaw life in Latchfield.

He would drop into Smith's store and spend hours over a purchase that both Smith and his pretty daughter believed was but a ruse to bask in the light of her eyes. He often stopped in Rankin's blacksmith shop, first to have his horse shod, and thereafter to talk. He frequented other stores, always building up his part. He stopped Webb's runaway team and made the acquaintance of Bartlett through a little kindness. Corny seemed to have an uncanny power to distinguish the honest from the dishonest inhabitants of Latchfield. He grasped that long ago honest settlers had taken up their abode there, ignorant of the nature of their neighbors. Corny had only to meet Mizzouri once to read in his speculative glance that he had a past. Bain, Cole, and the queer negro Johnson, apparently coranchers with Mizzouri, offered most alluring subjects for study. They had grown up with Latchfield. Corny began to dig into the origin of this settlement. He found it like digging in hard ground, until he happened to meet a man named Hep Poffer. This individual was a farmer and a grafter of fruit-trees, a genial old soul who saw no ill in anyone or anything. He had a loquacious wife who took a liking to Corny and scolded him for his lazy habits. Infrequently Corny ran into the Kiowa, Hawk Eye, to resume acquaintance with that fascinating Indian. Hawk Eye was something to Latch and nothing to Leighton, a fact Corny pondered over.

All through these summer days Corny did not fail to observe the comings and goings of the Latches and their guests. He watched from afar. He saw them drive by while he lounged on the porch of Leighton's hall, for anyone to judge him only another questionable character. He never changed his actions one iota to avoid meeting them. Once he ran into Latch, who fixed him with doubtful eyes and said: "You —— —— loafer of a cowboy! What kind of a deal did you give me?" And Corny had drawled: "Howdy boss. Don't you never think I stacked the cairds?"

Then the momentous time Corny had prepared for rushed upon him so suddenly that it left him breathless, his heart apparently stopped. Estelle confronted him in Smith's store.

Without any formality of greeting she said, in guarded voice:

"You have failed me."

"Wal! How-do, Lady," he drawled, removing his sombrero. "Aboot that job. I'm dog-gone sorry. But I hate work these hot days."

"Dad told me you wouldn't come," she went on, her face pale, her eyes dark in the shaded light of the store. "He said you were no good! . . . Oh, I was so sick—so furious. . . . But I hear things about you. Everyone runs to tell me. How handsome, how nice, how friendly you are! This Elsie Smith girl is crazy about you. They say what a pity you are only another rider on the dodge. Another hiding outlaw!"

"Dog-gone! I didn't dream I was so popular. I shore like that Smith girl. If I wasn't such a no-good hombre I'd shine up to her."

"According to gossip you have done so. And she's not the only one."

"Who else, Lady? I'm turrible curious," replied Corny, when indeed he was far from curiosity.

"That Fanny Hand!"

"Wal, what of it? Poor kid! She shore needs a friend. Leighton fetched her heah—promisin' her Gawd only knows what—an' makes a dance-hall hussy out of her."

"I don't want to hear," replied Miss Latch, hastily, her chin up. "I want to say this. I told Dad it wasn't true that you were no good. I tell you that you're a liar."

"Wal, that's short an' sweet, Miss Latch," retorted Corny, stung through his mask. There was no use trying to resist this girl. What did those proud dark eyes mean?

"You get this straight, now," she went on. "You promised to help me. My Dad *is* in trouble. You would not come. I've waited. To all appearances you are a drinking, gambling, flirting young outlaw, hiding away. But I don't believe it. I shall go on disbelieving it."

"Thank you. . . . How long?" queried Corny, huskily.

"I never will believe that."

"Wal! . . . Do you remember what I said to you —over my saddle that day?"

"I—I'm ashamed to say I couldn't forget."

"It's true. An' that's part why I've taken the wrong road heah in Latchfield. My other reason was to help your Dad. To find out who his enemies are—what they are doin'. . . . An' I'm on the trail."

"Oh, Corny—forgive me!" she faltered, her hand going out, to be withdrawn.

"Forgive nothin'," he returned, abruptly, fighting a mad desire to clasp her to his heart. "Your friends are waitin'. Run along."

"Will you come to my party?" she asked, eagerly. "Dad has invited everybody except you. Swears he will throw you out. Come—call his bluff. Will you?"

"Yes, on one condition. I cain't dance much. But I'll come if—if you'll slip outdoors a little—so I can talk to you," said Corny, getting the irresistible, preposterous idea out.

"What have you to tell me? Is it something about Dad?"

"Wal, yes. But that's not all."

"Yes, I will—I'll meet you tonight," she retorted, staggering him with flashing dark eyes, wide and wild.

"Tonight?"

"Yes. I couldn't wait. . . . It'll be moonlight," she whispered, hurriedly. "Say nine o'clock! Out in the walnut grove. There's a huge walnut tree with a crooked trunk. About three hundred yards straight out from our front porch. *Adios.*"

She was gone. Corny, standing motionless, aghast at his folly, amazed at a complete reversal of his original intention, watched Estelle's trim form as she left the store with her friends. If that girl really cared for him! While Corny was playing with this passionate thought, the clerk, who happened to be the proprietor, presented himself, and Corny had to flounder around in a disordered mind to recall what he had come to the store for.

Corny had a room on the second floor at the back of Leighton's hall. He climbed the outside stairway, went in to his room, and sat down beside the small open window. There he sat until dusk, a prey to thoughts and emotions he had never before known. Nine o'clock! He must make himself presentable. He had a rendezvous with the sweetest, loveliest, proudest little lady in all the land. At her wish! Latch would kill him, and deservedly.

Footsteps in the hall passed his door, out upon the landing, started down the stairs. That stairway descended directly under Corny's window. Corny could not see, but he could hear. More than once he had been intensely curious about the men who passed up and down this back stairway at odd hours. Leighton had rooms on the same floor, in the front, accessible by a stairway just inside the front door.

"Sho—sho I knows dat. But I feels sorta drove. What's he agoin' to do if I'se found oot?" Corny heard the words distinctly.

"Tumbler, ya won't be found out," came the quick low reply. "What in hell could Latch do if he did find out?"

"Wal, he could shoot. I knows dat man. I'se seen him, Kennedy. But Leighton's done got me ober a barrel. If I don't risk dis drive he'll squeal aboot de udders."

"Nonsense, Johnson. You're gettin' dotty with your gray hairs an' too much prosperity," returned Kennedy, so low Corny could not have heard if the speaker had not been scarcely five feet under the window. "This drive will clean Latch out of cattle. Then Leighton will close in on him. Leighton is close-mouthed. But I've a hunch ruin an' death for Latch wouldn't be enough for Leighton."

"He sho hates de boss. I wasn't dere when he got dat brand on his face. But I knows de brander. I sho does."

"So thet's it!" ejaculated Kennedy, in sibilant whisper. "Latch shot him!—What for, Tumbler?"

"Aboot a woman. But I'se been loose-lipped enough. Dat whisky is sho pepper hot. I'se gwine home now."

"Wait, you —— —— nigger!" hissed Kennedy. "I've been your friend. An' if Leighton has you over a barrel, let's wait till he plays his deal, then put him over one. We can do it easier than he can to Latch."

"Wha—what? Double-cross Leighton same as he's double-crossin' de boss?"

"Exactly. We'll get rich on it. Believe me, Tumbler, Leighton won't ever come through this alive. . . . Tell me, quick, about the woman in the case."

"Man, I ain't swarin' it's de truff, but I got it from Black Hand, a mulatto who rode wid de boss when he was massacreein' wagon trains with Satana. Dat was years ago. I nursed Black Hand when he was dyin'.

He tole me. . . . Back durin' de war Latch an' Satana raided Bowden's wagon train. Dey was to massacree every one. But Leighton stole a woman an' fetched her along in a big Tullt an' Company wagon. Latch ketched him wid de woman an' shot him. Den Latch had a hell ob a fight wid his band, to keep dem from gittin' her. Dam' near wiped oot de band. Old Keetch could tell better dan Black Hand. Latch was married to dat gurl by a member of his own band. He fetched her to Spider Web Canyon, where dey all used to hole up. Dis chile of Latch's, Miss Estie, she was borned dere. Once years ago I heerd Keetch an' Leighton arguin'. Leighton was heah when dat chile was borned. He stole letters—proofs ob de chile's heritage. Dat's what Leighton had on Keetch—what Keetch never dared tell. Dis chile growed up now doan know her dad was boss of de bloodiest band ever on de border. But she's gonna know, I kin gamble on dat. 'Cause Leighton will tell her some day. I'se heerd Cole an' Mizzouri an' Bain talk aboot Leighton's revenge. Dey got him figgered. But Latch laughed at der talk."

"By God!" gasped Kennedy, his head making a decided thump against the wall. "Thet's what Leighton has on Latch. . . . Partner of Satana! . . . Bowden's lost wagon train! . . . I never heard the beat of it on the frontier. . . . Come on, Nigger. We need another swig."

The two men passed on down the stairway, leaving Corny crouched on his knees. The blood beat in his brain. Slowly he lay back, stretched out, and tried to relax his steel-like muscles. Then his mind cleared of shock. The tragedy of Latch's life stood out like letters of lightning. Murderer! Consort of the bloodthirsty Kiowas! Real love and honest life too late! The havoc in Latch's face—the burning in his eyes— all so clear now! Remorse, torture—lastly horror at the fear of Estelle's finding him out, shrinking from him as something loathsome, ending her ruined life!

Corny sat up to let the cool night breeze fan his hot face. It was dark and still at the back of the house. Music and voices came from the front. The evening star shone alone in the sky.

"Wal, he's a game old rooster," soliloquized Corny. "Fightin' for years to hide his low-down past! That's been done before. Ahuh. But fightin' for the little girl! It'd kill her. Poor kid! She has reason to worry aboot her dad. But she has no idee of the truth. . . . An' so help me Gawd she never will!"

Corny could not eat. He could scarcely stand still long enough to wash and shave and don some of his new clothes. His mind remained clear but had a tendency to race. He was to meet Estelle at nine o'clock— meet her with the tremendous weight of this revelation on his mind. But no inkling of it must reach her. One thing only knocked at the gate of his slowly mounting gladness as the certainty of saving Latch from ruin and thereby the happiness of Estelle, began to take definite shape, and that was the haunting fear that she might feel as strangely about him as he did about her. And he would have to spill more blood to free her father—then ride away.

Long before a pale light brightened above the bold bluff, heralding the rising moon, Corny paced to and fro under the great, spreading, walnut tree.

The trunk of this monarch split low down and the right fork curved away close to the ground. In the center of the bend a wide seat had been built. Corny ran a quivering hand over it, brushed it clean with his scarf. Never in all his life had he waited for a girl, by day or night. Fate was giving him a cruel and maddening initiation into the mystery of romance and love.

Corny paced a beat across the wide dark shade. Here and there the big walnut trees stood as nature had widely separated them. Under them he saw the lamp-lights at the ranch-house. Momentarily the pale glow above the black rim grew larger and brighter. Estelle would come before the moon topped the bluff.

The instant he would see her and realize this incredible thing was not a disordered fancy or an ecstatic dream he would leap out of this tumult of whirling thoughts and wild emotions, to become cool and sure again.

Corny remembered Weaver, his trail boss and friend, and that poor misguided and reckless devil he had been compelled to kill. Some inscrutable dispensation of chance had been at work then, directing his steps toward Latchfield. And every single event since had led to the betrayal of Latch's secret, of his peril, of

the menace to Estelle's home and honor and happiness. How Corny thanked those men of the trail who
had guided him hither. He was an obstacle in the
path of Leighton's revenge—unsurmountable, inde-
structible, inevitable. He was an instrument sent there
to frustrate this man. Corny flipped one of the darkly
shining guns in his hand, sheathed it to throw again,
with a speed inspired by ruthless passion and long
practice. The skill he hated, the name of which he was
ashamed, the sickening revolt in the pit of his stomach,
these for once in his life found in him welcome.

But Corny put away thought of an immediate forcing of the climax. He leaned toward waiting for
proof of the negro Johnson's rustling of Latch's cattle, and likewise toward a plan to recover whatever
Leighton possessed that would throw light on the
tragic fate of Latch's wife and Estelle's birth. No
doubt Latch was in ignorance of what his archenemy
had known all the years and could produce at will.

A silver disk of moon tipped the dark ragged bluff
and almost imperceptibly the valley underwent some
magical change. Coyotes were wailing out on the range.
The night wind stirred the walnut leaves rustlingly.
Corny faced toward the ranch-house. At once his eye,
trained by years of night-guarding the herd, caught
a dark bar crossing the lamplights. She was coming.
Life could never again be lonely, empty, no matter
what the issue. The doubt of love, of woman, that
had haunted Corny since Lester's disaster had ruined
them all, faded forever out of his heart.

He strode out into the open. The moon glided

higher. A white radiance moved toward him from across the valley. Then he espied a dark form flitting from tree to tree, to pause behind each one, and then come on, like an Indian.

A last tree—the last patch of shade! She stepped out, slim, stealthy, darkly clad, and espying him in the open, she ran headlong.

"Oh—you're here!" she panted, her hands outflung. "I was scared. . . . It's new to me—meeting handsome *vaqueros*—out on the range."

"Wal, girl, you've got nerve," he replied as he took her hand. "I wasn't scared till I seen you. I'm shore scared stiff now. Latch would kill me for this."

"Corny! . . . It was easy. We're safe. I told the girls I was—meeting you. They're tickled—to death. They'll watch. . . . But Dad is in the living-room. . . . Benson, Keetch, Mizzouri—I don't know who—else. Something amiss—cowboy."

"Ahuh. Come in the shade. . . . Heah, set down now, an' when you catch your breath tell me what's amiss."

"Lift me up on *this* tree—like you did on *that* one," she said, and stood for him, with her arms high.

Corny did as he was bidden. That left him head and shoulders below her, as he leaned on the huge branch. She sat partly in the moonlight, and if more were needed for his undoing it came with the ray of silver which caught her face.

"Very thrilling—to meet like this, isn't it?" she questioned, fathomless eyes upon him.

"Turrible thrillin', child," he replied. "An' for me —dangerous."

"You don't look scared."

"Wal, I am, though."

"Corny, I believe I like this better than if you came to my home—a-courting."

"Dear, I'm courtin' death. I'll welcome the heartbreak. But I shore don't want to die heah. I've got some awful important work on hand."

"Cowboy, you can't frighten me—now I've got you. . . . But—before I tell you anything—*you* tell me— if it's really true what you said—over your saddle that day."

How large and dark her eyes in her moon-blanched face! Corny had no background of experience by which to understand her. But he could feel her intensity; he could see that she was wholly unconscious of how trying an ordeal this was for him.

"Yes, Estelle—it's true," he replied, unsteadily.

She swayed back out of the moonlight and covered her face with her hands. He turned away a moment to let her recover. That she betrayed no evidence of surprise and affront at the brazen impudence of a trail driver did much to carry Corny over that bitter confession.

"Corny, I—I've doubted you," she went on. "That Smith girl said you were one of them cowboy ladykillers!"

"Wal, reckon it's news to me if I am," drawled Corny. "I been buyin' stuff in Smith's. An' natural-like I talked sort of pert to her."

"You didn't m—make love to her!"

"Estelle! I cross my heart I didn't," ejaculated Corny, bewildered.

"Nor flirt with her?"

"No."

"She gave me a different impression. . . . And worse, Corny, I've been told you have paid a good deal of attention to one of Leighton's dancers. The red-headed girl. Is that true?"

"Wal, I'm afraid it is, little girl. But you notice I'm lookin' you straight in the eye."

"Yes. . . . But, why, then ——"

"Estelle, I've been findin' out things heah in Latch-field. An' I've made no bones aboot how I went at it."

"Corny! All the time I've been miserable. I—I've despised myself because I was so little—so jealous. . . . Because in my heart I knew you wouldn't lie to me. Yet I—I doubted. . . . And all the time you've been working for my dad!"

"You bet I have, Estelle," replied Corny, helpless in the current. He had meant to strengthen her doubts —deliberately to damn his character in her eyes. And here he was proud to tell her the truth.

"Forgive me, Corny," she entreated, and then with hands on his shoulders she lowered her lips to a level with his.

Corny's response had the simplicity of her invitation. He kissed her without realizing the inevitableness of this moment. But the instant she shyly withdrew her cool sweet lips he knew.

"My Gawd, little girl!" he whispered. "Am I drunk—or out of my haid?"

"That's not flattering, Corny. I gave you my first kiss. . . . Honest!"

"But, child, you—you couldn't do that onless ——"

"Of course I couldn't," she interrupted, quickly. "But never mind about *that* now. I—I'm a little scared myself. You see, we're not very well acquainted. That's *my* fault, Corny Cornwall."

"Listen, wonderful little lady. No one but you heah knows my real name. I'm Slim Blue. Savvy?"

"Slim Blue! Well, I never. Where did you get that pretty name?"

"That's my trail name, Estelle."

"I think I like it. But, Corny, we're wasting time. I can't stay long. Oh! it's so—so sweet to be here. . . . Corny, there's something dreadfully wrong with Dad."

"Yeah. Wal, I'm listenin'."

"I've made it my business to try to find out what *is* wrong. But I can't. . . . Corny, Dad walks the floor at night. All hours of the night! I hear men come and go. Bain, Cole, Mizzouri, Webb, Bartlett.— I've seen or heard them all, visiting Dad at late hours. No ordinary calls, believe me. I've heard Dad cursing Keetch. Oh, I've listened shamelessly. But I could never make out what was said. Once I think I heard Leighton's name. Then there are *other* men who came —whose voices I didn't recognize. I looked in Dad's desk and discovered that most of the ten thousand dollars I brought home is gone. Gone! and not one of the many bills paid. Oh, Dad owes everybody. They are all dunning him. I can't understand it, Corny."

"Wall, it's easy to understand aboot the bills. He's hard up."

"But where has all that money gone?"

"Shore I don't know, Estelle."

"I want you to find out. There were a good many brand-new greenbacks. Fifties and hundreds. They would be unusual here."

"Wal, I might run across some if I snooped around. But why—what's the idee?"

"I'd like to know *who* is getting it. . . . Corny, Dad is failing. Oh, I know it. He has lost weight. He looks old, broken, harassed. But when he sees *me* he changes so that I gasp with wonder. He's all smiles. He is my old Daddy again. It's only when I spy on him that I can see the havoc. . . . Corny, it's breaking my heart. What does it mean?"

"Wal, go on, little girl, if you have any more to tell," replied Corny, coolly.

"There's more. The worst. I'm so ashamed. We— the Latches are losing caste in Latchfield! My own home. The town Daddy built! . . . When I first got home I sensed a difference. I was puzzled. Coolness on the part of former friends! . . . Corny, today I had my suspicions confirmed. Mrs. Webb sort of avoided me on the street. I used to be so fond of her. Then when I spoke to Edith Rankin about my party she said she guessed none of the Rankins would be there. I was dumbfounded. And terribly hurt. . . . Corny, there's something—range gossip—going around about my father."

"Shore. I heahed a lot myself."

"Against my Dad?"

"Nope. What I heahed was all good."

"Ah! Corny, I should have seen you long ago. . . . Well, the last is so—so disgusting that I wouldn't tell you if it weren't so amazing. . . . You know that young gambler partner of Leighton's. His name is Wess Manley. Good-looking in a bold sort of way."

"Yeah. I know Manley."

"He insulted me."

"Wal, you don't say," drawled Corny, averting his eyes from her lovely troubled face. For a moment he was concerned with an inward reaction.

"I bumped into him on the street. The girls were coming out of Smith's. That was the second time we'd gone in there. . . . Manley was as bold as his looks. 'If it ain't Estie Latch,' he said, halting me. 'Hello, kid. You sure have growed up. Am I in for some of your favor?' . . . Corny, I couldn't speak, I was so furious. But I whirled and he called after, 'Proud as ever, I see . . . Estie Latch, you'll come down a few pegs presently. I'll see the day you drink with me in Leighton's.'"

"Wall, Estelle, he was just drunk," replied Corny, with easy assurance, hiding the fury of his emotions. "Don't think aboot that another minute."

"But, Corny, drunk or sober, he couldn't say that without some reason. He must have been sure I wouldn't tell Dad."

"Shore he was. An' you won't, Estie?"

"I don't want Dad shooting the cur. All the same, Corny, it riles me. I'm Western, in spite of my Southern education. . . . How do you explain all this?"

"Simple as a, b, c, darlin'," rejoined Corny. Then he had to catch his breath at her response to his unwitting term of endearment. "Estie! . . . Dog-gone! Am I loco?"

"We're both loco. But go on."

"Wal, Latch is on the verge of ruin. He has given away prodigally. He has been a prince to settlers, Indians, travelers, outlaws, everyone who came to Latch's Field. He has not saved. He is land poor. Thousands of haid of cattle have been rustled. Leighton is his worst enemy. There's an old grudge, datin' back years. An old gamblin' debt—an' gun-play aboot it. Your Dad gave Leighton that ugly bullet mark. Wal, Leighton is at the haid of this rustlin'. He has a gang. Kennedy is his main pard. Manley is with them. Tumbler Johnson, the nigger rancher down the valley, is supposed to be close with your Dad, same as Mizzouri an' the others. I heahed Johnson an' Kennedy talkin' today. There's a deal on now to steal all the rest of your Dad's stock. That will aboot ruin him. For he cain't meet his obligations—all the bills you spoke of, an' I reckon outstandin' debts to Leighton. An' the plan is, of course, to force Latch off his ranch."

"Good Heaven! Is it possible, Corny?" burst out Estelle, passionately.

"No. It shore isn't. But Leighton doesn't know that. . . . I reckon there's only one man who does."

"*You!*"

"I hate to brag, Estelle, but I reckon I'm the little old hombre. . . . Leighton's plan is to ruin your Dad financially. He'll end by holdin' all these debts. An' if he cain't drive your Dad off the land, he'll kill him an' take possession after."

"Kill Dad! That mangy-faced lout!" cried Estelle, incredulously.

"Wal, from Leighton's angle it's not such poor figurin'. Leighton would never meet Latch in the open, man to man. He's too clever. He'll have some of his henchmen shoot Latch unawares. Shore they plan to kill Keetch an' Benson. Maybe Mizzouri, too, an' other men who owe your Dad so much."

"Murder!" gasped Estelle.

"Wal, that's a high-soundin' word, Estelle, for this border."

"How awful! . . . So *that* is the secret? Poor dear Dad! Fighting to conceal his trouble, his prospective ruin, from me."

"That's the whole story, Estelle."

"Oh, I feared I—I know not what," she cried, poignantly, throwing wide her arms. "Something weighed upon my soul! I never dared name it in my consciousness. . . . And it's only debt, hatred, villainy!"

"That's aboot all, I reckon."

"Dad *is* all I've loved since I was a baby. Since he came home—and I went to him—there!—at Mother's grave."

"Yes, girl, he is all you've loved. Latch is one of

the West's great men. Great as Maxwell or Chisholm or St. Vrain or Carson—any of them. Generous, fine, noble, a grand friend, a bad foe, hard in his early days because he had to be hard to survive. But honest, clean, good as gold! He has made enemies, not *all* of whom he has killed. Worse luck! An' now when he's gettin' on in years an' has you to make him tender, Leighton—the worst of his enemies—has plotted all this ruin, worked it through the years, nursin' his hate an' revenge. . . . Estelle, don't ever have another doubt of your Dad."

"Nev-er! . . . Slim Blue, I love you," she whispered, and slipped off the branch into his arms.

Corny held her off her feet, aware of clinging arms, of a heaving breast, of kisses, of sweet fire. But he seemed passive, obstructed.

"There! . . . Let me down. . . . Our—our love-making can wait. . . . Corny Cornwall, you have given me back something precious. Bless you! . . . I will keep your secret. I am no longer frightened sick. You are my friend and Dad's saviour. Don't let thought of me hamper you. I'm Western, Corny. I was born up that black canyon."

"Wal, it shore—was lucky—for me," replied Corny, haltingly.

"I must go now. . . . I'll see you soon. At my party? I've the loveliest dress. I want *you* to see me in it. . . . Corny, you don't speak!"

"How can I—when I'm struck dumb?"

"You will come?"

"Yes, Estelle, I'll come. Now you run back an' leave me heah to moon."

"Goodnight—Slim," she whispered, and made as if to lift her lips again. But she suddenly wheeled and fled out into the moonlight, a swift dark form, soon disappearing.

Chapter XV

LATCH had long been aware of the growing estrangement between him and his two best friends in the valley, Webb and Bartlett. He had tried to blind himself to this dismaying fact, as to so many others, but it would not down. Webb was not a Southerner. He had come from Illinois with his large family, and was a man of means and influence. Bartlett was a squaw-man and stood high in the good-will of the Indians. Latch could not afford to lose the respect and friendship of either if he were to continue to hold his own in Latchfield. He met them in town on the day before Estelle's party and thought it a good opportunity to learn his exact status.

"Bart, you're coming to my girl's party," he queried, heartily.

"Wal, I wasn't, Steve," replied the blunt rancher, his gray eyes hard on Latch.

"Why not? I'd take it as a personal insult if you didn't. And that goes for your wife and daughter. Estelle is fond of Wilda."

"Damn it all, Sam," rejoined Bartlett, turning to Webb. "Thet's true. An' I'm gonna stick by Latch, talk or no talk."

Webb had lived long enough in the West to understand the delicacy of the situation. But he was a forceful character. His light-blue eyes held a penetrating suspicion as he met Latch's.

"Sorry, Latch. My family is not coming."

"No? . . . Anybody ill?" queried Latch, slowly.

"All well. And the truth is they want to come. But I've about decided against it."

"Oh!—You have? May I inquire why?"

"Latch, I'll be glad to tell you," returned Webb, hurriedly. "It's this talk of Leighton's ———"

"Keep yore fool mouth shet!" interrupted Bartlett.

"Too late, Bart," said Latch, coldly. "What talk, Webb?"

"There's been strange whispers for a long time, Latch. But only lately could they be traced. Your past has always been sort of shady. You settled this valley and kept open house to all. I certainly didn't know Latchfield had been a rendezvous for desperadoes or I'd never have located here. Leighton is spreading this poison. Just hints and whispers! And they have not become general yet. But some of us are damned concerned, I don't mind telling you."

"So it seems," replied Latch, in biting tone. "You must be damn concerned to mention this to my face. I can only take it that you believe my enemies."

"Latch, I wouldn't go so far," said Webb, nervously. "It's just that I—I don't like it—I don't want my family to hear of it."

"I understand perfectly, Webb," responded Latch, curtly. "I've no hard feelings yet. But if you and your high-toned family don't come to Estelle's party

I will know on what side of the fence you sit. And in that case you can go for your gun when next we meet."

"Wha—at?" cracked Webb.

"Good-day. . . . Bart, I'm thanking you for your faith in me," returned Latch.

Whereupon Webb blurted out: "Why in hell don't *you* go for your gun—if this man Leighton is a liar?"

Latch strode on down the street, with that retort ringing like a bell in his ears. Why indeed? Why did he not finish the job he had once begun on Leighton? The answer paralleled every question of his life at that time—Estelle. She had seen him kill one man. She had been terror-stricken at the encounter and then shocked at the killing. That had been years ago. Estelle had begun to reveal an assimilation of the West if not a direct heritage. Delicate, sensitive, high-strung as she was, she was in no sense a weakling. To hurt her feelings probably could not be avoided. To lose her love, which was so precious to him, was not the vital thing. Her honor, her name, her happiness—these must be preserved at any cost.

Latch had reached the hitching-rail where he had tied his horse, when he encountered the young trail driver, Slim Blue. He sustained a violent shock. In the mood under which he labored, weighed upon by dread, to be so suddenly reminded of Cornwall and the bloody past was enough to make Latch furious.

"Howdy, boss," drawled the youth, leaning over the rail.

"Howdy yourself, you damned flour-flusher," retorted Latch.

"Yeah? . . . Wal, I shore haven't been drawin' any aces lately."

"I hear you are slick at slipping aces from the deck."

"Wal, boss, I see Webb an' Bartlett have riled you."

"I'm riled, all right."

"I heahed that last crack of Webb's aboot why'n' hell you didn't draw on Leighton."

Latch had been affronted before he encountered Blue. So that he did not need much invitation to inflame him unreasonably. He realized that his old cool nerve had failed him and he fought to get it back. This youth looked at him with Cornwall's flashing blue eyes, and that in itself was enough. Latch had loved his strange boy lieutenant. And this trail driver seemed to exercise the same baffling fascination. Another youth gone wrong! Another daredevil of the times! Then it suddenly flashed into Latch's memory that Slim Blue had followed up his service to Estelle by vague hints of the same to her father. Cowboy blarney! Only another bitter drop to Latch's overflowing cup of disappointment!

"Some more of your nosey work," declared Latch. "Blue, I'm reminded of queer talk about you."

"Shore. An' thet reminds me of the same I heah aboot you," drawled the trail driver.

"You insolent cow-puncher!"

"Latch, heah's another hunch," flashed Blue while

his piercing eyes transfixed the rancher. "Stay away from your old pards down the valley road. 'Specially Nigger Johnson! Stay away from town! Stay away from the corrals. . . . Better—stay indoors! Do you savvy, boss?"

"Hellsfire! I hear you, but I don't understand."

"Wal, you can figure it out. But don't never look for an even break in Latchfield. Not with Leighton holdin' the cairds!"

"Thanks, Blue. Naturally your association with the low-down outfit would result in your hearing things. Am I to assume that *that* is why you spend your days and nights in Leighton's?"

"Latch, you can think what you like aboot me."

"All right. And it'll be no good. I'll thank you to stay away from Estelle's party."

"Ump-umm, boss. You invited everybody in this heah valley. Good an' bad! An', by golly, I wouldn't miss it for a million."

"Blue, if you come I'll throw you out."

"Aw, boss, you just couldn't do that," expostulated the trail driver, spreading his hands.

"I could and I would."

"But you'd be most turrible damn sorry afterwards. Miss Estelle her own self would say that'd be strange Southern hospitality."

"You conceited loafer! Do you dare insinuate my daughter would think anything of what concerned you?"

"Shore. I'll gamble on it," drawled Blue, with his

slow winning smile. That smile alone saved Latch from slapping his handsome face.

"All right, Blue. You come, and see what happens," concluded Latch as he mounted his horse.

"Anyways, boss, you'll need me turrible bad when Leighton's outfit ——"

Latch heard no more. He rode away at a trot, hot and uncomfortable, wholly dissatisfied with himself. Little by little one thing and another had accumulated in a great whole which, added to the Nemesis that had overshadowed him for years, presaged inevitable catastrophe. What could he do? To whom could he turn? Keetch was faithful, but had an inexplicable fear of Leighton. Benson could not be told. There was no one else. If only that sharp-eyed inscrutable trail driver had lived up to the impression he had created! Latch rode toward the corrals at his wits' end.

Half a dozen dusty riders had just come in. Weary pack-horses attested to long and arduous travel. Keetch and Simmons, with the *vaqueros* looking on, were talking to the arrivals. When Latch's horse turned into the wide court all faces looked his way. Keetch swung awkwardly upon his crutch, heading toward Latch.

"Billy the Kid ootfit," he said in a swift undertone. "I know Charley Bondre. They're all right when you're friendly. I advise you to make good on your old rule."

Latch rode up to the group, his gaze centering upon the man he intuitively took to be the young desperado already infamous on the frontier.

"Howdy, men. Get down and come in," Latch greeted them, cordially. "Keetch will take care of you."

"Much obliged. We're shore fagged," replied the youth. He appeared no more than a stripling of eighteen. His garb was ragged. A lock of light hair stuck out of his old sombrero. He wore his gun on the left side, rather high, with the flat end of the butt facing out—a fact that struck Latch singularly. Billy the Kid, despite his youth, already numbered killings equal in number to his years. He had a remarkable physiognomy, and would have been good-looking but for a prominent tooth. His eyes would have lent decided character to any face. They were either light gray or blue, but the color was uncertain. It was the look in them that held Latch. Another Cornwall or another Slim Blue, magnified in all ways! Billy the Kid was only another manifestation of the extreme of character, of wild life, developed at a wild time.

"I don't need to ask if you've come far," went on Latch.

"You bet we've come far, Mr. Latch," replied the outlaw. "Sixty miles today, I reckon. An' all to see you."

"Well, that's complimentary, I hope," said Latch, easily. "I still keep open house to all riders."

"So we heard. But we didn't come to try your well-known hospitality."

"No? What for, then?"

"We took a bunch of Chissum's cattle down the

Pecos an' across at Horsehead, round to the north of the Staked Plains. Sold to a trail driver at Red River. Well, on our way up the Canadian we run plum into an outfit drivin' a big herd of long horns wearin' your brand. It may strike you funny that we steal one rancher's cattle, then ride out of our way to squeal on an outfit who's stealin' yours. But I, for one, didn't want this last laid on to me."

"Ha! Ha! Funny? Sure, it strikes me funny. . . . Keetch, what do you know about it?"

"News to me, boss," returned Keetch, intensely interested. "An' if it's true we're cleared oot proper."

"You can gamble on my word, Mr. Latch," returned Billy the Kid. "We didn't know the cattle were yours until a settler told us yesterday. So we rode up pronto. That's all I can say, Mr. Latch. An' if your invite still holds we'll be only too glad to stay an' rest up a couple of days. I've long heard of Latch's Field."

"You're welcome, and thanks for the tip. Drop over after supper, you and Bondre, and smoke a cigar with me. Maybe you might have some news of outside."

"Shore have. Been to Dodge, Old Bent, an' Fort Union lately."

Latch left his horse, and telling Keetch to come up as soon as the visitors had been made comfortable, he wended a thoughtful way toward the ranch-house, muttering to himself: "The plot thickens. . . . Last of my stock. . . . Leighton back of this. . . . It ruins me. . . . By God! I'm a driven man!"

He found Estelle and her friends in the living-room, so gay and merry that he transformed his gloomy face as if by magic. He would deceive his daughter to the last moment. But something had to be told her.

"Girls, we have a visitor—one of the most infamous of Western outlaws—a boy still in his teens. No less than Billy the Kid."

"How lovely!" cried Elizabeth, ecstatically.

"Billy the Kid?" questioned Estelle, puckering her smooth brow. "Dad, could we ask him to my party?"

"Certainly. It will be something to tell your grandchildren some day."

Estelle blushed and the girls launched into gay badinage.

"I think Billy just happened along Latchfield way," went on Latch. "But usually visits of his to any town result in excitement, not to say worse. Perhaps our sleepy village is due for some."

"I shall flirt outrageously with Billy the Kid," averred Marcella.

But Estelle's violet eyes took the old darkly troubled expression. She had heard something. Latch left the room with brutal blows knocking at the gate of his heart. Were all his years of remorse, of travail, of fight to go for naught? Must he see this lovely innocent lass plunged into blackest misery? He went to his room, and barring himself in, sat at a window, seeing nothing of the glorious panorama spread out before him. "Wages of sin!" he whispered. "Oh, God!—burn me in hell forever—but save Estelle! . . . Oh, Estelle, my lass—my lass! . . . Oh, Cyn-

thia, my beloved! Would to Heaven you had been
murdered that black day!"

Keetch sought him presently, coming with slow
thumps up the stairs, and knocked reluctantly.

"Come in," called Latch, and made no effort to
conceal his passion-spent face.

The crippled old outlaw entered, haggard and hard,
to fasten revealing eyes upon his master. Latch mo-
tioned him to a seat, poured out a glass of liquor, and
waited.

"Did your *vaqueros* substantiate Billy the Kid's
claim about my herd?" finally queried Latch.

"Ahuh! . . . No riders in from down the valley.
Reckon they've been shot or druv off. I've been worried like hell for two days. . . . Boss, the Kid didn't
lie. Fust off, Billy the Kid is not the kind of hombre
who lies. You can gamble we're cleaned of our last
stock."

"Sold out to a trail driver! . . . Keetch, is there
no redress? Think of a well-known brand three thousand strong!"

"Hell! If we could prove who done it there'd be
redress all right. But we also know thet riders strange
to us stole our cattle an' sold them to strangers on
the Old Trail. Before we could ride to Dodge or
Abilene they'll be gone. . . . You're oot forty-five
thousand dollars, an' we're robbed, done, stuck, ruined,
by Gawd!"

"Financially, yes. But that is nothing, Keetch,"
replied Latch.

"Man alive! You're broke. You're deep in debt. An' Leighton has got hold of all your papers. He will take your ranch away from you."

"Over my dead body!"

"Wal, Leighton has been layin' for sixteen years to see yore daid body. But he'll ruin you fust, disgrace you, blacken your good name. An' last, old pard, I know he has some hellish idee of torturin' you through Estie."

"How do you know?"

"I heerd him say so."

"To whom?"

"Me."

"When?"

"Last time I seen him. I may as well tell you that he gave me a chance to swing over to him."

"Keetch, what hold has Leighton on you?"

"I double-crossed you years ago. . . . The honor among thieves didn't work with me then. But it has been a thorn in my flesh. If I had my life to live over again I'd not do it."

"Ah! . . . Keetch, old pard, how did you double-cross me?"

"No need to tell now, boss. You'll know after I'm daid. An' I've a bloomy feelin' thet won't be long."

"You should have told me before. I'd have forgiven then. I do now. You have been most loyal to me. . . . So Leighton wanted you to jump me?"

"Yes, he shore did. I don't know his plot, boss. But it has had a long, long hatchin' . . . Now we got our backs to the ditch. I'm stumped."

"There's a way out," replied Latch, with a deep sigh.

"Shore. But where—how—what? You an' me ag'in a whole ootfit! What I'm so turrible feared is thet you'll walk oot to kill Leighton. Course I'll go with you. An' no use deceivin' ourselves, we cain't kill Leighton, save by a lucky chance which ain't comin' our way these days. Thet leaves Estie to these wolves. Leighton never goes out alone. He has his body-guard round him all the time. He's watchin' like a hawk for a gopher. Bruce Kennedy is Leighton's right-hand man. Crooked, or I don't know men. If you had enough cash you could switch Kennedy to our side. Smilin' Jacobs an' Wess Manley air both gun-slingers. Either of them could beat you an' me to a gun. An' they have their ootfit."

"Hard facts, Keetch. Have they made you show yellow?"

"No, by Gawd! I've a queer hunch thet some miracle will save us. I know what I feel, only I cain't tell you."

"Miracle! I wish I had your blind hope. But—I see —only ——"

"What, boss?" queried Keetch, hoarsely, as Latch faltered.

"Destruction for me—and horror for my lass."

"You might take her an' ride away . . . No, he'd trail you—ketch you oot on the prairie! Thet'd never do. . . . I wish I could figger like I used to. But my haid 'pears thick. Gawd! I wish Cornwall was alive an' hyar. . . . Forgive me, boss, but I've thought of

him a lot lately. He had brains—thet boy. An' nothin'
flustered him."

"Yes, Lester foresaw this. Many times he wanted
me to let him kill Leighton. I think I always wanted
to do that myself. . . . How fate brings things
about! Keetch, this is my punishment. I committed
crimes and they've worked out my destiny. I see only
one chance in a thousand. To face Leighton in his
den!"

"Jest throwin' yore life away."

"But I *might* kill him," rasped Latch, haggard and
fierce.

Yet on the morrow, when the first guests began to
arrive from down the valley, Latch had never been
more the courteous Southern gentleman, hospitable to
friend and foe alike.

His invitations had gone far beyond the limits of
Latch's Field. Some of the arrivals had been three days
on the trip. Cowboys rode in from Findlay, and one
trail driver deserted at Red River, just to attend a
party given to the golden-haired daughter of Latch.
By noon, to Latch's amazement, Saronto, the fiercest
of Comanche chiefs, came with a full force of his
wild-riding braves, brilliant and colorful in their
beaded buckskins and eagle plumes. Hawk Eye, now
a chief of the Kiowas, with many braves Latch remembered only too well, rode down from Spider
Web Canyon. A caravan from Texas rolled in under
Scout Hennesy, who announced that several of his
party had declared Latchfield was the spot of their

dreams and they would settle there. A detachment of soldiers arrived from Fort Union. By mid-afternoon the wide level park in front of the ranch-house resembled a great encampment, and festival was in the air. All the Mexicans in the valley and many from outside were employed in getting ready the sumptuous feast which was to be held outdoors for the many. Latch's long dining-table was reserved for guests of prominence. It seemed a singular coincidence that Black Jack's gang of outlaws, second only to Jim Blackstone's band, made Latchfield that same day, by design or accident. Latch's word was welcome and the creed of the border prohibited anything but good will.

All of Latch's old allies except Nigger Johnson were in attendance. The Webb family, girls gaily resplendent and boys spick and span in bright scarfs, new suits, and shiny boots, preceded the guests from town. Leighton rode over, surrounded by his dark-garbed men. Latch's kinsman looked the dandy of the age in his flat-crowned sombrero, his long black frock coat, flowered vest, and flowing tie. But the hideous disfiguration of his face made him unpleasant to gaze upon.

Billy the Kid and Bondre, with their men trailing behind, rode out to the picnic grounds, more evidences of the good business Latch's party had brought the merchants in town. In a complete new outfit, clean-shaven and with his ragged locks trimmed, the famous boy desperado of the frontier looked like any other boy, smiling and gay, thrilled at the prospect ahead.

"Howdy, Mr. Latch. Shore is a treat," he called out. "Where do we check our hardware?"

"Hello, Billy. Glad you came. . . . See Keetch, there. Don't be offended if he slaps you all over looking for concealed weapons."

"Gosh no! It's nice to come to a decent party where a fellow needn't look to be drawed on."

It was indeed a unique social gathering. The Comanches held aloof from the Kiowas, the several outlaw groups kept to themselves, the ranchers, of whom there were a hundred or more, congregated in one great circle under a huge walnut tree, and everywhere were scattered little bunches of Mexicans, Indians, cowboys, *vaqueros*, and men whose calling was not manifest in their garb.

Latch went among them, picking out here and there a guest for the big living-room, where plates were laid for seventy. Sunset, the most beautiful hour of the day in the valley, was the one in which all were called to supper. Outside, hostile Comanche and honest rancher, or wild cowboy and murdering desperado, sat side by side in the huge circle to be served.

And at this moment Estelle came running out to be presented by her father. She wore white and her lovely flushed face beamed upon all. Latch, swift to catch any mood or action of hers, saw her violet eyes sweep the circle, linger over the cowboys, as if she were looking for some one in particular. It was the same when he let Estelle into the great dining-room, where her girl friends, the neighbors, the chiefs, and the outlaws all rose from their seats to greet her. Whom did the girl miss? Latch felt his heart contract. Slim Blue! Every person in the valley except Blue was present.

Latch bade his guests be seated while he remained standing. "Neighbors, friends, enemies, chiefs and outlaws, strangers within my gates, be welcome at my daughter's party. This is her birthday. She is sixteen. She belongs to the West. Eat, drink, and be merry."

"Oh, Dad!" whispered Estelle, with shining eyes on him. "I was afraid you were about to say, 'for tomorrow we die'!"

All through the wonderful meal Latch had assurance that Estelle still expected a late guest. Her dark eyes continually sought the door. Only he, perhaps, could read the disappointment in them. For all, then, except father and daughter, the sumptuous feast was a huge success. Then when chairs and table were moved out to make room for the dancers, and the fiddlers had begun to tune up, a slim strikingly handsome youth entered. It was Slim Blue. Not only the blush that dyed Estelle's cheek hurt Latch; this trail driver broke open a sealed chamber of memory. He seemed Cornwell come back from the grave.

Slim Blue was easy, graceful, cool when he greeted Estelle, and she presented him to her friends. Marcella and Elizabeth made much over the trail driver. Acquaintance had gone so far as friendship here. But it was the radiance in Estelle's eyes that broke the troubled knot in Latch's breast. Cynthia had looked at him with such light in her eyes.

Latch gave no consideration to the bitter rage that

consumed him. He strode across the great room to face them.

"Blue, I told you not to come," he said, loud and cold.

"Shore, Mr. Latch, I wasn't likely to forget. An' fact is I came to see you."

"Bah! You can't soft-soap us, cowboy. Now you rustle or I'll throw you out."

"*Father!*" cried Estelle, her face flaming red.

Blue sustained a subtle change. Latch had seen eyes like those before—eyes that veiled cold thought of death.

"See heah, Latch, you cain't insult me like that," said the trail driver.

"I couldn't insult you at all, Blue."

"Yeah?—Wal, we don't agree. I told you I came to see you."

"Get out!"

"Ahuh. . . . Everybody welcome heah but me!" ejaculated Blue, bitingly. "Greasers, redskins, bandits, cow thieves an' hoss thieves—all welcome but me?"

Latch waved the trail driver to the door. "Begone!"

Estelle confronted Latch with white face and blazing eyes.

"Father, have you forgotten that this boy saved my life?"

"No. I offered to reward Blue. But I will not have him here."

The trail driver dropped his head and turned to the door. Estelle ran to halt him, appeared to entreat him, and even caught his arm. Blue was not proof against that. Shamed and pale, he gazed down upon her, and then turned eyes of fire upon her father. Estelle led him out upon the porch. Latch stood petrified at the significance of that action. A terrible fear assailed him. Could his beloved child have become seriously interested in this handsome wild youth? She returned almost immediately.

"Father, all my life you have said 'yes' to me," she announced, with the first anger she had ever expressed to him. "It's too late in the day to start with 'no.'"

"But, Estie dear, listen," he burst out.

She pierced him to the heart with Cynthia's eyes, proud and dark and grieved, and passed on to join her friends.

Latch sought among the remnants of his self-control for something to preserve his dignity, to carry on in the face of this last and unexpected blow. The young folk, boys and girls, white and red, began to respond to the fiddlers. The Mexican *vaqueros* and *señoritas* entered in their colorful costumes. Latch left the clever Mrs. Benson in charge and sought the crowded porch, where he could watch unseen. His delight in Estelle's party had almost been extinguished. But he might have exaggerated his fears. Still, his love and pride were so great that he could not but thrill to see her dance, to revel in possession of her, to yield momentarily to the old dreams for her happiness. It was a big moment for Latch, and no doubt for all, especially Estelle, when Mrs. Benson presented Billy the Kid to the daughter of the house. Estelle gave no sign that he stood apart from the other youths of her village, and graciously gave him a dance. The border desperado did not look his fame and he certainly made the most of his opportunity. Estelle got him a dance with each of her friends. Soronto, the great chief, held her hand and pranced a little for her, his dark fierce face lighted with the spirit of the hour. Leighton stood outside one of the windows in the shadow. Perhaps only Latch noticed the passion in the Southerner's eyes.

A gay, dancing, crowded hour had passed when the sharp-eyed Latch saw Estelle slip out through the throng on the porch and flit away down the shaded path. He followed, amazed and sorrowful. What should he have expected? Had he not been young and hot-blooded once? The moon shone bright, so that Latch had no difficulty following the white form. Out in the garden, along the edge of the orchard, Estelle glided until she came to the edge of the first pond. Here she halted as if to peer into the shade of the trees. Latch tortured himself with the query— had she made a rendezvous with Blue? Preposterous! Yet Estelle had reached woman's estate. She was Cynthia Bowden's daughter. And Cynthia Bowden had loved a renegade, a bloody partner of the ruthless Satana. Latch realized that he was a fool. But he had to prove his suspicions. Estelle's white form dimmed into the shadows.

Latch went swiftly around the pond, to slip like a stealthy Indian along the border of willows up to the outlet where the water spilled over the mossy stones. Here was a nook under a large oak much visited by the dark-eyed señoritas and the riders.

Suddenly Latch froze in his tracks. He had come nearly to the opening before he discovered what he sought—the slim white figure of his beloved. Aye, he saw it—and all havoc seemed proved and ended. Estelle stood wrapped closely in Blue's embrace and she had her arms around his neck. She was kissing him with a wild abandon that left no doubt of what this obscure youth, this fiery-eyed trail driver, meant to her.

"Oh, darl—ing—I thought I'd missed you," she said, low and poignantly. "Or that you'd left in a huff."

"No, sweetheart, I came heah an' I'd have stayed heah till mawnin'," replied Blue, despondently. " 'cause I reckon it's the last time."

"Last time—you'll meet me!"

"I reckon, honey."

"No! No! . . . Slim Blue, have you made me love you—only to desert me?"

"You child! I didn't make you love me an' I—I'm turrible scared an' troubled 'cause you do."

"You *did* make me love you. . . . I mean so—so— Oh! . . . like this . . . and that!"

The soft contact of lips accentuated the latter broken end of that speech.

"Dog-gone-it, darlin'! I cain't help myself. You're a witch—an' I love you turrible. But, Estie, funny as it may 'pear, I've got idees of honor."

"Honor! Well, I just guess you have. . . . Boy, don't mind Dad's insult. Oh, he was a beast. I'll make him suffer for that. I'll make him crawl. But it was nothing to make you desert us."

"No, I reckon not. But I'm deceivin' him right heah. Makin' myself oot just what he believes I am. An' I cain't do it any more."

"Dearest, am *I* not deceiving him, too? My daddy! Oh, he'll kill me when I tell him—we're engaged."

"My Gawd, Estie! . . . Shore you cain't mean that?"

"Don't you love me?"

"Aw, quit your teasin'."

"Don't you worship me?"

"I reckon, Lord help me!"

"Didn't you say it'd be heaven you'd never dreamed of—to h—have me—yours—your wife—and ——"

"Of course I did," expostulated the trail driver, sadly. "But that was only dream talkin'."

"Sir! I took it you asked me to be your wife . . . Didn't you?"

"No! Why, Estie, I never dared think aboot that really."

"Then let me go. You swore you had honor. It is not honorable to make sweet eyes at a girl—to smile at her—to tell her you love her—and then hug and kiss her very heart out of her body."

"Estie, I cain't let you go this minute. I'll be strong enough—maybe—after a little. 'Cause this will be good-by."

"Oh no!"

"I reckon. Your father would never consent to us marryin'."

"Well, I'll marry you without it. I'll elope with you. We can always come back. Oh, he'll forgive us."

"Cain't you have mercy on a poor fellow?"

"Mercy! Cain't *you* have some on a poor girl?"

"Estie, all this is fool talk. It'll only make it harder for you. An' shake my nerve, darlin'!— Think what I've got to do! An' my nerve mustn't be shook!"

"Listen, you wild trail driver," she responded, running her white hands through his hair. "Once settle this—this awful affair of ours—then I'll give you all the nerve any man might need to be another Jason or Hercules or Goliath."

"Yeah? Who was those geezers?"

"Darling, don't call them geezers. They were great heroes!"

"Estie, we're gettin' away from the point. An' you should rustle back to your dance."

"I am dancing now—in your arms."

"Cain't you be serious, honey? This is hard on me."

"It should not be," she replied, sweetly. "I'll be serious. Listen. You saved my life—more than life. You helped me to be brave. You gave me back my faith in *him*. You made me love you. And you could never have done *that* if you hadn't loved me first. I'm a Latch. Then you told me the story of your life —about your mother—oh, I would have loved her!— and your brother! . . . You come from as fine a Southern family as does my own father. And just because you're poor—because you haven't had much schooling—because your great gift is guns—your great fault is spilling blood—because of these you imagine you're not good enough for me. Well, you are. . . . And right now you had better prove the respect you swore you had for me."

"Aw! . . . Estie, if—if I ever come oot of this turrible mess—will you—marry me?"

"Yes. And you will come out of it. Dad showed the cloven hoof tonight. He seemed a stranger. Sometimes I felt that I never *knew* him. But you dispelled that, bless you!"

"Lass, don't ever think nothin' but that Steve Latch is the biggest an' finest man in the West."

"Indeed, darling, that old conviction has come back. Tonight, of course, he hurt me. But it's only his care of me. And he believes you a no-good trail driver. Oh, when he learns the truth! Oh, what revenge I'll take."

"Wall, Estie, you set me on fire. I reckon I could do anythin'. . . . But it's been hard for me—settin' quiet as a mouse in my room, hour after hour, night after night, waitin' for a chance."

She spread wide her arms and leaned back from him.

"Think of me while you wait. . . . Take me now, darling—take all the kisses you need for all the nerve you need. . . . Oh!"

Her arms closed round his neck as Blue clasped her as if to make her one with him. Latch, gazing with abated breath, with fixed eyes upon the slight white form pressed so closely to the tall dark one, saw back into the past, saw Cynthia Bowden in his arms, even as his daughter now lay spent and still on the breast of the trail driver.

"There—Estie—forgive me," he whispered, huskily. "I'm a new man, an' yours—by Gawd! Whatever comes. Run back home now—an' dance your pretty haid off."

"When shall we meet again?"

"I don't know. Not soon. But trust me."

"I live in you. . . . Adios, Slim Blue. Oh, I love that name. To think I never can be Mrs. Slim Blue!"

She laughed happily and low and, slipping from him, ran out into moonlight, flashed across an open space, to vanish behind the shrubbery. Blue stood like a statue until she was out of sight, then glided away behind the willow hedge toward town.

Latch sank down as one becoming aware of unstable limbs. This revelation was the end for him. The last catastrophe! It broke his heart yet left him free. He passed over the many puzzling remarks that had been exchanged between Blue and Estelle. He had no way to divine their meaning, except to realize that the youth must be worthy, else he never could have won Estelle's devotion. Latch fought with a horrible might to wrench himself away from jealousy and selfishness. Estelle was amazingly like Cynthia. She had made her choice. Her father must abide it. His first strange impressions of this mysterious firebrand of a trail driver returned with a redoubled strength. Another boy from the South like Lester, only soft-hearted instead of flint

—another Billy the Kid in bold action, but not gone the road of the criminals!

Latch sat there a long while, until he sensed a release from fetters. Estelle would not be left alone now. That young man could protect her, else Latch's years of judgment on the border had gone for naught. A husband, a fighter, a Texan—these were infinitely to be desired. Estelle would love so deeply and passionately, as had her mother, that life would still be worth living, even if ruin and disgrace befell her.

Against these Latch girded up his loins for a last battle. All agony, it seemed, had been his, except the agony of seeing the daughter of the woman who had worshiped him, the blood of his blood, learn of his infamy and turn from him in loathing. That would be too much for human endurance. He must forestall it; and freed from the terror of leaving Estelle alone, he rose like an old battle-scarred lion, ready for a last charge.

Chapter XVI

IN THE gray dawn the ranch-house was dark and quiet. A pale moon, yielding to the break of day, hung over the bluff. Fires still smoldered in the encampment of the Indians; dogs belonging to the caravan bayed the yelping coyotes; oxen grazed over the obscure meadows. The last dark group of riders filed out upon the trail to the north.

Latch sat by his open window where he had lingered for hours. When the sun tipped the prairie horizon far down to the purple east he would be on his way to execute the tragic plan that had evolved from his travail. Leighton and his inseparables, after a night of gorging and drinking, would be asleep. Latch meant to force entrance to the room he had located long ago and kill his archenemy and the others. He had accepted his own death as the cost of this sinister deliverance. There seemed still time to forestall Leighton's extreme machination. Latch saw clearly that proof of his crimes would pass with Leighton and his associates. There would be left only the old doubt of his early years on the frontier. It was the eleventh hour and a terrible ruthless peace settled upon his soul. Thought of Estelle he banished.

Soon a red rim of sun peeped over the purple land. He welcomed it. Buckling on a heavy belt weighted with two guns and a ring of shells he left his room, stole down the back stairs and out into the yard. He made a point of securing a double-bitted ax from the woodshed. Then he cut across the orchard into the meadow, and circling the west end of town he worked his way through shacks and brush to the narrow lane that led in to Leighton's place.

The high gate was open. He heard horses thumping in the barn. He saw the stairway leading up the back of the big structure. An open door—dark, inviting! As he strode swiftly across the yard he thought he heard voices. But he closed his ears. Looking neither to right nor left, he gained the stairway and started up stealthily. Every step seemed to carry him higher and closer to the old Stephen Latch. He changed back in the climb. He retrogressed to the primitive which had found such terrible expression in the days of Satana. He was true to the stronger self now. All the love, the remorse, the strife were as if they had never been. His veins swelled with swift-gushing rivers of hot blood. Leighton! If luck favored him, this double-bladed ax would bury its shining head in his kinsman. Latch would rip the revengeful fiend open from throat to groin. Latch burned with unholy and unquenchable hate—with longing to have Leighton recognize his executioner—to suffer a horrible passion of defeat and agony of flesh while his heart's blood flooded out.

Latch reached the landing. He stepped into the hall. Door open on the right—room in disorder—bed had not been slept in. Other doors along the hall were not shut. Suddenly Latch saw a man's head and shoulders lying across the threshold of the last door on the left. Leighton's room! Latch rested the ax against the wall, and drawing a gun he leaped forward. One swift glance showed Leighton's room empty. Then Latch looked down. He straddled a dead Mexican—one Jaurez, long attached to Leighton. His skull had been split. Next Latch's swift sight took in the smashed door, the scattered articles of clothing on the floor, bureau drawers thrown to the right and left, and in a corner a demolished trunk. An old-fashioned trunk of French make—that had surely come from New Orleans! It had been forced open with the bloody ax which lay near, and rifled. A ruthless and powerful hand had preceded Latch. Some one had robbed Leighton while he and his comrades had attended Estelle's *fiesta*.

Latch rushed out and down the stairs, his plan disrupted, his thoughts in a whirl, his emotions undergoing another cycle. Once out in the lane, he slowed his gait and sheathed his gun. He went back the way he had come and hid in a clump of willows. From passion to reasoning was in this hour a slow process. But in the end he achieved it.

Latchfield had been full of outlaws the preceding night. He was logical to suppose that one of them had killed Leighton's man and ransacked the room. Yet the idea did not hold in Latch's consciousness. Something uncanny entered into all conjecture. Latch began to conceive that the slaying, the robbery, the evidence of tangible hostility to the powerful Leighton, bore some strange relation to himself.

"Slim Blue!" muttered Latch, as if struck by an arrow of thought. "What did he mean by waiting? Waiting! . . . He told Estie. She understood. . . . Last night—this morning—what a queer look! . . . So help me God!"

He heard horses go down the road at a gallop, and others trot by in the opposite direction. The town had awakened. Had it ever gone to sleep? Latch emerged from his hiding-place, and crossing the creek to the road, he faced town and stalked like a man whom it would be dangerous to meet.

But Latch did not get halfway down to the center of town. A knot of men, suddenly disintegrating in excitement, to turn back out of sight, dull pistol shots coming from indoors somewhere, hoarse shouts—these gave Latch pause, though they did not stop him. Smoke from guns, probably, was rising in the street. The hour might not be an auspicious one for his own purpose.

As Latch faced about to return to the ranch he saw the long line of canvas-covered wagons and yokes of wagging oxen stretched across the flat toward the break in the hill. The caravan was on the road to Fort Union with its escort of soldiers. Then Latch remembered that Estelle's friends were to travel with this caravan as far as the fort, and then transfer to a south-bound caravan. No doubt one of the many riders alongside the wagons was Estelle, who had promised Marcella and Elizabeth that she would ride to the top of the hill with them. Latch felt relieved that he need not expect to face her soon. Could it be that only last night the long-planned party had taken place? Then straightway in the press of his dark, fixed thoughts he forgot her.

He did not notice that it was hot, though he stopped in the shade of the cottonwoods around the second lake. He sat down the better to think. In this peaceful secluded spot the glare of valley, the bray of burros, the clip-clop of hoofs, were shut out. Still there seemed an unnatural tension in the very air. Again he arose to plod on to the first lake where the shady nook, the big oak, the gurgling water over the stone steps, recalled Estelle's incredible rendezvous with the trail driver. He could not linger there. He paced up and down an aisle of the orchard. Presently he smelled smoke and imagined he heard the distant hoarse voices of men. But he paid no particular attention. What he strove to recapture in its entirety was that mood of the night.

Nevertheless, disturbances from outside broke into his great distraction. Yells of a kind not to be ignored brought Latch to his feet, thrilling and chilled. Again he heard horses, this time on a furious run. Incredible as it seemed, something must be amiss outside of his own mind. He hurried toward the house, and when he got out in the lane espied Simmons running toward him. The bow-legged cowman, unused to such mode of locomotion, did not make fast time. At sight of Latch he shouted. The rancher had only to see his foreman's pallid sweaty face to grasp at catastrophe. As of old, his nerve and force rose to meet it.

"My Gawd—boss—I been—huntin'—you all—over!" gasped Simmons as he panted to a stop.

"What's up, man?" queried Latch, sharply.

"Hell-to-pay."

"Where?"

"At the corrals. . . . Come."

Latch lined up beside the cowman and waited. He was perfectly sure of Estelle's safety for the present, and nothing else mattered.

"Boss, lissen . . . I was sleepin'—in the barn. Was woke up about seven by loud talkin'. Somebody razzin' Keetch. I peeped out an' seen Keetch standin' ag'in the corral fence—facin' half a dozen men . . . Didn't recognize nobody—till I heard Leighton's voice. Seen him then—only one on foot. He was wavin' a gun— an' his fist in Keetch's face. He was as hoarse as—a bull—an' so mad I couldn't git the drift of his talk. But I understood Keetch—all right."

"Hurry. Go on," ordered Latch as the man stopped to catch his breath.

" 'Leighton, you're drunk,' says Keetch, sarcastic as hell. 'I jest got oot of bed. Slept in my clothes.'

" 'You're a —— —— liar,' bawled Leighton. 'Nobody knew I had those documents. You sneaked over to my room—last night—when we were all makin' merry—you brained José—an' robbed me. No money gone—nothin' but thet leather wallet—which only you knew about.'

" 'Leighton, there was two hard-nut ootfits in camp last night. Gone at daybreak!'

" 'But —— —— you! I tell you nobody else knew

about that wallet. . . . You dig it up pronto or I'll shoot your guts oot!'

" 'Sorry I cain't oblige you. I was asleep till you rousted me oot. An' I can prove thet.'

" 'You haven't got it!' screamed Leighton, poking his gun in Keetch's belly.

"Then Kennedy chipped in, nasty like: 'Lee, you're wastin' time on your old pard. Thet job was done too swift for a man on a crutch. . . . But fer Gawd's sake plug him if it'll fetch you to your senses."

" '—— —— the luck!' roared Leighton, foamin' at the mouth. 'It *had* to be Keetch who stole my wallet. There wasn't any money. Only he knew those papers an' letters were worth a million to me!'

"Then Kennedy cussed Leighton good, an' Manley added some. They wanted to get out of here. But Leighton was beside himself. I never seen a man so furious. Somethin' more'n fury, too, believe me. He just couldn't give up hectorin' Keetch about the stolen property. All the same, whether Keetch seen thet wallet or no, thet was his finish. I'll bet if he'd been packin' a gun he'd a mixed it with Leighton's company right there.

" 'Once more,' he bellared. 'I'll give you ten thousand dollars for my wallet.'

" 'Say, Leighton, if I'd knowed it was so valuable I'd stole it myself long ago,' replied Keetch, cool as a cucumber. 'But git over the idee no other man knowed you had it.'

" 'Who?' screamed Leighton, dancin' up an' down.

" 'Wal, I ain't tellin',' laughed Keetch.

" 'Latch! I'll burn the secret out of him with a brandin'-iron!'

" 'Nope, not my boss. I was feared to tell him.'

" 'Did you tell any man?'

" 'Haw! Haw! . . . Leighton, you're barkin' up the wrong tree. You've waited too long with your deal. An' I've kept my mouth shet too long.'

" 'Then, by hell! you'll never open it *to him*,' yelled Leighton, an' he turned thet big Colt loose on Keetch. When Keetch slid down Leighton piled on his hoss an' all of them rid away. I run out, yellin' for anybody. Kneelin' by Keetch, I seen he was all in. But he made me understand he had somethin' awful important to tell you. So I run after you—an' I've been huntin' ever since. Nobody at the house or in the camps had seen you. Miss Estie an' José rode out with the caravan. . . . I reckon we'll be too late."

"Simmons, you should have taken Keetch's statement, then come for me," declared Latch, grimly, as his dark imaginings leaped to conclusions. Swifter he strode on until he was almost running. They reached the corrals, crossed the court to the great barn where a group of *vaqueros* had congregated. Keetch lay inside the door, covered with a blanket. Simmons drew it back to expose the old outlaw's face. Whatever had been his wrong to Latch and the secret he had withheld, Latch forgave him in that moment. Considering all circumstances, Keetch had been exceedingly faithful. Latch gave orders to bury him out under the walnut tree that shaded his wife's grave.

At this juncture Benson rode into the court, the

iron-shod hoofs of his horse ringing on the stones. He scattered the riders and leaped off, his blue eyes gleaming.

"Latch, your party last night upset Latchfield," he began, hurriedly, and then, espying the dead man, he gave a start and gaped while his perturbed face turned gray. "*Keetch!* . . . Who shot him, boss?"

"Leighton. Did you see him in town?"

"Ha! I reckon. An' if I'd been blind I'd have heard him," declared Benson. "He's a ravin' lunatic. Somebody set fire to his house before he got back. Nothin' saved but some liquor."

"Fire!"

"Gosh! I should say so! Where have you been? All the Indians were there. An' the town turned out. Leighton was burned clean. Also half the block on his side of the street. Damn good riddance! But that isn't all by a jugful. It appears there's been shootin' since early mornin'. Nobody I seen knew much about it. One of Billy the Kid's outfit shot a member of Black Jack's gang. That must have been to get up an appetite for breakfast. Both outlaw gangs sloped pronto. I met Mizzouri, an' he had a heap to say about the killin' of Nigger Johnson. He said . . ."

"Johnson!" ejaculated Latch, startled in spite of the steely calm that had settled upon him.

"Yes. Johnson is dead as a door nail. I seen him lyin' on the sidewalk. Shot plumb between the eyes! Back of his head blown off, where the bullet come out."

"More of Leighton's work?"

"I guess not. Mizzouri said thet trail-drivin' cowboy, Slim Blue, was crazy drunk an' runnin' amuck.
Thet was before Leighton's saloon was fired. Early
this mornin', Mizzouri said. He was with Johnson
an' they'd stopped at the Smith store. They had a
hoss hitched there, an' also a buckboard. Blue came
slouchin' along, wild-eyed. 'Howdy, Niggah!' he
yelled. 'Throw thet gun you're packin',' so my borin'
you won't look so bad.' . . . Johnson tried to reason
with the cowboy. But it didn't do no good. Mizzouri
made tracks to one side. Then it seems Blue cussed thet
nigger somethin' scandalous, dared him to draw, swore
he hated all niggers an' wouldn't have none in Latchfield. Johnson went in Smith's store. Blue followed,
kickin' him as he'd kick a mean dog, drove him out
again. Then Mizzouri said Blue went close to Johnson an' whispered somethin' nobody else could hear.
But half a dozen men swore they seen thet black
nigger turn white an' go for his gun. He never even
got it out."

"Slim Blue!" cried Simmons. "Thet cowboy from
the Chisholm Trail? . . . Gosh, boss, but all this has
a funny look!"

"Strikes me as it struck Mizzouri—damn queer,"
retorted Benson, after waiting in vain for a comment
from Latch. "But let me go on. . . . Blue staggered
on down the sidewalk, an' finally disappeared, accordin' to Mizzouri. Well, thet's all from him. But
listen to this from me. When I rode into town Rankin
wasn't up. Nor his sons. Too much party! My hoss
had thrown a shoe on the way over an' had gone lame.

I went to Martinez, the greaser who has a shop back of Leighton's. An' while I was there I seen Slim Blue come ridin' up the alley. Say, he was movin'. I had a good look at him, an' if he was drunk, so am I right this minute. Martinez was bendin' over his job, so didn't see Blue. A little later I seen smoke rollin' up from the back of Leighton's house. Then come a big puff an' a roar. Thet old wood house busted into flames. Martinez had the shoe half nailed on when I lit in the saddle an' sloped. I shore didn't want to be caught behind thet burnin' house. I rode around an' come up the street, tied my hoss way down an' walked. Not many people seen the fire fust off. Only a few men run in to pack out kegs. I wasn't one of them. Then the Indians came, an' after them the townspeople. In half an hour Leighton's place an' four other houses were burned flat. About this time Leighton an' his outfit raced up the street. I happened to be near where they piled off. Leighton looked hell bent. I reckoned it no longer any place for me, so I hustled back to my horse."

Latch kept his deductions to himself. They were bewildering and subject to change with each new angle of thought. Simmons and Benson exchanged wondering conjectures and queries, while Latch paced to and fro beside the covered body of his old ally. What would Keetch have advised him in this climax? Latch divined that he must speedily anticipate a thunderbolt in shape of Leighton's next move. Instead of hunting down his enemy, Latch now waited to be hunted. And similarly he must look for paralleling action from the mysterious Slim Blue. Too late Latch realized his blind attitude toward that youth. With what a shock did he place this Slim Blue on the same plane with Lester Cornwall! Only it began to dawn on Latch that Blue was subtler, deeper, which traits added to his terrible skill with guns, made him more dangerous to Latch's foes. If Blue turned up again, as seemed inevitable, Latch would know beyond doubt that through Estelle he had gained the most formidable ally who had ever in all these desperate years shed blood for him. And the mounting conviction began to take hold of Latch's maddening thoughts, to work order out of chaos, to burn away the ever-encroaching tendency to despair, to inspire, to uplift, to rouse the drum of old passion, to flash again the lightning of his once unquenchable spirit.

"Simmons, saddle a fast horse and ride at once up to the house," said Latch, suddenly. "I want you to take a note to Estelle. You should intercept her on the way home. You will see that she goes on with the caravan to Fort Union."

"Yes, sir," replied the foreman, and with a yell to the *vaquero* he ran into the barn.

He was about to give orders to Benson when new arrivals across the court gave him pause, while a hand gripped his gun. But the riders were Mizzouri, Seth Cole, and Jerry Bain. Latch watched them approach. At last the old guard had proved true to the past.

"Howdy, Steve," drawled Mizzouri, as he reined in. "Mebbe we're a little late in the day, but hyar we air."

"Thanks, Mizzouri, I appreciate it, late or no. But what sent you?"

"Wal, it was thet son-of-a-gun of a Blue fellar. Boss, so help us Gawd if we ever knowed Nigger Johnson was rustlin' yore stock till Blue proved it to us. Thet was after he shot the nigger. Leighton an' Kennedy engineered thet last raid, an' Nigger Johnson pulled it."

"So Johnson double-crossed me!" rang out Latch, stung as of old at being betrayed.

"Shore. It's downright humiliatin', boss, for us to find thet out. Only lately did I get leary. But soon as we knowed it an' figgered what was to foller, we come pronto."

"Mizzouri, if you lined up with me in the fight that's coming, wouldn't that lend weight to claims Leighton might make?"

"Hell yes. But daid men tell no tales, boss," returned the little outlaw, grimly.

"No, they don't. All the same, I'll not risk jeopardizing the lives and reputations of you men. It cheers me to see you here. But go back home. Don't fear for me."

"Wal, have it yore way, Steve, old man. I was sort of itchin' for a fight. Too much peaceful livin'. Reckon, though, you won't need us a hell of a lot. Where'd you pick up this Slim Blue fellar? Boss, if he ain't the . . ."

Latch, with a wave of farewell, plunged away out of hearing. He did not care to have his old men see how deeply stirred he was. How that late loyalty warmed his veins! He rushed to the house and hurriedly penned a note to Estelle, and inclosed the last money he possessed. The clatter of Simmons' fast-moving horse greeted his ears.

"Ride, Simmons," he said to the waiting cowman.

"I seen riders top the hill, boss. Must be Miss Estie an' the *vaquero*. I'm off," replied Simmons, and with a clash of spurs he was gone like the wind.

Chapter XVII

SLIM BLUE leaped his horse over two fences and an irrigation ditch, running at full speed, Brazos might have taken his spirit from his master. The lazy days at Latchfield had palled on the greatest of cow horses. Gaining the open, Brazos stretched out and soon reached Spider Web Creek. Blue halted him on a high wooded bank and for the first time gazed back at the conflagration he had started.

"Wal, I reckoned thet loose hay would come in handy," he drawled, in cool satisfaction. Lurid flames were rising under the pillar of black smoke. The trail driver wiped his sweaty face. Then without taking his eyes from the fire he rolled a cigarette. He was a slow smoker. When that cigarette had been almost consumed Leighton's saloon and the building adjacent were down. In another half-hour only light yellow clouds of smoke marked where they had stood.

Blue had kept a vigilant lookout for riders. Evidently in the excitement no one but the rider in Martinez's smithy had seen him race away from town. A few horsemen had ridden into town on the road. Blue calculated it was about time some should be riding out. And what he meant to make sure of was who they were.

"Thet hombre I winged was Kennedy, I'm almost

shore," soliloquized Blue, as he reloaded the two empty chambers of the gun he had used. "Wal, considerin' the way he ducked to get under cover, I was shootin' some to hit him atall. . . . It's a safe bet Kennedy knew who was shootin', so the cat's oot of the bag now. Thet stall aboot me bein' drunk didn't work with Niggah Johnson. My Gawd! I'm shore glad thet waitin' deceitful game is over!"

Blue had at last come to the end of his long vigil. He had played his part. This day would mark him as Latch's ally and an enemy to the Leighton gang, and all who had any relation to them whatever. It had scarcely been necessary for Blue to pretend to be on a drunken rampage. He had indeed been wild with the frenzy of his success and his release from the maddening watch.

The treasure Leighton had guarded with such unremitting care was a wallet containing letters, marriage certificate, papers, pictures, and jewelry that had been the property of Estelle's mother. Blue had not had time for anything save a hurried scanning of the contents, but that had been enough to establish the relation of Cynthia Bowden to Stephen Latch, and the child Estelle.

The trail driver had not yet solved Leighton's plot as far as the contents of the priceless wallet were concerned. But they were to be used in the man's plot to ruin Latch, take possession of the ranch, and betray him to his daughter. Leighton would not stop at revealing the hideous fact of Latch's bloody past to Estelle.

"Wal, I've forced Leighton's hand," went on Blue,

grimly. "He had the cairds stacked on Latch. An' I spoiled his deal. Niggah Johnson daid, thet greaser Jaurez daid, the wallet gone, the saloon burned, an' Kennedy nursin' a bullet hole! Now what?"

Action had to be prompt. That very day Leighton must do his worst. He must beard the old lion in his den. It did not seem likely that Leighton would admit any more of his outfit into the intimacy of the strange deal. Bruce Kennedy, Smilin' Jacobs, and Manley— these men, all seasoned, hard-shooting outlaws, quick of wit as well as of trigger, were Leighton's accomplices. And of these Bruce Kennedy was a traitor, waiting for a chance to shoot Leighton in the back and take over the deal himself. In all probability Leighton would use these three men in his conflict with Latch and Keetch. The rest of the outfit Leighton would surely put on the trail of Slim Blue.

"Latch, poor devil, has shore got his back to the wall," mused Slim as he watched every avenue leading out of the town. "Game, I'd say! An' all to save the kid's happiness! Wal, he cain't know what I'll be doin'. I reckon he'll never heah aboot me till it's over. But I reckon I'm to be figgered on heah. I shore am. An' it's Leighton's turn to deal cairds, with me holdin' these aces up my sleeve. An' one of them aces bein' thet Kiowa Hawk Eye! Aw, I guess I'm not so slow."

That ended his soliloquies. An hour had passed, and before the end of another much would have happened. Hawk Eye was watching Leighton. The Indian had been slow to respond to Blue's advances. But gifts and kindness had made approach to Hawk Eye's friendship. Then a blunder of Leighton's turned the Kiowa against him.

The first rider to catch Blue's quick eye was one leaving the ranch on the road toward the hill. He was mounted on a fast horse, a sorrel Simmons always rode. Latch had sent his foreman out on some errand. What? How that cowman was raising the dust! Estelle had told Blue she was going to ride out with the caravan, to have a few more hours with her girl friends before they parted. This decision had not struck Slim as wise, but his objection was feeble, owing to the exquisite feel of two soft bare arms around his neck, and sweet lips on his. No doubt Latch had let Estelle go, with attendants, of course, and now had begun to be concerned about her. If he had sensed the crisis coming, he might well have dispatched the rider to advise Estelle to go on with the caravan.

Six horsemen in a bunch turned down the road toward Latch's ranch. Soon they left the road for the lane which led by the lakes. Blue lost sight of them in the green. They were ranchers, evidently, and the one mounted on the big white horse was undoubtedly Seth Cole. Their calling upon Latch at this eleventh hour held a significance not lost upon Slim Blue. In less than a quarter of an hour they reappeared! And about the same time Blue became aware of another horseman, riding an Indian mustang across the meadow toward the creek. Its rider was the Kiowa.

Slim stepped out into an open space where Hawk Eye espied him. The Kiowa had important information to which he gave brief utterance. Leighton had killed Keetch and had dispatched Jacobs and Manley to intercept Estelle on her way back to the ranch. Blue made two queries and Hawk Eye replied that Leighton's two men had left just after the caravan, and that the wound Slim had given Kennedy was in the left shoulder and had not seriously incapacitated him.

"You are one good Injun, Hawk Eye," declared Blue. "Go back. Watch Leighton."

The trail driver slid off to tighten his saddle cinch. Then mounting again, he swept an appraising eye along the willow-bordered creek to the brushy bluff. He had fairly good cover all the way around to where the road wound up the hill.

"Wal, Brazos, you been itchin' to run. Get oot of heah!" called Slim to his horse. Keeping well to the left of the creek, where the going was level, the trail driver made fast time to the mouth of the narrow canyon. Its dark portal seemed to call him. Crossing there, he took to the rougher brushy ground and half circled the ranch before he started to zigzag up the slope. Brazos was fresh and strong, but Blue saved him on that climb. Well might the great horse have need of stamina before the day ended. Once on top of the cedared escarpment Blue kept off the road and out of sight back in the trees. He calculated that Leighton's men would not go far along the road, but ambush it at a likely place and waylay Estelle upon her return. They would not be paying particular attention to their rear. Besides, neither Jacobs nor Manley was a cowman. Blue had not traveled more than a couple of miles up the gentle slope when he sighted a saddled, riderless horse tied under a cedar.

Slim dismounted to halter Brazos in a thick clump of trees. Then keeping behind brush and rocks, he advanced with extreme caution toward the road. That sorrel horse belonged to Simmons. If Blue did not miss his guess, Simmons had been shot from its back. But Blue could not locate the foreman's body anywhere in the vicinity. Presently, however, the trail driver's exceeding vigilance and genius for such work located two other horses hidden in the green and gray of cedars. A rocky eminence, half concealed by trees and brush, stood on the right of the road. Bandits would have chosen that place as an ideal one for a hold-up. Jacobs and Manley would never go far from their horses. They would be concealed in the brush under that flat rock.

Blue went back to his horse, and divesting himself of scarf, vest, and boots, he hurried far down on that side of the road, and crossing at a turn he made a wide détour to come up behind the rocky eminence. As soon as he located it and made sure the horses could not sight him from that side, he sat down to regain his breath and choose his further progress. As luck would have it, he could crawl under cover all the way to the ledge.

Blue did not tarry long. On hands and knees, stopping every few moments, he soon crossed the last hundred yards or more to his objective. That side of the little hill afforded a view of the road. Even as his sweeping gaze met the horizon two riders topped the line to show black against the sky. Blue experienced the thrill sight of his sweetheart always gave him, only this time it seemed to add something vital and tremendous to his passion. Estelle and her *vaquero* were two miles distant. Long before they came within sight or sound of that rock he would have had the unpleasant little business settled.

Wherefore he listened. He smelled cigarette smoke before he caught low voices. He decided it would be easier and safer to go up the ledge instead of around. Pulling a gun he crawled like a snake up to the flat narrow top. The rock was scarcely six feet wide. Tips of cedars reached almost to a level with it. Blue rested a moment.

"Smiley, I tell you I heard something," Manley said, low-voiced and quick. "Come back hyar."

Footsteps rustled below Blue, almost under where he lay.

"Ground squirrel," replied Smiley, contemptuously. "Gawd! you're a skeery cuss!"

"Ahuh. Mebbe thet's why I've lived this long."

"Aw, forget it. Hyar comes our party. Take a peep round the rock."

Jacobs whistled low.

"Smiley, I've an idee. Leighton gives us a lot of dirty jobs. Let's make him pay handsome for this one."

"Hell man! He always pays handsome."

"Not handsome enough. My idee is this. Listen. Instead of takin' the girl to Spider Web, let's hide her somewhere else. Then you brace Leighton an' ask for ten thousand. He'll pay."

"What? . . . He'd kill me!"

"Nope. Not while we got the girl. Can't you figger why he wants her taken to the lonely canyon?"

"Manley, you're low-down. I wouldn't double-cross Leighton."

"Why not? He'll leave you holdin' a sack in the end."

"I've a hunch none of us will hold anythin' very long—with thet —— —— cowboy runnin' amuck."

"Bah! You make me sick!"

"Manley, you're a tenderfoot, compared to me an' Bruce. An' he . . ."

Slim wormed his way out on the rock, over to the edge, and peeped down. The men were close enough together to suit Blue. Jacobs sat on a slab of rock with his left side toward Blue, an unfavorable position for gun-play. Manley was standing almost in line with his companion, a few steps beyond, and he was peering out between the corner of ledge and the brush.

Shoving his gun over the rim Blue called sardonically: "Howdy, men."

Smiling Jacobs stiffened as if steel rods had been shot through him. Manley froze in his tracks. Then Jacobs warily moved his head slightly and looked up to see Blue above, with only head, arm, and shoulder exposed. His dark face with its set ferocious smile turned a ghastly hue. He had hazel eyes which emitted oscillating gleams.

"Howdy, Blue," he replied, cool and slow. "I was jest tellin' my pard hyar to expect you."

"God-Almighty!" panted Manley, piercingly.

"Shore. Thet'd be you—prayin' when it's too late," said Jacobs, scornfully.

"———— —— you, Jacobs—you got us into this. . . . I wanted to keep to—the open road."

"Ahuh. Wal, pard, jerk round an' meet hot lead."

Blue interposed: "Don't bat an eyelash down there, . . . Smiley, will you talk?"

"Nix," retorted Jacobs, violently.

"How aboot you, Manley?"

"Yes—I'll talk," returned Manley, swallowing hard.

"What's Leighton's idee sendin' you with the Latch girl to Spider Web?"

"He says he'll use her to lure Latch into a trap. Promisin' to free her if Latch makes over his ranch holdin's. But I know Leighton means ———"

Jacobs interrupted with a terrible curse and suddenly spun round like a top, throwing his gun. As Blue fired, the outlaw appeared flattened by a battering-ram. Blue's swift second shot took the whirling Manley high up and knocked him into the brush, which upheld him as he swung his gun into action. Blue ducked back and rolled over twice on the ledge. Then he lay flat a moment, listening to the bang of Manley's gun and the *spang* of lead off hard rock. The outlaw's last three shots, at random, showed extreme terror of derangement from a serious wound. Blue never took unnecessary chances. He waited. Threshing

of brush, gasping breaths, a quivering jingle of spurs—
then silence! After another moment Blue peeped over
the rim. Manley had slumped down in the brush with
his boots higher than his head.

Rising guardedly to his feet, Blue peeped over
again, to make sure his work was done, then he
turned to locate the riders up the road. They were still
a mile or more distant. Whereupon Blue, with a de-
cisiveness that presupposed previous thought, made
his way to the ambushers' horses. He removed saddles
and bridles to turn the horses loose. Both saddles bore
a small pack and a blanket. Possessing himself of one
of these, Blue hurried off through the cedars in the
direction of Simmons' horse. He did not locate it at
once. Presently, however, he caught sight of the red
color of the sorrel, and hurrying up to him he slipped
the bridle and gave the horse a cut on the flank that
sent him tearing down the road. Blue searched for
Simmons' body, but in vain. Then not wishing to use
up any more valuable time, he ran back to where he
had tied Brazos.

"By gosh! I shore am a tenderfoot," soliloquized
Slim, as he rubbed the members that had not taken
kindly to rock and cactus. He pulled on his boots and
donning vest and scarf, he mounted Brazos to ride out
into the open. He wanted to intercept Estelle at some
point beyond the ledge of rock. Latch's *vaquero* had
sharp eyes and Blue did not want him to discover any
sign of what had happened.

Estelle was in sight, but farther along than Blue
had expected. He cantered on, thrilled when he saw

that he was recognized. She reined in her horse, as if startled, and waited. The *vaquero* slowed to attention.

It was then only that Blue experienced a sudden sharp relief. He had the situation in hand. Slowing up some paces from where Estelle sat her horse, he leisurely proceeded to light a cigarette.

"Corny!" cried Estelle.

She was white of face and the dark purple eyes were distended with expectation.

"Mawnin', sweetheart," he drawled, and doffed his sombrero.

"It's afternoon. . . . Oh my! did you ride out to meet me? . . . Are you all right? . . . And Daddy?"

"Wal, ootside of a turrible yearnin' to see my promised wife I reckon I'm tolerable," he drawled.

"Slim!—This boy understands English," she protested, with a vivid blush. "Oh, you are fooling me—about something."

"Estie, your dad was fine an' chipper when I seen him a couple of hours back. Nothin' atall to worry aboot, darlin'."

"You swear that?"

"Shore I do."

"But you—you look so different from last night."

"Wal, thet was in the moonlight an' I was sort of glorified by a certain young lady's confession. This is broad day, Estie, an' I'm pretty serious."

"If I could only trust you!" she murmured, divided between intuitive doubt and irresistible gladness.

"Wal, honey, it's too late now for you to back oot of your promise."

"Mr. Cornwall!" she replied, tilting her chin, as again a red tide suffused her cheeks. Slim appraised her with the sure possession-taking eyes of an accepted lover. It certainly was a little soon after his dark passion and deadly action to affect his nonchalant self, but he had to do his best, and sentiment seemed his cue.

"Estie! Don't spring my real name around heah," he protested.

"Then—you rode out because you wanted to see me?" she retorted.

"Why shore I did."

"You couldn't wait till tonight?"

"Wal, to be honest, sweetheart, part reason was 'cause I didn't want you runnin' right into trouble at home."

"Corny!"

"Don't fly off the handle now. Dog-gone-it, you're a Western lass! You gotta face things sometime."

"I can face anything, if you'll only *tell* me. I *knew* something was wrong—the instant I laid eyes on you. . . . Oh, Slim!"

"Hold your hawse, Estie," he returned, a little sharply. "Now listen. It's nothin' much. . . . Leighton has picked oot the day after your party to throw your dad off his ranch an' take possession."

"Leighton? . . . Oh, outrageous, Corny!"

"Wal, it shore is. But Leighton has got hold of

lot of your dad's papers an' like as not he'll try to force him off. I reckon thet may lead to some stiff arguin'."

"Arguing? Slim Blue, it means guns . . . and yours!"

"Wal, darlin', I haven't a lot of time to argue with you. My idea was for you to ride back, catch up to the caravan, go on to Fort Union with your friends, an' have a good time till this darned mess is settled."

"I won't do it," she flashed.

"No? Wal, supposin' we was married—then would you obey me?"

"Yes, I would. *But*, Mr. Trail-driver, we are not married yet . . . and there's many a slip 'twixt cup and lip."

"Dog-gone! Wonder what you mean by thet?"

"Don't be hurt, Slim. But you make me furious."

"How come? I haven't done or said a thing oot of the way."

"Oh, it's your infernal, cool, baffling way. Slim, you're a liar!"

"Aw, Estie ——"

"I won't go back to the caravan. It'd be wonderful to have more days with Marce and Elizabeth. But my play days are over, Corny. And the sooner you and Dad realize that the better for all of us."

"Yeah?—Wal, I'm glad you're woke up. If you marry me, Lady ——"

"Not if. . . . *When?*"

"All right. When you marry me, in the dim an' distant future, you'll have to work."

"I'm not afraid of work. . . . It is very evident,

Mr. Cornwall, that you do not expect to marry an heiress."

"No. We're gonna be poor an' you'll have to milk the cows."

"Lovely! Which means, my cowboy, that you expect Dad to lose all."

"I can't believe that. Anyway, if Latch has lost all, I reckon he'll get it back. Leighton has done some crooked work, Estie."

"Can you prove it?" queried Estelle, eagerly.

"Yeah."

"Oh, Corny, all my trust and hope is in you!" she murmured, her eyes glistening in tears.

"Wal, Estie, thet cain't be calculated to shake my nerve or lose my haid. . . . You won't trust me an' go back to the caravan?"

"It's not a question of trust. You want to spare me fright or pain. I won't go."

"All right. Then will you do this? Let me take you down the valley to Bradley's. He's a good friend of mine. He's a squaw-man, shore. But I've seen worse white women than his red wife and daughter. They'll make you comfortable."

"Slim, you want to *hide* me until it's—over?" she queried, aghast.

"Wal, yes, if you want to call it thet," he agreed, with a smile.

"Why?" she asked, gravely.

"Aw, I'd just feel freer, you know—more myself— better able to help your dad if I knew you were safe hid."

"You are afraid of Leighton."

"No, Estie."

"You are. You are afraid he will kidnap me to get even with Dad."

"Say, whoever put thet idee in your haid?"

"Keetch. What's more, Keetch told me never to ride out alone."

"Thet old son-of-a-gun! Wal, I reckon there's more men in love with you than me. An' oot heah, darlin', possession is nine-tenths of the law, an' the other tenth is a gun."

"Leighton makes my flesh creep. But I'm more afraid of that gambler dude, Manley."

"Yeah. Wal, you needn't be, Estie. . . . An' now how aboot my takin' you to Bradley's?"

"I will go, my lord and master. But are you quite sure you appreciate what a tremendous sacrifice this is for me?"

"I reckon—you wonderful lass!" exclaimed Slim, with warm gratitude. "My Gawd! but I love you turrible!"

"Indeed? You might have told me *that* sooner."

"Don't tease, Estie. Come, let's rustle along."

"You will not keep me hidden more than a few days?"

"Gosh, no! I cain't live any more without you."

"But you will come often—to see me—to tell me?"

"Shore. Often as I can."

"I must have clothes and my things. May I send Lopez for them?"

"Yes. Come now, Estie. Let's ride."

Estelle sent Lopez ahead, and riding beside Blue she extended a gauntleted hand and babbled of romance. Blue heard, but had no more to say. He watched the rider ahead as he passed the rock ledge and the cedars beyond. Lopez looked up at circling buzzards far overhead, but he did not see anything to excite suspicion.

Blue and Estelle rode hand in hand to the hill top. To his relief, no smoke marked the recent fire in the town. The ranch appeared to drowse under the afternoon sun. How significant that Latch's gray-green valley was not dotted with cattle! They rode down to the level, where Blue asked Estelle to send the *vaquero* in with news that she was safe and would soon be home. Estelle complied after giving Lopez instructions about what to bring her, and presently she and the trail driver were riding down the north side of the valley, under the rugged bluff. Owing to scarcity of water on that side there were but few settlers in all the thirty miles down to the open prairie. Bradley had located in the mouth of a canyon where narrow green fields attested to the labor of his hands. It happened that the squaw-man was in town. But Blue left Estelle with the Indian women and was about to bid her farewell when he happened to remember Leighton's wallet.

"Say, Estie, considerin' all this talk of yours aboot trust—can *I* trust you?"

"Why, Corny!"

"Wal, I mean will you promise to keep this by you an' not forget it till I come back."

"I promise, Slim. What's in it? Money?"

"Somethin' more precious than gold, dear. But you're not to open it! . . . Go to bed, honey. You look daid for sleep."

"Oh! . . . Good-by, Slim. . . . Be careful. Come back soon."

Blue waved to her as he raced across the valley. He had to decide whether or not to hunt up Bradley and prevent him from frightening Estelle with details of what had taken place since her party had ended at dawn that day. Blue wondered what further had happened in town and at Latch's ranch during the several hours since he had parted with Hawk Eye. Estelle's long-planned party had precipitated events. There were a few that Leighton had not dreamed of in his scheme of things. He had made sure of his trusted allies carrying Estelle off to Spider Web Canyon. Blue had long heard of that almost inaccessible rendezvous of outlaws. Leighton, no doubt, had more than one reason to lure Latch into the fastness of that wild canyon. At length the trail driver decided it would be wise to see Hawk Eye before making another move.

Chapter XVIII

BRAZOS ran the several miles to the lower Latch lake in short order. Here ended the open ranch and the green of trees, gardens, orchard, vineyards began like a wall. Blue deliberated a moment. The hour was getting along well into the afternoon. He would risk taking a look around the barns and corrals, possibly even the ranch-house, before going on to the creek in search of Hawk Eye.

Tying Brazos in the willows, Blue kept to the inside of the hedge and proceeded warily. The distance was far. But the cover grew thicker along that fence, which served as a wind, snow, and dust break. Arriving at the corrals, Blue kept behind the high fences until he reached the barn. He entered the back barnyard. It did not present the usual colorful scene. The back door of the barn had not been slid aside on its rollers. Blue found a crack to peep through. He was quite prepared to see Leighton's outfit in control of the ranch, and to force the issue if he could surprise them.

Cold and sure of himself, Blue drew the deep long breath that had become habit in such tense moments, and placed his eye to the aperture. At the far end of the barn where the runway slanted from the wide doorway into the court he espied a group of men. Beyond them two prairie schooners stood with their unhitched horses feeding on hay. Strangers had arrived, perhaps members of a caravan. Blue's survey took in two dusty, road-clad men, unshaven and dark, heavily booted. A tall, lank man, whose lean face appeared familiar, stood talking to Benson, and another whose garb proclaimed him a traveler but not a participant in the labors of travel. Several *vaqueros* were also present.

Blue drew back, to hurry out of the barnyard and halt around the corner of the big structure. In such an hour nothing could surprise the trail driver. But he did not know what to make of this. Pioneers, settlers, travelers, as well as more doubtful characters, were far from rare at Latchfield. Three of these new-comers packed guns. Blue's one deduction was not unfavorable to the Latch predicament.

He strode along the wall of the barn and around the far corner. A *vaquero* ejaculated, "Santa Maria!" All the men turned, but Benson's jump indicated nervous strain. Blue had halted, his right hand on his hip.

"By gad! it's Blue!" exclaimed Benson. His tone, his look, betrayed two things—an acquaintance with at least one of the trail driver's feats of the morning, and that sight of him, however startling, was welcome.

"Howdy, Benson," spoke up Blue, relaxing.

"Hello Blue!—Where's Latch?" blurted out Benson.

"I was aboot to ask you thet," returned Blue, sharply.

"Don't you know?"

"Shore don't. But I bet I can make a good guess."

"Where?"

"What I was lookin' for has come off. Leighton's ootfit has got him corralled."

"Blue, I don't think so," replied Benson, quickly. "In fact I am certain not."

"Wal, I'm darned glad to heah thet. But you gotta talk fast an' strong to convince me."

"Blue, I rode with the boss an' Pedro as far as the mouth of Spider Web Creek, less than an hour ago," announced Benson, impressively.

"Hell you say!" ejaculated Blue.

"Yes. Latch was in a great hurry, believe me. He did not want anyone to see where he was headed. Luckily he got away unobserved, I'm sure . . . and I've been riding all over to find you. My instructions were to fetch half a dozen men back to the ranch to hold Leighton off. Bradley is coming with two of his riders. I met Mizzouri, and he swore he'd come, whether Latch liked it or not. These freighters from Independence will set in with us. Simmons ought to be back soon. Then with you ———"

"Simmons won't be back, Benson. He's daid."

"Dead? My God, Blue!—How—who?" ejaculated Benson, horrified.

"Some more of Leighton's deal."

"Blue, the boss sent Simmons to catch the caravan and tell Miss Estelle to go on with it to Fort Union. If Simmons is dead he never got that far. We must ride out to meet her."

"Come heah, Benson," replied Blue, tersely. And taking Benson aside, he told him: "Estelle is safe. I left her at Bradley's to keep hid till whatever comes is over. Bradley wasn't home. I don't want him to tell her what has happened. Savvy?"

"Bradley ought to be here now."

"Wal, if I don't stay you tell him. I gotta see Hawk Eye pronto. But what the hell did Latch ride off for?"

"Blue, the boss sure was het up," declared Benson. "No wonder! Listen to this. Some time before noon these freighters from Independence drove in to town with this stranger. His name is Bowden. He's a lawyer from Boston. His business with Latch was to find out some clue as to what happened to one Cynthia Bowden, supposedly lost years ago with Bowden's lost wagon train. It seems a lot of money has been left to Cynthia Bowden. And the object of this lawyer's trip West is to find her, if possible, and whether or not she left a child. Latch saved Cynthia Bowden's life and married her. Estelle is her child. . . . All that money will come to Estie! My word, but it's great news! At this time when Latch is ruined. Talk about providence!"

Slim Blue gaped in mute astonishment.

"Well, Latch has to show some kind of proof," went on Benson. "Bowden has been months on the quest. He found out that Cynthia left Independence with her uncle in a prairie-schooner especially built for Bowden. It was a magnificent boat on wheels. Built by Tullt and Company. Old man Tullt is still living. He remembered that prairie-schooner. Remembered Bowden and his niece riding away on it. The front end had big letters in red, 'Tullt & Co. No. 1 A!' . . . Latch said he thought he might find that wagon-head as proof. The Indians drove all the caravan's wagons over a canyon wall. Latch thinks he can find it—his only proof that he saved Cynthia Bowden from the Indians and married her! The lawyer says he will accept that as proof. No wonder Latch packed light and rode off like mad! He was simply beside himself. Strange how things happen. Estie's fortune, and name, in fact, depend upon an old wagon headboard painted in red letters. Lord! What a forlorn hope! But I know Latch told the truth. Bowden believes him, too. Still, he must have one tangible proof that Latch ——"

"Wal," interrupted Blue, his voice like a bell, "tell your lawyer man thet there air written an' printed proofs of Estelle Latch's parentage. Jewelry, picture, marriage certificate, too! . . . Fact, by Gawd! But I can't explain heah an' now. I gotta rustle up Leighton an' stop him before he scents this deal oot. He's got a nose like a hound."

"Blue!—It'd be terrible if Leighton trailed Latch up Spider Web!" exclaimed Benson, aghast.

"Turrible! . . . Wal, it shore would. I'd say thet'd be the last straw for the old man. He's had a load, Benson."

"Here comes Bradley now. And Mizzouri. Gawd! —But what'll we do without you, Blue?"

"Rustle up to the ranch-house an' hold Leighton's ootfit off—if it comes. No fear of them destroying property. Leighton wants the ranch."

"Blue, you shouldn't brace that gang—alone," returned Benson, huskily.

"Wal, I won't walk up on them careless-like. . . .

Watch sharp now, Benson. Trust a lot to them freighters. An' shoot before askin' questions."

Blue wheeled to hurry back the way he had come, more wary than ever, stern and tense, his emotions in check, yet now and then flooding him with awe and rapture. He could not plan what to do until he had established the whereabouts of Leighton. At last he got back to his horse. When mounted once more, he raced away across the fields, leaping the ditches and pounding up the dust. When he crossed the road he had a look down its length into town. Bunches of horses and men lined the sidewalks. He flashed on, headed for the creek.

Again Hawk Eye failed to be at their rendezvous. Blue rode up on a ridge from which he soon espied the Kiowa riding across from the Indian encampment. Blue rode down in the open to meet him.

"Uggh!" grunted the impassive redman. "Latch go Spider Web. Leighton see—track um."

Blue swore.

"Hawk Eye, how many men with Leighton?"

The Indian held up two fingers.

"Who?"

"Keeneedy one. Dog-face man two."

"Kennedy shore. But thet slinky Breese!" muttered Blue, thinking fast. Leighton, for years so keen, subtle, implacable, was putting his own head in a noose. "Hawk Eye, how long take go Spider Web?"

"Leighton take long—me go short."

"Latch went up Spider Web to find the caravan wagons run over canyon wall years ago. Can you find those wagons?"

"No go water trail. Me climb—go round—find way down."

"Pack some meat an' bread, Hawk Eye. Meet me heah after dark. We go."

"Uggh!"

They parted. Blue went sweeping away across the creek and over the flat. The sun was setting red over the black domes in the west. One moment he felt exultant and the next oppressed. Estelle would come into her own, whatever happened to her father. The disgrace and ruin that had imperiled her happiness would be hidden forever up that mysterious Spider Web Canyon where she had been born. Leighton's one chance consisted in sticking to his outfit and staying in the open. But his abnormal hate and plan for revenge, his weakness to hold prisoner the daughter of his enemy, had hatched his doom. Leighton's bones would bleach in the lonely fastness of that outlaw retreat. But the oppression which weighted Blue's heart came from realization that Latch had made the same fatal blunder as Leighton. Bruce Kennedy and his canine-faced ally had their dark and secret plot. If Latch escaped Leighton he would scarcely escape these two traitors. What amazed and depressed Blue was the extraordinary way the deal had stretched on and on to this singular and fatal climax. He had an intense desire to learn the truth about these old outlaws.

He rode straight for Bradley's ranch, and as he drew near he caught sight of Estelle, who, no doubt watching for him, had seen him from afar. He answered her wave. Thick and heavy his heart beat in his ears. The sweetness of the moment confounded him. Her hair gleamed red-gold in the last rays of the setting sun. Whatever he had been, however hard and grim and desperate he was, and poor and unlettered, he was her choice among men, her sweetheart, her husband-to-be. And such a thrill came over him that it ended in pain. Long before he reined Brazos before the cabin he saw that Estelle had changed her riding-garb to a comfortable gray dress. This meant, of course, that one of the *vaqueros* had come from the ranch. Blue searched the sweet face for signs of trouble, but saw nothing save delight. She came skipping off the porch and was upon him almost before he dismounted.

"Oh, you dear boy—to come so soon," she cried, gayly. "If there were no one to see I—I'd kiss you."

"Evenin', Mrs. Cornwall," drawled Blue as he took her hand.

"Not quite yet—Corny," she replied, shyly.

"Do you reckon you will be ever?"

"If I'm not, there's going to be trouble for a certain young man."

"Estie, I'm shore hungry an' so is Brazos."

Blue had always found a welcome at the Bradleys'. The rancher's Indian wife, and her daughter, a pretty dark-eyed girl of sixteen, came out to greet him.

"Wal, I'm shore a tough-lookin' hombre to call on a lady," he said as he made for the wash-bench. "Haven't washed my face an' hands for three days."

"You dirty little boy! . . . I'll have to teach you a lot of things presently."

"Yeah."

"Slim, I'll see about your supper."

"Rustle, darlin'. I cain't stay long."

In a few moments Blue was experiencing how marvelously strange and sweet it was to be served by
Estelle Latch. She had brought his supper out on the
porch. The long twilight was slowly darkening.

"Did you see Dad?" she queried, eagerly, as if un-
able longer to withstand anxiety.

"No. But I saw Benson."

"Corny, you have bad news."

"Wal, it could shore be worse. Before tellin' you,
though, I'd like to ask you somethin' turrible intimate."

"What?" she whispered, intrigued by his earnestness.

"Air you goin' to persist in your ridiculous engagement to a no-good trail driver?"

"Corny! . . . Are you going to be the faithless
one?"

"Answer me, Estie."

"Yes. I shall persist—unless you ——"

"Could you be happy on a little ranch like this?
Keep house an' mend my socks—when I had any—
milk the cows an' all such pioneer woman's work—
while I raised a herd of cattle?"

"Corny, I could be perfectly happy with you anywhere. And I'd not be afraid of a pioneer woman's
job."

"Darlin', it's turrible hard. An' you've been used to
comfort and luxury."

"Dad has spoiled me, Corny. But I'm sure it's not too late."

"You could stand ranch drudgery, bein' poor, an' not havin' so much as these Bradleys—no money, no trips anywhere—just ranchin' it all the time, every day like the last? . . . Course I love you as I reckon no wild hombre ever loved a girl before."

"Corny, that would make up for everything else in the world," she replied, softly.

"My Gawd! . . . I cain't see how. But if you feel aboot me as I do aboot you it's easy to understand."

"I feel that way, Corny."

"You could marry a Southern gentleman an' live on a big plantation an' ——"

She trilled a laugh. "I want my West and my trail driver."

"You might even marry one of them millionaires in the East."

"Listen to you. Slim Blue, are you trying to tempt me?"

"No. I'm just bein' square. You could marry any man you wanted."

"Very well. It's settled. I want you."

Slim dropped his head on his hands and sat silent a moment. The gods of fate had certainly uplifted him to a love and life infinitely beyond his merits. But since they had!—he uncovered his face to meet her eyes dark and compassionate and loving in the dusk.

"Let's get my horse. Then you can walk oot with me to the big tree yonder."

It was Estelle who led Brazos. Presently she said:
"Corny, I gather from your seriousness—your concern for me—that Dad has lost all."

"Wal, I didn't mean thet. I was just supposin'."

"Then we still own the ranch?"

"Yes."

"You were just testing my love—my faith?"

"I reckon."

"Oh, Slim! How could you?"

"Wal, you see, sweetheart, you happen to be worth about a million. An' it worried me."

She faced him in the dusk, let the bridle fall, sought his arms.

"Dear, you have talked queer ever since you got here. Have you been drinking?"

"No. Never was so sober," he replied, smiling down on her.

"Worth a million! . . . You must be out of your head, darling."

"Aboot you, shore. But not aboot the million. . . . Estelle, you air heiress to a million dollars from the Bowden estate, down East."

"Heiress . . . Bowden? That was my mother's name. . . . Corny, what has happened?"

"Wal, heah. Lawyer from Boston rode in today. Name's Bowden. Some kin of your mother's. He had clues thet brought him to Latchfield. Your dad, you know, saved your mother from the Indians. Married her. Rumor of this has got out of late years. Bowden heahed it somewhere. At Independence, where your mother an' her uncle started with the caravan, old

Tullt remembered the very wagon they left in. In fact, he built it. Big prairie-schooner with red letters painted on the front. *Tullt an' Company No. 1 A.* . . . Wal, your dad told the lawyer thet he saved Cynthia Bowden an' had married her. Thet you was her child. The lawyer had to have some substantial proof. Latch reckoned he could find thet very wagon your mother crossed the plains in. The Indians had dumped it over a canyon wall west of heah. He could fetch that lettered haidboard. Bowden, the lawyer, agreed to accept thet as proof. So your dad packed an' rode off with Pedro."

"How perfectly wonderful!" she cried.

"Wal, it is—sorta. Buffaloed me, all right."

"But, Corny, it seems absurd to expect to find that wagon. After all these years! . . . Oh, it must have been Dad's very last hope. If that were the only proof he had to establish my right to mother's name! Oh, how heartrending it will be if he fails! Poor old Dad! There has always been something so aloof, so inexplicable, about him. But he is a great Westerner. He has been the best Dad in all this world. For his sake—to save the ranch he loves so well—I hope he finds the proof. But I can stand the disappointment, Corny."

"Wal, if you air not the game kid! . . . Listen, Big Eyes! Your dad don't need thet Tullt an' Company No. 1 A wagon to prove you are Cynthia Bowden's daughter an' heiress to this fortune."

"O—oh—Cor—ny!" she faltered, clinging to him, her great eyes shining in the gloom.

"If I could only have seen Latch before he left!" went on Corny, hurriedly. "But I didn't. An' after all, I reckon it'll turn oot best this way. Estie, thet wallet I gave you for safe-keepin' contains proof of your parentage."

"What?" she whispered.

"Letters, papers, pictures, jewelry, marriage certificate. They belonged to your mother. Latch never saw them, for purposes of his own. Your mother died. An' Latch never came back for five years. . . . Wal, I got on to Leighton's plan to ruin your dad. Revenge! An' I spied on Leighton. I heahed him speak aboot these proofs. An' as I once told you, I hid in my room for weeks, waitin' for a chance to steal them. Thet chance came night of your party. I had to muss things up a bit. But I got them, an' burned Leighton's saloon down afterward."

"You knew all the time?"

"Wal, I reckon."

"You can prove I'm Estelle Bowden Latch?"

"I should smile. When you go back to the cabin, look in that wallet."

Suddenly she flung her arms around his neck. "O-oh—Corny, darling. I've got to cry my heart out. But I'll hold in—till you've gone. . . . Oh, it's so unbelievable."

"Wal, it shore is. You cain't never be a poor homesteader's hard-workin' wife now."

"Oh, Slim, you won't go back on me because I'm rich," she entreated, and fell to kissing him.

"Reckon I didn't mean it thet way," he replied, unsteadily. He could understand her abandon. She kissed him and hugged him until she was utterly spent and lay on his breast, white and quivering.

"Now, Estie, you've had your spell an' if you'll brace up an' listen I'll say a few more things an' then rustle."

"Yes," she whispered.

"I'm leavin' at once with an Indian to trail your dad. I reckon Leighton might get a hunch an' follow. If they meet—wal, let's not borrow trouble. I'll try to prevent thet meetin'. Only you prepare yourself for anythin' an' be the game kid you've been all along. Stay heah till I come back. Thet ought to be less'n three days. An' don't worry, Estie. Our luck has changed."

She could only gaze up at him with darkly distended eyes and hang on to him with tight little hands. He kissed her a last time, and breaking their hold leaped on Brazos and rode swiftly off into the gathering darkness.

That was a ride like the trail driver made on stampede nights. The action seemed in harmony with the force of his emotion and eased it—helped him grow away from it—to give all his cunning to the desperate task of saving Latch from Leighton.

Hawk Eye waited in the melancholy gloom. He bestrode one mustang and held the halter of another that carried a pack.

"Uggh! Which way go, Blueboy?" was his greeting.

"Which way best, Kiowa?"

"Far way. Leighton no watch back trail. Me see um."

Hawk Eye made a slow gesture, indicating a long ride and détour.

"Go, Hawk Eye. Blue give hawse, silver, plenty rum."

"Good," grunted the Kiowa, and led away toward the west at a brisk trot. Blue followed, his eyes seeking to penetrate the gloom ahead. They crossed the creek and the road, and keeping out in the open, passed Latch's ranch-house and gained the bluff. Hawk Eye climbed a little-used trail and, once up on the plateau, turned to the west into the cedars. Blue could tell by the stars that the Indian rode straight as a beeline, only departing from his course to head draws or go around thickets, rocks, or other rough places. The hours flew by. The sense of certain guidance and the miles slipping by under a steady trot satisfied the trail driver. They rode through the scattered cedars, out upon the rolling bare ridges, down into shallow dips, and across stony levels, always in a straight line. Wolves mourned and coyotes wailed from the lonely ridge tops. Some stars sank behind the black rim of the earth and others took their places. Late at night a misshapen weird moon came up to change the dark gloom to opaque gray.

Blue knew neither weariness nor drowsiness. His trail-driving nights numbered into the thousands. He felt no impatience. Something of the Kiowa's impassiveness seemed added to his own iron calm.

Chapter XIX

RAY dawn streaked the east. By its light Slim Blue began to discern the dark confines of a ragged canyon along the rim of which he had been following Hawk Eye.

The broken ledge-floored plateau sloped down to a rent in the earth. Cedar and piñon trees grew thickly in soft ground, sparsely out of the rocks. Broad daylight came. What a wild and wonderful vista greeted the trail driver! Long slants of gray stone sloped down to the canyon rim. The bottom of the deep gorge could not be seen. Across the blue abyss the opposite wall stood up, ragged and split, green and gray, with a heavy growth of timber on top. Beyond rose high domed peaks. It was a lonely, desolate region, silent as the grave.

Hawk Eye swerved to the right, working away from the rim. Halting at a point where the rocky slant resembled a mill-race cut in stone, he said, "Wagons go down."

Blue gazed with a start. He grasped the significance of the Kiowa's assertion. Here, then, was the place where Latch and Satana had disposed of the stolen prairie-schooners. The hard granite left no scar or scratch; the canyon yawned like a bottomless pit. There did not appear to be any point near where it would be safe to crawl down to the rim and look over. The edge of the precipice was a long way from where the trail driver sat his horse.

The Indian led on. Blue followed, conscious of a pondering blight upon his thoughts.

They had to head many intersecting ravines that jumped off into the canyon. The sun rose. Wilder and rougher grew the traveling. There was not the slightest sign of a trail. But the Kiowa was not at a loss. He knew the rocks. At last he led down into a crack, steep, of washed, bare, slippery steps of stone where Blue preferred to walk. Deep down, this crack opened into a narrow canyon as tortuous as a crawling snake. The walls were rugged, cracked, caverned, and as they sheered higher they leaned closer. No sunlight touched them low down. A slender stream of water meandered among the great boulders. Progress was exceedingly slow. Every detail of that canyon appeared magnified with each mile, and especially the fantastic wildness. But for ferns and moss, flowers and vines, sage and dwarfed trees, it would have been a ghastly, whorled grave of solid stone. A certain kind of beauty began to manifest itself.

Hours passed. Blue wearied in spite of his tremendous incentive. How long? Noonday had come and passed. Soon Leighton would have had time to overtake Latch. Then when Blue seemed on the verge of desperation Hawk Eye led out of a crack, scarcely wide enough to squeeze the horses through, into a luxuriously green canyon valley, magnificently inclosed and insulated by walls like pictures, melodiously mur-

murous with stream and hum of bees and song of mocking-birds. Far below a white waterfall fell like rising smoke over cliffs. Eagles soared above lonely crags. Deer lifted long ears and stood motionless. Grass and flowers reached halfway up the legs of the horses.

"Spider Web," said Hawk Eye, gruffly. And indicating that Blue should look to the horses and wait there, he vanished among the spruce trees. Blue tied the horses back out of the open, and seeking shade along the edge of the timber, he took off spurs, chaps, boots, his vest and sombrero. Then he drank from a crystal bubbling spring. He lay back on the moss and gazed up through the foliage at the blue sky. His strength seemed to come back. This was the notorious Spider Web Canyon, hiding-place for outlaws and savages. Latch was below somewhere, with Leighton on his trail. The hour had almost come. Blue rested, cooled off, but could not restrain a mounting impatience. He drew his guns, added a shell to the empty chamber in each, weighed them, flipped them over and over. That far he got. Impossible to set any course of procedure! Yet many swift plans transgressed his stern resolve not to think until the right moment.

The Kiowa appeared, a buckskin-clad shadow, gliding out of the green spruce. His action was stealthy, his bronze face as impassive as that of a statue. But his piercing black eyes brought Blue to his knees, with a hot gush of blood swelling his veins.

Hawk Eye knelt beside Blue, to take up a twig,

evidentiy to trace a map in the clean brown needles close to the trunk of the spruce.

"Good," said the Kiowa, with the fire of intelligence in his sloe-black eyes. "Me find wagons. Latch there. Leighton ketch um——tie um up. Make heap wardance."

"Gawd! Has Leighton got Latch tied?"

The Indian nodded.

"Good!" he ejaculated, so emphatically that Blue realized it must be good. "You come me. Like snake. Me go close. Leighton heap loco. Watch Keeneedy—dog-face man. Bad hombres."

"How far, scout?" queried Blue, tightening his belt.

The Kiowa studied the canyon wall below. Then he pointed to a notched section of rim, and indicated where the wagons had been rolled over, and that Latch, prisoner of his enemies, was there at the base of the cliff.

"How close we get?"

"Heap close." Following these terse words the Kiowa made signs that Blue construed to mean the grass was deep and soft, the brush thick, and that they could shoot and not be seen.

"All right, Kiowa. Go slow. An' no shoot till I yell."

"Leighton heap slow. He powwow."

"Ahuh—the —— —— —— ——! It's his last —by Gawd!"

Hawk Eye glided away in among the slender wide-spreading spruces with Blue at his heels. The grass gave forth no sound; the foliage scarcely trembled as they slipped through the aisles. The Indian strode swiftly for a quarter of a mile, then grew cautious. He would look ahead, then turn his ear and listen. Blue heard only the murmur of waterfall and the music of mocking-birds. Hawk Eye zigzagged among the spruces, glided around the immense blocks of rocks, along the base of the cliff, to halt at open sunny lanes, look and listen, then dart across like a swallow. In his bare feet Blue followed silently. Slower went the Indian, until at last he got down on hands and knees. They were drawing close. A loud raucous laugh —Leighton's—made Blue's blood leap. He filled his lungs by a deep intake of air, then, kneeling, he soon was on the Kiowa's heels. No need to tell that savage to go slow! He was a snail. He made no more sound than a snail. He scarcely moved a blade of grass. This was the Kiowa's game and Blue blessed all that he had foreseen in kindness to him.

Blue did not look up again. He paid attention only to Hawk Eye's moccasined feet, and to the exceeding caution with which he followed. He brushed the ferns and tips of spruce branches that softly closed over Hawk Eye's body. The fragrance of spruce needles was permeated by the pungent odor of smoke. All grew densely green ahead. He hoped there would be no more uncovered patches to cross! He felt the presence of the overhanging cliff to the left and the open valley to the right. Water was tumbling off the cliff close at hand. Rustling of birds made Blue stiffen. Slower crawled the Indian until he scarcely moved. Voices grew distinct. Blue raised his head to see points of light through the brush. Spruce had given way to hackberry and scrub oak. It furnished as good cover as the spruce, and gave more room low down. Inch by inch the Kiowa wormed his way under the low-branching foliage. Blue, cold and sure now, with tight lips and nerves taut, made absolutely certain that he would not stir a leaf or snap a twig. He devoted all his faculties to this end. Once where he could see these outlaws close at hand, where he could command the element of surprise, he would be grim destiny itself for them. And this now seemed inevitable. All Leighton's calculating years of hate had led to this.

The green canopy overhead brightened. Blue looked up to see that Hawk Eye was crawling into an open glade toward a narrow strip of thicket. Voices beyond this point indicated the whereabouts of the outlaws. Wood smoke came from a camp fire. To the left a yellow curving wall sheered up, so high that Blue could not see its rim. Under the wall lay an enormous gray and russet pile that at first glance Blue had taken for a slope of talus or disintegrated avalanche from the cliff above.

But a second glance petrified him. The enormous pile, which extended beyond his line of vision, consisted of ruins of wagons. He raised himself upon a shaking elbow. He stared. Was this sight a distorted scene from a nightmare? Wheels! Wheels! Wheels! Rusty tires, broken hubs, myriads of spokes, wagon-tongues standing up like denuded saplings, wagon-seats, wagon-beds, hoops and ragged bits of canvas, rusted brake-handles, boards with faded paint, every part of hundreds of prairie-schooners, made up this enormous pile of wreckage.

It seemed to shout with many piercing voices at the trail driver. It was haunted. Gray ghastly ruin of caravans! How many lives sacrificed to the bloody greed of the border? Faces of rugged pioneers, scalped heads of women, nude bodies of children gazed mournfully out of that pile upon Blue. Had he not met thousands of caravans? Did he not know the lion-hearted men, the courageous quiet-eyed women, the innocent playing youngsters of the tide of empire that moved west? No man could know them better than the trail driver. And he sank down shudderingly sick, struck to his soul, momentarily warped from his relentless purpose. He had seen the work of Satana and Latch. Bloody devils! He ground his teeth in irrepressible rage. But the fierce Kiowa chief could be understood, for the white man had driven him into the waste places, robbed him of meat. But not so Latch! What a monster! This was the secret of Spider Web Canyon, this the shadow on Latch's past, this the end of Bowden's lost wagon train.

Blue felt only hatred for Latch in that moment. He repudiated his stern resolve of rescue. Let Leighton work his will on his great enemy. Let Latch take his due. However brutal Leighton's revenge, it could not be enough. Then into Blue's righteous wrath flashed thought of Estelle. His flower-faced Estelle, with her innocence and sweetness, was this border murderer's daughter. A storm of conflicting emotion shook Blue to the core.

At the moment he felt the Indian's moccasined foot upon his outstretched hand. Blue raised his head. Hawk Eye made a slight gesture, imperious and warning. Slowly Blue expanded his lungs in an exhaustive breath. Then he crawled silently in the wake of the Kiowa, glad to get under cover again.

This last tedious approach ended in a little covert on the very edge of the thicket. Here and there apertures in the foliage emitted bright light. The open was less than an arm's-length away and the barrier only leaves.

Blue took his cue from the Indian, who cautiously rose on one knee to peep out through a hole. Only then did Blue give attention to the voices beyond the green screen.

"Ho! Ho! and a bottle of rum!"

That was Leighton's harsh voice, vibrant with an exultant ring. Then followed a clinking crash that nonplused Blue.

"Listen to that music, Bruce. . . . What ho! Gold! Gold! Gold!"

The long metallic tinkle ending in a ringing crash came indeed from gold. Blue recognized a sound he had become familiar with in the gambling-hells of Dodge. It thrilled and astounded him. Gold here in Spider Web Canyon? It had to do with that pile of wagon wreckage. Rising on one knee beside Hawk Eye, he found a slit between leaves.

Less than fifty feet away, against the colorful background of the open sunny canyon, he espied Leighton, nude from the waist up, radiant and hideous of face, in the act of lifting a double handful of gold coins from a basin which lay upon a flat rock, to let them slide out in a glinting stream back into the sounding tin. A number of little canvas sacks tied at the neck lay clustered on that flat rock. They told an incredible story. Latch, adventuring back to this canyon for the proof he required, had found gold neither he nor any of his band had ever known had slid over that wall with the wagons.

Blue had to force his gaze away from Leighton. The second spectacle to rivet it was the headboard of a prairie-schooner, leaning against a sapling. It appeared to be in a remarkably good state of preservation. Red letters on a background of green were legible. *Tullt & Co. No. 1 A.* Latch had found the proof he had sought and a fortune in gold besides. Leighton, tracking him to his lair, had surprised him and captured him in the act.

Farther on a few steps, Breese was puttering round the camp fire. He was a little wiry man with a weazened face, and a formidable look. Though the day was hot, he still wore his heavy gun belt; the rapt Leighton had dispensed with his.

Hawk Eye nudged Blue and directed his attention to another peephole in the foliage. Through this one he espied Bruce Kennedy, dark and mask-like of countenance, sitting on a rock, with inscrutable eyes on Leighton. A few steps to his right appeared Latch, bound upright to a spruce tree, the lower branches of which had been trimmed off. Latch's gray head drooped, so that Blue could not see his face. It struck

Blue that the man's hair was distinctly grayer than when he had seen him last. Latch made a picture of abject, hopeless despair.

Blue's next move was to find a longer slit in the foliage through which he could have all the men in sight at once. This took him six feet or more from the Kiowa, who followed to give him a warning gesture. It was lost upon Blue. The great Kiowa scout had done his work. Blue was almost tempted to laugh. The game was his. The miserable Latch in his collapse, the mad Leighton in his triumph, the traitor Kennedy absorbed in his scheme—these men were beyond suspicion of their environment. But Breese had to be catered to and watched. An unusual sound in the brush, the chatter of a squirrel or squall of a jay, would not be overlooked by him. Blue knelt on one knee, gun in hand, and peered stealthily out, resolved to go the limit in patience. This drama was one to see played out. Pity for Latch knocked at Blue's heart, but did not gain entrance. Once more he lent keen ears to the talk of the outlaws.

"He never knew the gold was in that wagon," declared Leighton, evidently addressing Kennedy. "When I slipped up on Latch he was digging the bags out of that old wagon-bed. Couldn't have heard the crack of doom."

"Ha! Reckon it *was* the crack of doom," replied Kennedy.

"Bruce, you don't seem wild with joy over this find," complained Leighton. "There's all of fifty thousand dollars in those bags."

"I won't be yet awhile."

"God! to think that gold was hid in the bottom of the big schooner all the time!" exclaimed Leighton, and walked out of the sun to wipe his sweaty face. "I remember that Tullt wagon. Something different all the way through. It had a false bottom. But I was too crazy over the Bowden girl to look at anything else."

"Ahuh. Wal, loosen up, Lee," returned Kennedy, with sarcasm. "You been close-mouthed all these years. It's time you spilled over."

"I will, you bet, soon as my old pard Latch perks up enough to see and hear."

Breese manifestly heard, for he left his task to come over and speak, "Your idee is to stay hyar awhile?"

"I should smile."

"How long?"

"Days, anyhow."

"It's a no-good idee."

Leighton guffawed with the intolerance of the master who had conquered all.

"Sam, it's the best idee I ever had in all my life."

"Ahuh. Wal, we don't agree. You left thet damned trail driver alive back there to muss up your plans."

"Lee, I'm agreein' with Sam," interposed Kennedy, curtly.

"I see you are. Well, what do you agree on?" replied Leighton, impatiently.

"We wouldn't stay in here too long," went on Kennedy.

"Hell, man! With Manley and Jacobs bringing the —" Leighton choked off the end of that ejaculation.

"Wal, *you* reckon they are. But *I* don't," rejoined Breese, significantly.

Leighton turned purple in the face and cursed at even a hint of defeat to his plans. They could not fail. This was his hour.

"Get your deal with Latch over," suggested the cold Kennedy. "Then talk turkey to us."

"What?"

"Yes, what. What do we get?"

"Bruce, I don't like your tone," replied Leighton, soberly.

"An' I don't like your slow deal. It's revenge you want. You don't care a damn for land an' stock an' money. But Sam an' I do. Moreover, this unexpected gold fall makes a difference."

"I'll divide that with you," said Leighton, grandly.

If he expected his two allies to exhibit rapture over this generosity he was disappointed. Kennedy was not impressed, while Breese walked back to the camp fire.

"All right with me, if Bruce is satisfied," he called back.

"Say you're both —— —— uppish all of a sudden. . . . Bruce, can't you stand prosperity?"

"Never had a chance to try. Suppose you give me one."

"We'll all have one. . . . How'd you like this.

Soon as Manley and Jacobs come you can all go down to take charge of the ranch for us."

"I'll think that over," returned Kennedy, ponderingly.

Leighton stood up. He appeared to expand. He wrestled as if with some spirit of procrastination. He threw it off and stood transfigured.

"Cousin Steve, are you ready now to talk terms?" he burst out, in stentorian voice.

Latch lifted a haggard face, and fastened dull eyes upon his captor. Blue concluded that Latch had been knocked senseless and was just recovering.

"I have all your papers," went on Leighton, waving a hand toward his saddle and pack. "Every debt you contracted in Latchfield you owe me. Same in Dodge City and Abilene."

"Suppose you—have?" replied Latch, hoarsely, breathing hard. "I can't pay now."

"You will sign over your ranch property to me."

"No—you—rustler!" flamed Latch. "You stole my cattle. You stole the herds I sold!"

"You can't prove that, Latch."

"I know a cowboy who can."

"That —— —— —— —— Blue!" rasped Leighton, violently.

"I'm not saying heah."

"You needn't say, Latch. We know," replied Leighton, passionately. "We're on to your sleepy-eyed, slick trail rider. Another Lester Cornwall. We slipped up on him, I admit. He fooled us all. . . . By God! I don't know how much. But he killed Nigger Johnson and Lopez, robbed me and burned my property, crippled Kennedy—all of which you've got to pay for."

"I can't pay—I told you."

"Lee, I'm buttin' in to say mebbe we ain't done yet slippin' up on Slim Blue," interrupted Kennedy, sourly.

In weary amaze Leighton swore roundly at his henchman.

"Listen! I heerd somethin'," cracked out Breese, peering all around.

"Mebbe it was the last kick of thet greaser I shot," said Breese, as if to himself.

"Might have been a horse. Jacobs and Manley ought to be here," returned Leighton, hopefully, and gazed with basilisk eyes down the canyon. Silence ensued. After a while the men relaxed. Leighton went to his saddle-bag, from which he carefully extracted parcels wrapped in an oiled skin. The contents of these, spread upon the flat rock, proved to be papers with pen and ink.

"I've everything ready, Latch. All you do is sign. . . . Bruce, when he gives in untie his hands and get something flat for him to write on. Ho! The wagon-board! Just the thing. . . . Latch, why in the hell did you risk all to come up heah after that old Tullt haidboard?"

Latch made no reply. He was difficult to gauge just then. Blue knew that the ranch and the bags of gold just found, strong factors in this situation, were not the determining one.

"What is your deal, Leighton?" Latch queried, curiously.

"Sign over all your holdings."

"And if I don't?"

"I'll force you off," flashed Leighton. "And I'll betray you to your daughter and the range."

"Betray me how?"

"I'll give away your partnership with Satana. I'll prove your complicity in the massacre of Bowden's lost wagon train and of other caravans."

"You can't—prove—" panted Latch, with a mounting horror in his gaze. Sweat dripped from brow and hair. He strained on his bonds.

"Hell! Look at that pile of wagons there. If I needed more proof they would be enough. But I don't need—I can prove it in other ways. Yes, Latch, I've got you at last. I will prove to your daughter that you were boss of Satana's murderers and scalpers—that you were long a border outlaw—that you built Latchfield with bloody money. . . . I will prove to her that you were married to her mother by an outlaw—that she is a bastard."

"Leighton, if I agree to sign—what guarantee have I—that you never will betray me?" asked Latch in a husky whisper.

"Ha! You'll have to take my word, Cousin Steve," declared Leighton. "But the fact is I could settle down to ranching easier in mind—if the truth about you is never told."

"How many living men know that truth?"

"Not many, Steve. Outside of me there's Manley,

Jacobs, Bruce heah, and Breese. Also that old Kiowa scout of yours, Hawk Eye. Mizzouri and the other members of our bank, long turned honest—they'll never squeal. So with our lips shut you're safe."

"I'll—sign," said Latch.

Leighton appeared strung on vibrating wires, as he strode to the rock and gathered up a large, legal-looking document and carefully unfolded it. Then he dipped the pen in the bottle. Breese had fetched the wagon-board while Kennedy, armed with a Bowie knife stood ready to cut Latch's bonds.

"Aha! We're quite business-like, heah in Spider Web," babbled Leighton. "Sam, brace the board against him . . . lower . . . there, hold it. . . . Bruce, don't cut the rope; we may need it. Untie his hands."

In another moment Latch was rubbing his wrists. He went over to the board, his tragic face white, his di-shevelled hair hanging down, and studied the paper Leighton held under his eyes.

"Sign—heah," ordered Leighton, in a high-pitched voice.

Latch took the pen and wrote with a steady hand. When he dropped the pen Leighton snatched up the paper, read the signature gloatingly, waved the paper to and fro to dry the ink, and seemed to have diffi-culty in getting his breath. But at the moment he did not look at Latch.

"Bruce, tie his hands again," he ordered, presently, and wrapping up the deed in the oiled skin, he went to his saddle-bag and put it carefully away. He knelt there a moment after the talk was completed.

"I heerd thet damn noise again," muttered Breese.

"What kind of noise?" asked Kennedy.

"Damn if I know. Funny little noise! Not a hoss. . . . I reckon this canyon is haunted."

Leighton leaped up, suddenly transfigured.

"It will be haunted, by God!" he cried, and with giant strides he went back to Latch. "You squared one debt. But there are two more."

Latch shrank against the tree and sagged in his thongs. He nodded his shaggy head as if to give affirmation to a fact his mute lips refused to speak.

The dignity of great passion sat upon Leighton's brow like a crown. In that moment of revelation a terrible sincerity, born of wrongs, shone from his face. He placed a quivering finger upon the livid scar that marked temple and cheek on the left side—that defaced his features so hideously.

"Steve Latch, you will pay for this with your life," he rang out. "But not until you've paid the other debt."

Latch's lips framed a query that never breathed into sound. He knew. He read his foe's mind. And a gray blight spread over his countenance.

"You stole Cynthia Bowden from me." In the fury that replaced his former dignity, Leighton almost screamed the words. "Latch, you'll live to see me strip her daughter—heah—before this day ends!"

"God-Almighty! . . . Leighton—you could not —be so vile! . . . Kill me! Make an end—of all!

. . . Remember your mother—your sister. . . . Don't debase—that innocent girl!"

"Burning you alive wouldn't satisfy me. I know your weakness. Through Estelle I'll get even with you, Steve Latch. . . . Jacobs and Manley are fetching her heah!"

No human being could have doubted Leighton. Certainly Latch did not. Right there he faced a hell that rendered null his other trials and sufferings. He could not die or even faint. But his mortal spirit seemed to consume his flesh. He grew old while Blue watched. Torture visibly rended and racked him. It was so tremendous that it would not let him collapse. Whatever had been his crimes, he paid in full measure for them in this last hour of retribution.

Blue could bear no more. One more moment he waited to steel himself against the drum and stride of passion not his own.

"Listen!" called out Breese. "I heerd thet funny noise again."

"Horses comin'," jerked out Kennedy, nervously.

"Horses!" Leighton fairly screamed the word. He ran out into the open, his bare back shining in the sunlight. In his fury of eagerness he went beyond a clump of spruce which obstructed the view down the canyon.

Suddenly Kennedy leaped in front of Latch, struck him a hard blow in the chest, shook him violently, shoved up the hanging head.

"Latch, wake up," he said, sharp and low. "Leighton will do as he swore. He's got your girl. Jacobs an' Manley went out on the road to waylay her, fetch

her here. . . . It's too dirty a job for Sam an' me.
. . . If I cut you loose—leave this knife in your hands
—will you make thet same ranch deal with us?"

Latch strangled over a rumbling consent. Life and
fire returned to the dead hollow eyes.

Kennedy leaped around behind Latch, moved
swiftly, bent low, and stood straight again. Blue saw
the tight ropes loosen.

"Drop your haid," flashed the keen Breese. "He's
comin'."

Leighton appeared, charging back, like a disappointed bull. He marched straight for the flat rock,
and snatching up his gun he confronted his men.

"No horses coming. You both lied. Something fun-
nier than a noise heah!"

"Aboot as funny as death, Leighton," taunted
Bruce Kennedy.

Latch lunged from the tree, an appalling spectacle of a man inspired with a superhuman will to
kill, the wicked blade high. Leighton heard and
wheeled. His wild scream mingled with Latch's terrible roar. He shot as the knife descended. But up
went the knife aloft, dripping blood, and on the instant Leighton seized the arm that held the knife
while Latch gripped Leighton's gun hand. They
whirled like spinning tops, kicking up the dust. Blue
could not have shot had he been inclined. He was not
sure of himself. Latch would kill his kinsman. No
mere bullet could stop that magnificent regurgitation
of will. He was the stronger. He jerked Leighton off
his feet and fell with him, to roll and thump over the

ground. Suddenly the gun went flying. Latch had sheered his blade into contact with Leighton's gun arm. Blood streamed down it over the naked shoulder.

"Cut his guts out!" shrilled Kennedy, standing bent and stiff, his face working.

"Break loose, Latch. Let me bore him!" yelled the traitor, dancing around with his gun low.

Leighton heard. He screamed like a madman. Here, instead of satiation of a life-long lust, loomed death. It worked upon him as horribly as had his ultimatum to Latch. He fought mightily. But he was in the hands of a superman to whom life was nothing. Both Leighton's clutching hands on that blade arm, with all his weight, could not stop its movement. Latch dragged him off the ground, and suddenly reaching up with his left hand he seized the knife out of his right. The blade gleamed down. Flashed up! It caught Leighton low in the abdomen—lifted him as he let out an awful cry—flung him to his knees.

Blue sprang out of his ambush, his gun shoved forward. But not one of the three standing men saw him. Their eyes were riveted on the spectacle of Leighton, disemboweled, gory-handed, trying to stop the flood of life blood.

The sight held Blue only for a glance. He leaped aside to get Breese and Kennedy in satisfactory alignment, then he vented his intense restraint in one shrill yell. Breese whirled, his gun describing a half circle, and at Blue's shot he buckled, firing into the ground. Kennedy was slower in turning, somehow obstructed in action, his hand halting at his hip.

"Howdy, Bruce," drawled the trail driver.

"Blue!" whispered the outlaw.

"I reckon. An' tolerable accommodatin'. I should have shot you in the back."

Kennedy's nerve failed even as it drove him to draw. He never pulled trigger, but sank under Blue's fire, open-mouthed, wide-eyed, failing at the last in the desperate spirit by which he had lived.

Blue strode over to the gory Leighton, now prostrate, dying fast. Latch joined him, to gaze down with a stifled gasp. The Kiowa, last to line up, exclaimed gutturally: "Uggh!"

Leighton was wholly conscious as he looked up. Where were his driving passions now? He was in the shadow and felt it.

"Leighton, I'm tellin' you thet Jacobs an' Manley never got the girl," said Blue, deliberately.

The outlaw understood, but the failure of his great coup mattered little now. His convulsive face smoothed. His unfathomable eyes swerved from Blue to Latch, then rolled and set.

Chapter XX

NEAR sunset next day Latch saw home again, as a man in a dream sees the scene of his boyhood.

Blue and Hawk Eye had packed him down out of Spider Web Canyon. Benson, Mizzouri, the lawyer Bowden, the freighters, Bradley and the *vaqueros*, flocked from house and corrals. Latch seemed far gone, but was still conscious. They carried him to his room and laid him on the bed near the big west window. Whisky revived his failing strength.

"Blue, am I going to cash?" he asked, weakly.

"Dog-gone if I know, boss," replied the trail driver. "If you do, it cain't be from loss of blood. Thet gun-shot of yours wouldn't keep me from ridin' trail. But you're acting damn funny."

"I have no pain—no sensations whatever. I feel dead."

"Wal, I'll ride over to fetch Estelle," replied Blue. "Benson, call your wife. Get his boots an' clothes off. You'll have to cut that blood-caked shirt. Dress his wound. I couldn't dig the bullet oot. Shave him an' spruce him up. . . . Rest of you men rustle. You'll heah all aboot it in the mawnin'."

"Blue . . . look!" whispered Latch, indicating with weak hand a great pillar of smoke rising far away, to obscure the sunset.

"Awful pretty. Thet's a big fire, boss," said the trail driver, peering out.

"You set fire—to the wagon pile?"

"Shore did. Lot of dry wood there. Been no rain for weeks. Thet fire'll be so hot it'll melt every bit of iron . . . Nothin' left but a patch of ashes an' thet'll soon grow over."

"The last—trace destroyed!"

"Yes, boss, an' your last enemy daid," rejoined Blue. "You're a lucky hombre."

"God did not forsake—her!"

"Wal, I don't know aboot Gawd," drawled Blue, with his dry smile.

"Blue, I misjudged you."

"Natural. I'm a hard gazabo to figure. But the hell's over now. Let's never speak of thet again. It's range life—cain't be helped. . . . I'll go now to fetch Estelle. See that you air her old Dad!"

Latch lay quiet, watching the far-distant rolling clouds of smoke, shining red and gold against the black mountains. He was happy. At the last he had asked only one thing of fate and of life—to spare his daughter. But he had been granted many things.

Dusk had mantled the valley scene and the plateau to the west when, an hour later, Mrs. Benson lighted the lamps and propped Latch up on pillows.

"I hear horses," she said, suddenly.

Indeed, Latch had already heard the tearing beat of swift hoofs. They grew louder. With scrape and pound they came to a stop under his window. Rapid footsteps pattered up the stairs. Then a lovely face, pale but radiant, flashed in the doorway.

"Estie! . . . My girl—my girl!"

"Oh, Dad!" she cried, and rushed to the bed, to fall upon her knees, to inclose him in loving embrace and lay her face against his.

When Blue clinked up the stairs a little later Latch was holding Estelle's hand as she sat beside him.

"Wal, how aboot it?" he drawled.

"Slim, darling, I was afraid you had lied—again," she replied. "But if you did, Dad swears to it."

"Slim, darling?" asked Latch, with smile and show of surprise.

"Yes, Dad," she answered, with a vivid blush. "That is something *he* must explain when you are well again."

"Oh, I see."

"Boss, nothin' much to explain," interposed Blue, far removed from his cool, nonchalant self. "Thet very first day I went crazy aboot her. It fetched me heah an' kept me heah."

"No explanation is necessary, Blue. The Latch family owes you more than it can ever repay."

"Aw! . . . Say, but my name's not Blue."

"No, Dad, it's not. I just liked the name he gave himself here. Slim Blue is pretty."

"Well, then, if I give my consent, what will your name be instead of Mrs. Blue?"

"If! . . . Daddy! You couldn't refuse."

"Estie, I couldn't indeed. But I'm happy to give

you my consent and blessing. Slim's name might be Red, White, or Blue. It wouldn't matter. Names are of little account on this frontier. What counts is what a man *is*. I always wanted you to marry a Westerner. You will be rich. You will inherit a great ranch. And I have never known a boy—except perhaps one—to whom I would have given you as willingly as I give you to Blue."

"Except perhaps one!" exclaimed Estelle. "I never guessed that. Who was this wonderful boy, Dad?"

"He was like a son to me. Saved my life more than once. Blue reminds me of him. . . . He, too, was a Texan. His name was Lester Cornwall."

"My Gawd! . . . Boss, what you—sayin'?" burst out the trail driver, his lean face turning pale.

"*Daddy!*" cried Estelle, in great excitement. "Slim's name is Cornwall, too. And *he* had a brother called Lester."

"Shore, boss, I'm Lester's kid brother," interposed Blue, huskily. "Years ago I took the trail—huntin' for him. An' I never stopped huntin' until I met your daughter. Thet changed my life. . . . If you can tell me anythin' aboot Lester ——"

"Son, I can tell you all," replied Latch, swiftly. "Lester came to me in 1863—during the war. He joined my band of rebel guerrillas. He was the coldest, most reckless boy I have ever met on the plains. I doubt if even Billy the Kid had more nerve. . . . After the war I drifted—from one fort to another— from trading-post to cattle town. Lester stuck to me. He did not care to settle down. But when at last I decided to develop Latch's Field into a great ranch, he agreed to come with me—work for me . . . Alas! that was never to be. . . . He was killed."

"Would you mind tellin' me how, boss," asked Cornwall, huskily, his face bowed in his hands.

Latch caught his loosened tongue in time. He saw again that vile gaming-hall in Dodge—the girl with the eyes of a hawk—the scornful Lester.

"Son, he died as so many Westerners have died," replied Latch, with a ring in his weak voice. "Back to the wall—a gun in each hand. . . . In my defense!"

"Wal, now—I'm glad to heah—at last," quavered Cornwall.

"Oh, Dad, you've seen such terrible times," murmured Estelle, sadly. "I do hope they're over. . . . Corny, don't grieve. He was brave. He never drifted into dishonor. He was with my father."

"Estie, go into my closet," directed Latch. "In the corner. That old leather valise. . . . Search under things to the bottom. You will find two belts. One holding two guns. Fetch them out."

When Estelle came forth carrying the belts, Latch resumed.

"Give them to him. . . . There son, is all I saved of Lester's outfit. One belt contains money. It has never been opened. Take it and the guns. I'm glad to have these keepsakes for you. Happy that the boy who loved me like a father was the brother of the boy who is to be my son."

Latch was out and around in a few days, walking

with a cane. In answer to solicitude about the bullet left in his shoulder he replied that he would let it remain, to keep company with the one already in his hip, and also to remind him of something.

"Corny, what's your idea about running this ranch?" Latch inquired, returning from the corrals to find him and Estelle on the porch.

"Wal, I shore got a good idee," drawled the trail driver.

"Say idea, darling," interposed Estelle.

"All right . . . ideea, darlin'."

Estelle threw up her hands in despair.

"What is it, son?"

"Wal, I don't know, but I reckon it's good. You say Estie an' I have to go East to corral this dog-gone inheritance of hers. Wal, suppose we ketch thet caravan bound south in a few days. At Santone I'll pick the best trail drivers I ever trailed with. . . . Bim Weaver, Gawd bless him! an' Reddy Westfall an' Long Tim Archer an' Fox Huggins an'—dog-gone it yes! Gunsight Sharpe. I can make him go straight. I'll make a deal for life with thet ootfit an' send them heah with the five thousand haid of long-horns you wanted."

"Corny, I like your idea," declared Latch.

"They're a wild lot. But, boss, we'll need 'em. Rustlin' has just come into its own. Cattle-stealin' as a business has got to be contended with. For years, I reckon. . . . Wal, Estie an' I will come back quick . . ."

"We will not," interrupted that young lady, spiritedly. "Let Dad and your wild outfit run the ranch. This trip is our honeymoon, Mister Cornwall. And I'm going to make the most of it. You should be thrilled, instead of wanting to hurry back here to shoot rustlers."

"Estie, I'm shore thrilled, but also scared stiff," replied Corny, humbly. "Only can I wear my boots an' pack my gun?"

"I should smile you can't."

"Dog-gone!— Wal, if I can wear my sombrero I'll go."

"You can wear a new one, as wide as this porch. I don't want you to lose your Western look altogether. . . . Dad, have you ever been to Boston?"

"Yes, lass. That is where I met your mother and fell in love with her."

"Oh! But I thought you saved mother from Indians."

"Indeed I did. I'd met her before, however."

"You must tell me all about her some day. . . . Are there lots of beautiful girls in Boston?"

"Thick as hops."

"Corny is such a fickle, no-good trail driver," she said, demurely. "Do you think I can hold him, Daddy? —*after* we're married, I mean."

"Lass, I rather think so."

"Then perhaps we'd better settle it—and *him*," she went on, her eyes bright, her cheeks rosy. "We'll ride south with that caravan. Get married in San Antonio. Go to New Orleans. See my school friends there. Take the boat up the Mississippi to St. Louis. Then the train to Boston. Corral that dog-gone inheritance! Then try to spend it all in New York before starting west again. How's that idea, Dad?"

"Great!" ejaculated Latch.

"Wal, Lady, I don't know aboot you," added Cornwall, dubiously, his wonderful eyes flashing their light upon her. "But whatever you want goes with me."

After they left Latch endeavored to get back in the rut of his old work. But he soon discovered that his working-days were past. He could not stick at anything. He loved the ranch; still the old interest and industry were lacking.

In due time the great herd of long-horns arrived, in charge of the finest, wildest sextet of young Texans that Latch had ever met in a bunch. Weaver, however, was no longer a boy. Latch took to him at once and the interest seemed mutual.

Weaver and all the boys had a story to tell about the wedding of Corny and Estelle, which they had attended. Estelle's letter to her father was long, loving, poignant, and incoherent, especially where it dwelt upon these infernal cowboys and their tricks. But she was safely married and inexpressibly happy, and on her way.

This letter marked a crucial time for Latch. It seemed to be the end of some phase of his life. He took no more active interest in anything, unless the current events of the frontier, to which he lent a strange and eager ear.

He walked about the ranch most of the cooler parts of the day, and spent hours in favorite spots, one of which was the shady bench at the first lake. He liked to walk out under the huge walnut trees where the Kiowas had been wont to camp, or across the meadows where he had seen the herds of buffalo graze. Little things held his attention for long, birds and bees and rabbits, and the live stock about the ranch. He dreamed a great deal, and always in the dusk he sat beside Cynthia's grave.

He never invited guests to the ranch-house again. The hospitable dining-room that had sheltered so many famous and infamous characters of the West, red and white alike, knew them no more.

More travel than ever passed through Latchfield that summer. The town grew apace. The burned block soon boasted of showy new edifices, not all of which were a credit to the community. Hard-eyed, hard-lipped men still rode to Latchfield.

Events of the period possessed extraordinary interest for Latch. He drove to town often, always to meet the stages or an incoming caravan or troop of soldiers. The hanging of Black Hand, the fight at Adobe Walls where Texas Rangers held off repeated charges of hundreds of Comanches, the strange disappearance of a small wagon train somewhere between Fort Larned and Apache Pass, the rise to notorious border fame of the killer, Billy the Kid, and the forecast of the terrible Lincoln County War, the duel of Wild Bill Hickok with five cowboys at Hays City, the gossip that old Kesse Chissum had once been a cattle thief, and that the Old Trail Chisholm could confess to a few pilfered long-horns in early days, the hanging of the rich rancher Settlee at Laramie, to the horror of a community who had held him high—these rumors of range happenings, and many more as news drifted in from week to week, seemed to obsess Stephen Latch and remain in his memory, where already was stored a vast lore of the border. But Latch was one of the frontiersmen who did not talk.

The fact was that he grasped to his broken heart every stray bit of fact or rumor connected with the making of frontier history. How wild men at a wild period, in a wild country contributed to the progress of the western movement of civilization! He never condoned or excused his past, but as the days multiplied he grew to understand it. Not all was he to blame! The fur-trappers, the discovery of gold in California, the freighting caravans across the plains, the Civil War, the white invasion of Indian territory, the massacre of the buffalo, the cattle-driving—all these had contributed their share to the evil of the West.

Moreover, Latch was haunted. He had a sleepless and eternal remorse. Agony indeed had died of its own stupendous force that inevitable day in Spider Web Canyon. But as he drifted and dreamed on toward what he divined was dissolution more and more did he live in the past. In the dark hours of night he lay awake—not alone in that chamber. In the gray dawn when the birds first twittered, he remembered his awakenings in Spider Web Canyon with Cynthia by his side. Those days so brief were all of happiness he had to remember. Days that could be no more here or in the hereafter! For in the spirit world he would be denied the companionship and love of his wife. He had transgressed laws that even God could not forgive. In his prayers for Estelle he had bartered even divine salvation and he had to pay. His must be the lonely naked shingle of a darkened shore, the winged demons overhead, the twining rocks beneath, the fiery thorns, and always, forever, the mournful blast driving him with the horde of evil spirits onward in the gloom.

Estelle's first letter from the East cheered him, made him happy for many a day. It had been written in midsummer. And now it was frosty autumn. How the days passed! The letter read:

HANOVER HOUSE,
BOSTON
July 21

DARLING DAD:

We've been here two weeks and I've been so rushed I haven't had a minute to write. I'm so happy I can write now. Just look! But I think of you often, love you always, pray for you every night.

We have been a sensation to our relatives, most of whom have been nice, I'm bound to admit. But there's one Bowden who's a cat. It's a niece of Uncle John Bowden, who has been so lovely to us. She is a tall brunette—simply gorgeous, and a dog-gone flirt (as Corny says), and hell-bent on breaking my heart. *She* would have inherited the Bowden fortune if *I* had never been found.

Well, Dad, Corry is some one to be proud of. . . . But I

must tell you important things. The matter of my income has been determined. The principal is held in trust until I am twenty-one. I get the income—some forty-odd thousand dollars a year. And I can draw what I like. Hurrah! The legal documents are all in the hands of the administrator, but duplicate copies will be given to me to bring home.

Tremendous curiosity was evident among the Bowdens and their kin as to the proofs of my heritage. You bet I did not show them to everybody.

I must tell you about Corny. He's the handsomest fellow you ever saw in stylish clothes. But he *is* a little bowlegged and he *will* wear that big sombrero. They're all crazy about him. I've suppressed his trail driver's speech considerably, but nothing could ever change that drawling Texas accent and his cool, easy, careless air.

Uncle John adores Corny. Just listen to this. The other night Uncle invited us to dinner at a fashionable hotel. Corny looks perfectly grand in a full-dress suit *after* you get him in it. Well, we went to dinner. There were four guests besides Corny and me. Uncle John asked us if we'd like some of the famous Cape Cod oysters, and of course I said "Yes." Then he asked Corny if he liked tabasco sauce. My beloved said: "Shore! I like thet fine." Well, what do you think? He spilled about a quart of tabasco over his oysters, in spite of my kicking him on the shins. I'm always doing that, though.

Then Corny forked one of the oysters—as he afterward said—and swallowed it whole. Merciful Heavens! You should have seen his face. It went bright red—then pale. His eyes almost popped out of his head. Tears streamed down his face. He gulped.

Uncle John asked: "How do you like the tabasco?" And that dear brave cowboy came up with a smile: "Shore is the best tabasco I ever tasted." Then heroically he picked up another and a larger oyster, more generously spread with tabasco (which he afterward told me he thought was catsup), and he swallowed that.

The result was terrific. I thought Corny would burst. I feared he'd die. But I helped him to a drink of water. One glass—then another! . . . He didn't eat any more oysters.

The funniest part, though, came after. Corny was not his usual self that night. He appeared very thoughtful. Next morning he did not get up for breakfast, and when I called him he just lay there.

Uncle John had news at breakfast. He positively beamed upon me. He could scarcely contain himself. "Estelle, your husband awakened me at four o'clock this morning. 'Please come to the door,' he said. I went, fearing from his sober voice that you might be sick. He looked as sober as his voice.

" 'Uncle John, what'n hell was that red stuff I put on the oysters at dinner?'

"I replied that it was tabasco sauce.

" 'Tabasco sauce, huh?' he repeated. 'Wal, it shore was turrible hot. I'm gonna pack a lot of it back West and pour it all over the range. Then there never will be no more snow an' ice to freeze us cowboys!' "